EVERY
STAR A
SONG

ASCENDANCE SERIES BOOK TWO

EVERY STAR A SONG

A NOVEL

JAY POSEY

Skybound Books / Gallery Books

New York   London   Toronto   Sydney   New Delhi

Skybound Books/Gallery Books
An Imprint of Simon & Schuster, Inc.
1230 Avenue of the Americas
New York, NY 10020

First Skybound Books/Gallery Books paperback edition October 2021

SKYBOUND BOOKS/GALLERY BOOKS and colophon are registered trademarks of Simon & Schuster, Inc.
Skybound is a registered trademark owned by Skybound, LLC. All rights reserved.

For information about special discounts for bulk purchases,
please contact Simon & Schuster Special Sales at 1-866-506-1949
or business@simonandschuster.com.

The Simon & Schuster Speakers Bureau can bring authors to your live event. For more information or to book an event, contact the Simon & Schuster Speakers Bureau at 1-866-248-3049 or visit our website at www.simonspeakers.com.

Interior design by Davina Mock-Maniscalco

10 9 8 7 6 5 4 3 2

Library of Congress Cataloging-in-Publication Data has been applied for.

ISBN 978-1-9821-0777-2
ISBN 978-1-9821-0778-9 (ebook)

For David, a man who faithfully endures

ONE

Elyth felt the warning, a sudden sharpening of her senses, before its cause formed in her conscious mind. A few moments later, out of the corner of her eye, she caught the man glancing her way for two seconds too long and her heart sank. It wasn't the first time they'd tracked her down. But there'd been no sign of them for so long, she'd almost begun to believe she'd escaped at last. With that man's glance, all such hope vanished. The consequences would be violent.

She took a sip of her strongly spiced and mildly alcoholic tea, placed the cup back on the small table in front of her smoothly, casually. No need to alert the man that she'd marked him. Not until she'd identified his friends. And she knew he would have friends. At first, Elyth kept her eyes slightly lowered, centered on the steam swirling and tumbling up from her drink while she allowed her vision to expand out, to take in the wide energy of the common room. Then, she let her attention drift, and made note of where instinct drew it.

The place was a two-story affair, half bar, half restaurant, with the upper section open and overlooking the main floor below, where she now sat. It was about three-quarters full. Patrons stood in clumps near the bar, or sat in close groups around other tables. Elyth sat back in her chair and swept her gaze in a lazy arc around the restaurant and then back again, careful not to let her eyes rest even for a moment on anyone in particular. But now that she'd spotted one of her hunters, the others gradually became apparent. A man and a woman feigning intimate conversation at a corner table by the entrance. A lone woman, lingering over a tall mug of a once-hot beverage that no longer steamed. Above, in the upper section, a pair of men arguing animatedly in friendly debate.

Hezra agents, all.

It'd been over three years since her self-inflicted exile from the First House of the Ascendance, since the protection of that great House had been withdrawn. The Hezra had been after her from the first day. And though Elyth knew they would never truly abandon their search, she'd been on-world almost long enough to begin to hope that maybe she'd at last found a place far enough out of the way where she could live the quiet life she'd envisioned for herself. But the Hezra's reach was as long as the galaxy itself, and now she was a hair's breadth from their grasp.

Worse still, Elyth knew what the appearance of these agents portended. This was no brief moment of crisis. It was only the opening salvo in what would be weeks, if not months, of relentless pursuit. Once more she would be forced to burn her world to the ground in yet another attempt to disappear and reemerge on some other planet, with another name and another life. Her coat hung on the back of her chair. At her feet sat the small pack she kept with her at all times, containing the few personal belongings she'd taken when she'd left the House; most important among them, her journal of the work she'd performed in its service, and the vials of earth she'd saved from each world she'd killed. And now, the only possessions that would leave the planet with her.

It had become a cycle, birthed on the planet Qel, now destined, it seemed, to echo through the cosmos. Since then, all she'd wanted was time and space to reconcile what she had been raised to believe with what she had witnessed, and indeed participated in, on that world, by the side of the man she'd called Grief. Sacrificing her status in the House, giving up all she'd been and ever could be in that seat of power, should have been penance enough. But it seemed that the Ascendance authorities would never forget nor forgive her for Qel.

They'd stationed six inside; two at the front entrance, one each near the side and rear exits, two on overwatch from above. If they'd risked putting that many of their own in such close proximity to her, it was a sign that they weren't likely to try to kill her outright. They could have done that from a much safer distance. Another capture attempt, then. Small comfort.

Elyth carefully replayed what she'd observed of the agents since her arrival nearly an hour before; the relentless training of her former life had made the practice of tracking the people around her automatic. Five of them she could recall seeing enter. But the sixth, the woman by the side entrance, had already been at the table when Elyth first came in. They'd gotten here ahead of her. Either they were getting better, or she'd allowed herself to become predictable.

Undoubtedly the rest of the team was already positioned outside, waiting for their moment. But what moment?

Elyth glanced around again. There were maybe sixty or so others in the establishment. Too many witnesses, too much potential for collateral damage. The settlement was large enough to hide in, but still small enough for news to travel fast. If they didn't want too many questions being asked, it was a safe bet they wouldn't make their move until she was outside.

Unless she forced their hand.

Elyth took a long drink of her tea, while she surveyed her mental map of the surrounding area, the buildings, the avenues, the alleys. Any escape route she identified, she had to assume they had as well. Though the agents were uncomfortably close, it was their containment strategy that posed the biggest threat. Beyond those in the restaurant, she had to anticipate a tight perimeter around the establishment, and a second, looser cordon beyond that. Would they have a third? Undoubtedly. The rings they'd formed around her might extend all the way to orbit.

Twice before she had narrowly escaped their capture. The cost of doing so again seemed almost more than she could bear. For a moment, her last sight of *eth ammuin* flashed in her memory. His gentle acceptance of the rough hands that had seized him, the quick grin he'd given her as they dragged him away, as though it was all the consequence of some small mischief, or perhaps just the beginning of a prank he'd planned all along. He'd allowed himself to be taken. Elyth hadn't been able to fathom why. Until now. He must have known the toll it took to live hunted. Maybe his had been the wiser choice.

Even if immediate escape was possible, this latest attempt all but proved Elyth would never experience the true freedom she'd thought she'd purchased with her exile. Unless she could persuade the Hezra to give up their obsession with her. Her hope of such was slight beyond measure; the outcome of any attempt to negotiate seemed all but inevitable. But *eth ammuin* had taught her the value of being open to the great impact often hidden in small probabilities. Unfortunately, she had no means to communicate directly with the Hezra.

Except, perhaps, the agents in the room.

To escape, she first needed to disrupt them, paralyze them just long enough to seize the initiative. To send a message, she needed them to be willing to suspend action long enough to hear what she had to say.

Maybe there was a way to do both at the same time.

Elyth stood, gathered her things, picked up her tea, and carried them all with her toward the lone woman watching the side entrance. As she approached, the woman kept her eyes studiously on the round table in front of her, seemingly lost in thought.

"Excuse me," Elyth said, stopping at the table. The woman glanced up, her expression placid, tinged with the suspicion one might expect from someone approached by a stranger. The signs of surprise and anxiety were apparent to Elyth's acute eye, but well controlled. The woman was truly a skilled professional.

"I'm sorry to bother you," Elyth continued. "Would you mind if I sat with you for a few minutes?"

"Not really looking for company," the woman replied.

"Me neither," Elyth said. "And a guy over there's been giving me weird looks all night."

"Yeah? Which guy?"

"Back over there," Elyth said, bobbing her head discreetly toward the first Hezra agent she'd spotted. "Dark hair, beard, brown coat."

The woman flicked her eyes toward the man. Her partner. A

critical moment. She would suspect she'd been made, but would she let the situation play out to see where it led? Elyth readied, in case the woman made a move.

"Oh yeah, him," the woman said. "Why do you think I'm sitting all the way over here?"

She pushed the chair opposite her out with her foot. Elyth nodded, gave a quick bow, and touched her heart in casual greeting.

"I'm Evani," Elyth said.

"Evani," the woman repeated. "Beril." She dipped her head and tapped her heart in the bare minimum of greeting that could pass for manners.

Elyth pulled the chair around to the side of the table, closer to Beril and angled so she could keep an eye on the common room and the exit. She sat down and, just like that, removed one link in their chain of communication and took a casual hostage. In doing so, she knew she was pushing the Hezra team into high alert. The woman Beril might not be able to report directly on Elyth's movement, but undoubtedly her channel was open to the other Hezra operatives. Elyth had been under their observation before; now she knew every eye and ear was intensely focused on her every motion and word.

The trick would be to stretch the uncertainty of the moment out, to keep them off balance as long as possible, without tipping them into action.

"Thank you, Beril," she said.

She sat calmly, her expression pleasantly neutral. At first, she didn't initiate conversation, just watched Beril with an expectant openness. The posture put the other woman in an awkward gap of silence, where Elyth could observe how quickly she could process the situation and respond. After a few moments, Elyth gestured to a nearby attendant, and then to Beril's mug, now only a third full and probably room temperature. Beril shook her head, but the attendant had already disappeared.

"Least I can do to show my gratitude," Elyth said.

"It's really not necessary," Beril answered. "I've never minded helping a sister in a time of need."

"Courtesy deserves to be repaid," Elyth said, "and I carry no debts."

Beril twitched a smirk.

"None at all?"

"I'm all paid up."

"Must be nice."

The two women sat in quiet showdown for a moment, Elyth watching as Beril scrambled to find her footing in the face-off. The contrast between Beril's calm expression and the tension pouring from her impressed Elyth.

The attendant briefly broke the silent standoff as he returned with a fresh mug, this one steaming, and placed it in front of Beril with a quick bow. After he departed, Beril lifted the mug to Elyth, dipped her head in thanks, and took a sip of her drink. Elyth noted the way she held the mug, grasping the narrow handle with two fingers rather than hooking it with her thumb, the way the locals did.

"New to town?" Elyth asked.

Beril's eyebrow raised involuntarily, though whether her surprise was due to the fact that Elyth had noticed or had dared to ask wasn't clear. She hesitated a moment, trying to decide whether to stick with her cover story or admit the truth.

"That obvious, huh?" she said, after the hitch.

"Local attire," Elyth said, with a quick smile, "but not custom. It's always the little details that take the longest."

Beril flashed a thin smile of her own. Elyth read in her expression the working of her mind, as she tried to discern Elyth's intent.

"Recent arrival, actually," Beril said. "About three standard weeks, I think. Seems like longer. But I hate to look like a tourist."

"You do better than most."

"This your home world then?" Beril asked, gently testing the situation.

"No, I've only been here a few months," Elyth said. "But I'd like to stay. The people are good. Cordial, not overly interested in your business."

Beril's eyes narrowed slightly, sensing how Elyth was steering the conversation.

"Spoken like someone with a past," she replied.

"Everyone's got a past."

"Some more than others."

"I've just been looking for a place to settle down," Elyth said. "Somewhere I could keep to myself, be left alone. I'm doing everything I can to lead a *quiet* life."

The last traces of doubt melted from Beril's demeanor. She understood the game now, understood that Elyth was negotiating with her, and with the Hezra at large.

"Consequence is hard to outrun," Beril said.

"Not when it's already run its course. And when no one's seeking to drive it beyond its natural limits."

"Well, that is the trouble, isn't it? Those who cause harm usually want to forget, while those who suffer it tend to remember."

"Revenge rarely works out."

"Justice usually does," Beril answered. "Eventually."

"It's important to know for certain which one you're looking for."

"You might believe your debts are paid. But some of us answer to a higher authority."

"We all do, whether we care to acknowledge it or not," Elyth said. "But authority and wisdom are two different things."

"It would be wise to submit to both."

Elyth bowed her head. Beside her, Beril tensed further, undoubtedly well briefed on Elyth's physical prowess, and fearful of what she could do with her voice. Elyth was almost out of time.

"I'm no threat to either. I'm a woman of peace, content in obscurity," she said quietly, and then looked back to Beril. "And I don't want to hurt anyone."

"Then maybe you should go out the side door, instead of the front."

Elyth knew that exit led to a narrow alley that filtered into a small courtyard between several of the buildings. Isolated from the main traffic of locals.

The two women stared into each other's eyes for a hard moment, and Elyth saw the granite resolve that the Hezra had forged within Beril. They would never let her go, even if the pursuit destroyed them.

Elyth's hope for a different outcome had been vanishingly small to begin with, but at least she'd honored the chance. She spread her hands open before her, where Beril could see them, and slowly rose from her chair.

"Well, Beril," she said, as she put on her coat. "Thank you for the company. Good luck."

"With what?"

"With whatever happens when I walk out this door."

Beril smirked. "If it's any consolation, if it were up to me, you'd already be dead."

Elyth picked up her small pack and slung it over her shoulder. As she turned to go, Beril raised her mug and dipped her head in salute.

"See you soon, Elyth."

Elyth looked Beril in the eye.

"Probably not."

She crossed the few steps to the side door with even stride, not knowing how many agents would be waiting for her when she opened it. Ten or a thousand. It would make no real difference. The outcome would be the same.

In the three years since her exile from the First House of the Ascendance, Elyth had carefully investigated new avenues of the Deep Language and its power to influence time and space. Though *eth ammuin* had opened her eyes to a multitude of possibilities, her long years of training had seared within her the inherent risks of tampering with the fabric of the cosmos. Still, she had found techniques hidden within techniques, secrets masked or perhaps forgotten, connections implied by the gaps between House teachings. Three years of exile had only grown her understanding.

And her willingness to act.

She drew in her breath, long, steady, and cleared her mind of all but one image. And in her exhale, she formed quiet words in the Deep Language.

"Lightning seeks its course."

Elyth paired the words with a hand gesture of her own devising, amplifying the fullness of the words. As she reached out and opened the door, the power of the Deep Language took effect, multiplying the breadth, depth, and quickness of her perception. It wasn't that time slowed for her, exactly. Rather her senses opened and unified with new dimensions of clarity; sight, sound, touch all joining together in a single experience that could be processed faster and more completely. From an outside perspective, her ability to see the Hezra's plans unfold and react accordingly would give her finely tuned reflexes the unnerving appearance of supernatural foresight.

The narrow alley beyond the door was empty. Elyth stepped out and glanced left, toward the main street. A light rain had begun to fall. In her altered state, she could perceive the individual drops, and the space between them. Heavy foot traffic passed by the mouth of the alleyway, citizens going about their evening routine, oblivious to the coming clash. But she saw no sign of any Hezra agents or troopers.

She turned right, followed the side street to the courtyard, the nexus behind several buildings. There, she found them waiting. Twelve heavy troopers standing in a shallow arc, armed and armored.

But in the center of the courtyard, about twenty feet ahead of the others, stood a woman fully suited in some type of light powered armor that Elyth had never seen before.

The suit bore Hezra markings, done in their traditional crimson and black, and though it showed no signs of damage, it nevertheless looked well-used. In stark contrast with the taut knot of her companions hunched over their weapons, she stood upright, unmoved by the circumstance, almost casual. A veteran of the most dangerous missions.

Their champion.

The opaque faceplate was a matte crimson; featureless, implacable.

"Exile," the suit said. The mask gave her voice a synthetic, graveled edge. "You are summoned."

A strange greeting, coming from the captain of a Hezra grab team. Elyth could feel the tension streaming from the others, the fear of what might come next, and of what failure might mean. Or success, for that matter.

"You brought an awful lot of friends just to make an invitation," she said.

The suit made no reply.

"And if I decline?" Elyth asked.

"Death."

The answer came so quickly, so surely, Elyth knew it was no bluff. They meant to take her if they could, and kill her if they couldn't. She wondered how they would know when to pull the trigger.

"For us both," the suit added.

The claim caught Elyth off guard. The Hezra didn't punish its own troops for failure. And the weapons carried by the troopers around them didn't seem capable of penetrating the woman's armor. That thought sparked another in her mind, of the lengths they'd been willing to go to before, back on Qel. The Contingency. Were they so desperate to stop her now that they would destroy an entire planet rather than see her escape again?

In that one moment of thought, the woman crossed the gap with impossible speed, a strike leveled at Elyth's throat. It would have ended any other conflict. But to Elyth's enhanced mind, the intent of motion signaled its inevitable outcome; she easily parried and sidestepped.

But the suit seemed to anticipate the movement, and pivoted into a follow-up strike. Elyth deflected the attack, reflexively reached to catch the arm. But the armored limb wrenched from her grasp, the motion flowing directly into an elbow strike that narrowly caught Elyth on the cheekbone. The power of even that glancing blow tipped Elyth's balance to her left. Instinctively, she tucked her arms in to protect her head and body, and not a moment too soon. Another attack impacted her forearm, as the suit relentlessly followed through. Elyth slipped under another strike, checked the assault with an open palm to the faceplate, and took two quick steps back to create distance.

Her heightened awareness enabled her to see the strikes as they developed; yet the woman's attacks seemed almost equally able to predict her own counters. A skilled combatant, far beyond the usual Hezra trooper.

And there was nothing Elyth could do with her bare hands to damage the woman through that armor. But she wouldn't need to. Already she'd formed her plan of escape through the line.

For a few seconds, Elyth allowed the woman to press the attack. As long as it appeared that their champion was winning, the others seemed content to hold their fire. Elyth dodged and redirected her foe, feigning a scrambling retreat while carefully guiding the fight toward the arc of troopers around them, near the center of their line. Once they were close enough, Elyth would launch the armored woman into the nearest shooters, fold the arc in on itself, and escape in the momentary confusion. She guessed she would have three, maybe four seconds, before the troopers would gain a clear shot. Even as the fight continued, she planned her route through the center alleyway, predicting when and where she would face her next encounter.

But only a few steps away from where she had expected to spring her ambush, Elyth found the exchanges increasingly easier

to anticipate. As the fight extended, the woman's combat style became more apparent. And it wasn't typical of a Hezra trooper. It
was smoother, more fluid, loops and arcs rather than the lines and
angles of standard Hezra technique. And though the intensity was
severe, the energy driving the combat fell into a rhythm that felt
strangely familiar.

Acutely familiar. Elyth suddenly felt she'd fought this opponent before, hundreds of times, over many years. Impossible. But
even as her mind tried to reject the concept, her body moved to
test the theory.

When an opening appeared, she feinted a high-line attack toward her foe's face that she'd used too often against her longtime
sparring partner. And the reflexive counter she expected began to
unfold, as she knew in her heart it would. As it did, she slipped
low, sweeping a leg behind her opponent and unleashing all her
might in a powerful open palm strike to the woman's solar
plexus.

The suit absorbed the impact easily, but it could do nothing
against gravity.

The woman tumbled backward with a startled cry made unearthly through the mask, scattered the two closest shooters, and
impacted heavily on her back.

Elyth's scant window presented itself, her half moment to escape, if she seized it.

Instead, she stood paralyzed.

"Nyeda?" she said.

The woman in the suit sat up quickly, but did not regain her
feet. And though the faceplate had not changed, Elyth knew the
expression behind it just as surely as she knew her own reflection.

Her training partner. Her sister-in-arms. And now, apparently, traitor to the House.

The shock coursed through Elyth but before it could fully manifest, a hard blow struck her from behind and plunged her into emptiness.

TWO

Elyth emerged in fragmented consciousness. Her first awareness was that of the sterile, thin scent of cycled air. Next, she noticed gravity too was subtly different, thin in the same way the air was. It was several seconds before those sensations connected to any sense of meaning. When they did, she realized she was no longer on a planet, but rather on a ship.

The pain followed soon after, dull but full and wide, strongly contrasted against the thinness of everything else. Her entire body felt drained of all but a deep, pulsing ache. She dared not open her eyes. That didn't prevent the person by her side from noticing she had awakened.

"Elyth," a woman said, warm, kind, a soothing voice speaking from her previous life. Her first life.

Nyeda.

In the haze, it took a few moments for the echo of the past to re-form into the call of the present. For the voice that had once been loved to transform into one to be hated and, perhaps, feared.

"Elyth," Nyeda said again, and though the tone was the same, it struck Elyth now like cold steel.

She refused to open her eyes.

"I know you can hear me," Nyeda said. "Does it mean nothing to you that I would violate my oath by speaking your name?"

As Elyth's consciousness returned fully, the memories reorganized and clarified, and she saw once more in her mind's eye Nyeda standing before her in black and crimson armor. Elyth didn't want to acknowledge the woman, but the words came anyway.

"What oath of yours could possibly remain intact," she said, "now that you bear the Hezra colors?"

Nyeda made a sound somewhere between disgust and a chuckle without humor.

"I can forgive the accusation, Exile, despite the arrogance. But in this room, there is only one traitor to the House."

Elyth allowed her eyes to open then, but did not turn to face the woman by her side. There was scant light in the chamber, yet it seemed to bore directly into the back of Elyth's brain. In her brief glimpse, she judged the size and furnishings of the space. Tight quarters, even for a ship. She closed her eyes again against the assault of meager light, as the rest of the image formed in her mind.

Not quarters. A cell.

"The nerve agent will take time to leave your system," Nyeda said. "You're fortunate they didn't kill you."

"I don't feel fortunate."

"Then you still haven't fully grasped your position in the world."

Elyth drew a long breath, pushed back against the wall of pain that invited her to remain silent. The thin cot she lay upon felt more like a stretcher than anything one was meant to sleep on; its surface seemed designed only to aggravate the tension in her muscles.

"I had a place," she said. "You took me from it."

"With good cause. Each day of your exile, the threat you pose to the Ascendance grows."

"If I posed a threat to the empire, I would have chosen a different path," Elyth answered, anger slipping through. Nyeda could not fathom what power Elyth had turned away from, and how costly it had been for her to do so. At the time, Elyth herself had scarcely understood the toll her choice would take. "All I want is to be left alone."

"An impossibility, I fear."

Elyth tested her eyes against the light once more, and this time found the discomfort bearable. Still, she kept her gaze on the ceiling.

"I've done nothing to warrant First House's concern. But you must know that already. If I'd been doing anything dangerous, the Paragon would have seen it."

"Perhaps. We couldn't be sure."

"You'd have me believe that you still serve the House, then?"

"Believe whatever you like," Nyeda said. "But I remain an Advocate of the Voice and servant of the First House, as you once were. My duty is to serve alongside the Hezra. For a time."

The thought that Nyeda was a traitor had been difficult to accept, but it had presented itself as more likely than the claim she was making now.

"An alliance," Elyth said. "Because you feared what I might become?"

"No, Exile," Nyeda said. "Because we fear what you already are."

The silence lay heavy upon Elyth, as Nyeda gave her words time to fill the space of the room. There was a rich economy to the statement, an implied proclamation of judgment that followed behind. The First House hadn't merely withdrawn their protection from Elyth. They were actively partnered with the Hezra in this. In hunting her down.

"And," Nyeda added a moment later. "Because we need your help."

Elyth looked at Nyeda for the first time. The woman was dressed now not in the black and crimson of the Hezra, but in the simple gray of her House. And in her tearful eyes, Elyth saw the great distance between them, how deeply betrayed she felt, mingled with fear, and the genuine love she somehow still clung to, or that clung to her, perhaps. It was the depth of that love that had made it possible to wound her so completely. Despite the circumstances, Nyeda was glad to see her. And terrified.

"What help could you possibly need from an exile and high enemy of the Ascendance?" Elyth asked.

"When you're strong enough, we'll show you."

Though it seemed to set every nerve in her body ablaze, Elyth forced herself to sit up, and then struggled to her feet.

Nyeda smiled in spite of herself.

"Perhaps you haven't changed as much as I'd thought," she said. She stood as well, and stepped to the hatch. "I have no doubt your will is sufficient, but your mind needs rest. At least another hour, to ensure the toxin is cleared. I'll return for you."

Someone outside must have been observing the entire event, because as Nyeda was turning toward the door, it chirped and unlocked, and then slid open. Four Hezra troopers stood guard in the corridor.

Elyth remained standing by her cot after the door closed, defying the cry of her muscles to give in, to lie down, to return to the temporary oblivion of sleep. An aching fog seemed to envelop and penetrate every aspect of her mind and body. Gradually, as she confronted the pain that clung to her very being, she felt the edges of it begin to recede.

Though she was no longer a daughter of the First House of the Ascendance, Elyth had not abandoned its many useful ways. She forced her body into the moving meditation that she'd first learned as a young girl, taking each pose in turn, extending the time for each as long as she could bear. Silence Unveils the Heavens. Arrow Seeks the Heart. Warrior Summits the Mountain. Watcher Greets the Storm. Titan Bears the World. Orual Releases the Dove. Servant Awaits with Gratitude. With each transition, she mastered a little more of herself, and by the end of the sequence, though the pain had not fully ceased, it had quieted enough for her to focus on other things.

Not that there was much to focus on in her tiny cell. And the brief glimpse she'd had of the corridor and the guards beyond had only confirmed the obvious: They were keeping her in a proper brig rather than an improvised holding cell, and thus she was on a military vessel. All that really told her was that this was a Hezra-run operation, supported by the House, and not the other way around.

As her mind became clearer, one detail emerged that should have struck her immediately as strange. They had not restrained her in any way. Once, when she still served the House long ago, she had been captured by the Hezra and they had fit her with a device that prevented her speech. They certainly feared what she was capable of; Nyeda had taken pains to make that much clear. There was no mere prison that could hold an Advocate of the Voice for long, if she desired freedom. The fact that they'd done nothing to prevent her from wielding the power of the Deep Language could not have been a careless oversight.

Shortly after she'd completed the sequence, the door to her cell slid open. Nyeda stood in the corridor alongside a tall, thin man, and flanked by a four-man armed escort.

Nyeda stepped inside first, followed by the tall man, who had to duck his head to enter. He was perhaps six and a half feet tall and had the look of an endurance athlete, slender but broad-shouldered and clearly fit. And his uniform told Elyth all she needed to know. It was a crisp black trimmed with subdued crimson elements, and a single, understated Hezra emblem on the high collar.

He was an Envoy, an emissary of the supreme authority of the Hezra, the Hezra-Ka.

The escort remained outside, and no one spoke until the door had closed and locked once more.

"Is this the tiny thing that has caused us so much trouble?" the man said, smiling down at Elyth. He was easily a foot taller than her, and his forceful presence magnified the difference. "They tell me I shouldn't speak your name. What do you think of that?"

"I don't think of it," Elyth replied.

"I don't much either," he said. "But your former siblings are a touchy bunch. I suppose I shouldn't upset them without *some* cause. My name is Sardis. You know who I represent."

He stated it plainly, but waited for acknowledgment nonetheless. Elyth gave a curt nod.

"Good. Then you understand the severity of your situation. I've been told you're smart, so I won't expound too thoroughly. Suffice it to say that if at any point I become concerned that you pose a threat to anyone on this ship, from captain to cook, I will have you separated down to your base atoms and distributed into space, and no one will even bother to ask why."

He said it all with the same smile, somehow neither genuine nor condescending. It looked like an expression he'd seen other people use, but didn't understand the function of.

"I am but your humble servant," Elyth said, with a mock bow.

"Ah, that it would be true," he replied. "Perhaps in time. First, a conversation, before you make such promises."

He made a signal with his hand, and the door opened behind him.

"This way," he said, exiting.

Elyth glanced at Nyeda, who held out a hand inviting her to leave first. As Elyth stepped by her, Nyeda leaned forward.

"I hate that man," she whispered.

Elyth stepped out of the cell and followed Sardis through the ship, with the guards forming a tight knot around her and Nyeda behind. After an elevator ride and a brief walk, the Envoy led her to a cabin on one of the uppermost decks. An additional pair of sentries stood at attention by the hatch, but it was significant to Elyth that when Sardis led Nyeda and her inside, neither the guards nor the escort followed them into the cabin.

Once inside, Elyth saw that the cabin had been converted into a workspace of sorts, though judging from the scattered material and number of floating holographic displays, it'd either been done hastily or by someone with zero sense of organization. A moment later, the answer clearly emerged as the second, when a man suddenly stood up from behind a makeshift desk.

"Hello, sorry," the man said. "Sorry, a quick nap helps clear the mind. For me anyway."

He was a short, stocky man, with golden-brown skin and a mass of white hair that seemed more like a hat than anything naturally grown. On first impression, Elyth had no idea what to make of him. He had a broad face, rounded, with prominent cheekbones, and his stark white hair was at odds with his otherwise youthful look. And though the hair would have been perfectly at home sitting on the head of any proctor of mathematics, his frame was that of a military man, used to hard, physical labor. His jumble of physical characteristics defied any educated guess at his age. But his appearance seemed more or less in line with the state of his improvised office: a sort of loose collection that shared a single purpose, even if that purpose wasn't exactly apparent.

"Envoy," he said by way of greeting.

"Arbiter," the Envoy replied.

The Arbiter smiled placidly at Elyth and Nyeda, apparently waiting for the Envoy to introduce them. After a few awkward moments of silence, the Arbiter finally took it upon himself to do so.

"Arbiter Oyuun," the man said to Nyeda, and then again to Elyth, offering a courteous bow each time. Elyth returned the bow, but neither she nor Nyeda returned the offer of a name, and Oyuun didn't seem to expect one.

Sardis addressed Elyth.

"We're going to share some information with you that is not widely known. It's important that it remain so. But it's necessary for you to know it, so do please pay attention."

He motioned to Oyunn.

"Arbiter," Sardis repeated. "If you would, please."

"Certainly, of course. Delighted."

He turned immediately and rummaged among the floating displays hovering over his desk, sliding several into an overlapping pile in apparent search for a specific one.

"Ah, here we are."

He pulled the display closer and expanded it, angled it so the others could see it, a professor preparing to deliver a lecture.

It was a small audience. The Envoy, Nyeda, Elyth. And both the Envoy and Nyeda seemed more interested in watching Elyth's reaction than in anything Oyuun had to say.

"Are you familiar with this world, Advocate?"

"Arbiter!" Nyeda said sharply.

Oyuun reacted with surprise, at first not realizing what he'd said that triggered the harsh response. But then it occurred to him.

"Oh yes, my apologies," he said. "Are you familiar with this world . . . must I call her Exile? *We* didn't exile her."

"We ask that you not honor her with the title she herself renounced," Nyeda answered.

"I've never been much of one for formalities," Oyuun said. "I have a hard time keeping all the rules of etiquette in mind. But very well." He addressed Elyth intentionally, once more.

"Are you familiar with this world, dear?"

Elyth looked at the display, scanned the few details, then shook her head.

"I'm not sure if that's a relief or not," he said. "This is *ru het* eleven-seventeen. Technically speaking. Back at the lab, we've just taken to calling it Qel's Shadow. It's a strange planet. Very curious. About five months ago, it showed up roughly ten light-seconds from Qel."

"Showed up?" Elyth asked. The Ascendance empire spanned the entire galaxy, and had long ago cataloged every planet within its borders. The idea that they had somehow missed one was absurd.

He nodded. "Fully formed, out of nowhere."

"I don't understand."

"Neither do we," Oyuun said. "A few folks around the lab thought maybe you'd made it."

He smiled, but Elyth couldn't tell if he was joking or not. Oyuun didn't seem to be sure either.

"I'm not sure what you mean."

Oyuun nodded again.

"In most regards, the planet is quite indistinguishable from any other habitable Ascendance world. Stable atmosphere, plenty of liquid water, carbon-rich. A bit on the smaller side, maybe half the size of Qel or so. But if we wanted to settle it, we wouldn't even have to terraform it. Quite the gift, really. A whole new planet, from nothing.

"The only thing I don't like about it is, of course, that it shouldn't be there. And I mean beyond the obvious weirdness of *poof*, new planet. Specifically, I mean there's no disruption of the neighboring worlds, no orbital disturbance, no gravitational signature. If you didn't know it was there, you wouldn't be able to tell, really, except from the light bouncing off it, and there's not much of that. Even the worlds nearby don't seem to notice it. And then, even more strangely, it's tracking Qel's orbit. Not *orbiting* Qel, mind you. Just trailing along behind it. Hence 'Qel's Shadow.' "

Elyth couldn't make sense of what Oyuun was telling her, or why, for that matter. But a deep dread was beginning to form in her bones, that here, at last, was the unforeseen outcome of *eth ammuin*'s work on Qel. Something birthed from his thoughtless exploitation of the Deep Language, the unintended consequence of his twisting of the fabric of reality. And, if she were being honest, wrought with her help.

"I'm looking forward to seeing what you can tell us about it," Oyuun said.

"We hadn't gotten that far yet, Arbiter," Sardis said.

"Oh. Well. Do you want to tell her, or should I?"

Sardis sighed mildly, and Elyth got the sense that he'd given the Arbiter strict instructions, none of which had been followed. She also started to suspect that Oyuun knew exactly what he was doing. And was enjoying it.

"You might as well continue," the Envoy said. "Since you've already started."

"Certainly." He turned back to address Elyth again. "We've learned everything about the world that we can from a distance. Which, as you can see, hasn't been much. So we're sending an expedition to investigate. I was hoping you would join it."

Elyth looked to Nyeda, then to Sardis. They were both still watching her intently.

"You make it sound as though I have a choice in the matter," she said.

"You do," Sardis answered. "I'm sure it's more than you deserve, but in this matter, it truly is left to you to volunteer. We're looking to solve a puzzle, and we believe you may have some of the key skills and knowledge that we're missing. It would do us no good if you were to spend all your energy looking for every opportunity to escape."

The suggestion seemed preposterous on its face. There was no way they were offering her a genuine choice.

"You want me to travel to this world, to investigate it on your behalf. And then what?"

"If we're successful and satisfied with your aid," Sardis said, "we're prepared to commute the standing order, and grant you regular citizenship. Assuming you live the quiet life you claim to want, we won't see each other again."

For someone in Elyth's position, the offer of reinstatement as a proper Ascendance citizen was a high reward indeed. But she didn't understand why they'd spent so much effort to bring her in, or why they would make her such an offer. The Hezra already had entire armies of scientists and technicians. They didn't need her help to understand the planet. There was one skill that she possessed that might make her particularly valuable. She was an assassin of worlds. Or had been, once. But that, too, did not make her unique. The House had others of her former order who could have carried out such a mission.

"And what, precisely, do you mean by 'successful'?" Elyth asked.

"Survival would be a good start," Oyuun offered. "Beyond that, well. Practically anything you learn would be more than we know right now. I have a running list of questions around here somewhere—"

"We could define a few, more concrete, goals, if you prefer," Sardis said, cutting in before Oyuun could say more. "To make sure all parties agree on the outcome. I understand you may find it difficult to trust our intentions in this. But it is the Hezra-Ka's directive that you be offered the choice."

Elyth looked to Nyeda. The older woman nodded; the House had assented. If Elyth accepted and performed her duties well, she would receive full, proper Ascendance citizenship. No more running, no more hiding, no more living hunted. She could live openly, travel freely.

It seemed too clean, too easy.

"And if I decline?" she asked.

"We drop you off on a world of your choosing, no hard feelings," the Envoy said. "And we give you a standard day's head start. As a courtesy." He flashed his emotionless smile.

"And, I assume, continue to track me the entire time."

"*We* won't," Sardis replied. "We're a special detachment. In this matter, the Hezra is especially compartmentalized. We would not be able to communicate your whereabouts, because we cannot communicate *our* whereabouts, nor our contact with you."

"I find it hard to believe that the Hezra would go to such lengths to find me, only to release me again based on my personal whims."

"I don't care if you believe me or not, Exile. Logistical matters aside, you have the assurance of the Hezra-Ka himself that you are to be released unharmed, if that is your choice. My word is the word of the Hezra-Ka."

The last phrase struck Elyth with its intended forcefulness. An Envoy who falsely claimed to speak the word of the Hezra-Ka could be put to death for the violation.

"Personally, it makes no difference to me," he added. "I'd be delighted for you to return to being someone else's problem. I strongly advised against this whole direction anyway."

Elyth scanned the faces of the three others in the room. Sardis showed no signs of deception. Despite his earlier threat to separate her into her atomic components, he truly did seem to want nothing more than to get her off his ship and out of his way. She wondered how long he'd had to search for her, just to deliver his message.

Oyuun, on the other hand, had a warm, lively expression, as

though this was all exciting and enjoyable. He clearly wanted Elyth's help in this strange matter.

Nyeda's face would have been unreadable to an outsider. But as her once sister-in-arms, Elyth saw the subtleties of her conflicting emotions. She was torn, ashamed of being forced to seek the help of an exile, but anxious for the aid nonetheless.

Elyth looked at the display hovering nearby, showing this planetary enigma. Qel's Shadow. A mystery to be solved, in exchange for a fresh, new life. A life extended to her by the gracious hand of the Hezra-Ka.

And beyond the Hezra, she saw, too, the Paragon of the First House. Her former sovereign, the Hezra-Ka's mirror image. They stood as the twin powers animating the Ascendance's authority, long at odds and now, it seemed, joined in purpose. But Elyth knew all too well the cunning and subtle designs of the Paragon, the many-layered intrigues she spun for her own intentions. Whatever threat this new world might pose, whatever alliance it appeared to have forged between the two arms of Ascendance might, Elyth knew that it must all be merely one facet of the Paragon's secret purpose.

And hers was an authority to which Elyth would never again submit. She turned back to Sardis.

"I think I'll take my chances," Elyth answered.

"Just as I anticipated," Sardis said, irritated but clearly not surprised. "I advised them that this would all be a waste of time and resources, but I suppose at very least you've given me the pleasure of being right. Perhaps next time others will be more willing to listen to me."

His response surprised her; she'd expected him to give her an ominous warning or explicit threat, to make at least one attempt to bend her will. But after his response, he stooped down and picked something up off the floor from beneath Oyuun's workstation and held it out to her. Her pack; all the belongings she had left now. Nyeda stepped forward, a half step ahead of the Envoy.

"Consider carefully," she said. "Think of the lengths we've gone to. Think of all we're offering, and what it must mean."

In Nyeda's words, Elyth sensed a desperation deeper than the woman's expression had revealed. But even now, Elyth could perceive how the Paragon would use this to draw her back once more under the House's control. For all her power and cunning, the Paragon never bore the risk of her designs, instead always working through others, ordering their steps, manipulating them into carrying out her will while concealing her true intent, and shielding herself from its consequences.

"I made my decision years ago, Nyeda," Elyth answered, taking her pack from Sardis.

"Very well," Sardis said. "I'm sure I don't need to impress upon you the importance of not speaking what you've learned here. It would make you particularly easy to find. We'll make arrangements for your travel."

Elyth glanced once more at the image of *ru het* 11-17. Though they called it Qel's Shadow, she couldn't help but see it as *eth ammuin*'s work. Some unforeseen consequence of his long effort to unravel the full power of the Deep Language. And the result of the Hezra's secret project. This was more their doing than hers. And she had already played her part. She would leave it to someone else to rise up and meet whatever challenge this little world posed.

Sardis opened the door, and stood next to it, waiting for Elyth to exit.

"Sorry to see you go," Oyuun said, sincerely. "I was really hoping to work with you on this. I think you have a lot to offer."

"I wish you all success, Arbiter," Elyth answered. "May you ever ascend."

"May we all," he replied. Nyeda remained standing by his side, unwilling now to meet Elyth's gaze.

"It was good to see you again, Nyeda," Elyth said, truthfully. Though she had no desire to return to the House, she couldn't deny how much she missed her sisters. The other made no reply, didn't raise her head. Elyth looked on her for what would be the last time, savoring the moment even in all its brokenness. In her exile, she'd never expected to see anyone from the House again, and though the circumstances were strained and confounding, she counted this final chance to be in her once-beloved sister's presence a gift.

"Goodbye."

Elyth turned to follow Sardis out, but before she took a step, she said, "You know, Envoy, if this matter is truly so important, you should talk to the Paragon herself. She's really the one you should be sending."

The man gestured for her to exit first, but as she began to move, Nyeda spoke from behind.

"We did," Nyeda said. The words caught Elyth, prevented her from crossing the threshold.

"Advocate!" Sardis snapped.

Elyth half-turned, saw Nyeda looking at her now, and saw the truth on her face. Despite the Envoy's warning, Nyeda continued.

"We did send the Paragon, Elyth. She didn't come back."

THREE

Elyth surveyed the vast array of gear laid out before her, a magnificent display of the Hezra's technological ingenuity and power. There seemed to be a tool or gadget to cover every possible situation one might meet in an unexplored land, and many more that had such specialized purpose, she couldn't fathom why someone had gone to the trouble to design it. The only thing conspicuously missing was any sort of weapon.

The Hezra procurement officer waited patiently, answered her questions politely, made his recommendations humbly, as though he were guiding her through his finest selection of wines. It was all on offer, for her to equip herself as she saw fit for the task ahead. Nyeda stood nearby, silently observing.

The moment after Elyth had agreed to join the task force, a whirlwind of activity had swept her along so quickly that she barely had time to process how radically the decision had altered the direction of her life. Her change of heart had happened almost unconsciously, reflexively. Nyeda's forbidden revelation had shocked her, of course. But beyond that, it had transformed in her mind the reality of the situation they were facing.

Sardis had made it abundantly clear in both his words and his displeasure with Nyeda that the Paragon's disappearance was to be kept utterly secret. Arbiter Oyuun had already known, which told Elyth how highly ranked the man was even within the obviously top-tier structure that had been put in place for this secretive operation. Officially, however, the mission was one of scientific investigation and intelligence gathering, not search and rescue. It still wasn't clear to Elyth what its true, unofficial purpose was.

She took her time selecting her load-out for the expedition. No one could tell her how long they expected to be on Qel's Shadow, nor what they might find there. During her service to the House, she'd been through the same process countless times, predicting the unpredictable, evaluating her likely needs against the cost of weight and bulk. The main difference now was that she wouldn't be operating alone.

Elyth didn't yet know how many others she would be joining, and still no one had explained to her what role she was expected to play. But she could guess. She would study the planet as only an Advocate of the Voice could. And then, if called upon, she would kill it. It was her experience with Qel that set her apart from any of her former sisters, and she suspected that was the key that the Hezra needed, and that only she possessed.

After she'd completed her preparations, the procurement officer took careful inventory and informed her that he'd personally oversee the transfer of her equipment to the ship they'd be traveling on. Elyth thanked him, and joined Nyeda.

"Sardis is assembling the team at the staging area," Nyeda said. "I imagine he'll have some sort of speech prepared."

Elyth nodded, and the two left the armory, Nyeda leading the way. The silence between them felt strained, its edges bulging beneath the weight of all that they wanted to say to each other. Elyth sensed that neither of them knew how to begin. Or perhaps both feared that once begun, they would not know how to stop.

As they rode together in a lift, though, Elyth finally brought herself to test the boundaries.

"Are you going to call me 'Exile' for this entire trip?" Elyth asked.

Nyeda remained silent long enough for Elyth to think that she wouldn't respond. But then she spoke.

"I don't know," Nyeda said. "It is hard to be with you."

She paused and looked down. After a moment, she shook her head, looked to Elyth, and added, "But it was harder to be without you."

Tears rimmed her eyes, and Elyth felt her heart stir. In her long exile, she'd worked to set the memories of her past life aside, to drain them of their emotional significance and mark them as dead. Here, now, reunited with Nyeda, the warmth and bonds of sisterhood rekindled unexpectedly, and she found tears of her own rising in response.

"I did miss you, Nyeda," she said. "I don't regret my choice, but I am deeply sorry for the pain it caused you."

Nyeda returned her gaze to the doors of the lift, the bitterness of the wound overshadowing any lingering bond she might have felt with Elyth.

"The pain wasn't just mine," Nyeda said. "I'll never understand how you could abandon the House, after all it has done for you."

"You would," Elyth replied, "if you understood all I had done for it."

They lapsed into sharp silence for a few seconds more, the quiet hum of the lift providing the only buffer to soften the edge. Nyeda could not have known the truth of what the Paragon had put Elyth through, nor of the confrontation between them. Least of all, could she have suspected how Elyth had prevailed in that final test. Even if Elyth explained it, Nyeda would never believe it. The gulf between them was too great, and the distance was magnified by the closeness Elyth had felt only a moment before.

"I still don't know how you found me," Elyth offered.

"I'm not sure we ever would have on our own," Nyeda said. "But we had help."

They arrived at the proper deck and the doors slid open before Elyth could ask more. A long, wide hangar stretched before them, buzzing with crew. Nyeda led her out, walking a few steps ahead of her at a pace that made it clear she didn't want to continue the conversation.

It would have been difficult to do so anyway, given the amount of activity on the deck. As they walked, Elyth saw three ships aligned and waiting on launch platforms, and it appeared that all of them were being prepared for deployment. The largest of the three had a less aggressive bearing than the others, and though it was clearly of military design, several of the external features gave Elyth the impression that it was primarily a research vessel. The two smaller craft seemed like siblings, one larger, bulkier, the other lean and scrappy. A transport and its supporting gunship. For a science expedition, the Hezra was going in heavy.

Palettes of supplies and equipment lay neatly arranged near each ship, and Hezra crewmembers moved efficiently to load and ready the vessels. Judging by the look of it all, Elyth guessed their launch window was fast approaching. And based on the size of the craft and the way they were being prepped, she noted that none of them were equipped with aspect drives. Ascendance vessels of sufficient class used Hezra-engineered aspect drives to cross vast distances near-instantaneously. That the three vessels lacked drives of their own told her one of two things: Either they were already within their launch range of Qel's Shadow, or their current vessel would be serving as their mother ship for the operation. That also meant that once they launched, they'd be dependent on the greater ship's support for their return.

Nyeda continued on through the middle of it all, to the far side of the hangar opposite the bay doors. There they passed through a double-sealed chamber that opened to a short corridor, which was lined with a pair of cabins on either side.

They entered one of these and from the proximity to the hangar and the layout of the space itself, Elyth identified it as a final point of assembly for crew and troopers before deployment. Compared to other cabins she'd seen on the vessel, this one felt quite large and had been designed with mixed purpose. The front third was arrayed with perhaps forty or fifty seats arranged in gently curving rows, focused around a raised platform, equipped for formal briefings. But the rest of the space had an almost recreational atmosphere. The middle portion was casually furnished, comfortable seating arranged in various clusters, with a few stations for refreshments scattered throughout. The rear of the room was mostly open space, and there Sardis stood talking with two other men, alongside a metallic, cubic container that Elyth took to be some sort of special supply crate.

"Ah, good," Sardis said when he saw them. "Our guests of honor."

He waved them over. The two women crossed the space to join the group.

"This is my agent in charge of security," the Envoy said, introducing the man on his right. "Wari Korush."

The instant she'd seen him, Elyth had identified the man as an Azirim, a member of the force that served as elite bodyguards for both Hezra command personnel and Ascendance Grand Council dignitaries. He was short and wiry, with head shaved bald and the braided beard iconic of the Aziri, groomed with acute precision. Even in his relaxed stance, his bearing made him seem as hard as an iron rail, a man of stone made flesh. A thin strap across his chest held sheathed a rare and storied weapon, a technological wonder the Hezra called a void-edge. It was the size and shape of a wide-bladed field knife, worn high near the shoulder with the grip downward. Elyth knew it was a fearful device, granted only to certain members of the Aziri, but hadn't ever seen one in person.

But for all the impact the man himself made, it was the name that marked him most in her mind. *Wari* was not only name but also title, identifying him as one of an extremely small group within the Aziri. To carry the name of *Wari* was to be trusted and skilled enough to serve as personal guard for the Hezra-Ka himself. The select group had much in common with First House's own Advocates of the Voice, though their purpose and training were completely different. Though Elyth had met a few Aziri before, she'd never encountered one of this man's status. They were peers, in a way. Most trusted, and most burdened, in service to their sovereigns.

Korush bowed crisply, the perfect demonstration of courtesy and respect. But Elyth could read in his eyes an emotion directly opposed to his display; there was no doubt he considered her an enemy. She returned the bow, but didn't offer her own name. It was clear that everyone here already knew who she was.

"And his little pet machine god," Sardis added. "I forget its designation."

The crate beside them stirred. Elyth took a reflexive step back at the motion, as the cube-like shape softly clattered and expanded, its once-solid exterior swarming and shifting into a vaguely humanoid-shaped mass of technology, like the blurred shadow of a man.

"Its designation is Subo," it said, its voice polite and quiet, tonally identical to that of a human. It towered over her, standing a few inches taller than even Sardis. She saw now that what she'd initially taken to be large square panels of metal were actually comprised of hundreds, possibly thousands, of individual components, intricately tessellated with no sign of how they were joined or held together. Apart from speech and the astonishing ability to shift shape, Elyth had no idea what its other capabilities were. Given what she knew of the Hezra's capacity, there was little doubt that it was a weapons platform of dire magnitude.

The man on Sardis's left chuckled at her reaction.

"Don't worry, it won't bite," he said. "Unless Korush tells it to."

He was dark-haired and dark-eyed, and from his build and uniform, Elyth could tell he was a Hezra officer who spent more time in the field than in command centers. He had a casual demeanor at odds with the usual tight professionalism of Hezra troopers, like a man on vacation in the midst of a war council. His uniform bore no identifying insignia.

He stepped forward to greet the two women.

"Captain Ames," he said, with a broad smile and an informal bow. "Pleasure to meet you finally."

Elyth returned the greeting, and realized he was talking specifically to her.

"Finally?" she said.

"Yeah, I'd hoped to do it a lot earlier, but I just never could quite catch up with you."

There was a playful glint in his eye that suggested some inside joke or deeper meaning that she missed. But Sardis didn't give them time to talk more.

"Ames will be primary navigation once we're on-world," he said. "But for the moment, he'll be setting up for the final briefing while the rest of us talk."

"Sure thing," Ames said, taking the dismissal without skipping a beat. He smiled at both Nyeda and Elyth again, gave a quick bow, and then headed off toward the front area.

Sardis waited until Ames had busied himself setting up the station for the upcoming final briefing before continuing with the others.

"I'll be bringing in the rest of our segment shortly," he said. "Before I do, Exile, I thought perhaps I should afford you the chance to reconsider, now that you've had some time to contemplate matters more fully. Even now, you are under no obligation. But once we depart from this ship, you will be committed. There will be no turning back until our task is done. For any of us."

He wouldn't say it aloud, but it was clear enough that he truly didn't want her on the team. Though it defied her understanding, Elyth knew what authority must have demanded it of him. Only the Hezra-Ka wielded such power over an Envoy.

"I committed when I made my choice," Elyth replied.

"Which choice?" Sardis asked. "The first, or the second? You seemed so certain each time, it's hard for me to be sure."

"Envoy," she said, "I'll hold up my end of the deal. You need worry only about keeping yours."

He rocked back on his heels, disappointed and resigned.

"Indeed," he said. "Very well. I suppose we should get on with it then. Korush."

Subo folded itself back into its cubic form with a soft-edged clicking, as its articulated outer shell reconfigured. The process was disconcertingly fast, like watching a tree decay in time-lapse. Elyth got the distinct impression that the machine's initial self-presentation had been for her benefit, a threat implied.

Others began filtering into the room as the rest of the team started to arrive. Arbiter Oyuun was among them, a few of his staff in tow. He waved, to Elyth specifically it seemed, but he was in continued conversation with one of those at his side, and his face remained serious with concentration.

"For the sake of our little group, we're going to have to find something else to call you besides 'Exile,'" Sardis said. "A handful of us know your identity, but it's already difficult enough for some to cope with having members of the First House embedded with their unit. There's no need to alarm them further. Advocate, do you have an acceptable alternative?"

Nyeda looked at Elyth for a long moment, wrestling with the decision. Any title would suggest a certain standing within the

House, and according to law and tradition it was forbidden to honor an exile with the name they'd been granted by its elders. But Elyth could see, too, that there was something more going on.

"Let her have her own name," Nyeda finally said. "I'll not speak it. But as a token of our grace and hope that she'll fulfill her promises, the others may. As far as they're concerned, she is an Aspirant, my attendant."

"Fine," Sardis said, flatly. He turned abruptly, headed toward the front of the room. "I suggest you both sit in the back."

Korush bowed to them both and followed Sardis, leaving the two women alone. Elyth turned then to Nyeda. Though it had been lost on the others, she knew what it meant for the older woman to permit the use of her name.

"Thank you," Elyth said.

"Earn it," Nyeda answered. "And perhaps one day, to utter it won't be such a curse in our halls."

She walked away, and made her way to a seat in the rearmost row of the briefing area. Elyth followed after her and sat beside her, readily adopting the humble position of attendant that Nyeda had assigned to her. Though Elyth had once held the higher rank and standing in the Order of the Voice, it was no matter to her ego to now be considered the lesser of the two. At least it would make it easier to fade into the background, to be overlooked and underestimated by those who did not know her already.

Over the next few minutes the remainder of the team members joined the assembly. Several people glanced their way as they entered, but most showed no sign of recognition or even interest. Elyth watched the way they self-organized as they filed into the briefing area, and without conscious effort began mapping the connections she could infer. There were about half as many people as seats, perhaps forty or so, and though they might all have been Hezra, the clusters they formed and the quiet conversations within them revealed some of the boundaries between those gathered. Even among the troopers, she picked up clear signs of the professional but subtle testing that always happened when top-tier veterans first met. It was obvious that personnel had been drawn together from a variety of units to create this task force.

She noticed, too, how Captain Ames moved easily among the groups, greeting several by name and receiving equal welcome from the disparate groups. Elyth couldn't tell if his widespread recognition was personal or by reputation only, but either way, he was clearly both respected and liked by a majority of the team. The opposite appeared to be true for Nyeda and Elyth. Though no one looked their way or made any audible remarks about them, it also seemed to be no accident that the two rows in front of them remained empty.

Sardis stepped up onto the platform at the front of the room and activated two large holographic displays, and the conversations dwindled to silence in a matter of seconds. One display showed a standard Hezra operation order, listing key details about timing, communication protocols, and command structure. On the other sat a full-screen view of the target planet from close orbit. It was vivid in green and blue, splashed and streaked here and there with the white of clouds. Inviting. Nothing about it suggested its anomalous origin, or the threat it represented.

The Envoy took a few moments to carefully scan the individuals gathered before him, his eyes resting on each long enough to suggest he was either comparing each face against a mental checklist or that he was memorizing them for future reference. When he reached Nyeda and Elyth, however, his gaze brushed past them almost as if they weren't there.

"Each of you gathered here has been hand-selected for this task, because of your service to and your standing within the Hezra hierarchy," Sardis began. If that statement had been intended to serve as praise or recognition, he undercut the sentiment immediately with his next one. "So I'm not going to waste time going over the details that you should have already reviewed in the packages you were issued.

"One item bears mentioning, however, that has not up until this point been disclosed. Ours is not the first deployment to *ru het* eleven-seventeen. We will be the *second* attempt to conduct such an operation on the world."

An intense silence gripped the room; no murmurs or whispers, though in the quick exchange of looks among several troopers, Elyth could read the surprise and the questions raised.

"First House volunteered a number of personnel to serve as an advance scouting party. To aid them, we provided a Hezra asset of some value. We have no further information to share on the composition of the first task force, nor on its outcomes, other than to say it was a House-led initiative. You may notice that *we're* running the operation this time, and infer from that what you will."

Sardis didn't look to the back row when he said it, but the chuckles and quiet comments throughout the room left no doubt that he'd meant to ensure that Elyth and Nyeda knew their place within the group.

"Now, now," he said, in mock conciliation. "We all serve the Ascendance, in our own particular ways. Some more than others, perhaps, but certainly we appreciate the support of the First House." Here, he gestured to Nyeda and Elyth.

"They have graciously supplied us with two advisors. Nyeda, of the First House of the Ascendance, Advocate of the Voice."

Several heads turned to look their way now, and a few murmurs signaled the recognition of Nyeda's special status. Though Advocates of the Hand and the Eye regularly interacted with Hezra personnel, Elyth doubted that anyone in the room had ever had direct contact with an Advocate of the Voice before.

"And her attendant," Sardis continued, as though it were a throwaway comment. "You can address her as 'Aspirant,' I believe. They will be attached to Captain Ames's group for the duration, to serve in an *advisory* capacity."

He emphasized the term, though whether it was for Elyth's sake or the rest of the team wasn't apparent. Captain Ames turned around in his seat and gave the two women in the back row a broad smile and a genuine salute. Whatever anyone else might think of them, at least they seemed to have an ally in him. Elyth still wasn't sure why.

"The quarantine fleet is stationed at standard intervals, five light-seconds from eleven-seventeen," Sardis said, the displays shifting behind him to show a strategic representation as he spoke. "We will stage deployment four and a half light-seconds from the forward line. And we will be making a direct-line jump to that point of departure."

The general reaction to the statement was one of restrained surprise, a feeling Elyth shared with the others. It meant they were not yet within their launch range to the planet and would be using their aspect drive to reach their designated deployment point. But that was not the part that had surprised the members of the task force. Due to the great power and method of operation of the aspect drives, standard protocol called for transitions to be made in areas of space with substantial distance from any significant gravity wells. Final approach was always completed on standard radiant propulsion. In this case, however, it seemed they would be transitioning directly to proximity with their target world. An unusual and potentially dangerous maneuver. But Sardis gave the reason for its necessity.

"In case it was not made abundantly clear in your materials," Sardis continued, "our involvement in this matter is unknown to the hierarchy at large and should remain so. Our unorthodox travel plans should help mask our arrival. And if all goes according to specification, our subsequent departure will also go unremarked upon. When we reach our destination, we will deploy immediately. Following dismissal from here, each team should proceed to its assigned vessel and prepare for the shift. *Clariana* will serve as our command craft, and will remain in synchronous orbit for the duration. *Aterin* and *Vanquin* are our surface crafts. Teams assigned to those vessels should expect to make first landing, and then be prepared to stay on-planet until our work is completed.

"From the moment we deploy, we will be on task. If any of you are feeling apprehensive about what lies ahead, I can provide you the following reassurances. I assure you that our progress will be slow, that our task will be difficult, and that the risks to our personal lives will be extreme. There is no way to know how long it will take for us to perform our survey, nor to predict what we will encounter while we do so. If you require any further reassurance, you signed up for the wrong job."

Sardis paused and scanned the group again in his manner, as though judging for himself each individual's resolve. This time, however, when he reached the back row, he locked eyes with Elyth and held her gaze for long seconds. She did not look away.

"I cannot overstate the significance of this operation," he said, finally addressing the group as a whole. "The Hezra-Ka is watching."

That final statement apparently served as Sardis's dismissal. He closed the displays and stepped off the platform, headed directly for the exit. The expectation was clear enough. Apart from a few sensitive details, the teams had all been briefed in advance, and the assumption was that they were prepared for immediate deployment. All that remained now was to board their respective ships and wait for the signal to launch. The members of the task force moved into crisp action, with little conversation.

Elyth alone, it seemed, had been left without clear instruction. As the personnel filed out of the room, though, Captain Ames remained to one side. Nyeda and Elyth joined him and stood by until they were the only ones remaining.

"It's my privilege to have you both under my care for the trip," he said. "But I think it's probably wise to take it slow for the first little while. These guys are all pretty slipstream, used to moving fast and not having to deal with a lot of overhead and baggage. They're going to sniff around you a bit, to figure out how much trouble you're going to be. Try not to take it personally. I don't think it'll take them long, though, once they see how good you are on the ground. And word to the wise, politeness is not generally among their skill set. But with certain folks, it doesn't hurt to be able to give as good as you get."

"We'll follow your lead, Captain Ames," Nyeda said.

"Not too closely, I hope," he replied with a wink. "I'm kind of a knucklehead."

He gestured toward the door and escorted the two women to their waiting ship. As was to be expected, the majority of the personnel were boarding the largest vessel, *Clariana*. But Ames took them past it, to the smaller transport, dubbed *Aterin*.

Though his encouraging aside had seemed motivated solely by his friendly nature, Elyth noted the separation it had opened between them and the rest of the team they were joining. Clearly that had been part of his plan. The man was sharper than he purported to be.

By the time they arrived at the ship, everyone else had already taken their places closest to the rear hatch, leaving the forward-most seats available. Ames led Elyth and Nyeda up the center aisle, through the midst of the team, past the empty seats, all the way to the front. When they reached the farthest seats, he directed them to sit there.

Elyth glanced down the length of the vessel. She estimated the *Aterin* had capacity for forty or so, and a quick count put the team at a dozen troopers, excluding Ames and the ship's crew. It was impossible to ignore the number of empty seats the captain was putting between his troopers and the women of the House.

"VIP status," Ames said with a smile, in response to Elyth's glance.

"Your kindness is appreciated, Captain," Nyeda said. "But so is your candor."

His smile shifted sideways, good-humored even with the breaking of his polite fiction. He looked at the men and women at the back of the ship.

"They've got a lot to deal with right now. I figured it's best to let them run their usual routine as much as possible, without having three walk-ons in the middle of it."

"Three?" Elyth said.

Ames looked back at them and gave a quick nod.

"Joint op. I'm a guest, same as you. Well, not quite the same, they all know me well enough. But it's not business as usual for any of us. Anyway, don't worry, we'll get all mixed in together soon enough.

"For now, go ahead and get settled in. I'm going to check in with the crew real quick. Once we make the shift, things are going to move pretty fast, so try to relax while you can."

He slipped off toward the cockpit, leaving the two monastics to buckle in for the journey ahead. Despite all the questions that still swirled in Elyth's mind, she didn't try to speak with Nyeda. The details would come in due time, and the order in which they were provided to her would tell a story of its own.

As unimaginable as it had been only hours before, it was now clear to Elyth why the House and the Hezra had gone to such incredible lengths to find her. They were being deployed to confront whatever the first team had encountered there. And Elyth couldn't ignore the fact that no one had called it a rescue mission. The implications sat heavy upon her.

The relative hush as they waited told of the gravity the others felt as well. Apart from a few quiet comments, there was none of the casual banter or good-natured ribbing she would have expected from the troopers at the back of the ship.

A few minutes after he'd disappeared, Captain Ames returned, but passed by without addressing them. He took a seat in the middle of the craft, alone, with space between both parties. Maintaining his neutrality. Or, perhaps, reinforcing his position as a bridge between them.

It was roughly an hour before Elyth felt the subtle shift in her sense of time and place that signified the activation of their mother ship's aspect drive, as it transported them across an unknown distance to within half a light-second of Qel's Shadow. She knew Nyeda had also sensed it, and she knew, too, that no one else aboard the vessel had the capacity to do so.

The aspect drive was the great gift of Hezra technology that had opened the path to the Ascendance's expansion throughout the galaxy, making trivial the interstellar distances that had once been incomprehensible. And though Elyth didn't know the exact mechanism behind the drive's operation, she knew well enough its foundation. The device drew upon the limitless potential of the cosmos, just as she did when she spoke the Deep Language. And though the two methods of contact to that source were vastly different, those trained in the arts of the First House possessed a special sensitivity to its use.

Less than a minute after the shift, the interior lights dimmed and switched to red, signaling imminent deployment. The craft was silent with waiting.

"Hold up," a gruff voice eventually said from the rear. "I forgot to pack socks."

The comment was perfectly timed. At almost the same moment that the last words had been uttered, the acceleration of the launch pressed them into their seats. A couple of chuckles sounded in the cabin, and then fell silent again, any further commentary lost in the deep hum of the ship as it made for its destination under radiant propulsion.

Sardis had told them that once they launched, there would be no turning back. And though Elyth had meant it when she'd said she was committed, as the distance between the mother ship and their tiny vessel stretched open, she felt the familiar fear of the unknown rising within her to match it. She herself had once beheld the full strength of the Paragon and had scarcely withstood it. Now, she would discover what terrible power existed within the universe that might dwarf even that of the ancient matriarch of the First House of the Ascendance. And as the distance between them and that mysterious planet diminished, so, too, did her confidence that any of them would survive.

FOUR

There were no viewports or displays for Elyth to watch as they made their final approach to *ru het* 11-17, but she felt the transitions as the vessel staged its radiant deceleration, and again when it shifted to atmospheric flight. Though there was no obvious signal, shortly after they entered the atmosphere, she heard movement among the team behind her. As the craft slowed for its final descent, all twelve troopers rose, fully geared in the Hezra's sleek, flexible armor and armed with long rifles of several different classes. Had they been deploying to an area of open conflict, they would have looked no different. The group moved to stack up by the rear hatch. The moment the craft touched down, the hatch opened, and the team flowed out with practiced precision. Ames stood by for several minutes before giving them the all clear.

When their turn came, he gave Elyth a quick wink, as if to say everything was under control. But the tension in his jaw and the hardness in his eyes told her of the fear he, too, was fighting. Previously, Ames had always allowed Nyeda and Elyth to pass through doors ahead of him, a mild but uncommon deference to their status within the House. This time, however, he took the lead through the hatch, leaving Elyth to be the last to step out of the craft.

So it was that her first real view of the planet came through her own eyes, as she stepped up to the hatch and looked out at the landing site. Her immediate impression was that it couldn't possibly be real.

The landscape was familiar enough, a wide clearing ringed with trees, hills rolling away. A bit idyllic perhaps, but not out of sync with the general features of any other Ascendance world. The colors, however, were so vivid and striking that they seemed hyper-real, as though they'd been tuned through some filtering process to maximize their impact. Elyth felt that she was now, for the first time, seeing what *green* truly was; that here, on this world, *green* had its source, and everywhere else she'd ever seen it had merely been a thin shadow or husk of the real thing. And the same was true of all the colors across the landscape. The reds and yellows of the wildflowers that dotted the clearing, the clear blue of the sky, even the tans and browns of the earth, every shade and hue created the same impression of a reality fuller and somehow more substantial than any she'd witnessed before.

Elyth inhaled deeply, and noted the crisp freshness of the air. It was intensely so, fragrant with the health of its earth and trees, but so clear and clean that it seemed to have been created only moments before she'd breathed in. *Fresh* hardly captured the quality. *Newborn* was more accurate.

She walked down the ship's boarding ramp in a mild trance. A light breeze rose briefly and swirled, a gentle greeting gust that stirred the sun-warmed air around her in playful welcome. The troopers had formed a security perimeter around the landing site and though they were all stationed at their designated posts, they, too, seemed to be feeling the same effects of this springtime world. As Elyth's foot touched the planet's surface, it struck her suddenly that she was breathing air that until recently had been completely devoid of human breath.

She wasn't quite sure how much time passed before she came fully back to herself, a few seconds or a few minutes. It was the sound of Captain Ames's voice that recalled her to the moment, and to their task.

"Team Banger's on the ground and secure," he said, speaking into his communicator. His tone was professional, but subdued, as though he were hesitant to disturb some sacred silence. "You're clear to bring it down."

A few moments later, a distant grumble became apparent, and then grew into a growling roar as *Vanquin*, the supporting gunship, approached. As they descended, Elyth noted how flat and dull they seemed now compared to the vibrant life of Qel's Shadow. The intrusion seemed vulgar in that setting, but the ship's arrival appeared to break whatever gentle spell had fallen over the security team. Their activity became sharper and quick conversations more frequent, as the gunship touched down nearby.

The *Clariana*, the third, largest vessel, remained somewhere above them in close orbit, and Elyth guessed Sardis was up there now, watching everything unfold, making his condescending comments from the safety of his command-and-control station.

She was quite surprised, then, when the gunship touched down, and the Envoy was the first to step off, with Korush and Subo close behind. Apparently she'd misjudged at least one quality of the man. And though she hadn't imagined it possible when she'd first met the Azirim, Korush looked even more formidable, outfitted now in the sleekest suit of armor Elyth had ever seen. It was reminiscent of the armor Nyeda had worn when she'd captured Elyth, though his was more elegant and he wore no helmet. As before, his void-edge hung grip-down on his chest, and from the way he and Subo moved, it was clear they served as close escort for Sardis.

Watching their approach, Elyth wondered what connection Korush shared with the machine; whether they were in some sort of constant communication enabling the Azirim to command it, or if, rather, Subo were fully autonomous and tuned to read and follow Korush's intent. Or there was some other mechanism, beyond her ability to discern. Whatever the case, she got the impression that the pair operated in tight coordination, and might as well have been two limbs of the same mind.

Captain Ames met them halfway, and they held a brief, quiet conference. Despite the ease of their landing and the serene environment that had greeted them, Elyth could tell from the intensity of their expressions that something had already gone wrong.

After a couple of minutes, Sardis returned to the gunship with Korush and Subo in tow. Ames walked over to one of the troopers and spoke for some time before joining Nyeda and Elyth.

"Bad start?" Elyth asked as he approached.

Ames shook his head, but his look was troubled.

"No, start was just fine," he said. "Just trying to decide whether or not we set up base camp here, or if we should load back up and check around for another spot."

"Isn't that the kind of thing you usually decide *before* you set down?" Nyeda asked.

"Sure is," he answered. "But usually our data's better."

He scanned the landscape around them, and the sharpness of his focus gave Elyth the impression that it was no casual survey. It

seemed more like he was either memorizing the geographical details or comparing what he saw against some previously prepared mental map.

"The location doesn't match what you expected," she said.

"No it does not," Ames said, continuing his slow inspection of the surroundings for a few moments longer.

"This is where the first team made landing. Or, at least, that's what we thought. But as you can see," he said, sweeping an arm out toward the tree line, "no ship, no camp, no sign that anyone's ever been here or anywhere nearby."

Elyth and Nyeda both turned to face the open expanse between their ship and the first line of trees.

"Topography's different, too, from the scans they sent back before they entered the atmosphere," Ames added. "So either we got the coordinates wrong or they did."

"You think they fell off course?" Nyeda asked.

Ames shrugged.

"Possible. Unlikely, I'd think, but possible. Could just be they didn't want us to know where they actually were."

"I'm certain you're not suggesting they would have purposely sent back false data?" Nyeda said. She kept her tone even, but Elyth knew the woman well enough to hear the anger at the accusation.

"Me? Not really," Ames said. "That's the Envoy's take on it, though. I think he's already under the impression that First House knew more than they wanted to share. And if we're all being honest, I think we can at least agree it wouldn't be *that* unusual, given the House's usual mode of operation."

Nyeda didn't like the implication, but she didn't argue it either.

"Seems like we could narrow the possibilities down easily

enough," Elyth said. "A landing site can't be too hard to find. Or a crash site, for that matter."

"Yeah, but that's, uh . . ." Ames said, trailing off, not quite sure how to finish whatever it was he'd been about to say.

"That isn't a priority," a voice said from behind them. They all turned to find Sardis walking the last few steps to join them.

"We'll set up here," Sardis continued. "It seems foolish to abandon our plan quite so quickly. Particularly when I'm certain we'll have much greater cause to do so later. Captain Ames, what measures remain before we can begin?"

"Scans all looked clear coming in," Ames answered, "but I'd still like to get over and walk the perimeter for myself before we commit."

"An hour?" Sardis asked.

"Two would be better."

"An hour then," Sardis said. "I want Arbiter Oyuun's detachment on-site and working within three."

"Understood," Ames said. He gave Elyth and Nyeda a quick bow, and headed off to talk with one of his troopers. Elyth watched the interaction, and noted how it seemed to play out more like a negotiation between peers rather than a superior officer giving orders. The trooper listened to whatever it was that Ames had to say, then offered some counterpoint or suggestion of his own, to which Ames acquiesced. They parted; Ames headed to the transport and the trooper toward the security line the rest of his team was still holding.

Elyth recalled what Ames had said about being a guest, just like them, and now the arrangement started to become clearer in her mind. Whatever Captain Ames's background was, she gathered that he was serving as an advisor or in some specialist capacity. The

troopers were in support of him, but not under his command. She didn't know how that would play out as the operation unfolded, but later, when the initial rush of activity had settled, she planned to see what more she could learn of Ames.

As Captain Ames entered the transport, a second group coming from the gunship caught Elyth's attention. Korush and his ever-present machine companion, Subo, were at the head, leading a pair of troopers toward the Envoy.

"I should accompany Captain Ames," Nyeda said.

"Out of the question," Sardis answered, so quickly it was as if in reflex.

"I'm not here to stand around and watch, Envoy."

"Oh, you most certainly *are* here to watch, Advocate. Until I decide otherwise."

Korush and his contingent arrived, but waited silently at a respectful distance.

"Do not forget who I serve," Nyeda said, with some heat. "I'm not beholden to your Hezra-Ka and—"

"It's simply logistics," Sardis said, cutting her off. "A practical matter. This may be difficult to imagine, but the two of you are the least of my concerns at the moment. I don't need the distraction of keeping track of your whereabouts. . . . Particularly if events necessitate a hasty relocation."

Sardis glanced away, his gaze drawn by motion. Elyth looked too, and saw that Ames had returned from the transport. He was now armed and kitted up, but instead of returning to them, he was moving out to meet a group of four Hezra troopers who'd come off the security line. When he reached them, they headed out together toward the tree line some five hundred yards or so distant.

"Make the most of your downtime," Sardis said, turning back

to Nyeda and Elyth. "You're not likely to have much more of it once we get started."

He turned to address the troopers standing off to one side who had been serving as Korush's escort.

"You two, come with me. I'm going to take a look around for myself. Korush, you stay here."

"I cannot advise it, Envoy," Korush said.

"Recall that you have *two* purposes to attend to, Azirim," Sardis said. "Neither of which is to *advise*. You should remain on hand in case your work is required. Don't worry, I'm not the helpless sort of thing you're used to playing nanny for."

"As you say, Envoy," Korush answered with utmost respect, despite clearly disagreeing with Sardis's self-assessment.

Sardis flicked a hand at the two troopers, signaling for them to join him, but started marching off without waiting for them to do so. He took a path roughly perpendicular to Captain Ames's direction of travel, his strides long and purposeful, as though he knew exactly where he was going and what he was looking for. Watching him go, it was hard for Elyth to judge whether that was true, or if it was an act intended to maintain his status among the hard-edged troopers under his command.

Korush, too, watched the Envoy for a span; his posture was relaxed, but Elyth got the impression that if anything moved to harm Sardis, the Azirim would respond as quickly as if he'd been anticipating it. Eventually, he turned briefly back, looking first at Nyeda and then at Elyth. The intensity of his look had an almost physical weight to it, but he said nothing to them before he turned his attention outward once more. He'd made it clear that he had no intention of addressing them; that didn't prevent Nyeda from speaking her mind.

"Envoy or not, that man shouldn't get used to issuing commands," she said. After a moment, she added, "Or, at least, to expecting them to be followed without question."

Elyth glanced at Korush to gauge his reaction; there was none. He seemed to take no more notice of them than the silent, hulking machine of his that stood nearby. But she could tell that he was alert and attuned to their every movement, even as he scanned the horizon.

For the next ten minutes, the odd group stood in strained silence, until Korush reacted to movement off to his right.

The others followed his gaze, and saw Captain Ames already returning with his team. Both Ames's pace and his expression suggested he'd found something he really didn't like.

As he drew closer, they could hear him speaking into his communicator, and though he was maintaining his professionalism, it was obvious he was arguing against whatever he was hearing from the other side.

"No sir, I'm not . . . I understand, Envoy, I'm not suggesting we wait for guarantees," he said. He reached the troopers holding the close security perimeter and signaled for everyone to group up while he continued his response. "Sir, you asked for my expert opinion, and my expert opinion is that we should give it a full day cycle before we ask anyone else to come down here."

He stopped a few yards away from Elyth and her companions, excluding them from the others, but apparently not concerned about them overhearing what he had to say. Ames was silent for a few moments, listening to the reply, and he held up a finger to hold off any questions until the conversation was done.

"Yes sir," he said. "Yes sir, I understand. Will do."

He shook his head before addressing the troopers gathered

around him. They all kept their voices lowered just enough to keep Elyth from being able to discern exactly what they were saying, but given what she'd already heard and what she could read from their body language, she picked up enough. They were moving ahead with establishing a base camp, even though whatever Ames had found had spooked him enough to advise against it.

Resigned, Captain Ames continued over to Elyth's group to give them a quick debrief. His demeanor was sharp, intense with focus and clarity; his easy, casual nature had completely evaporated. She recognized that look, knew what he was feeling. She'd felt it herself many times before. It was the weight of duty, forcing an advance into danger over the caution advised.

"We're going to go ahead and bring the research vanguard down," he said. "It's going to be a couple of hours of scramble and dust while everything gets set up. Until then, Korush, any chance you can persuade the Envoy to get back to the gunship?"

Korush dipped his head in acknowledgment, and then turned and strode off to retrieve Sardis. As he passed Subo, without any obvious signal or command, the machine flowed into an escort position just off the Azirim's shoulder and slightly behind.

"And, Daughters of the House," Ames said, "if you will, I need you to load back up on the transport until we get squared away out here."

Ames held out a hand to direct the two women back aboard the transport.

"Everything okay, Captain?" Elyth asked.

"Doubt it," he answered. "I don't mind if you two hang out by the ramp, if you want to keep an eye out. But do *not* wander off. Not even fifty feet. Is that clear?"

"What did you find out there?"

Ames glanced back at the tree line, hesitated for a few seconds.

"It's not what's out *there* so much," he said. "It's the ground *here* that I don't like."

He started to lead them toward the ship but stopped after a couple of steps and shook his head. He turned, leaned closer, lowered his voice, as though confiding more to them than he ought.

"*Clariana* ran narrow atmospheric analysis and picked up particle traces from the first team's ship, local to here. So while we were out there, we shot bearing back to them from five separate locations. And every single one of them confirmed the coordinates."

He paused, troubled by the implications. Elyth interpreted his message. The Paragon's ship had indeed entered the atmosphere along the vector they'd communicated back to the Hezra. But there was no sign anywhere that they'd touched down.

"You mean they set down somewhere nearby?" Nyeda asked.

"No," Ames said. "I mean, as far as we can tell, they set down right here. *We're* in the right place. It's almost like . . ." He shook his head again, scowled at the horizon. Wrestling with whether he should tell them or not. Or, perhaps, just trying to find the words to describe it.

"Like what?" Elyth prompted.

He looked her in the eye. "Like it's the *land* that's changed."

FIVE

Elyth and Nyeda remained aboard the *Aterin*, seated on the deck at the top of the boarding ramp and watching as the Hezra personnel scurried around the landing site to finish establishing the first footprint of their base camp. Shortly after Ames had directed them back to the vessel, a small fleet of automated craft from the *Clariana* had made landing. On their approach, Elyth had initially taken them to be shuttles for the rest of the team, but as they touched down, she realized they were all too small and too flat to carry any crew. They'd landed in formation, a central cluster with an outer ring. Even before the troopers had begun their work, Elyth had discerned the ships' actual purpose. Some were supply craft, but most were self-deploying structures. It was a ready-made camp, dropped from orbit.

Watching them work, Elyth estimated that within an hour the small team would have transformed the grassy clearing into a spartan but functional base of operations. For all the technological prowess of the Hezra, still nothing impressed Elyth as much as the hierarchy's logistical efficiency.

A third landing craft had joined them not long after the first of the structures had been fully deployed, this one a small shuttle pod from the *Clariana*. Arbiter Oyuun had stepped out, followed by two assistants that Elyth hadn't yet met, but they'd quickly disappeared into the centermost structure along with Sardis. They hadn't reemerged, and still no one had given Elyth or Nyeda any further instructions.

The two women sat together in an active silence, until at last Elyth let slip the first of the many questions that haunted her mind.

"Did you know, Nyeda?" she asked. "That the Paragon herself was leaving the Vaunt to come here?"

Nyeda didn't respond at first. For a few long seconds, she just continued to watch the activity on the ground. But Elyth knew her former sister deeply, and saw in her hesitation the tumble of questioning, of memory reawakened and often rehearsed. She guessed an answer before Nyeda spoke it.

"You did know," Elyth said. "Because she asked you to help prepare the plan?"

Nyeda glanced at her. "No," she answered, and then looked away again. "No, the plan was in place before she spoke with me. And when I volunteered to join her, she wouldn't allow it. She charged me with a different task."

The pain of the admission shone through. Elyth understood then the churn of emotion she saw in Nyeda. The regret of having been left behind. The guilt of survival, when others were lost. And the weight of that guilt hinted at the magnitude of the loss.

"How many went with her?" Elyth asked.

"Sixteen," she answered. "Eight of the Hand, four of the Eye, two of the Mind. And two of the Voice."

The loss of so many Advocates was a tragedy almost unimaginable for the House. But to lose two from the Voice cut even more deeply; their numbers were already so few. Elyth sat quietly, her eyes fixed intently on Nyeda, waiting for her to speak the names of her sisters.

"Umarai," she said. "And Dmini." Her head tipped forward, bracing against a gale of sorrow.

The fingers of an arctic grief clasped Elyth's heart. Umarai and Dmini. At the mention of their names, long-neglected memories erupted, peppering her with fragments of emotion.

Umarai was a few years younger than Elyth, and though the two had never been especially close, Elyth had always liked her, and knew how highly regarded she was within the Order. That she had been trusted to accompany the Paragon was no surprise.

And Dmini. After Nyeda, Dmini had been the dearest of Elyth's siblings. They had been Aspirants together, had trained together, studied together. And though Elyth had been brought into the Voice much earlier, when it came time to decide Dmini's place in the House, Elyth had served as her sponsor, and championed her before the elders of the Order.

To lose them both was a devastating blow. Elyth had lost sisters before, but she realized in that moment how naive she'd been during her exile. Despite knowing intellectually that it couldn't be true, she saw now that after she'd left the House, she'd allowed herself to behave as though her former Order would continue on just as she'd left it. That her sisters-in-arms would live forever exactly as they'd been when she'd departed. Though she'd said goodbye to them in her heart when their ways had parted, she'd never properly embraced the idea that their lives, too, would follow their own courses, and might find their own end.

In the midst of her unexpected grief, Elyth saw Nyeda's great burden, knew how she must have wrestled with the thousand different *if only I had . . .* thoughts that plagued her mind. Indeed, as gifted and devoted as Umarai and Dmini had both been, neither of them stood above Nyeda in the Order. That the Paragon had denied her the chance to serve in their place must have led her to a crisis of self-doubt of near-crippling magnitude. And though Elyth no longer served alongside her, she still loved Nyeda dearly.

"Nyeda," she said. "The Illumined Mother alone made her choices, and nothing you could have done would have swayed her from her own purposes."

"I know," Nyeda said quietly. After a moment, she raised her head again and, with eyes clearer, gazed out at the surface of the planet once more. "I didn't understand it at the time. But I believe I'm beginning to."

"Surely she knew the Order would need your strength and leadership in her absence."

"No," Nyeda said. "I think she knew I'd have to be the one to find you."

For all the certainty in Nyeda's voice, the words didn't clear any confusion in Elyth's mind. That the Paragon herself would have anticipated her involvement, to say nothing of having planned for it, only added further mystery to already complicated circumstances.

"I don't see how that could be true," she said. "I don't understand why she would think I would have any part to play in this."

"Neither do I," she replied. "Only you know what passed between the two of you before you chose to leave."

Before you chose to leave. Those last words held the greatest weight. Until now, Elyth had assumed that her exile from the

First House had been presented as an edict from the Paragon. In truth, Elyth had rejected the path offered by the Paragon that would have allowed for her to continue to serve the House. Not only rejected it but prevailed against the Paragon's efforts to command it of her. Elyth had believed those events remained known only to the two of them. But Nyeda's claim that Elyth had chosen to leave made it plain that she, at least, knew something of the truth.

"Is it known to the House? That I chose this path for myself?"

"Not by many. The Illumined Mother revealed it to me, just before she left. Whether she's told others, I can't say."

Nyeda paused briefly, but then added, "It was a strange time, to be taken into her confidence that way. To be singled out, charged with so heavy a duty, to keep so deep a secret, when all our lives have been so strongly commanded toward openness and connection."

Elyth knew well the feelings of both inclusion and isolation that Nyeda described. The honor and burden of the Paragon's trust. She'd experienced it herself, when she'd been dispatched to Qel. And she knew, too, how the Paragon had used those tools to manipulate the situation to her own hidden ends.

"I have no doubt you've told me the truth as you've seen it," Elyth said. "But I still can't see the Paragon's true purpose in all of this. No matter what threat she foresaw, I can't comprehend why she would choose to lead a team herself. It has never been her way, to put herself at risk when she has so many others at her command."

Nyeda bristled at her words.

"The Illumined Mother has never hesitated to give any measure of herself for the sake of her House, and for her daughters," she said. "She felt responsible. Felt it was her duty, or her penance, perhaps. For having failed to adequately control you."

"So she did believe I was the cause of this?"

"She thought it possible. And you must consider it too. Whatever happened on Qel, whatever it was that you did, it shook the Ascendance at its roots. Our House had to be the one to step forward, to account for . . . for whatever this is." She waved her hand at the land outside the ship.

Elyth looked at the surface of the world before them, pondering what secrets the Paragon had perceived in its earth. No matter what Nyeda told her, Elyth could not bring herself to believe that the Paragon's motives for being first on the planet were so purely noble and willingly self-sacrificial.

"Then why would she not seek me out first, Nyeda? Why risk herself, if she believed I was the one responsible?"

"Because she feared you, Exile," Nyeda said, heat rising. "Do you still not understand? The Paragon of the First House of the Ascendance *feared* you. In a way I have never witnessed in her before." She paused again, settled herself. "But I think, too, that she knew something deeper. Either about the Deep Language itself, or, more likely, about you. Something she saw in you that no one else can perceive. Not even yourself. . . . Certainly not me."

"And yet you sought me out."

"*Something* gave her courage enough to at least consider the possibility that you might not prove an enemy after all."

"It's her job to consider all possibilities. And to choose her course from among many paths. That's the responsibility of the Paragon."

"Spoken like someone who has never known the weight of that burden," Nyeda answered, and though her tone was even,

Elyth heard the anger seething beneath the words. Nyeda could get loud when she wanted to, but she was most frightening when she went quiet. "You've never had to confront the kind of uncertainty that the Illumined Mother navigates on our behalf, never had to discern what action to take, knowing the consequences will reach far beyond *anyone's* ability to see. You were a tool in her hand, an instrument forged for *her* purpose, and I will *never* understand how you could turn against her. How you could turn your back on our way, and on our House . . . on me."

"Nyeda," Elyth said.

"Don't, Exile," she answered, with the quiet sharpness of a keen blade. She remained perfectly still, but the effect was the same as if she had stood up and angrily walked away. Elyth had pushed her too far, had awakened too many wounds. In her effort to draw the strands of truth together, she had forgotten how her relational distance from the Paragon was not shared by Nyeda, who still suffered under the loss and uncertainty. Anything else she might say now would only serve to deepen their pain.

Elyth rose to her feet, lightly touched Nyeda's shoulder in silent consolation and apology, and descended the ramp. She stopped a few steps away from the craft, drew a deep breath of the pristine air, held it in her lungs. Somewhere on this world, the Paragon and sixteen women of the House had vanished. And for all the appearances that something had gone catastrophically wrong, Elyth just could not find herself fully convinced that she wasn't somehow still trapped in a cosmic web, weaved by her former sovereign.

She scanned around her at the transformed landing zone, where the Hezra personnel seemed to be in the final stages of setting up their camp. The two main ships flanked the southern end of the site, with a compact but stout structure in between that had an aggressive, bunkerlike appearance. In fact, now that the structures were all arranged and deployed, the location looked more like a tiny combat outpost than any sort of research station. Typically, it would have struck Elyth as being classic Hezra overaggression. Given what they knew of the planet so far, though, she had to admit that in this case it might not have been the wrong approach.

Four troopers maintained security, each posted in pop-up towers at the edges of the site, that were little more than platforms raised six feet off the ground. Under their guard, the rest worked on the finishing touches, some unloading supplies from the back of a utility skimmer, others distributing gear with the aid of sleek powered exoskeleton striders, still others testing power distributors to ensure they had good coverage across the camp. But Elyth noted how all of them kept their weapons close at hand, and how alert they remained to their surroundings. A few moments later, she understood why they were so on edge.

Off to the west, a strange noise arose some distance away. A knocking sound from deep within the surrounding woods, like two large trees driven together in the wind, slow but rhythmic. It lasted only ten seconds or so. But while it lasted, every single person in the camp was completely still. And after it stopped, it took a few moments more before anyone resumed their activity. Elyth hadn't heard the sound while she'd been in the *Aterin*, but based on the reaction of the others, she could tell it wasn't the first time that they had. She wondered if it was closer now than it'd been before.

She glanced back up the ramp to gauge whether or not Nyeda had heard it as well, but her former sister was no longer sitting there, having apparently retreated somewhere deeper into the craft. When she looked back, motion from the center of the camp drew her eye, and she saw Captain Ames coming out of the center structure, followed by Sardis and Arbiter Oyuun. The trio paused a few steps outside and formed a half circle facing the direction of the sound, clearly in discussion about it. Elyth had had enough of sitting around. She decided to insert herself into the conversation.

Ames was the first to notice her approach, and he acknowledged her with a quick nod and a subtle gesture for her to join them. Sardis glanced in her direction, but didn't seem to take any particular note of her as he continued on with whatever he was in the middle of saying. Elyth took the lack of a clear demand to halt as tacit approval of her presence. She stopped next to Oyuun, who gave her a brief smile in greeting.

"Anything I can't handle on my own, I'm certain Korush can manage," Sardis said to Ames. "If that's your concern."

"It's *one* of my concerns, yes," Ames replied. "But there's still so much we just don't know, sir. And not all threats can be shot to death."

"Clearly you haven't seen Subo in action," Sardis said. "But, very well. I will acquiesce if you agree to keep the contingent small enough. I want this site operational and I'm not willing to lose time just so your friends can go stomping around in the woods."

"Sure, I can keep it real small," Ames said. "As long as you agree not to argue with me about who I bring along."

The knocking came again from the woods, from roughly the same distance and direction as before. Conversation ceased for the duration. Though it didn't continue as long this time, Elyth was struck by the consistency of both the sound and its rhythm. Each individual knock had a benign, natural quality to it that wouldn't have seemed out of place to anyone who'd spent as much time in the wilderness as she had. Close-grown trees swaying out of sync, or thick branches meeting in the wind. But it was much too loud. And taken together in sequence, the steady rhythm and identical amplitude of the knocks seemed tinged with intent. It was the suggestion of purpose that produced such an unsettling effect.

"Fine," Sardis said as the sound faded. "Go pick your best. And be quick about it."

"Great," the captain said, and then his eyes went to Elyth. "How do you feel about a little scouting trip?"

Sardis shifted his gaze back and forth between the two of them.

"No," he said.

"You literally *just* agreed not to argue with me," Ames said.

"Because I assumed you were speaking of bringing one or two from your assigned unit."

"First off, she *is* part of my assigned unit," Ames countered. "Second, we can take one of her, or eight of the others. You want to keep things small, she's the smart choice."

The Envoy clearly didn't like the argument, but the fact that he didn't have an immediate reply suggested he might actually be considering it. Ames pressed his momentary advantage.

"All due respect, sir, you're the one all hot to get things moving here. If we're going to be out there poking around anyway, might as well get her started too. Leaves the rest of the crew here working, just like you want."

Sardis turned his full attention on Elyth then.

"It seems the captain here would like to provide you with your first opportunity to fail us," he said. "I don't suppose you are wise enough to decline?"

His towering stature combined with the intensity of his stare would have been oppressive to any normal person. But Elyth was a woman who had beheld the infinite cosmos and the power that held it all together. To her eyes, in that moment, he seemed small and insubstantial.

"I'm here to serve," Elyth answered, with a precisely respectful bow. "And I wouldn't dare refuse the direction of the officer whom you, in your wisdom, placed in authority over me."

Sardis grunted, and though it happened so quickly she thought she might have imagined it, the shape of his mouth twitched in what might have been a millisecond show of surprise or perhaps even something bordering on amusement.

"Your graciousness astounds," he said, all trace of positive emotion replaced with his usual acidic tone. He pointed to the westmost bunker. "Fifteen minutes, meet there. I will depart on time, regardless of who is with me."

He turned to address Oyuun.

"Arbiter. Dare I believe that you possess the capacity to maintain order for as much as an entire hour?"

"Chaos is fundamental to the universe, Envoy," Oyuun said. "And I don't like to make promises. But I don't think I'll manage to burn the entire place down in that short window."

Sardis fixed him with his hard stare.

"It would take me at least two," Oyuun finished. Sardis lingered a moment longer, apparently searching for a sufficiently biting reply and unable to come up with one.

"Fifteen minutes," he finally said. He swiveled abruptly and set off with his long strides toward the *Vanquin*.

"I'm not entirely sure he likes us," Ames said.

"He is . . . not a nice man, at heart," Oyuun replied, briefly watching the Envoy walk away. He then looked back to Ames and Elyth, each in turn. "But nice and good aren't the same thing, and he *is* effective. It's not without reason that the Hezra-Ka charged him with this task. It would be a mistake to underestimate him."

His expression was deeply serious, and his warning clear. After a moment, though, in characteristic fashion, he smiled and added, "Though it *could* be a mistake to believe everything he says about himself."

He reached out a hand to each of them, clasped their arms just above the elbow, and squeezed. Even in gentle encouragement, the strength in his grip told Elyth he hadn't spent his entire life in a lab.

"Be careful, watch yourselves," he said. "And take good notes! I can't wait to hear what you find!"

"I'll be sure to bring you a little something back, Arbiter," Ames said, clapping Oyuun on the shoulder.

Oyuun nodded, and headed back to the central structure.

"Nothing wriggly," he called over his shoulder. "Or with too many legs!"

"Roger that," Ames said. Once Oyuun had gone, he turned his attention to Elyth. "You sure you're good with this?"

"Of course," she answered. "I'm dying to do something useful. And I assumed you had a good reason for suggesting it."

"Not sure it's a *good* reason, but *a* reason, yeah," he said. He motioned for her to follow him, and started leading her back toward the *Aterin* as he continued. "Now, as you've probably noticed, I'm not the most educated man, so admittedly, I'm pretty ignorant of how you folks do what you do. But I do at least understand that you can see things in a way that's different from how any of us can. I got a little sense of the area my first time out, but I'd really appreciate getting your perspective on this place."

Elyth found herself glad to hear that Ames apparently wanted

her along just to get her read on the nature of the planet. Whatever else the Envoy might have had in mind for her, helping investigate the ecology of the strange world seemed like something
useful and beneficial she could do in the meantime.

"Just point me where you want me to go, Captain."

"For the moment, I want you right beside me," he said. And
then he flashed a smile. "Maybe a few steps ahead, actually. But
first, let me run you back to the *Aterin* and get you kitted up. I have
no doubt Sardis will leave without us if we give him any reason."

He picked up his pace and led her back to the transport at a
half jog, and spoke into a communicator along the way.

"Hey Tal, you on board *Aterin*?" he said. "Great. Can you pull
a standard rig for me real quick? I'm taking one of our VIPs out
for a walk. . . . No, the other one. . . . Yeah, just the kit. Thanks."

They slowed to a brisk walk as they approached the ramp,
and by the time they reached the top, one of the Hezra troopers
was already walking down the main aisle carrying a small pack
by its straps, and a bulky bundle under one arm. Elyth recognized her as one of the troopers that had accompanied Sardis on
his first trip out; Tal, she assumed.

"Hey pops," Tal said. Elyth spotted the insignia on her uniform, identifying her as a sergeant, first class, which made her one
of the higher-ranking enlisted troopers of the task force. They met
in the middle, and Ames continued past her, while pointing back at
Elyth.

"Get her set up for me, will you? We're racing the Envoy."

"Hey, no pressure," she replied. Ames disappeared through a
hatch, and Tal set the gear down on two of the empty seats nearby.
She unrolled the bundle first, revealing it to be a soft-bodied vest
striped with attachment points for other gear. A pair of gloves

made of matching material flopped onto the seat. "You ever wear one of these?"

"No, I haven't, Sergeant," Elyth answered.

Tal held up the vest and turned it quickly to show both front and back. It was matte black, but looking closely, Elyth saw the material was comprised of small hexagons tightly joined through some invisible mechanism. The sergeant tossed it to her.

"Right arm through first," she said, gesturing as she spoke. "Wrap and seal from the left."

The vest was open along the left side; Elyth slipped her right arm through as directed, and then Tal helped her pull a flap around beneath her left arm. When the edge of the flap met the body of the vest, the tiny plates shifted together so completely that it appeared to be crafted from a single, unbroken piece of material. The weight was noticeable, but not uncomfortably so, and Elyth could see how one could wear the vest for long periods, if only it hadn't been quite so large on her. She wasn't sure if it was the wrong size, or if it'd been designed to be worn over heavier attire. Just before she asked, though, Tal ran a quick finger along the top of her left shoulder, and the vest responded to the gesture by gently constricting, and fitting her form more snugly. Elyth tested the comfort, inhaled deeply, twisted at the waist back and forth. It didn't seem to restrict her movement in the slightest.

"Don't let the weight fool you," the sergeant said. "It's nice and breathable, but apart from heat and sweat, there's not much that can get through it." She thumped the front of the vest with a heavy fist, and then picked the gloves up from where they'd fallen.

"Same stuff," she said, offering them to Elyth. "Main difference is sensory pass-through. Keeps your sensitivity, up to a point, dampens anything that gets too far up into your pain threshold.

Takes a little getting used to, especially when you're touching something real hot or cold. The most important thing, though, is to remember when you're *not* wearing them. Seen a few corporals in the field pick stuff up with their bare hands that they shouldn't have. Usually only takes once to learn, but it's hilarious every time."

Elyth slipped the gloves on, and just as the vest had, they subtly reconfigured to fit. With each hand, she tapped her fingertips against her thumbs in succession, pointer to pinkie and back again, testing the impact on her sense of touch. To her surprise, if she hadn't been looking at her hands, she wasn't sure she would have been able to tell she was wearing gloves at all.

She looked up from the gloves to find Tal holding her small operations pack.

"Pretty sure this one's yours?"

"It is, thank you," Elyth said.

"I didn't check it, since I didn't know what you put it in anyway, but whatever procurement got for you should all be there."

Elyth accepted the pack and slipped it onto her shoulders. As she adjusted the straps, it occurred to her that she hadn't seen Nyeda leave the craft, but neither was she in the main cabin.

"Have you seen," Elyth said, and hitched just a moment, nearly having forgotten to use the address proper for her supposed station, "Advocate Nyeda?"

"Sorry, no, really haven't been keeping tabs on you two. You need her?"

"No, thank you," Elyth said. "Though if she's looking for me, could you inform her that I was asked to assist Captain Ames?"

"Oh . . ." Tal said, and she looked momentarily concerned. "You sure she'll be okay with that?"

Since Elyth had been presented as an attendant Aspirant, the Hezra personnel considered Nyeda the authority between them.

"I am," Elyth answered. "My role is to provide whatever assistance is requested of me."

"All right," Tal said, though she didn't seem entirely convinced. "I'll have to remember that when my feet get sore."

She produced a small device from a pocket, and attached it to the front of Elyth's vest, near her collarbone.

"Comms run through the vest," she explained. "This little guy here will match channels with the captain for you." She held out a second component, this one a thin arc about an inch long, flattened at either end. "And this piece goes over an ear. Either one, whichever's comfortable. Press the ends against your head."

Elyth took the component and placed it over her ear, then pressed on the flat ends as directed. It wasn't exactly clear how, but the device felt firmly attached and didn't shift around when she turned her head back and forth.

"It's bone-conducting, so it won't interfere with your normal hearing," Tal said. "And it's range-dependent. Boosts signal only when it's needed. If you're next to each other, you won't hear anything different. Farther away, this little guy kicks in. Only weird part is when your guy's too far away to hear with your own ears, this thing kind of makes voices sound like they're coming from inside your head. You get used to it, eventually."

Tal stepped back and gave Elyth a quick once-over. As she did so, Ames reappeared, similarly geared up, though he had his short rifle slung across his chest.

"You set?" he said to Elyth.

"I don't know. Do I get one of those?" she said, nodding to the weapon.

"Only if the rest of us are dead," he answered. "But if it comes to that, you can absolutely have mine."

He slapped Tal on the back as he passed.

"Thank you, Sergeant."

"Sure, pops. You guys need any company out there?"

"You looking to hang out with Sardis some more?" Ames replied.

"Oh, no sir," she answered. "Too much to do here. Busy busy."

"Yeah, I figured," Ames said. "Do me a favor and don't take off without us."

"Wouldn't think of it."

"I bet you already have."

"Well, yeah . . . but only because of the Envoy. You be good out there, Captain," Tal said. "Keep your comms up."

"Yep. See you in a bit."

Tal nodded and headed back to whatever job she'd been doing before they'd interrupted her. Ames turned and started toward the ramp, and Elyth followed along.

"Good kid," he said. "Tough as they come."

"Seems friendly enough," Elyth said. "Or does everyone call you 'pops'?"

"Just her," he said. "On account of my great wisdom and experience."

"I admit I wasn't expecting to be treated like I actually belonged here."

"Don't expect it to be universal," Ames replied as they walked down the ramp. "Tal's got more sense than most, though, and she gets a pretty quick read on people. She doesn't have much patience for useless folks, no matter how high their rank or station might be. But she'll respect anybody that can do work, no matter where they come from. My guess is she can tell you're the real deal."

He started to say more, but something caught his attention and changed his focus.

"He said fifteen minutes," he said to himself, and then to Elyth, "Come on, we're going to have to double-time it."

He picked up the pace to a full jog. Elyth fell in just behind him and, looking ahead, saw that Sardis had already crossed halfway to the western tree line, with Korush and Subo flanking him. The trio was walking, but at a determined pace. Ames and Elyth caught up with them just as they were reaching the scrub brush border of the woods.

"I thought you said *fifteen* minutes," Ames called.

Sardis paused and turned.

"It didn't take us as long to prepare as I anticipated," he said. "But now that you're here, would you care to take the lead?"

"Yes sir, I would. And I'd appreciate it if you wouldn't follow right up on my heels. Keeps the bears from getting us both at the same time. If they're going to get a meal that big, they ought to have to work for it."

"By all means," Sardis said, dipping his head. "Please show us how it's all done, Captain Ames."

Ames flipped some internal switch, and his easygoing demeanor transformed immediately to all business.

"I'm on point," he said. "Elyth next, leave me about ten yards. Envoy, behind her at the same interval, and Korush, you're with the Envoy. If I tell you to stop, stop immediately. And if I tell you to run, don't ask why."

As if in response to his words, the knocking sound came once more, louder this time. The group remained at the border until it stopped again.

"Yeah, all right," Ames said. "We're coming."

He stepped forward confidently, but with care, tuned to the environment like a man following the tracks of a wounded animal. Elyth held her place until he'd gone ten yards in, and then followed behind. And together, the small group left the relative safety of the camp, the vanguard striking out to confront the lurking unknown.

SIX

They kept a methodical pace for about half an hour, pausing every so often whenever Ames went still to survey their surroundings. As they stalked through the forest, Elyth found herself increasingly impressed by the others in their small group. Though it was no surprise to her that Korush could move with such fluid quiet, the fact that his machine companion could flow across the terrain with similar grace was astonishing almost to the point of being unnerving. More than once she found herself looking back to verify that Subo's feet were in fact touching the ground, and that it wasn't just floating above the surface like some metal cloud.

And even Sardis was competent in the wild, moving with quiet steps and sure footing. It clearly wasn't his natural environment, but he avoided the clomping mistakes of the novice she'd expected him to be, and demonstrated a level of attentiveness that put him on par with a seasoned hunter. Though she didn't want to admit it, the more she saw the Envoy in action, the more respect she felt building for him. She doubted she'd ever be able to admire the man, and she certainly would never trust him, but witnessing firsthand his alertness and skill in the wilderness gave her some measure of confidence that he wasn't the blustering, bumbling bureaucrat she'd first taken him to be.

As good as they were, though, none of them were in the same class as Captain Ames. He was among the best movers she'd seen, including her own former sisters from the Order of the Voice. He seemed to intuit the natural rhythm of their environment, and moved effortlessly through it, with it, as though he was as much a part of it as the wind or the trees. And when he stopped moving, he might as well have been part of the landscape.

His skill was made all the more impressive by the otherwise uncanny stillness of the wood. She had noticed it the instant they'd crossed the threshold of the tree line. Despite the vibrancy of color and lushness of plant life, there was an emptiness to the forest that made it feel like a brightly lacquered mausoleum. And the longer they walked, the heavier that sense became, until it was almost oppressive. It wasn't silent, exactly. The trees whispered and rustled in the light breeze; their gentle footsteps stirred the air as they padded over the dead limbs, leaves, and needles cast off and scattered on the forest floor. But for all the appearances of healthy vegetation, Elyth couldn't shake the feeling that they were the only truly living things in that wood.

"The thing I don't get," Ames said, his sudden words shocking after so long a silence, "is where is all the wildlife?"

He stopped and turned back to face them. His posture straightened and fell relaxed, giving up on trying to remain unnoticed for the moment, as though the game of hide-and-seek had been declared over and he the winner. The rest of the group caught up to him, while he stood looking around. He shrugged and shook his head.

"I get that maybe we're the first humans to walk these woods," he said. "So maybe every bird and beast ran off to hide. But all this, and not a single print? No nests, no beds, no runs, no scat? I haven't even seen a single insect."

He looked over to Elyth.

"This feel right to you?"

She shook her head.

"Yeah," he said. "Me neither."

"It does seem odd," Sardis said. "Particularly when so much else seems familiar. I'll inquire of Oyuun when we return. This strikes me as the sort of detail one would have noted if one were being thorough in one's research."

"The knocking stopped," Korush said.

Elyth had been so intent on the moment to moment of her surroundings that it hadn't registered with her that she hadn't heard the strange sound since they'd entered the wood.

"I couldn't hear it while I was on the *Aterin*," she said. "How frequently had it been happening?"

"Started up a little while after the supplies touched down," Ames said. "Got more active over an hour or so."

"And then gave up, as soon as we came out to find it?" Elyth said.

"A shy spirit of the wood, perhaps," Sardis said. "Whatever it was, can we assume for the time being that it does not represent a threat to our humble camp?"

"I don't know, sir," Ames answered. "Not finding a thing doesn't mean there's not a thing to find."

"Oyuun's sensor array should be functional in another . . ." Sardis said, and paused briefly to check the time. "Hour at most. I'm inclined to let him take up the search for the source. There doesn't appear to be much point for us to continue pursuing it, if it doesn't care for our presence."

"Might as well get a couple of readings while we're out," Ames said. "Give the Arbiter a little something to work with."

Sardis glanced around the woods, still seeming impatient, as though they were running behind some unspoken schedule. But Elyth was starting to get the impression that that was just his normal state of being.

"Fine," he said. "Ten minutes, and then back to camp."

Ames nodded, and gestured to Elyth. "I don't guess that happens to be time enough for you to do your, uh . . . ?" He held up a hand and waggled his fingers.

"Analysis?" Elyth said.

"Sure, I guess."

"It isn't magic, Captain," she said. "Just a different way to read than you're used to."

"I'll take your word for it."

"That's not a bad policy. But no, not nearly enough time. If I'm working steadily, it usually takes a couple of days to get a baseline, and then after that, it can be a week or so to build a comprehensive profile."

"How comprehensive does it need to be?" Sardis asked.

"That depends on what you want me to do, exactly," she answered. "Care to tell me what that is?"

"*That* depends entirely on what we find," Sardis said. "Nine minutes."

"All right," Ames said, and he waved a hand at Sardis, Korush, and Subo. "You three hang tight here for nine minutes, while the Aspirant and I take a quick look around. Wari Korush, I trust you'll keep the Envoy from doing anything silly."

Korush dipped his head in acknowledgment. Ames nodded, and escorted Elyth away from the group.

"I guess do what you can," Ames said. "We'll try to get a proper trip put together once the Envoy settles down."

"It won't be much," Elyth answered. "But I can get a start."

They parted, with Ames headed off toward something that had already caught his attention a few yards away.

Elyth walked several paces from the others, and then stopped with her back to them and took a long inhale. She closed her eyes for a few moments, settling into a sense of the place, felt her connection to it expand beyond the borders of her self. It was true that establishing a baseline for her planetary analysis would take about two standard days, if she were following normal First House protocols. But during her time on Qel with *eth ammuin*, he'd taught her a new way to interpret the vital energies within a world. And afterward, in her exile, she'd reevaluated the techniques of the House, explored the edges and gaps of her teachings, and developed an enhanced method of her own.

It would bring her neither quantifiable data to evaluate nor hard scientific evidence to assess. But if she executed the technique properly, then the world itself might tell her where to begin.

She fixed her mind on her purpose, and let the words of the Deep Language rise to her lips.

"Dawn chases shadow; blossom greets the day."

When she opened her eyes again, she let her vision go wide and unfocused, to absorb the sweep of view before her, the impression of the place taken all at once. For several minutes she held still, allowing the unique quality of sensation that the wood created to imprint itself on her, to sink into her being.

This was her first true introduction to Qel's Shadow, the first genuine moment of greeting free from the distraction and confusion created by the presence and activity of all the others. And as she opened herself to what this unique world had to offer, she felt it, too, begin to unfurl itself hesitantly before her. It would take days of careful study to discern the foundational patterns within the planet's composition. But in these first few minutes Elyth allowed the wide-band ripple of the terrain, the sharp-edged freshness of the air, the trace humidity in the breeze on her cheeks to all mingle together to shape a sensation within her, like a tide rising timidly to meet her. The broad strokes washed over her, each revealing a subtle touch of the signature of the world, each drawing her by gradual degree into greater alignment with its singular form of self-expression.

No matter how many times she had done it, Elyth had always been awed by the complex vitality deep within the heart of each world. Even in the sickest of the planets she'd had to put down for the Ascendance, there was something radiantly precious about the unique story of its formation, buried within its many layers, told by its intricate pattern of threadlines running throughout. And Qel had taught her how to truly listen to the silent anthem each world lifted in reverence to the cosmos.

But here on Qel's Shadow, the first notes of its resonant song generated the barest hint of a discordant overtone, a harmonic variation at odds with her many years of experience with nature. The impression struck her something like hearing a voice humming a familiar tune, but with the wrong rhythm. Someone singing the echo of a song, or perhaps mechanically repeating a sacred hymn without having grasped its meaning.

It was a wisp of smoke at the edge of perception, and she knew reaching for it would only obliterate the fragile strands. Her training kicked in, held off the temptation to strain her senses, and Elyth rested in the moment, knowing her stillness would allow space for the impression to grow sharper, more apparent.

"Four minutes," Sardis called from behind her.

The slow wave of energy building within Elyth collapsed completely at the harsh edge of his voice.

"In case you actually wanted to *do* something while we are here," he said.

Elyth resisted the urge to turn around to address him. Whether she answered with a cutting response or a humble one, either would acknowledge the provocation. Sardis seemed to thrive on the reactions he induced in others; ignoring him seemed to be both the wisest course and the cruelest.

Whatever she'd begun to sense about the place was lost for the moment, the impression too ephemeral for her to hold in her mind. It would be difficult to recover until she could find some measure of genuine solitude. Until then, she'd have to make do with the more technical side of her analysis. Fortunately, even in the immediate vicinity, there was sufficient botanical diversity to begin.

She pulled her set of collection instruments from her pack and gathered a few samples of the most easily accessible variety; a scrap of papery bark, a bit of spongy gray moss, a segment of a woody fungal bloom. While she did so, she gained a deeper appreciation for the gloves Tal had provided her. They left the sensitivity of her touch so intact that she was able to handle the delicate bark with care, and feel the velvet texture of the moss through them. Yet when she tested her fingertip against the fine point of one of her tools, the sharpness somehow remained apparent without ever passing into pain, no matter how hard she pressed against it. And the ill-advised experiment left no trace or mark on the glove.

For a brief flash, Elyth wondered what instruments the House might be able to develop with the Hezra's aid, if only the blending of their two disciplines had not been forbidden at the founding of the Ascendance. But the thought quickly vanished. Whatever discoveries or progress might have been accelerated, there was no doubt that humanity would have soon after erased itself with such power.

Captain Ames returned as she was capping a sample of surface soil. And though his pace suggested he hadn't found anything dangerous, his expression still showed focused concern, while he tried to work out the strangeness of the wood.

"No bears, Captain Ames?" Sardis said as he approached.

"No bears, no spiders, no wasps," Ames answered. "Which normally I'd be glad of."

Elyth chuckled at the response, at the unusual combination of creatures in his list, reading in it something of his personal distaste for them. For a warrior so at ease in the wilderness, he seemed unusually uptight about bugs.

"Hey, those are the three great terrors of the wild," he said, mock seriously. "Everybody knows that. It's just science."

"Your courage is truly inspirational, Captain," Sardis said. "What's your assessment?"

"My assessment is that this place is weird, sir. That's about all I've got so far."

"It looks familiar enough," the Envoy said. "To my admittedly amateur eye, at any rate."

He stepped to a nearby tree with his hands behind his back, leaned closer to inspect it. It was tall, slender-trunked, with a sprout of leaves high at the top, and coiled by a thin vine with delicate blossoms.

"Tendril rose, I believe," he said, identifying the vine. "This forest could be on any of a thousand Ascendance worlds I've visited."

"That's probably why it feels so weird," Ames said, looking up at the patchwork canopy above them. "*Looks* like what you'd expect, without actually being it. I don't know."

Sardis let out a quiet grunt, a sound Elyth initially took as acknowledgment of Ames's statement. But when she glanced at the Envoy, she saw he was looking at the fingers of his left hand. A moment later, he removed his glove and revealed a crimson streak along his pointer. He pressed his thumb against it, and a bright bead formed near the fingertip.

"Well," he said. "That's unexpected."

He held his finger up and turned it to show them the drop of blood.

"I'll have to file a complaint with my tailor. Went right through the glove."

Ames was by his side in a moment.

"What did you touch?" he said. "Show me exactly."

Sardis pointed to the offending plant, and started to reach toward it, but Ames stopped him.

"Don't touch it again!"

"Captain, I'm not fool enough to let it bite me twice," Sardis said. And despite Ames's warning, he gently raised the head of one of the flowers on the vine to show the stem beneath. To his credit, he did avoid injury this time.

Ames produced a knife from his belt and then carefully slid the blade under the stem to support it while he gently pushed the Envoy's hand away. He continued to move Sardis aside, farther back from the plant, and then stepped in to study the stem up close. Elyth watched him work, noted how intently he studied the vine's features and read its structure.

"These little devils," he said. "I see why you didn't notice them, they're almost clear, like glass. I can't tell if they're thorns or just really stiff bristles. They look worse than needles, though."

He turned back to Sardis.

"How do you feel? Any light-headedness? Heart rate increase? Blood rush of any kind?"

"I am in excruciating pain, Captain, as you can see," Sardis said flatly.

"Sir, this isn't a joke. Your body just got compromised by un-identified flora."

"It's a tendril rose. They're on ten thousand worlds."

"It *looks* like a tendril rose. *Looks* and *is* aren't the same thing."

"I'm fine, Ames." He held his finger closer to Ames's face. "Already stopped bleeding. And it didn't even leave a splinter."

"Still shouldn't have gotten through your glove."

"I concur. Hence my complaint."

Ames turned back to the plant and studied it for a few moments longer.

"Yeah," he said finally. "Yeah, I think I see the one that got you. Doesn't look like it broke off. It's still got a little blood on it. Or hmm . . . *in* it, maybe . . ." He turned his head, checked the stem from multiple angles. "It does look like it's inside. Interesting. And maybe good. At least maybe that means it didn't inject you with anything."

Ames gingerly took hold of a tendril and excised a portion of it with surgeon's hands.

"Still, better get toxicology on this," he said. "And we better head back right now, just in case."

"We're three minutes behind anyway," Sardis replied, donning his glove. "I assume our return can be at a quicker pace than our timid entrance?"

"We can pick it up, sure. I don't think we need to worry too much about making a racket now. Just watch your footing. And don't touch anything else."

Sardis made an exaggeratedly dramatic gesture to invite the captain to lead the way back. Ames moved out, and the others followed closely behind, no longer leaving the gaps between them that he'd enforced on their way into the wood. The brief exploration and the lack of wildlife had made the forest seem less threatening, but something sinister remained in its emptiness. They kept the pace up, a more purposeful walk than the stalking approach they'd taken before. But even with Ames's explicit statement about no longer needing to be concerned about noise, each member of the group still seemed compelled to make themselves as small as possible. Elyth felt the pressure to move quietly herself, beyond her normal, natural propensity for it, as though the wood demanded it of them.

They had traveled about twenty minutes when the knocking sound started up again, somewhere behind and to the left of them. Ames froze in place at the first occurrence, and the others followed suit, but turned to face the direction of the disturbance. The knocks continued in their slow rhythm, identical in interval just as before. But the nature of the sound had changed. Closer, certainly, but now with a subterranean quality, a deep cavernous thrum underlying each dull wooden impact.

After several seconds, a second source joined the first, this one coming from the opposite side and somewhat farther away. The intervals of each seemed the same, though their rhythms were slightly offset. The effect created an unmistakable impression of a heartbeat. But gradually, though the change in timing was imperceptible, the rhythms unified, and the sounds merged until Elyth lost the sense of directionality and instead felt that she was at the center of a single drum.

Both continued for nearly a minute, the longest she'd heard thus far. When the beats finally ceased and the wood fell quiet again, the emptiness of the place seemed magnified, as did the sense that none of them belonged there.

"I don't think I liked that," Ames said.

"Korush," Sardis said. "Did you happen to get a range on that?"

"No sir," Korush answered. "Waveforms were indeterminate. Too broad to pinpoint."

"Of course they were. I'm really not certain why we bother to invest in such . . ." Sardis replied, waving a dismissive hand at Subo while he searched for a term, ". . . instruments if they're no better than our own ears."

"Indeterminate origin," Subo said politely. Elyth thought the machine was repeating Korush's report, until she saw Korush's head snap to look at it. "On vector."

"Acquire," Korush said.

"Acquired."

"Am I supposed to understand any of that?" Sardis said, but Korush ignored him, stepped past him with an intense look. Elyth felt the hair on her neck stand on end, without understanding why.

"Range?" Korush asked.

"Two hundred meters," Subo replied. "Thirty-two seconds."

"That sounds bad," Ames said. He brought his rifle to his shoulder, muzzle pointed to the ground but ready to engage in a heartbeat. If only he knew with what to engage.

"Korush?" Sardis said.

Korush didn't reply. But Subo responded in surprising fashion. The machine stepped behind Sardis and unfolded its outer shell, its innumerable micro-segments blossoming and streaming out in a manner somewhere between a swarm of insects and the roots of a tree growing at hyperspeed. The components formed a dense latticework encasing the Envoy.

At the same time, two small pods emerged from Subo's core chassis, rolling up and to either side, to where its shoulders would have been if it hadn't refactored itself.

"Korush!" Sardis shouted. "Korush!"

But still Korush took no notice of the Envoy. He stood ten feet ahead of Subo, and though his stance was relaxed, he had the look of a storm cloud summoning its power to unleash a thunderbolt.

"Korush!" Sardis called again. "This is unacceptable!"

"Fifteen seconds," Subo said, its voice perfectly calm.

"Korush?" Ames said.

Korush raised a hand, actually acknowledging the captain and gesturing for him to wait.

"Ten seconds," Subo reported.

The shape came over a rise forty yards distant, directly in line with Korush and Subo. Ames snapped his weapon up, but Korush shot his arm out sideways, signaling for the captain to hold fire.

At first sight, Elyth took it for a large mammal. But almost immediately that impression gave way to one more insectlike. What it was, she couldn't tell, but the way it moved sent a surge of revulsion through her, like witnessing a serpent in its death throes or the twitching of half-crushed spider. It made barely any sound, other than a clicking sort of shuffle across the forest floor. And it covered the ground way too fast.

The thing rapidly closed the distance to Korush, twenty yards away, but he stood motionless, waiting. His void-edge hung on his chest, ready for sudden and devastating deployment. And though Elyth felt certain that's what he was preparing to do, the creature was so close and so fast, she doubted even he was quick enough to draw it in time. To her surprise, he didn't even twitch a hand toward it.

Instead, when the creature got within ten yards of him, Subo emitted a brief, low hum. An instant later, the pods on its frame sent forth six ribbons of purple-tinged light, silent, luminous beams that arced and then converged, passing like wraiths through the beast and into the ground beyond.

The creature collapsed instantly and impacted heavily, its momentum carrying it a yard or two before it came to a complete rest. They all stood in silence for a few moments, staring at the thing lying in a heap before them. Sardis, as usual, was the first to speak.

"Korush, let me out of this thing!"

Korush made no acknowledgment, but the latticework surrounding the Envoy retracted as Subo assumed its typical form. As soon as he was able, Sardis strode out of his protective cage and within arm's length of the creature.

"I am not a child, Azirim," he said as he passed Korush. "You absolutely may *not* have your pet do . . . *that* . . . again."

"It is the will of the Hezra-Ka that you be protected," Korush answered. "And I serve his will."

His delivery of the response was the epitome of etiquette and respect, but the message was clear; when it came to fulfilling his duties, he was not the Envoy's to command.

"There's no shame in getting buttoned up, sir," Ames said,

approaching the creature cautiously. "I would've gotten in there with you if there'd been a door."

Elyth joined the two men by the carcass, and though its twitching movements had ceased, the sense of revulsion it created continued. Even up close it was difficult to identify. The creature was a mottled gray-brown lump, a confused mass of features both mammalian and insectoid, lying on what Elyth guessed was its side. The majority of its body was covered in a spiny fur, like the quills of a hedgehog, punctuated by patches of sleek carapace around its joints. Roughly the size of a small bear, it had six limbs of different sizes, unusually arranged.

The rear legs were stout and slightly shorter than the others. The remaining four were paired on each side, one thick like a beetle and one thin like a spider, and joined together at the creature's shoulder. If it could be called a shoulder. The body wasn't segmented like an insect's, but its limbs and their mode of articulation were most similar to that of an arthropod. Except at their tips. The legs ended in a strange split-configuration that reminded Elyth of a partially open Venus flytrap, or eyelids with sparse lashes. Each half was ridged with eight long, fingerlike protrusions, and each protrusion had many joints that appeared to give them grasping capabilities somewhere between a human hand and a tentacle. Whether hand or foot, there was something undeniably rootlike about their look, as though plant life, too, had been incorporated in the creature's development. And now that she'd made that connection, her perception of the body shape shifted to include not just mammalian features but fungal ones as well, like an enormous mushroom cap.

If it possessed eyes or mouth, Elyth couldn't readily recognize them.

"Well. It would seem this place isn't totally devoid of wild-life," Sardis said. And though he spoke calmly, Elyth detected a hint of a tremor in his voice. "Captain Ames, what precisely are we looking at?"

"Scientifically speaking?" Ames said. "My new worst nightmare."

"That's not particularly insightful."

"No sir, it is not. But it's all I got at the moment. Looks like someone took the awful parts of a bear, a spider, and a wasp, and squashed them all together."

"Do you have a hypothesis on why we didn't detect it before?"

Ames stared at the abomination for a few moments, before shaking his head.

"Because I have no idea what we'd even be looking for, I guess?" He pointed to various features as he spoke. "Body shape makes me think it'd be a nesting critter, but no guess on where. Could be underground, could be in the rocks, could be in the water for all I can tell. No mouth I can see, so I couldn't tell you what it eats. And feet, or whatever those are, like that, I'm guessing they don't leave much in the way of tracks. At least not that we'd recognize as such. I'm not even sure it's normally ground-dwelling." He glanced up at the trees above them. The implication sent a shiver through Elyth.

"Its intent was undoubtedly hostile," Sardis said.

"Territorial, maybe," Ames replied.

"Or a hunter," Korush said.

Ames lifted his weapon and examined it briefly, and then extended his foot and hazarded a gentle poke of the beast's back with the toe of his boot.

"I'm glad you were here, Subo, old buddy," he said. "I'm not sure I could've put this thing down on my own."

"It seems so . . . out of place," Elyth said. Sardis looked at her.

"Elucidate," he said.

She gestured at the landscape around them.

"As you said before, everything else here looks like it could be on any of a thousand Ascendance worlds. But this . . . thing . . ."

She shook her head.

"Yeah, never seen anything like it," Ames finished.

"No," Elyth said. "That's not quite it. We *have* seen things like it. You said it yourself. It looks like a composite of different species, of different kinds of life. But not like life itself. For all the nature out here, there's nothing *natural* about it."

"And yet it is not entirely alien, either," Sardis said. He was watching her intently, but not in his usual challenging way. His mind was working in parallel to hers, integrating her thoughts with his in rapid analysis. "Indeed. Indeed, I believe I see what you mean, Exile. A curious world, this. *Like*, but not *same*."

Elyth nodded.

"Well," he continued. "Our little excursion has not been a total waste of time, then. Captain Ames, if you'd be so kind as to drop a marker at this location, I'll have the Arbiter direct his initial efforts to this area."

"Sure thing," Ames answered. He glanced down and tapped at a small device attached to his harness. "When we get to camp, I'll bring some of the troopers out to haul this thing back too. Oyuun's going to want to get a personal look at it."

"I do not share your confidence that he'll *want* to," Sardis said. "But yes, I concur that he should. And let's expedite our return. One such sample is sufficient."

The Envoy still projected his usual confident disdain, but the implication was clear enough. He didn't want to wait around for another one of those things to show up any more than the rest of them did.

"Yeah, roger that," Ames said. "Korush, you want to take rear guard?"

Korush nodded his consent, and dropped to the back of the line as Ames led the way to camp. Elyth noted, though, that Subo remained by Sardis's side for the duration of the journey.

By the time they returned, the base camp appeared to be fully operational. Several Hezra troopers stood watch in their towers and at points around the camp's perimeter, but the other few who remained in sight were sitting together in a casual clump at the center, recovering after their labor. Everyone else, Elyth assumed, had disappeared into the various structures.

One of the troopers stood as the patrol came in; Elyth recognized her as Tal, the woman who'd helped her get her gear together.

"Hey pops," Tal called. "Good hunting?"

"The best," Ames replied. "And lucky you, you get to help me bring it in."

"Seriously?"

"Yeah, we bagged a specimen. Big one. Do me a favor and grab a sled. And bring your friends. . . . And arm up."

"You want to take the skimmer?" she asked, jerking her thumb at the flatbed utility skimmer parked to one side of the camp.

Ames shook his head. "Tempting. But I want to stay agile, just in case."

Tal nodded. Elyth could see the weariness on the sergeant's face, but the trooper made no complaint as she went to work. With that exchange, the group broke up; Ames to gather his team for another trip out, Sardis with Korush and Subo to Oyuun's structure, undoubtedly to debrief the Arbiter. Elyth started to follow the Envoy but he waved her off.

"I'll summon you if I deem it necessary," he said.

Her instinct was to protest, but she stopped herself, and instead just nodded. As much as she wanted to hear Oyuun's initial reaction to their findings, she knew she'd have a better chance of getting deeper information later, without the Envoy around. She wasn't sure what more was expected of her at that point, and she wasn't quite ready to face Nyeda again. Instead of returning to the heart of the camp, she found a quiet spot near the edge and sat down on the ground with her back against one of the bunkerlike structures. She stayed there for some time, watching the wall of trees across the clearing, allowing her mind to wander where it would as it processed all they'd experienced on their brief excursion.

Her unguided thoughts continually returned to the Paragon and her sixteen companions. And to Umarai and, most of all, to Dmini. She recalled the tune that Umarai hummed absentmindedly whenever she performed any sort of manual labor, a liltingly soothing melody, somewhere between work song and lullaby, from the woman's pre-House childhood. And Dmini's laugh, and her terrible jokes, and the sadness that only showed at the corners of her eyes when she was trying to conceal her feelings. And the Paragon. The Illumined Mother herself. Though their parting had been a sundering of relationship, Elyth found her heart deeply stirred at the thought of the great matriarch of the First House lost in this place.

And yet, for all the strangeness she had already encountered on the world, nothing thus far had struck her as anything beyond the Paragon's ability to control or withstand. No matter how she turned it over in her mind, it still seemed incomprehensible to her that the first team's disappearance was purely the result of accident or misfortune. Even so, she knew there was a great deal about the planet yet to be discovered, and she tried to leave a little door open in her thoughts to account for the unknown that might have been the source of the unthinkable.

Elyth was still reflecting and contemplating when Captain Ames returned with his party, leading their low-hovering sled along behind them. When she first spotted them, she thought from their pace that they were hurrying to return the creature to the Arbiter. But when she glanced again at the sled, she realized it was empty.

She rose and met them as they reached the perimeter. Ames was uncharacteristically dark.

"Run into trouble?" she asked.

"Not exactly," Ames answered. "But I'm sure we're in it anyway. Couldn't find the thing."

"Your marker didn't take?"

"Marker was fine. We were in the right spot, no doubt about it. But whatever that thing was, it's gone now," Ames said. "And I mean gone. Vanished. *Poof.* Not a single trace."

He continued past her and on toward Oyuun's central lab. And Elyth knew, just as Ames did, that they were only just beginning to discover how deep the well of trouble ran on this impossible planet.

SEVEN

Elyth lay awake on the cot, staring up at the gentle arc of the ceiling. Exhausted as she was from the day, sleep would not come. And though she didn't want to admit it, the encounter with the horror from the wood and the creature's subsequent disappearance clung to her, filled her with a dark anticipation, as though a horde of its siblings might erupt from the trees at any moment. Beside her, just over arm's length away, Nyeda slept soundly on a simple cot of her own, sweetly oblivious to the nebulous dread that Elyth felt but could not name, and thus could not command.

The Hezra troopers had generously given the two of them quarters to share, separate from the rest of the unit. And though the structure was small and clearly designed for storage, the relative privacy it provided was an unexpected luxury on such an otherwise spartan site. It may well have been the result of the Hezra's distaste for mingling with them, but in light of the generally kind reception that Ames, Tal, and Oyuun had given, Elyth chose to receive it as a nice gesture.

For a time, she tried to steer her mind toward solving the

puzzle of the creature's arrival and disappearance, thinking that if she could treat the mystery rationally, it might steal away the instinctual fear that hovered over her. To no avail.

After a solid hour of lying sleeplessly, Elyth decided her pure will was insufficient to draw sleep down upon herself. There wasn't room enough in the structure to run through her moving meditation sequence, so she quietly rose and slipped out beneath the night sky of Qel's Shadow. The day-night cycle here was roughly thirty standard hours, nearly evenly split between light and darkness. Though the air had cooled, it remained pleasantly mild, and called to her mind springtime in the Vaunt, the walled city, home and sanctuary of the First House.

The camp was still, dark, and quiet. But not unguarded. Though she couldn't see them all, Elyth knew troopers were standing watch while their comrades slept. The clear sky above offered meager starlight, supplemented by the weak shine of Qel hanging out there in the void. Too small to serve as a proper moon, too muted to be taken for a star.

But seeing the planet reminded Elyth of how the two worlds shared a sky, at least in impression. The stars, of course, weren't the same here as she had come to know them under Qel's nightly veil. But in the broad sweep, it would be easy to mistake one for the other. Out here on the edge of the galaxy, at the farthest ends of the Ascendance's empire of worlds, the heavens displayed the vast gulf between life and emptiness. The stars were all crowded toward one half of the sky, huddled together as the last brilliant refugees escaping the infinite darkness.

On practically every other planet inhabited by citizens of the mighty Ascendance, the night served as a reminder of humanity's astonishing mastery over the physical universe. From deeper within the empire, it was nearly impossible to see a star that hadn't been reached, studied, cultivated by their collective hand. And for every star touched, worlds followed, majestic dwellings for the ever-growing populace, nurtured through the wisdom of the First House and the power of the Hezra, under the beneficent direction of the Grand Council.

But out here, at the very end of its reach, even that galactic span seemed insignificant against the backdrop of all that remained beyond its grasp. For all its local dominance, the Ascendance had still not unlocked the secret to crossing the void between galaxies. And so that which seemed so incomprehensibly omnipotent from within was revealed as weak and inconsequential from without.

She lingered a few moments longer by the entrance to her quarters, breathing the mild night air, listening to the gentle sounds of the environment as the light wind stole through grass and trees, seemingly reluctant to draw attention to itself. It was impossible for her to ignore the absence of other common signs of life; insect chirps, or the occasional call or cry from nocturnal birds and beasts. The land bore a winter's stillness.

"Trouble sleeping?" a quiet voice said from the darkness. Elyth startled at its sound, snapped her head in its direction. A dark silhouette stood five yards away, and though she couldn't distinguish features, she recognized the shape of the man. Arbiter Oyuun. His body was turned, facing outward from the camp, but he seemed to have his head turned in her direction. How long he'd been standing there, or how she'd failed to notice his presence, she had no idea.

"Sorry to startle you," he said. "I wasn't sure how else to announce myself."

Elyth approached with careful steps, glancing around to see who else might be lurking under the stars.

"I'm usually much harder to surprise," she said. "Must be losing my edge."

"Long day," Oyuun answered. "Strange circumstances. I wouldn't judge yourself too harshly."

It was too dark to read his expression, but she could hear the kind smile in his words.

"I'd like to say it's because I have so much on my mind," Elyth said, "but that seems like a silly excuse to offer a man in your position. I can't imagine what you must be dealing with."

Oyuun chuckled and shifted. She could see his face in profile now, as he looked off into the black wilderness beyond their camp.

"Oh, I don't know. When you get right down to it, it's all just a little science with a good dose of math. This would probably be trivially easy, if I were any good at either."

"Forgive me if I don't take you at your word, Arbiter. I suspect you're misrepresenting yourself by several orders of magnitude."

"A matter of perspective, my dear. If you compared what *I* know to all that there is that one *could* know, I assure you that you would find the delta is practically infinite. For all intents and purposes, I know nothing."

"You are a man great in both intellect *and* humility, I see."

"Not humble enough to reject your flattery, I fear," he said, his smile shaping his words again. "You are kind. And I can hardly tell you're patronizing me."

"That certainly wasn't my intent—"

"Oh, think nothing of it. You are being polite, and I take no offense. But I'm fully aware that your understanding of our universe dwarfs my little scratchings at its surface," Oyuun said. He drew a deep breath and raised his head to look at the heavens above them. When he spoke again, his voice was lower, his words pensive, tinted with melancholy. "I may be able to describe it crudely, on a good day. I know the formulas for the basics, I suppose. But, if I were brazen enough to think I knew anything, I might suggest that you understand it in a way that defies description. I've done little more than read about it. You have *lived* it. I might be tempted to say I was envious, if I didn't also suspect that there's a price you've paid for that understanding. One far beyond my capacity to bear."

Elyth stood silent at the Arbiter's surprising response to her. The words came from him so easily, she could tell that the thoughts he was sharing weren't impulsive or unconsidered. They had the weight of deep rumination, almost of confession, as though he'd long waited for the chance to speak them. And they seemed built upon a foundation of genuine respect for the First House and its work as keeper of the Deep Language.

"But listen to me rambling on," he said, lightening the moment. Unexpectedly, he sat down on the ground as he continued to speak. "Or rather, don't. Sorry, I'm a foolish old man up well past my bedtime. I probably shouldn't have taken all those naps while the Envoy was away."

Elyth sensed the implicit invitation, and after a moment's hesitation, she joined the Arbiter on the ground, sitting cross-legged beside him.

"You are a fascinating man, Arbiter," Elyth said. "I don't believe I've ever had the pleasure of meeting another quite like you."

"Lucky for me. I'm sure if you had, you wouldn't be so forthcoming with your praise."

"Given your rank and the caliber of the others assembled to support your work here, somehow I doubt you're the fool of the Hezra, sir."

"The Hezra-Ka may disagree with your assessment," Oyuun said.

"The Hezra-Ka would disagree with many of my assessments," Elyth replied. "That doesn't mean he's right."

Oyuun chuckled.

"Well. You didn't hear it from me, but those who sit in authority are just as given to misjudgment as the rest of us," he said. And as though it struck him as an afterthought, a moment later he added, "As I am certain you are all too well aware. I admit I can't fathom why the First House would release a woman of your quality into the wild. Let alone force her there."

"Only because you don't know me, Arbiter."

"Perhaps. But I may know you better than you think. Varen certainly thinks highly of you."

A lightning surge coursed through Elyth at the mention of Varen's name. It was so unexpected, so out of place, it seemed like a carefully planned, precisely timed emotional ambush. And though the Arbiter didn't turn to look at her, she knew he was intently tuned to her reaction.

"You've spoken with . . . him?" she asked. She had known him as *eth ammuin*, and could not call him by the other name.

"I have," he answered. "At length."

Oyuun put subtle but unusual emphasis on the words, and with their implicit meaning, Elyth saw the conversation up to this point in an entirely new light. This was no casual midnight banter. He had something to tell her. Something he was sure the Envoy didn't want her to know.

"Since his capture, after Qel?" she asked.

"And before," he answered. "Long before."

Long before. That would mean the Arbiter hadn't just known about the Hezra operation on Qel. He'd been part of the secret work there to dissect Varen's understanding of the Deep Language, and to incorporate what they learned into Hezra technology. The blending of the two had been expressly forbidden since the founding of the Ascendance. In a flash, Oyuun's admission transformed him in her mind, from a kindly researcher to the worst sort of architect of destruction. A man who understood the potential for catastrophic harm his work could unleash, and who undertook it anyway.

Elyth kept her words as neutral as she was able.

"You were involved with the work on Qel."

"It's worse than that, my dear," he said. "I was the chief technical officer for that initiative. When we began our . . . collaboration with Varen, I was the one who selected Qel as the site for his release. And our research."

Elyth sat quietly, absorbing the information, letting it swirl and settle into place, allowing it to integrate with all she had known up to that point, and all that she hadn't.

"So," Oyuun said, after her lack of a response. "Perhaps now you see how I am indeed the fool of the Hezra."

"You were in charge of Deepcutter?" Elyth asked. The covert program had been the Hezra's prime initiative for untold years, the project to at last crack the secrets of intergalactic travel, to open the universe to the Ascendance's continued expansion. She had only known about it because of her high rank within the First House, and even that had been unauthorized.

"Deepcutter? Hmm, I've never heard that name," he said in a tone that clearly indicated he had, and then leaned toward her briefly. "But yes, that was the one."

"And Varen taught you the Deep Language?"

"I'm not sure I'd say that, exactly. In his way, I suppose. But only enough to show me how little I actually knew."

He sat back and sighed heavily.

"The universe has a way of chastening us in proportion to our hubris, and mine was perhaps the greatest in the history of our ancient race. So my time here on Qel's Shadow is my penance. Mine, far more than yours. I fear, however, that it is beyond my capacity to repair on my own."

"I'm not sure why you're telling me any of this," Elyth said, allowing a measure of her disgust to seep into her words. "I have no absolution to offer you."

"Oh, of course, yes. Sorry, I'm not looking for anything from you. I suspect the full measure of my punishment is yet to be meted out. But I do feel it's important for you to know the truth, or as much of it as you can, anyway. I hold a strong belief that you can't find the optimal solution to a problem without first properly identifying the actual problem you're trying to solve."

"Then I don't see how any of that is relevant to the problem at hand, Arbiter. Unless you're planning to tell me precisely what it was that . . . *he* taught you."

Oyuun chuckled again, but without humor.

"Ultimately, he taught me that I didn't even know the right questions to ask," he said. "I worked on Deepcutter for almost thirty years, always chasing the idea that our challenge to intergalactic travel was one of distance. That it was the same problem set we had already solved, just of a greater degree. It was only recently that I came to understand there's something else going on, something too subtle or too . . . fundamental, perhaps, for our instruments and techniques to notice. The nature of space within our galaxy is different from that which lies beyond it. And I suppose that's where Varen was most helpful. If nothing else, he showed me that I was trying to solve the wrong problem."

"While he was helping you, did you know he was also changing Qel?"

"Yes," Oyuun said. "And no. I knew he was doing something. He was meticulous, deeply thoughtful, testing his concepts with great care. We were monitoring the health of the planet, and his work didn't appear to be destructive. It wasn't until the First House took interest that we realized we might not know what exactly we should have been watching for. Hubris, again."

"And then rather than letting the truth be known, you tried to destroy it."

"In part. I can't speak to what percentage of that decision was based on protecting the reputation of the Hezra. Greater than zero, certainly. But we did realize the danger of losing control of Qel. If there'd been any other way, I would have preferred it. Unfortunately, the Contingency was the only tool we had at the time to fully correct the situation."

"That seems to be a hallmark of the Hezra," Elyth said. "To assume you're capable of controlling things beyond your comprehension."

"A fair assessment. If we were being charitable, I would say the hierarchy had a pretty good track record of doing so, up until recently. But your point is well taken."

"And we're repeating the mistake here, on this world. Trying to control it, without understanding what it is."

"It does appear to be our way. But I hope you see now why we need you here. We're learning that we still have more to learn, late though it may be."

Elyth shook her head in the darkness.

"What makes you think I could find anything that the first team couldn't?"

"A hunch, only," Oyuun replied. "I have a hypothesis that this place was born out of the interaction between the power of the Contingency and whatever it was that you and Varen did on Qel to protect it from destruction. If that's true, perhaps there's some affinity between Qel and its Shadow. Something inherent that only you would recognize."

"Strikes me as an awful lot riding on a hunch."

"Indeed. But that's the nature of my work. Making my very best guesses, and then proving myself wrong."

He leaned forward and took a deep breath. In it, Elyth heard both relief after his confession and also resolve for what lay ahead.

"When morning comes," Oyuun continued, "my work will begin in earnest. I've told you all of this to give you a more complete picture of our situation. But I have also told you all of this in hopes that you'll understand the strength of my commitment to correcting whatever imbalance I've invited into our empire. The fault is mine, more than anyone's. And so must be the responsibility to repair the damage.

"I know I said I wasn't looking for absolution, and that remains true. But, for whatever it's worth, I *am* sorry that you are bearing the burden of my mistakes, my dear. If I believed I could fix this without involving you, I would. But because my errors have caused such hardship for you, I want you to at least know that I'm willing to face whatever I must to correct them. I am here until the end. Whatever that end may be."

The two sat quietly in the darkness for a time, Elyth pondering the many revelations, and Oyuun apparently content to let her do so. She'd spent the past few years reflecting on the chain of events that had led her to exile. Now, she saw how much further back in time that chain of causality stretched, and how much smaller her role in it all had been than she had previously believed. Within that new expanded context, she felt more like a cog in a great, galactic machine than the commander of her own fate that she'd thought she'd become.

If the Arbiter had been waiting for a response, she wasn't sure what to offer him. Her thoughts were too many and her emotions too complex to distill them into any meaningful statement. Neither judgment nor forgiveness seemed fully appropriate. If nothing else, Oyuun's admission did at least tell her that this was no mere scientific curiosity to him, and revealed the depth of his resolve. Whether or not his resolve could truly withstand the pressure of the Shadow remained to be seen.

Given enough time, either of them may have had more to say to the other; as it was, the moment was fractured by a brilliant sheet of white light casting out from the northeastern quadrant of the camp. The light poured across the clearing all the way into the first few feet of the tree line beyond. The camp's interior lights glowed to life. A piercing alarm followed, and only a handful of seconds later, the site erupted with troopers.

Both Elyth and Oyuun shot to their feet, but stood frozen in place, unsure how to respond. The Hezra troopers showed no such uncertainty. Despite the late hour and the mind-breaking sound of the alarm, the Hezra personnel moved like a single, clockwork unit, some snapping into position to focus on the threat area while others secured the flanks. It was speed without haste, smooth aggression in motion.

Nyeda came out of her quarters, eyes half-wild with the shock of violent waking.

"What's going on?" she called.

"No idea," Elyth answered.

"Let's go see," Oyuun said, and without waiting for a reply, he started off at a trot toward the front line.

Elyth and Nyeda exchanged a brief look, and it was hard to know which of them had the greater fear. Elyth's mind conjured the image of a rolling wave of those abyssal creatures rushing the compound. But Nyeda had only heard tell of the beast; there was no knowing what she might imagine emerging from that black wilderness. Elyth was the first to turn to follow after Oyuun. Nyeda's footsteps fell in close behind.

Vanquin, the gunship, spun up its engines as they crossed the site, lending a low growl to the sound of the alarm. Elyth and Nyeda caught up with the Arbiter as he was being intercepted by Tal, a few yards behind the perimeter.

"Return to your quarters, sir!" she ordered as she stepped in his path. She was fully kitted up, armed with a large rifle, and her eyes showed battle intensity. "All of you, get back to your quarters!"

"What's happening?" Oyuun asked.

"Sir, you need to get inside, it's not safe for you—"

"Sergeant, you do not give me orders!" Oyuun interrupted, and the authority and booming volume of his voice took Elyth, and apparently Tal, by complete surprise.

"Sir," Tal said in acknowledgment. "I'd request that you at least stay behind me."

"What exactly is happening?" Oyuun said, stern but quieter.

"Not sure yet," Tal answered. "Picked up motion out there, headed this way. Something massive."

She glanced at her comrades stationed at the edge of camp,

poised to engage the threat closing in on the site. Elyth and the others with her all followed Tal's look, watching the wood line for the first sign of whatever terror it was about to unleash. *Vanquin* leaped off the ground and swept into a supporting position, holding a low hover just outside the camp and angled to lend its overwhelming power to the troopers below.

"Are the drones up?" Oyuun asked.

"Any second," Tal said. And as if they'd been waiting for her command, three small craft rose out of a housing bay nearby and then zoomed off toward the tree line.

The bright floodlights of the camp only filtered into a few rows of trees of the forest; beyond it a wall of night stood impenetrable. The drones added their support from above, switching on broad-sweeping searchlights as they fanned out across the clearing. Elyth followed the intense oval starlight of the drones' searchlights racing across the ground, scanning for the first sign of the threat. When the drones reached the limit of the floodlights, however, there was nothing else beyond to be seen.

Literally nothing.

Elyth watched intently, as the blackness of the wild swallowed any attempt to peer deeper. Whenever a drone returned to the tree line, its pool of light reappeared, but as soon as the craft moved farther into the wilderness, its light vanished once more from the surface of the ground.

After a minute or two of zipping back and forth, the drones settled into loiter, following lazy orbits around the threat area. *Vanquin* left its station then, roaring off to investigate. Shortly after, the alarm ceased, and the troopers around the perimeter eased up. No one left their positions, but several people clustered together, undoubtedly discussing whatever had just happened.

"False alarm?" Elyth asked.

"Not exactly," Tal said, shaking her head. She listened to the chatter on her comms for a moment, and then signaled to Oyuun. "Sardis is looking for you. By the tower up there." She pointed to a guard platform nearby.

"I'm sure he is," the Arbiter said.

Oyuun headed off toward the platform, and Elyth followed without hesitation, Nyeda by her side. The Envoy was waiting for them, flanked by Korush and Subo. He glanced at the Arbiter's uninvited escort as they arrived, but neither greeted nor dismissed them.

"Arbiter," he said. "We're going for a ride."

Oyuun nodded his consent, but said nothing further. His eyes were fixed on the tree line.

A few moments later a utility skimmer cruised up, the ground-hugging variety with a doorless, bubble canopy and open-top flatbed that the Hezra used for hauling supplies. When it came to a stop in front of them, Elyth saw that Captain Ames was in the pilot seat with a hard look on his face. Sardis hopped into the other seat in the open-air cockpit, and Oyuun, Korush, and Subo climbed into the back. While they were still getting situated, Ames glanced over at Elyth and Nyeda, and then gave a quick jerk of his head toward the skimmer's bed. That was all the prompting Elyth needed.

She grabbed the side wall of the bed and lightly levered herself up and in. Korush flashed a questioning look, which she answered by sitting down next to Oyuun.

"Aspirant!" Nyeda said, and Elyth realized her mistake.

"My apologies, Advocate," she said, standing once more and turning to address Nyeda with a formal posture of deference. "Will you permit me to accompany the Arbiter?"

"In or out, we gotta move," Ames answered before anyone else could.

"Very well, you may," Nyeda said. "Report back to me immediately on your return."

"Yes, Advocate," Elyth replied, as she retook her seat. Nyeda kept her eyes fixed on Elyth for a moment, and then briefly flicked her gaze to Korush. Elyth followed the look, saw Korush staring back at Nyeda with a subtle expression Elyth couldn't read. He dipped his head in a shallow nod, acknowledging Nyeda. There was something between them Elyth hadn't seen before. Nyeda remained standing by, her arms crossed as the skimmer accelerated and everyone's full attention went to the fast-approaching border between light and darkness.

Ames brought the skimmer to a stop within ten yards of the tree line. Sardis was the first one out, marching with such purpose toward the woods that Elyth had the impression the man was about to unleash a stinging verbal rebuke on the wilderness itself. He had a sidearm in hand, the first time she'd seen him armed at all.

Korush and Subo flowed out of the back of the skimmer and quickly caught up with the Envoy. Ames, Oyuun, and Elyth dismounted and followed, a few steps behind with a greater measure of care. Sardis stopped where the light did, and stared into the blackness, posture suggesting anger at whatever was out there. When Elyth reached him, it became apparent why he'd stopped, and why the light did as well.

The ground was gone.

A chasm had opened, sheer and of unknown depth. But the edge wasn't jagged, or unstable. The earth hadn't broken open or collapsed, as in an earthquake or vast sinkhole. It was as worn and weathered as though the terrain had been shaped by natural forces over centuries, rather than violently created mere minutes before.

"Well," Ames said. But he didn't continue.

Sardis snatched a device off his belt and stabbed a few strokes on it with his finger. A few moments later, one of the drones loitering overhead swung over and began a slow descent, illuminating the face of the wall below them as it went. Elyth leaned out to peer into the fresh canyon; Ames took hold of her arm with gentle firmness to keep her steady. The chasm appeared to have a rocky face, with a few strange shapes jutting out here and there that didn't look fully natural. They were too smooth and rounded in places, too many angles and straight lines in others. But the top-down perspective and the shifting light from the descending drone made it difficult to judge what she was seeing.

The Envoy fiddled with the device again, less violently this time, and the drone below paused, rose a few feet, and then hovered with its light trained on one of the angled shapes. He was the first one to recognize what they were looking at.

"It would appear we have discovered the landing site of our first expedition," he said. And once he'd said it, recognition came. It was a winglet from a craft, partially merged with the landscape but undamaged as far as Elyth could tell.

"And," Oyuun said quietly, "it looks like my work begins now."

EIGHT

Elyth ran her fingertips across the rough stone, studied the cliff face stretching some fifty feet high and washed orange-golden in the morning light. From her long years of study, training, and experience, she should have been able to easily discern what was wrong with the cliff. But no matter where she looked, everything about it seemed right. The cracks, the erosion from wind and rain, the layering. Even to the touch, it seemed as natural as any terrain she'd encountered. The stone was ancient and granitic, with some sedimentary limestone and other trace minerals at home in the composition. It was well-formed, without flaw or defect, as if the land had always been this way, and they had suffered from some strange collective delusion.

It would have been the most logical determination, if not for the scattered pieces of a once-mighty First House starship embedded within.

The whole situation was a mystery and a marvel. Everywhere she looked, from the top of the cliff down into the basin where she stood, the environment possessed all the signs and hallmarks she would expect from long-weathered features of the terrain. The forest at the bottom appeared undisturbed by the sudden change of topography; a buffer of open ground ran fifty yards between the foot of the cliff and the tree line, and even that was unbroken and covered in the plant matter and scrub brush one would expect.

But for all the awe the chimeric landscape induced, still nothing was so mind-bending as the state of the ship. Across the shallow bowl of the basin, parts and pieces of the First House vessel lay spread. Several components had already been excavated, but the majority remained strewn throughout the clearing, some fully exposed, most partially buried. The other task force members crawled over the site, which vibrated and whirred with the sounds of dozens of Oyuun's drones. It struck Elyth as a scene she had witnessed on many worlds, though at a larger scale: ants and flies swarming over a carcass.

"What do you make of it?" Nyeda asked from behind her.

"I'm not sure," Elyth answered. She looked up the face of the cliff again. "It's like ten thousand years of change happened in an instant."

"Not the land," Nyeda said. "The ship."

Elyth turned; Nyeda stood with her back to the cliff, surveying the field before her. The heaviness in her voice revealed the intent of the question. Against hope, hoping for some explanation beyond the obvious.

Elyth stepped closer, drew up alongside her.

"I can't see how anyone could have survived," she said, "no matter how strongly I want to believe otherwise."

Nyeda nodded slowly.

"It was the outcome I had expected," she replied. "But to see it confirmed is almost more than I can bear."

The two stood together in silence a span, before Nyeda added, "I've seen crash sites before, but never one this catastrophic."

"It wasn't a crash," Sardis said, approaching from Elyth's left, a gunmetal panel in his hands. Oyuun trailed behind him, clearly trying to catch up before he missed more of the conversation.

"What?" Nyeda asked.

"It wasn't a crash," the Envoy repeated, joining them. He held the panel out for them to see; Elyth recognized it as a section of a winglet from the craft. "No sign of damage, no stress in the material. Our technicians couldn't have done a more pristine job if they'd simply removed this for repairs."

"For the few parts we've located," Oyuun countered as he arrived. "But we shouldn't assume that's true for the bulk of the craft."

"You're assuming there *is* a bulk of the craft," Sardis answered.

"We know there's an anomalous field around the planet," the Arbiter said. "Dampening gravity, preventing it from propagating as it should. Crossing the threshold at high velocity or too steep an angle, or some other such variable, could have caused a gravitic shock wave. Something like explosive decompression. A miscalculation in trajectory, produced by the unusual gravitational threshold."

"That would be a simple theory," Sardis said, clearly unconvinced.

"Hypothesis," Oyuun corrected. "But one I'd prefer to disprove before making other, wilder conjectures."

"Advocate," Sardis said, addressing Nyeda, "is there any First House operational protocol that would account for . . ." he paused to wave his hand at the field, "this?"

"For what, exactly?" Nyeda said.

"Oh, anything really. Just off the top of my head, say, dramatic measures to obscure a landing site, for example."

Elyth recalled the Envoy's briefing and his passing mention of the Hezra asset that had been sent along with the task force. She picked up the thread before Nyeda could respond.

"You think they destroyed the ship," Elyth said, "to cover the theft of your device." Sardis looked to her with an arched eyebrow and a fleeting glint of appreciation.

"Disassembled is more like it," he said, holding up the panel.

"That is a ridiculous, *moronic* accusation," Nyeda said sharply. "Even coming from a Hezra stooge like yourself."

"Perhaps," Sardis replied. "But it is a *hypothesis*. The asset on loan to the Paragon's task force is of experimental nature, and I believe we can all agree that forthrightness has never been the First House's strongest trait."

"I won't argue the Paragon's capacity for deception," Elyth said, "but I can assure you, Envoy, if she'd wanted to steal a Hezra device, her design to do so would have been far more subtle."

"And given the vast array of this planet's anomalous features," Oyuun added, "I believe our time is better spent focused on it, without the distraction of imaginary betrayals."

Sardis regarded Elyth and then Nyeda for several seconds each, his keen gaze searching for any sign of deceit.

"The mere suggestion is disgusting," Nyeda said, staring him down. "If you had any honor at all, you would be ashamed for having voiced it, let alone having thought it."

Sardis grunted.

"Shame requires ego, Advocate, and I am but a humble instrument of the Hezra-Ka," he said. "And I nevertheless would like to verify that it is still somewhere on this planet, even if it has been reduced to its individual components."

He started to turn to leave, but Elyth stopped him with a question.

"Just how experimental was it?"

He paused and glanced back at her.

"Beyond your need to know," he said.

"Enough to tear a ship apart?" she continued. "Or to cause the surface of a planet to change?"

"Also beyond your need to know."

"In the hands of the First House," Oyuun said, "the potential outcomes—"

"Arbiter," the Envoy said loudly, "we have a great deal of work, and we've wasted enough time talking."

Sardis marched off immediately, but Oyuun lingered a few moments, obviously debating whether or not to say more despite the Envoy's admonition. But he decided against it, offered a quick nod, and strode to catch up.

"That man is intolerable," Nyeda said. "And I'm disappointed that you would attempt to ingratiate yourself to him by slandering the Paragon. Disappointed, but I suppose not surprised."

Elyth felt no need to respond; her mind was elsewhere, working to incorporate the new information. Though Arbiter Oyuun genuinely seemed concerned with the planet, Sardis's role had become more apparent. His primary objective was the recovery of whatever piece of Hezra technology had been lost. She wondered just how much of the task force would abandon the world once that objective had been achieved.

Apart from a handful of troopers left behind to guard the

camp and a few at the perimeter, all the members of that task force were pitching in with the recovery effort regardless of rank or role; the cliff face was like an archaeological dig turned vertical. Elyth scanned the scene again with fresh eyes, to see if she could discern who among them might be solely concerned with locating the device, and whether by their method of search she could glean an idea of what they might be looking for.

Their engagement with the task was complete, and understandable: it was the first, real concrete objective they'd had since they landed.

But Elyth couldn't escape the sense that everyone else had homed in so thoroughly on that task in part because they were all eerily reluctant to look too closely at the geological phenomenon that had unearthed the remains of the vessel. As if by considering it, they would have to accept it, and accepting it was something like madness.

Oyuun shuttled back and forth between workstations, sometimes examining extracted portions of the ship, sometimes poring over data coming in from the drones' evaluation of the emergent cliff. His was powerfully internal work; Elyth noted how intensely focused he was, filtering out all the noise and threat of distraction around him as he processed all he was learning. Sardis, on the other hand, seemed the polar opposite, though to Elyth's surprise apparently no less effective. He ranged the entire site, in near-constant one-sided communication with the crew and staff in high orbit above them aboard the *Clariana*, coordinating both ground- and space-based efforts simultaneously. Seeing the two of them in action together revealed to Elyth the unquestionable supremacy of this Hezra task force in a way she'd not yet witnessed. Briefly, she wondered what the Ascendance might accomplish if not for the divide between her House and theirs.

But then she recalled that the shifting planet beneath her feet might very well be the result of just such an interaction.

As much as her heart longed to learn the fate of her sisters, she knew there was little she could do to speed that effort. So instead, she decided to confront that which the others seemed intent on ignoring. The land itself.

"Where are you going?" Nyeda challenged as Elyth began to move.

"Out there," she answered, nodding toward the tree line.

Nyeda shook her head.

"Out of the question."

"There's work to be done away from all this commotion," Elyth said. "And I'm of no use here."

"That will be even more true if you give the Envoy reason to keep you chained."

"Do you need to escort me?"

"No, I need to keep watch here, to see firsthand what they discover."

"Nyeda, whatever they find won't be an answer. At best, it might point in a direction. But the answer lies out there somewhere. I know you feel it too."

Nyeda regarded her for a moment.

"I'll stay within sight of the perimeter," Elyth added.

Nyeda returned her gaze to the Hezra troopers, scanning the site, apparently closing off the conversation. After a few seconds, though, she spoke.

"Don't leave the clearing."

It wasn't what Elyth had wanted, but even the edge of the

forest was likely to tell her more than she could learn from any further study of the cliff face.

"Yes, Advocate," she said, offering a minimal bow. She turned and left the cliff, headed across the open ground.

One of the troopers holding the perimeter reacted to her approach, but when he'd identified who she was, he gave her an expressionless nod and returned his attention once more to the woods. Elyth read in that brief look, though, the gnawing, formless anxiety that she, too, was feeling. He was a hardened veteran, but he'd never faced a situation like this one. None of them had.

The bizarre change in the terrain was here, in the basin at the foot of the cliff. But its source, she felt, was much farther away. And possibly much, much deeper. She could hear the call clearly, but for perhaps the first time in her life she was hesitant to answer it.

Elyth could feel the trooper's eyes on her as she continued past him and crossed the twenty-foot buffer of open ground between him and the tree line. She stopped within arm's length of a tree, reached out with a delicate touch. Its bark was silvery-gray, papery and smooth in appearance but textured beneath her fingertips as though coated by fine-grained sand. Branches stretched some fifty feet above, turned upward as if to paint the sky with its foliage, yellow-green and vibrant. All along the trunk, from root to the reach of Elyth's gaze, fine cracks ran, etched like lines of laughter and sorrow in an aged and weathered face, or armor scarred through many battles.

She stepped closer and crouched, running her fingers along the top of an exposed root, down to where it slipped beneath the earth. Unbroken, undisturbed, with no sign of traumatic movement of the terrain.

And yet it wasn't quite right.

Elyth glanced up to the top of the tree again; though she couldn't identify the species, the pattern of its branches suggested it had grown surrounded by other trees, not at the edge of a clearing. She looked down the length of the tree line. From that vantage, the transition from clearing to forest seemed too abrupt, as though the trees were a tide receded from its shore, or a veil drawn back.

She stood and walked slowly along the border, letting her fingers slide along the trunk of each tree she passed. On any other world, their stories would be encoded in their roots and bark and leaves; here on Qel's Shadow, Elyth was no longer certain she could trust those sources.

Her mind was only just beginning to work through the implications when her assessment was interrupted by a call from behind her. When she looked, she saw several troopers gathered in a cluster on the far side of the clearing, and others headed toward them. Sardis crossed the basin with his long, purposeful stride; Oyuun moved to the troopers at a trot.

Whatever they'd found was significant enough to stop all other work. As Elyth jogged over to join the group, a trooper left the cluster headed toward the utility skimmer parked near the cliff base. Korush stood with his machine guardian a few yards back from everyone else; he glanced at her as she approached and continued to watch her as she merged with the group. When she did, she understood the reaction.

They'd uncovered a capsule, eight feet long, with a slick graphite-colored shell and slender, transparent window; unmistakably a stasis module, for keeping critically injured personnel stable until full medical treatment could be rendered. It appeared to be perfectly intact and operational. Her heart leaped with an unfocused hope that someone, *anyone*, had survived.

"Who is it?" Elyth asked.

Sardis answered without turning to address her.

"It would appear we've located our asset," the Envoy said. "The question of the immediate moment is whether or not it is still functional."

His answer simultaneously deflated her hope that they'd found a member of the House and puzzled her as to why he called the asset "it" if *it* was actually personnel. She glanced at Subo then, and wondered if there might be a creation even more advanced, even more dreadfully powerful. Something not human, but nevertheless organic.

The troopers struggled to load the module onto the skimmer, until Subo moved silently over to assist. Elyth couldn't get a clear view between all of the bodies and Subo's hulking frame. Once the module was secured, Sardis moved toward the skimmer's cockpit.

"Wrap up operations here," he said as he entered the vehicle. "Return to base and await further instructions."

The skimmer pulled away before anyone could reply, question, or argue. As the vehicle passed by, Elyth finally caught a fleeting glimpse through the transparent canopy of the module. Her curiosity shattered in an instant. Though she saw the face only in profile, recognition struck her with the force of a thunderbolt.

The Hezra asset was no device.

No, the being in the capsule was none other than Varen Fedic.

NINE

"Did you know?" Elyth demanded.

Nyeda was seated on her bed in their shared quarters, hands clasped in front of her, head bowed.

"Nyeda, did you know that *eth ammuin* was part of the Paragon's team?"

"It would be wise to calm yourself, Exile."

Elyth ignored the mild challenge and Nyeda's response was answer enough.

"How long, Nyeda? How long have you known?"

"You know it now," Nyeda answered quietly, without raising her head. "When *I* learned of it is of no consequence."

"No consequence? If you knew before we deployed and you withheld something *that* critical from me, how am I supposed to trust anything you say?"

"You can trust that I will tell you whatever I deem relevant for you to know. Expecting anything more would suggest that I owe it to you, which I most assuredly do not."

"If I had known earlier, it would have impacted everything I've done up until now!"

Nyeda snapped to her feet, her face three inches from Elyth's.

"Exactly. And where would your focus have been then, Exile?" she said, hard eyes burning with an intensity that her voice did not betray. "Had you known, what would you have spent your energy pursuing?"

Elyth's instinct was to deny the implication, but the question pricked her heart. Nyeda was right. Had Elyth known, the thought of reuniting with *eth ammuin* would only have distracted her from . . . no, she admitted, would have *consumed* any other cares she had. Until she had learned his fate, she would have thought of nothing else.

"And you've made it clear that you still haven't learned your place," Nyeda continued. "Understand this: You are the *lowest* member of this team. You give no orders, you make no demands. You have no authority here, and you never will. As far as this team is concerned, you are nothing more than a tool. The sooner you accept that, the easier this will be for everyone."

She held Elyth's gaze until she was satisfied that the message had landed with its intended weight and then sat back down on her bed.

"We were brought here to deal with the planet," she added. "Not to restore old relationships."

The acid in the words made the double meaning clear; neither with *eth ammuin* nor the House.

The entire task force had been ordered to remain in their quarters ever since they'd returned to base, but the tiny space Elyth shared with Nyeda felt too tight, too oppressive now. Elyth turned and opened the door.

"Where are you going?" Nyeda asked.

Elyth didn't respond. She had to get out, had to breathe fresh air under an open sky. She stepped out of the shelter, intending to run through her meditation sequence. But as she exited the structure, she saw a figure approaching.

Korush.

Behind her, Elyth heard Nyeda stand and move to the entrance, undoubtedly to chastise her for her disobedience. She, too, stopped when she saw the Azirim.

"Wari Korush," Nyeda called. "What's the report?"

Korush didn't answer immediately; he waited until he was within conversational distance to reply.

"Advocate," he said, by way of greeting. And then to Elyth, "*Aspirant*," in a tone that had just a hint of distaste for the word. Whether it was a reaction to her personally or merely to the deceptive title, she couldn't tell.

"The Envoy has requested that you join him in the medical facility."

"Requested?" Nyeda said.

Korush didn't answer, just stood in place, looking at Elyth.

"All right," Nyeda continued. "Give me a moment to gather my things."

"No," Korush said. "Only her."

Elyth didn't turn to look at Nyeda, but she didn't need to. She could feel her once-sister's reaction.

"Certainly," Elyth said, with a bow. "Lead the way."

Korush nodded and headed back the way he'd come without addressing Nyeda again. Elyth followed but after a few steps glanced quickly back at Nyeda, saw the confusion and disappointment on her face as she watched the two of them leave.

Together, Korush and Elyth crossed the grounds to the medical facility; apart from guards stationed at the corners of the site, no other personnel were in the open. The Azirim didn't speak to her again, not even when they reached their destination. He ushered her into one of the isolation chambers, and then followed in behind her and remained stationed by the door.

The majority of the medical equipment had been shoved against the walls, hastily from the look of it. In the center of the room lay the stasis module, with Sardis on one side and Oyuun on the other. Subo stood passive in the far corner, somehow unobtrusive despite its hulking frame.

Elyth glanced at the window in the module, and the sight of *eth ammuin* lying within struck her with two barbed emotions. The disorienting dread of seeing a loved one laid in a coffin; its inevitable twin, the impossible but unavoidable hope that they would rise out of it and prove false the sorrow. In this case, she knew the hope was greater, that he really might come back to her. But she knew, too, that the greater hope might well be herald of a more devastating fall.

She averted her eyes from his face. The churning of her emotions threatened the clear mind and physical control she knew she needed to maintain.

"Ah," Sardis said. "And now we are four. Welcome, Exile."

"Envoy," Elyth answered. She offered no bow to him, but when she greeted Oyuun, she bowed with perfect etiquette. "Arbiter."

Sardis's thin smile showed he had not missed her subtle intent.

"Now, now," he said. "Let's not seek offense where none was intended. It was for operational security purposes, not a personal slight."

It was no wonder why Sardis had not revealed the truth to her about the "Hezra asset," but Elyth wondered how many other members of the task force had known. Oyuun, certainly. Korush, she guessed, though the man's demeanor was so uniformly flat, even if he had been *more* surprised than her, she wasn't sure she would have been able to tell.

"Why did you bring me in here?" she said.

"Straight to business, excellent," the Envoy replied. "The Arbiter and I are of differing opinion on a matter, and so we are looking for a third voice to break through our impasse."

"On what point?"

Sardis held out his hand toward the module, but said nothing.

"Obviously," she said. "Could you perhaps be more specific?"

"No," Sardis said. "We wouldn't want to contaminate your thoughts with ours."

Elyth looked back and forth between the Envoy and the Arbiter, trying to discern whatever she could from their faces. Sardis masked his emotions well, but the tightness at the corners of Oyuun's mouth suggested the argument entailed some matter of risk.

She took a deep breath to steel herself, and then approached the stasis module.

"Do be careful not to touch it," Sardis said.

Elyth scanned the module, evaluating its state. Like the other parts of the ship they'd recovered, there were no signs of damage, nothing to suggest a crash, or an explosion, or any other catastrophic failure. But the module itself was made of many parts, and yet remained fully intact. Everything else they'd found thus far had been separated down to a component level.

They'd hooked the module up to a base station; its projected display showed an array of readouts, only a few of which Elyth was familiar with. She forced herself to look through the window, at *eth ammuin*'s face and upper torso. He was dressed in an unadorned Hezra uniform, of the kind usually worn by field support staff. It took effort and several seconds, but she passed through the visceral, emotional reaction and evaluated him with a physician's eye, detached from the personal connection, focused only on the physical details she could observe.

From what Elyth could see, there were no injuries, no wounds, nothing to suggest any reason for such extreme medical measures. Ascendance vessels of sufficient class were all equipped to provide extensive treatment, and Advocates of the Hand were of the highest skill in the healing arts. Whatever had happened to *eth ammuin* must have been internal and devastating.

Or . . .

Elyth looked to the display, searched out the basic vital signs. She wasn't trained enough to interpret all that she was seeing, but from what she could tell his baselines were within reasonable ranges.

"How long has he been in there?" she asked.

Oyuun bent forward to look at the display, and then said, "Three months, ten days, seventeen hours. Approximately."

"And how long ago did the task force deploy?"

"Oh, about three months, twelve days. Approximately."

"So they put him in there soon after they arrived."

"So it would seem," Sardis answered.

"Or before," Oyuun added. Sardis gave him a quick look, and that gave Elyth a hint at what the two had been arguing about.

She pointed at the display. "Is this providing any details on his condition?"

"An excellent question," Sardis said. "As far as we can tell, nothing's wrong with it."

"With the module?"

"With the asset."

"Oh . . . you mean nothing's wrong with *him*."

"I prefer to think of *it* as property of the Hezra, as a precaution. But why do you ask? Are you considering removing it from stasis?"

Though she'd managed to stay analytical to that point, the Envoy's question broke her detachment; if there was nothing wrong with *eth ammuin*, then there was nothing to stop them from bringing him out of stasis. He could step out of his coffin, back into her life. Her heart leaped at the thought.

But she checked herself before she spoke, wrestled her way back to a clinical evaluation. It was unlike the Envoy to ask such a leading question. And the Paragon was nothing if not thorough in her calculations; she wouldn't have agreed to put *eth ammuin* in the module without very good cause. Unless they could determine what that cause had been, it seemed unwise to go against the judgment of the Paragon of the First House.

That line of thought triggered another, and Elyth realized what the point of contention had been.

"You don't need me here to make that assessment," she said. "You think he caused this."

Sardis arched an eyebrow, apparently impressed, but he kept his voice neutral.

"Oh? What suggests that I would think such a thing?"

"Your nature," she replied, and Oyuun chuckled. "I imagine you're more familiar with his capabilities than you are with this planet's. It'd be cleaner, if he were the problem."

"You would not agree, I take it."

"No."

"And why not?"

"Because none of this *feels* like his work."

"Unconvincing," Sardis said.

"If he had sabotaged the task force in some way, then you think what? They put him in here to contain him? Or he put himself in here, after the fact?"

"Either seems possible. Do you not find it odd that out of everything we've found, the only thing that has been left intact thus far just happened to have this inside?"

"Envoy, given everything we've experienced since we arrived, I'd say this is one of the *least* odd things we've seen. You have to consider it at least possible that something happened to him when they arrived. Or even that they knew they were in trouble, and this was their way of trying to preserve him in hope of recovery."

Sardis sighed dramatically.

"You disappoint me, Exile," he said. "But I suppose I should have expected you to side with the Arbiter."

"Which, I would like to highlight, she did without knowing what side I was on," Oyuun said.

"That's beside the point. Very well, Arbiter, I will concede that it is not yet conclusive. But let the record show that I still consider the asset to be the most likely cause of the first expedition's misfortunes."

"Yes, duly and *repeatedly* noted," the Arbiter answered. "And as I've said, there's a very simple way to gather evidence to support one view or the other."

"Your proposal would require us to wake it. And if I'm correct, it seems like that could be a very bad idea indeed."

"Less of one if we did it now, while we have Korush and our friend from the House here."

"And if it is as I suspect?" he asked.

"Then I will update my probabilities accordingly."

"By how much?"

"I would say it makes your hypothesis more likely by . . . seven percent."

Sardis weighed their options, and though he clearly didn't like the idea, his bias toward brute efficiency seemed to win out.

"Very well," he said. "Bring it out."

Oyuun nodded and moved to the module's base station, where he began making adjustments on one of the control panels. Sardis took a single step back from the module, and without taking his eyes from it, he added, "Korush, please be prepared."

Korush left his place by the door to stand next to the Envoy.

"We'll bring him up gradually," the Arbiter said. "If we see any instabilities, we can halt the process."

"How long?" Sardis asked.

"A half hour should be safe."

"And what are we looking for?" Elyth asked.

Sardis answered. "Whether or not it has its voice."

Elyth was uncomfortably familiar with the notion. She'd been captured by Hezra troopers before, back on Qel. To keep her controlled, they'd affixed some sort of collarlike device that paralyzed her vocal cords any time she attempted to speak. But she'd seen no such device on *eth ammuin*, and she wondered what method they may have used to constrain him. At that thought, she couldn't help but wonder what else he'd been forced to endure since last they'd seen each other.

She felt her clinical detachment slipping and, despite her efforts, as they waited, and watched, it came unmoored.

What if he didn't wake?

And what if he did?

She'd imagined their reunion many times, even while believing it utterly impossible. But in *eth ammuin*'s presence, she had witnessed things that could not come to pass. Now, here, on the cusp of impossibilty invading reality once again, possible futures branched and stretched before her to infinity. Her thoughts and emotions spiraled in on themselves, forming a chain that somehow looped endlessly, gaining intensity with each cycle until her very being felt inseparably enmeshed within its fractal whorls.

Each minute seemed to grow longer than the one that had come before.

"Stability is good," the Arbiter said. "Here he comes."

Elyth clasped her hands behind her back to hide their trembling.

The canopy of the stasis module retracted; for a minute or two, *eth ammuin* lay with his eyes closed, motionless except for the rising and falling of his chest with breathing deep and even.

"Well?" Sardis said. Oyuun just held up a hand, as if to impart a measure of his own patience to the Envoy.

And then, at last, the moment arrived. *Eth ammuin*'s eyes opened, as though reluctant to do so. His unfocused gaze wandered a small patch of the ceiling above him, and then gradually expanded its range, gaining clarity with each moment. When he finally began to take in the faces around him, awareness and recognition came quickly.

He saw Oyuun first; the Arbiter met him with a cautious but encouraging look. Then Sardis, whose glare didn't change. Then Korush. Elyth could tell *eth ammuin* knew these people, and well.

It was not until his gaze fell on her that he showed any surprise. He rolled over onto his side to support himself on his elbow, eyes wide, mouth open. Speechless.

"Hello, *eth ammuin*," she said. It was all she could think to say.

"It doesn't answer to that name anymore," Sardis said. "Nor at all, unless I permit it."

Eth ammuin still hadn't taken his eyes from hers, nor had he spoken. The Envoy watched intently a few seconds longer before bending closer.

"Varen," he said. "I am certain I made clear to you the consequences you would face if I were forced to retrieve you. What do you have to say for yourself?"

Eth ammuin's eyes lingered on Elyth a moment longer before he looked to Sardis. He opened his mouth to answer, but then shook his head and tapped his throat.

"There's no use pretending," Sardis said. "We already know you sabotaged the First House initiative."

To Elyth's eye, the look of shock on *eth ammuin*'s face was unquestionably genuine. He stared blankly at Sardis, and then looked to Oyuun for confirmation. When he turned back to the Envoy, *eth ammuin* shook his head again, this time out of confusion.

"The entire force was lost," the Envoy said. "All except you, of course. *Mysteriously*."

Eth ammuin sank back slowly, lying once more on his back, eyes searching the ceiling above him.

"We are returning to the Hezra-Ka this very moment, and

when we arrive you will face his judgment. If you have anything to say in your defense, now would be the time."

Elyth hadn't thought of it before, but the medical facility lacked any particular signs of being a field hospital; it was unlikely *eth ammuin* would be able to tell they weren't on a ship, and there was no reason to doubt Sardis's declaration. She wondered just what game the Envoy was playing, but held still lest she be accused of aiding *eth ammuin* in some way.

Eth ammuin shook his head a third time; now in disbelief. He reached up and touched his throat again, but weakly, and then let his hand drop to his chest.

"Envoy," Oyuun said.

Sardis didn't take his eyes off *eth ammuin*.

"Sardis," the Arbiter said, only slightly louder.

"Yes, fine," the Envoy replied. He stepped forward and, with his fingers held in a peculiar pattern, reached down to touch *eth ammuin*'s throat.

"Sardis," he said, "Envoy of the Hezra-Ka."

He removed his hand and stepped back to his previous position. There was no obvious change or indication of what he'd just done, but the words and the touch apparently served to remove whatever restraint prevented *eth ammuin* from speaking. He swallowed a few times, opened his mouth as if in a yawn, and then at last spoke.

"Arbiter Oyuun," he said, and the sound of his voice sent an unexpected wave of emotion through Elyth. Time or mistreatment had added a slightly ragged edge to his voice that hadn't been there before, but it took nothing away from the warmth of his tone. "How much time until we reach our destination?"

Oyuun glanced at Sardis before answering.

"Well, Varen, I suppose that depends on what you have to tell us."

Eth ammuin nodded slowly, but kept his eyes on the ceiling. His distress was apparent, but its source was not; he seemed trapped between the shock of the moment and the memory of whatever had happened before he'd been placed in stasis.

"I'm afraid there isn't very much to tell," he said. "We never even made it to the planet."

TEN

"Exile," Sardis had said. "You are dismissed."

That was how Elyth's reunion with *eth ammuin* had ended, and with it, any chance to learn what he knew about what had happened to the Paragon and her team. It had been over an hour since then, and still nothing. Sardis, Oyuun, and Korush hadn't yet emerged from the medical facility, and the rest of the site remained eerily quiet as the other task force members loitered in, or just outside, their quarters.

She'd had no desire to return to face Nyeda, knowing what questions would await her there. After having discovered that no one else seemed to care where she was, she had decided to take advantage of the temporary freedom and spent the better part of an hour lazily walking the perimeter of the camp. Now, she stood just outside the boundary, looking off to the tree line opposite the recently formed cliff.

Elyth's thoughts continued to churn, but they felt removed, or she felt numb toward them. They were adding nothing new or useful, and she allowed them to pass by without trying to follow where they might lead.

"Nice to get outside a bit," said a voice from behind her. She glanced back to see *eth ammuin* standing a few feet away, hands in his pockets, looking up at the sky. She hadn't heard him approach. "Been a while," he added, with a smile.

She turned to face him, as he scanned the sky above and then the landscape behind her. Korush and Subo hovered a few yards behind him, like a pair of storm clouds threatening to descend upon them at any moment.

"Well," *eth ammuin* said, at last letting his full attention rest solely on her.

His smile broadened, and for a long moment they stood beholding each other's faces, neither seeming quite able to believe the other was truly there or knowing what to do about it. Elyth had so many questions, and so much to tell him, and it was all so complex and interconnected that there was nowhere to begin.

"Well," he said again. "Here we are."

And somehow, that was the most proper thing he could have said. Though it seemed impossible, after all they'd been through together and then in their years apart, here they were.

"It's good to see you again, *eth ammuin*," Elyth said.

He reacted at her use of the name, a sort of amused pleasure touched by an echo of sadness, like a grown man hearing a familial pet name from happy childhood years long past.

"I'm just Varen now, Elyth."

"I can't call you that."

"You'll have to," he said. "They won't let me be anything else."

There was a tinge of sorrow to his words, a melancholy that seemed at odds with the man she'd known him to be on Qel.

"But I promise, whenever you say it, I'll hear something else instead," he added.

Her first reaction was that it seemed strange that he would allow anyone to dictate his own name to him. But at the thought, she recalled her own initial refusal to address him by his self-selected name, and how easily he'd accepted the nickname she'd forced upon him. She reinstated it.

"How about I call you Grief, then," she said. "For old times' sake."

"A compromise," he replied, bowing his head slightly. "Grief it is. For old times' sake."

He looked at her for a moment, bathing her in a warm kindness she hadn't felt in years. She'd almost forgotten what it was like to be known.

"You look well," he said. "I take it the House has treated you kindly."

Elyth exhaled a single, near-silent chuckle at the ridiculousness of the suggestion.

"I guess you didn't catch Sardis calling me 'Exile'?"

"Oh no, I did," he said, smiling his mischief again. "And that struck me as a great kindness. Mind if I join you?"

"Why would I mind?"

"Yes, why would you?" he said. "I'm quite charming and I've heard, to some tastes, possibly even handsome."

"And humble as ever," Elyth said, turning back to look toward the forest. Varen stepped up alongside her, about an arm's length distant. Neither of them seemed willing or able to face the intensity between them directly; standing next to each other eased the pressure and felt more natural somehow.

"I just wasn't sure if you were out here doing your thing," he said. "Didn't want to interrupt."

"Yet you did, which leads me to suspect you also, in fact, wanted to."

He chuckled.

"I've missed you, Elyth."

He said it casually, an effortless admission. But she felt the enormous weight of the words, the significance he bestowed upon them. It was true, but not in the common, light, shallow way. The words seemed to have risen unbidden from the deepest part of his soul, a mantra echoing from the loneliest moments of his isolation. Elyth stood silent, unsure what response to offer. He didn't leave her much space to answer anyway, apparently expecting nothing from her.

"So," he said, "what are we up to out here?"

"The Envoy give you permission to be talking to me?" she asked.

"Of course. I wouldn't have come out if he hadn't."

"I find that hard to believe."

"Well," he said, and his words hitched a half breath. He nodded to himself, not quite imperceptibly. "Perhaps a tiny bit of the Hezra's famed discipline found a way to rub off on me."

If she'd not known him so well, she might have bought the casual dismissal.

"What did they do to you?" she asked quietly.

He glanced at her, gave her a sad smile and a half shrug.

"Nothing significant, in the grand scheme of things," he

answered. He held her look for a few seconds and then turned back to the woods. "But enough about me. What do you make of this place?"

She lingered, watching his face, his eyes. But he kept both studiously turned toward the trees. That line of conversation was closed off to her. At least for now.

"Fascinating," she said, likewise turning her attention back to the tree line. "From a distance. I don't much care for it up close."

"Much like my sentiment toward snakes."

"And spiders, as I recall."

"Indeed. Have you seen either since you arrived?"

"No, not a single one."

"Well, then," he said, "it can't be *all* bad, can it?"

An image of the grotesque beast they'd encountered flashed through her mind, but Elyth saw no good reason to inflict a description of it upon him.

"I wouldn't jump to such conclusions just yet."

"Careful as ever in your judgment I see."

"Force of habit," she said.

"Runs in the family," Varen replied. Off of her look, he added, "I didn't get to spend as much time among your former House-mates as I would've liked, but it was enough to notice a few similarities."

"What were you doing with them in the first place, Grief?" Elyth asked. "And what happened?"

"As I said, I'm afraid there isn't much to tell. Envoy Sardis delivered me to the vessel maybe an hour before we deployed. Once we were underway, the Paragon told me I would be briefed when we touched down on the planet's surface. We were preparing to enter low orbit when . . . whatever happened happened."

He paused, eyes narrowed as he replayed the memories.

"I just remember losing my balance, and one of my keepers catching hold of me. Dmini, I believe it was. A kind soul. She asked me if I was all right, and then I heard her call for help. Her face is the last thing I remember seeing until you woke me."

The mention of Dmini's name pricked Elyth's heart, and Varen's simple description of her rang true. Elyth knew him well enough to know he was telling the truth; and also, to know he'd left something out. Something that still troubled him.

"The second to last thing you remember, you mean," she said. He glanced at her, a scant smile curling the corner of his mouth.

"You can still read me that well, even after all this time?"

"You're not as mysterious as you like to pretend."

He shook his head. "It won't make sense."

"Very little does."

"It was . . . I don't know how to describe it, but . . . it was like I was *hearing* the planet. But not with my ears. It was more internal than that."

"Like a voice?"

"No," he said. "More like a heartbeat. . . . I don't know."

Varen studied the tops of the distant trees for a moment and then said, "Or maybe it was just a really bad headache. At any rate, I feel fine now. I'm looking forward to getting to work. You know why they brought you here?"

"I have my suspicions, but no, no one's been terribly specific," Elyth said. "I don't suppose you know?"

"Actually I do," Varen replied, turning back to her. "And sorry, that's my fault. I told them I couldn't do this without you."

Elyth recalled Nyeda's earlier admission that they'd had help tracking her down. Though she didn't know what part Varen had played, there was no doubt that he'd been the key to the Hezra's successful search for, and capture of, her.

"Couldn't do what without me, exactly?" she asked.

"Whatever it is we're going to do while we're here," he said, with a quick grin. The brief flash of mischievous youth stole the years from his face. But the smile vanished as quickly as it had appeared, and he lowered his voice. "But you realize how much trouble we must be in, if they're letting us be here together."

Elyth nodded. "I assume it's because of what we did on Qel. They obviously think this has something to do with it."

"I suspect they aren't far wrong."

She studied his eyes.

"*Does* it have something to do with it?"

He shook his head vaguely.

"I wish I could say for sure. This is nothing I expected to happen. But you know how I am about plans."

"Someone told me they thought we might have created this world."

Varen swept a lingering gaze across the landscape.

"Oh, I don't think we can take credit for that," he said, distracted, wistful. After a few moments, he returned his attention to her.

"But wouldn't it be marvelous if we had?"

He locked his gaze on hers, and she saw there a familiar glint, a tumbling mixture of excitement, concern, wonder, and impishness. It was a look that had once angered and appalled her, the sign of his reckless willingness to wield the power of the Deep Language impulsively. But in time she'd discovered it also revealed his courage to stand in the midst of the unknown and the unknowable, and to embrace whatever may come. That part of him she'd learned to love. And there was no way to separate the two.

He was both creator and curer of chaos, the solution to the very problems he himself caused. Or at least had been up until now. Whether he could continue to be so remained to be seen.

He paused again for a span, then said, "You do feel it, though, don't you?"

"I feel a lot of things, Grief. Be specific."

"Well now, Elyth, if I could *describe* it, I wouldn't need to *feel* it, would I?"

He glanced at her sidelong. She returned the half look, waiting, expectant.

"It's . . . I don't know," he said. "You're the one in tune with everything. I was hoping you could help me define it."

She let him wrestle.

"Fine," he said, relenting. "On the surface, it's everything it should be. A new, pristine world. A wondrous gift of serendipity. But underneath. Underneath there's something in its call, in its voice . . . something that's . . . it's . . ." He held out a hand, waggled his fingers, grasping for a term.

"Alien," Elyth finally finished for him.

"Huh," he said, mildly taken aback. "Huh . . . I was going to say *pure potential*. But I could see 'alien' too, I guess. If you happen to be of the opinion that a planet should be only one thing instead of many possible things."

An invisible smile leaked into the words.

"You're enjoying this."

"Enjoying it?" he said. "I wouldn't say *enjoying*, no. Some mix of intrigued and awed, maybe. With a healthy dose of terrified on occasion, if I let myself think about it too much. But don't tell

Korush. I would hate for him to despise me for my weakness. He has so many other things to despise me for already.

"And I would be lying if I didn't admit there was something weirdly inviting to me about this place. Maybe not inviting. I don't know. I suppose this world might destroy us. Even so, I can't help but feel . . ."

He trailed off. But Elyth looked to him, and saw it in his eyes.

"Connected to it," she said.

"At home," Varen said, nodding. "At peace. Like this is exactly where I am meant to be."

He looked again at her then.

"You don't feel that way?" he asked again.

Elyth shook her head.

"No," she answered. "No, Grief, I don't. I don't feel anything like that at all."

He didn't seem surprised, exactly, but subtly puzzled, perhaps.

"Well. Maybe you'll warm up to it."

"Or maybe I'll have to kill it."

It took him a moment longer to respond than was comfortable.

"Maybe."

They stood quietly for a few long moments, surveying the silent forest together; its trees were a wild cascade of variety and beauty, both familiar and strange in the familiarity. Like the cliff, there were no obvious signs of anything out of place. It took effort for Elyth to recall that the loathsome creature that had ambushed them the day before was anything more than a disturbing dream. There was a slipperiness to the worst elements of the world, a shifting that made it difficult to grasp and retain.

"You've spent some time with Arbiter Oyuun then?" Varen asked, changing the subject.

Elyth nodded. "I got the impression that you're well acquainted with several members of our team."

"Certainly," Varen said. He glanced back at Korush. "We've been friends for quite some time."

"The Arbiter mentioned that."

"He's a good man," Varen continued. "Good heart. Probably the smartest man in the Ascendance. If anyone can figure out what's going on, and what we should do about it, it's him."

"And until then?" Elyth asked.

"I suppose we wait for him to tell us what to do."

He looked over at Korush again and raised his voice. "What do you think, Korush? In the meantime? Sleep late, go for walks, sit around and tell stories? That sort of thing?"

Korush remained impassive.

"Subo? How about you? Wrestle, maybe?"

"Do not address Subo," Korush said. The statement was mild, the polite rebuke of a museum curator preventing a child from touching a prized artifact.

"I suppose not," Varen said. "I don't mean to offend you, Korush. It's just my great hope that one day you'll be able to enjoy *something*, even if for but a moment."

"My joy is to serve the Way," Korush said, in his grave but utterly courteous manner. And then, without changing his tone in the slightest, he added, "But I confess that I do enjoy the moment when Sardis silences your voice."

Varen laughed aloud, a startling burst of mirth in that tensely near-sacred place.

"And all this time," he said, "here I've been thinking *Subo* was the funny one."

He leaned his head toward Elyth, but kept his eyes on the Azirim.

"Korush is a patient soul," he said, "but I do hate to try him unnecessarily."

Korush held Varen's look, but made no response.

"Subo, on the other hand, loves a good story," Varen said, looking over at the massive machine. "I think deep down, in its heart, it's actually a poet."

Elyth knew Varen well enough to know his purpose was neither mean-spirited nor solely for personal amusement. Based on her own experience, she guessed there was some work he was attempting to accomplish in the mind or heart of the Azirim. The unanswered question was whether Varen's true aim was for Korush's benefit or his own.

Korush, for his part, remained unmoved and unreadable.

The exchange struck an unexpectedly discordant note in Elyth's spirit. She remembered well the effect Varen had had on the people who lived on his mountain on Qel, how effortlessly he could put others at ease, how he'd wielded gentle command over them. Certainly she'd experienced it personally, fiercely for herself. When they'd parted ways, she'd believed the two of them shared a connection as deep as the cosmos itself. But witnessing how expertly he could weave his casual influence, Elyth felt a sudden prick of doubt as to whether or not their relationship held a truly unique place in his heart.

She'd assumed that Sardis's control over Varen's speech was a protection against his use of the Deep Language. Now she wondered if it was merely meant to prevent him from gaining allies.

"Anyway, I suppose we should be getting back," Varen said. "Sardis was irritated enough as it was when he saw you out here."

"Ah," Elyth said. "He sent you to get me."

"In a manner of speaking."

"He sent Korush to get me. And you tagged along?"

"I simply made the case that it would be difficult for Korush to retrieve you *and* keep an eye on me. I don't think we're in any particular rush, but I also would prefer not to give the Envoy any reason to think he needs to lock me up again."

Elyth nodded.

"I suppose I wasn't going to get a chance to enjoy any more silence after you showed up anyway."

Varen chuckled softly.

"It's interesting what we humans consider 'silence,'" he said. He closed his eyes, tilted his head back slightly. "Listen . . . the wind in the trees, and through the grass. And just at the edge of hearing, the sound of water tumbling. We call it quiet, but there's a music in nature, if we would but attend to it."

He listened a moment longer, then added, "But you already know that, far better than most."

He opened his eyes again, gave her a quick smile, and then turned back toward the camp.

"Thank you for your patience, Korush. You are ever the gentleman."

Elyth turned to join him, and as she did, a spit-spark of color flashed in her periphery; she reflexively looked to identify it, and was startled to find a small songbird no larger than her palm perched on the corner of one of the camp's structures.

Varen reacted to her movement, followed her gaze.

"Well, there's a fine fellow," he said. "I wonder how long he's been sitting there."

Elyth saw the bird in profile and from that angle it appeared to be mostly black apart from a few subtle scarlet markings at the tail and around the eyes. Neither sound nor motion of flight had accompanied its sudden appearance, and Elyth's first thought was that the chromatic display that had drawn her eye had been the delicate creature materializing from nothing. But after a few moments of her watching, it flared its wings, stretching them in the sun, and she saw the burst of color there again. What had seemed black was in fact an iridescent midnight blue; and beneath its dark wings, it was brilliant yellow, with greens and scarlet at the wingtips. The feathers of its sunshine belly rippled with dark, crescent accents that gave it an appearance like the scales of a fish. She guessed it was a finch of some sort, though the color pattern was one she'd not seen before.

It was the most natural thing in the world, a bird perched in the warm sun; it took a moment for Elyth to recognize the significance of the little songbird. It was the first wildlife she'd seen in that place, apart from the lone horror of the day before.

"And do you have any friends about?" Varen asked the bird, glancing around.

It occurred to Elyth then that maybe the reason there'd been no life in the wood before had been due to another, different dramatic change to the land before their arrival. Captain Ames had said something along those lines when they'd first landed. Though at the time, she hadn't fully grasped the genuine possibility in what he'd said, the full truth now settled on her.

She was just about to turn to find the captain when the bird let loose its song.

It trilled a long tune, some fifteen distinctive notes or so by her quick estimate, in clear, pretty tones, with a hint of rounding like that of hollow chimes. The sound was familiar enough and pleasant, but like the bird's coloring, the song itself was one she'd not heard before. She waited a few moments more, and it repeated the call.

"What a delightful little tune," Varen said. And he hummed it back to the bird, innocently; a lilting, soothing melody. And when Elyth heard it repeated, she realized she'd been mistaken. It was true she'd never heard the song from a bird before. But with a human voice behind it, she recognized it now for what it was.

Umarai's song.

She gasped at the realization, grabbed Varen's arm. The songbird fled at the sudden motion.

"What is it?" Varen asked, alarmed by her reaction. "Elyth?"

But she was already jogging back into the camp. She found Oyuun and Sardis huddled together near Oyuun's central field lab, talking with Captain Ames. Sardis looked up at her approach; he saw in an instant that she had something to tell them, but he sharply gestured for her to wait anyway. He was midsentence. Elyth quenched the urge to interrupt, but only barely.

"—because I believe it's a mistake to try to solve all the problems at once, Arbiter. Focus on one, and perhaps its solution will lead to others."

"*Your* work might be nearly complete," Oyuun countered, "but mine has hardly begun. I won't sacrifice the time."

"This will require further discussion," Sardis said, "and clearly our associate has something urgent she wishes to share."

"They landed safely," she said. "They were here."

Both men looked to her then. Oyuun open and receptive, Sardis, skeptical but listening.

"Explain," the Envoy said.

Elyth told them of the bird and its song.

"You're certain of this?" Sardis asked. "It was the *same* song, not just *like*?"

"Identical," Elyth answered. "No question."

"And what's your hypothesis, dear?" Oyuun asked.

"I don't have much of one. But my guess is the land changed after they touched down. Swallowed the ship. And I think we're extremely lucky that whatever opened this chasm up stopped when it did."

"Indeed, not much of a hypothesis at all," Sardis said in response. "But very well. Where did you see this bird?"

Elyth indicated the direction, and saw Varen standing some distance away, his back to them, with Korush and Subo halfway between the two groups. Sardis immediately began walking that way. Elyth followed.

"Captain Ames," Sardis said. "Join me please."

It was the first time Elyth could remember hearing the word *please* come out of the man's mouth. Korush fell into step behind Sardis as they approached Varen.

"Our friend here," Sardis said when they were gathered, indicating Elyth, "has a concern about a bird."

Elyth quickly described what she'd discovered.

"Little fella?" Ames asked. "About that big?" He held out a cupped hand, motioned with the other a rough size.

"Sounds right," Elyth said. Ames nodded.

"Yeah, I've seen a few of them flitting around, mostly out that way," he said, pointing toward the trees where Elyth and Varen had been. "First noticed it an hour or so ago, I'd guess. I wouldn't have known there was anything off about its song, though."

"Very good," Sardis said. "Let's see if we can find one."

"For what?" Ames asked.

"Between Oyuun, Varen, and our friends from the House, I should hope at least one of them can think of a way to make use of it. We certainly won't know if we don't try. Korush, is it too much to hope that your machine could help in this endeavor, or is it only made to destroy?"

"Subo is made to protect, Envoy. Its options are many."

"Excellent. Fan out, call Subo when you spot one."

Sardis walked toward the tree line then without further direction. The others glanced around at one another.

"Can't Subo track one for us?" Varen asked. "Save us the trouble?"

"They're quick, and don't like a lot of activity," Ames said. "By the time we got there, they'd probably be gone. But they don't seem all that shy. If you don't make too much of a ruckus, one will probably come to you, especially if we're in the woods. Just don't go far."

Korush and Elyth both nodded.

"And I have to go too?" Varen asked.

"Faster we find one, faster we come back," Ames said. Varen mimed weighing the choice, but Elyth knew it was just for effect. To her, he actually seemed eager to get into the woods.

The small group branched out as they crossed the clearing and filtered in among the trees, walking softly and watching the branches above. Elyth had gone twenty yards or so when the knocking sounds started up again. Close, and loud. The floor of the forest seemed to vibrate beneath her feet with each knock, but she couldn't tell if that was actually the ground or if it was herself. She stopped moving, crouched, and placed her hand on the earth. Closed her eyes.

"If another one of those creatures shows up," Sardis said, "I'm going to be displeased."

His words were clear through the communicator, but she could hear tones of his natural voice as well, some distance ahead and to her right.

"If another one of those creatures shows up," Ames replied, "I'm going to be running."

Elyth directed her focus down, through her palm, as she slowly compressed the leaves and fallen pine needles, until she felt firmly the soil beneath. And with each subsequent knock, she felt the thrum, like the tolling of an enormous stone bell.

"I've found one of your birds," Sardis said. "And in quite a picturesque scene, no less. Korush, if you'd be so kind as to direct your machine this way—"

He didn't finish the sentence, though it wasn't clear if he'd intended to say more. Nonetheless, Elyth heard him make a sound in his throat like a quiet gag or hiccup, a reflexive reaction like someone who'd nearly inhaled a bug. It was immediately followed by a louder noise in the environment, the soft, wet *splutch* of an overripe melon hitting hard ground.

"Envoy?" Ames said. He waited a few moments for a response, and then, when he got no answer, "Hey, Sardis."

Elyth opened her eyes, looked in the direction she'd heard the Envoy before. She couldn't see him from where she was, so she stood and started walking that way.

"I hope nothing fell on him," Varen said.

Elyth was the first to reach what she guessed had been the Envoy's position. It was indeed a picturesque little glade, no more than ten yards at its widest, with a stream flowing along one side. The trees stood tall around it, and most were wrapped in the blossoming vines of tendril rose that they'd seen before. There were no songbirds in the branches, however, and Sardis was nowhere to be found.

She heard someone approaching through the woods behind her, Ames by the careful sound of his footfalls, but she continued to scan the area to see if she could pick out which direction the Envoy had gone.

On the opposite side of the glade, on the ground near the tree line, four small mounds caught her attention, of unequal size but arranged in a line too straight to be natural. She moved closer to examine them. And when she at last realized what she was looking at, the cold shock of abject horror stole her breath.

"What *is* that?" Ames said in a low voice, from behind her.

Elyth fought through the sudden desiccation of her mouth and clenching of her throat before she answered. "I think it's the Envoy."

ELEVEN

Elyth was close enough now to identify the mounds and could not bring herself to move closer. And though she had seen enough for the image to be branded vividly forever in her mind, she could not force herself to turn away. The ghastly scene had a surreal nightmare quality that transfixed her in revulsion.

Bones, internal organs, skin, uniform, and gear. Neatly separated, placed in piles. From where she stood, his skin seemed to be all in one piece, as though it'd been a suit he'd decided to shed.

Captain Ames slipped past her, moved cautiously in a half crouch like a man approaching a wild, wounded animal.

Varen and Korush arrived at the edge of the glade and stopped, both surveying the scene. Elyth glanced over at them, read their reactions. Varen went pale, his hand to his mouth. If he had vomited, she wouldn't have been surprised, but he managed to suppress the impulse. Even the immovable Wari Korush couldn't contain his shock and horror. And, Elyth realized, something more. It had been his duty to protect the Envoy from harm; a duty he was now realizing he had failed at in the most catastrophic way.

"What . . ." Korush said, but nothing more.

Ames was in a full crouch now, a few feet from the mounds.

"No sign of a struggle, or animal. No prints apart from a couple of his." He glanced up at the trees, shaking his head. At a complete loss.

"I had no idea all of that could fit inside a human body," Varen said, in a mix of disgust and genuine amazement.

Korush wheeled to face him then, and to Elyth's alarm, the Azirim's hand went to the hilt of his void-edge.

"You," he said.

Varen held up his hands defensively, shook his head.

"No, Korush, no way," he said. "I had nothing to do with . . . that."

It was too late. Korush was going to cut Varen down where he stood, and Elyth was helpless to prevent it. Her mind raced to find the right phrase she could utter to intervene; she stood paralyzed in the moment.

But then Korush's hand relaxed, and though he did not remove it from the hilt, the coiled tension left his body and Elyth saw that he was not going to strike after all. It was clear, though, that if he had detected any sign of deceit in Varen, there would have been no such mercy. He glared at Varen a moment longer, then turned his attention back to the glade.

"I'm not saying I hadn't ever thought about it," Varen unwisely added, "but if I had tried to do that, I could never have been that tidy."

"Stop," Elyth said sharply to Varen, before Korush made a move. And then to Korush, "Did Subo detect anything?"

Korush shook his head. A few moments later, as if summoned by the mention of its designation, the device arrived and took a position by Korush's side like an obedient hound.

"Captain, what about you?" Elyth asked. "Anything you saw, or heard?"

"Where's all the blood?" Ames said to himself, either ignoring her or too focused to have heard the question. He was knelt now by the grotesque shrine, cautiously investigating the pile of bones with the blade of his knife. Elyth had been too repulsed to look carefully before, but at Ames's comment she forced herself to walk closer and observe. Clinically, she scanned each grouping in turn and discovered to her astonishment that Ames hadn't been exaggerating. Not only was the ground clear of it; as far as she could tell, the bones and organs themselves were completely devoid of any trace of blood, as though they'd been painstakingly washed and cleaned.

"We need to get off this planet," Ames said, standing and stepping back. He looked across the four piles one last time, and then turned and started back toward the camp. Elyth lingered a moment longer, scanning the ground and trees near where the Envoy must have been standing only a few minutes before. And seeing the tendril rose vines brought back a memory unbidden, of their first trip into the woods, when Sardis had pricked his finger.

"Captain," she said.

"Yeah?"

She walked around the gruesome display and closer to the tree line, half an arm's length from the nearest vine.

"Did Arbiter Oyuun ever give you an analysis of the cutting from the first tendril rose you brought in?"

"No," Ames said, walking over to her. "Haven't really had time to follow up on it. Why?"

Elyth knelt and peered under the blossoms, to the elegant

stems beneath. And, suspicion confirmed, pointed. Ames crouched beside her, saw what she had discovered. The delicate glasslike thorns weren't their usual crystalline clear. They were crimson.

"We need to get off this planet," Ames repeated. "Right now."

He stood again and once more headed toward the base, quicker now. This time Elyth joined him, and Varen fell in beside her.

But Korush and Subo didn't follow. Instead, they moved together toward the remains. Subo reconfigured slightly, its arms folding and fusing into a half-moon basket. Elyth paused, turned partially back; Korush knelt and began to gather the bones.

Ames was on the other side of the glade before he realized what was happening.

"Korush," Captain Ames called. But Korush ignored him. "Korush," he said again.

"I cannot leave him here, like this," Korush said.

"Wari Korush," Ames said, his tone quieter. "Buddy, I'm not sure you can even say it's *him* anymore."

"I *will* not," Korush answered, continuing his grim task.

Difficult as it was, Elyth forced herself to return, and aided the Azirim in the effort. Wordlessly, eventually, the other men joined in, and they completed the work with as much respect and silent dignity as any of them could offer in the situation. Soon enough they were all returning together, Subo bearing the remains, covered now by its metamorphic shell.

When they reached the field camp, Elyth found all the activity unnerving. The Arbiter had clearly given some order in their absence, and the rest of the task force moved with purpose, oblivious to the shocking tragedy that had befallen them. She wasn't even sure how to tell them what had happened.

"Arbiter!" Ames called as they approached. Oyuun looked over and took them all in at a glance; and in that brief span, he understood.

"Where's the Envoy?" he asked, even though his expression showed that he already knew the answer, at least in part.

"Subo has him in there," Ames responded, pointing. "What's left of him, anyway."

"But what *happened*?" Oyuun said.

For a time, the group was silent, unable to explain and, it seemed to Elyth, unwilling to speak of it. She stepped into the gap.

"The planet took him apart," she said. And as the words left her mouth, an adjacent thought struck her; the image of the ship scattered across the landscape rose to her mind. "It took him apart," she repeated, to herself.

Oyuun looked to her, and as usual made the connection immediately.

"Disassembled," he said. He fell silent for a thoughtful moment, until Captain Ames broke in.

"I'm not sure what you guys are thinking about," he said, "but maybe it's something we can all discuss when we're off-world. We need to roll this op up, get safe, and come up with a new approach."

"The Envoy understood the risks involved," Korush replied. "He would not wish us to abandon our task merely on account of his death."

"And there's no need for you to stay, Wari Korush," Varen said. "Your task was to serve a single purpose, and that, through no fault of yours, has become sadly unnecessary. Through *no* fault of yours."

Elyth understood Varen's tone and his intent; he was trying

to gently support the captain's recommendation while releasing Korush from both duty and guilt. But Korush didn't receive it that way.

"I was brought to serve *two* purposes," Korush answered. "*Now* I have only one."

He fixed Varen with a stare of both stone and flame, an unyielding intensity only partly subdued by his otherwise blank expression.

"Well," Varen said. "Perhaps that, too, has become unnecessary."

There was an implied threat in Korush's words that Elyth didn't fully understand; the tension between the two men added a new dimension of stress to the group.

"I'm not going to argue what Sardis would have wanted or expected," Ames said, to defuse or at least redirect the discussion. "But I'm here as an advisor, and I'm strongly advising that we jump off this"—he paused, shook his head, and waved his hand at the landscape around them—"this . . . demon rock before it *disassembles* anyone else."

Arbiter Oyuun did not look back at the group. Instead, he headed toward the field station and over his shoulder said, "I believe you may be right, Captain."

"Sir," Korush said, with respect, but clearly ready to challenge the elder man.

"I'm the ranking officer now," Oyunn said, cutting off any argument. "And this is *my* operation. I'll run it the way I deem best."

He turned and strode to an open-air communication station. The others followed him into the shelter; he was already at work on a terminal, activating a new display that appeared to show a series of Hezra command codes.

"The captain is right," he said. "The situation has become untenable. And we can't solve this problem if we're all dead. I'm authorizing immediate evacuation."

He punched in several codes, transmitting them back to the *Clariana*, still in orbit, and then opened a team-wide communication channel.

"This is Arbiter Oyuun. Due to a critical change in threat assessment, all personnel are to prepare for immediate departure. Rally at base center for further instructions. All personnel, rally at base center."

He closed the channel, and the impact of his message rippled through the troopers working the site; exchanging glances with one another, looking around at the surrounding woods to see what new horror might be descending upon them, taking offense at being ordered to retreat instead of advance.

Oyuun started off toward the central meeting point, and the others followed suit. Elyth caught up to the Arbiter and touched his elbow. He looked at her, and she spoke in a low voice.

"I can't leave," she said. "Not yet."

He regarded her for a moment, but said nothing. Whether he purposely ignored her statement or was merely too focused on other things to respond, he turned his attention to the gathering troopers without answering her. The Arbiter took his place in front of the group, and he began his address as the last team members trickled in. Elyth found Nyeda in the midst of the others; the question was plain on her face. Elyth shook her head, and a moment later Oyuun began. She was surprised once again to see the man transform from kindly scientist to intimidating military officer; when he spoke, his voice boomed with authority.

"Envoy Sardis is dead," he said abruptly. The shocking revelation stunned the members of the force, but Oyuun continued. "Killed by unknown means, by some force of this planet. The threat to our operation is now too high and too unpredictable to warrant continuation at this time. As ranking officer, I'm ordering your evacuation off-world until we can reevaluate and determine a better course of action. This is not a failure. Our operation is not canceled. I'm temporarily halting your work on the planet, but everyone should expect to return in due time.

"The order has already been transmitted to the *Clariana*, and departure will begin as soon as they respond with an all clear. There will be time for questions later. For now, grab whatever personal gear you need and then board the ship you arrived in. Leave everything else. Dismissed."

Everyone did as they'd been instructed, but Elyth noted how much more slowly they moved to carry out the new orders. Where previously the troopers had acted with crisp precision, now there was a clear reluctance. Quiet conversations began between pairs and trios, even as they prepared for departure.

Oyuun watched the team disperse and then turned toward his research station. Elyth followed after him, and when they had enough separation from the others, she called after him.

"Arbiter," she said. He paused long enough for her to catch up, and she continued. "I'm not leaving."

The man sighed, frustration clear on his face. But there was a kindness in his eyes that caught Elyth off guard.

"I know you don't like it, dear," he said. "But I *am* the highest-ranking officer here, now that Sardis is gone. By Hezra protocol, this is *my* operation, and I've ordered your evacuation."

Your evacuation. Elyth had noticed it the first time he'd said it, but the repetition made it clear it'd been no accident.

"You're not leaving," she said.

Oyuun held her look for a moment and then gave a subtle shrug.

"Now that the base is established, I have all I need to continue the work," he replied. "There's no reason to jeopardize everyone else. I'll call when I have a solution."

"It's madness to leave you here alone."

"There's plenty of madness on this planet already. A little more won't change anything. And I certainly would never ask anyone to do something I myself am unwilling to do first."

"Arbiter, no offense to your team, but there's no one else like you here. If we lose you, we lose everything. There's zero chance we can solve this without you."

"I appreciate the sentiment. But maybe we'll get lucky and these anomalies will subside once everyone else is off-world."

It took a couple of seconds for Elyth to decipher his thought process, but when she did, she asked, "You think all of this has been some sort of . . . reaction to our presence?"

"I'm not sure what I think yet. But it's a hypothesis worth testing. Our first team was seventeen members, and our own is larger. Perhaps a somewhat smaller group would experience smaller effects."

"Well, regardless of your plans, I'm not done here yet."

"I've given you a direct order, which it seems you are intent on disobeying. I could very easily have my troopers put you on lockdown for violating our agreement."

"The fact that you haven't yet makes me think maybe you'd be glad for the company."

Oyuun's eyes crinkled with a hint of a smile.

"I do not ask it of you," he said.

"You don't need to," she answered.

"If I'm leaving, then she must," a voice said from behind Elyth. Nyeda.

"Our circumstances have changed, Advocate," Oyuun said. "Our former plans should be reevaluated in light of what we've learned."

"Circumstances *haven't* changed, Arbiter. It's just that the dangers of this planet aren't so theoretical anymore. I won't argue with your order to evacuate the team. But I go where she goes."

"Umarai was here, Nyeda," Elyth said. "And if Umarai was here, then it's likely that at least *some* of the others made it too. If there's even a chance that the sisters of our House walked this planet, I won't be able to rest until I know for certain what became of them."

"You didn't seem to have any such concern when we first discussed it," Nyeda said. "It isn't even *your* House anymore, Exile."

"That may be," Elyth said. "But I'm here now, Nyeda, and I'm not willing to leave. Not yet."

"Arbiter," Nyeda said. "She is under my command, and I am under your authority. I will leave the decision to you, whether to force her to come with me or order me to stay with her."

"I'll order neither," Oyuun replied. "Elyth has given her answer, and I'll not contradict it."

"Then we are a team of three," Nyeda said.

"Four," said Captain Ames. When he'd wandered up, Elyth didn't know, but the little crowd they were forming had started to attract some attention. Looking around, she saw a few clusters of troopers crossing toward their ships, their eyes on the Arbiter and his conference. Varen was heading their way, with Korush and Subo close behind.

"Captain Ames, you should return with your team."

"All due respect, sir, you're going to need someone around for the manual labor."

"I considered all of this before I gave the order. And I *have* given the order. If necessary, I will have you relieved of duty."

"It won't be necessary, sir," Ames said, smiling and friendly as ever, with a stance that suggested he wasn't going anywhere no matter what anyone told him.

Oyuun looked skyward and sighed with exaggerated emotion.

"A single loss of life and our entire command structure is already coming apart at the seams," he said. And then he looked over Elyth's shoulder and said, "And I suppose you're here to argue that you should be allowed to stay as well?"

"Me?" Varen said. "No, I was just coming over to see what everyone was talking about. But now that you've offered . . . very well, I accept."

Korush drew up beside Varen wordlessly. The look on his face said enough. He would be wherever Varen was, no matter what. Subo stood silently by his side, arms returned to their normal configuration. They'd laid the Envoy's remains somewhere, though Elyth didn't know when or where.

Oyuun swept his eyes around the group.

"Six," he said. "Counting Korush and Subo as one, as it should be."

"Too many to test your hypothesis?" Elyth asked.

"No, just five more than I'd expected," the Arbiter replied. He glanced at the two vessels prepping to depart and shook his head. "But you were correct. I *would* be glad for the company." He looked back at her and added, "Truth be told, I've always been afraid I would die alone."

"I'm not in a rush to die together, just to be clear," Varen said. "Unless it's absolutely necessary."

The group lapsed into silence for a few moments, until Varen, of course, broke it.

"Why is everyone so glum? I know it's been a rough start, but we have no idea what else we might experience here. Maybe all the strangeness of the planet will grant us some unexpected benefits too."

No one else seemed to know how to respond, but Elyth did.

"Grief," she said, "your boundless optimism is, by comparison, making your intellect seem quite limited."

Varen smiled and made a brief gesture, fist at his side and an open hand stretched out. A reference to a pose in Elyth's meditation sequence; Watcher Greets the Storm, the physical mnemonic of a willingness to stand and confront the unknown.

"How far do you think the risk extends?" Ames asked.

"I have no clue," Oyuun answered. "I advised *Aterin* and *Vanquin* to return to formation with *Clariana*, beyond the gravity threshold. I hope that will prove a sufficient buffer."

Ames shook his head. "No good, sir. Travel would be an hour at least. If we get in real trouble, no one will be able to reach us in time."

"I came in on a *Clariana* shuttle. I intend to keep that here, in case of emergency."

"If what happened to the Envoy isn't an emergency, I'd hate to see one," Varen said.

"Shuttle's short-range," Ames said, ignoring Varen's comment. "No jump capability. And it'd be a tight fit for all of us."

"I wasn't expecting to carry more than one, Captain. But if you have a different recommendation, make it."

"I'd keep *Vanquin*. Gunship might come in handy."

"Not an option, unless one of you has a couple of years' worth of training I'm not aware of. Those gunships aren't easy to pilot, and I absolutely will not allow anyone else to stay."

"Well, I guess that's a fair point . . . but we should at least keep *Vanquin* in sync orbit for QRF."

"QRF?" Varen asked.

"Quick reaction force," Ames responded, and then continued making his case to the Arbiter. "If you change your mind and want more shooters, Tal and her team can drop back in. Still wouldn't be close enough to extract us in a hurry, but if things go even more sideways, we could hop in the shuttle and they could at least meet us halfway, and then jump us out."

Oyuun deliberated for a few moments then nodded.

"That sounds reasonable," he said.

He stepped away from the group and scanned the camp, more intently this time. From what Elyth could tell, it looked like the last of the personnel were loading up. A few troopers stood on the boarding ramps, watching the discussion.

The Arbiter returned his attention to the small team that had formed around him.

"I've clearly shown too much kindness that has been interpreted as weakness," he said with a stern look. "It would seem I'm unable to command anything of any of you. Last chance to change your mind, before I let our people go."

He looked each of them in the eye in turn, searching out their resolve. Under his gaze, no one moved or made a sound. Even Varen, for once, gave the moment its appropriate gravity.

"Very well," he said. "Captain Ames, would you make the

arrangements with *Vanquin*, or is that too much like an order for you to follow?"

"Sir, yes sir!" Ames said, snapping off a perfect salute, before turning and trotting off toward the gunship. "Hey Tal, you got a sec?" he said into his communicator as he went.

"I need to check in with *Clariana*," Oyuun said, addressing the others, "and then we'll discuss what comes next."

He turned and went into his station. The rest of them stood silently together, each reflecting on this newer, heavier commitment they'd made, and, off of Oyuun's last words, imagining just what *exactly* might come next. Elyth watched Ames; Tal had come out to meet him halfway, and from her body language, Elyth could tell she wasn't happy with the discussion. It appeared to be fairly heated, but Ames managed to prevail, probably through some mix of rank and good nature.

For some reason, watching Tal's reaction triggered a stab of sharp-edged fear in Elyth, reminding her that the planet could seemingly take any one of them at any moment, without warning or even obvious mechanism. But in the midst of that fear, she felt, too, the deep teachings of her former life welling up to meet it. *Sareth hanaan*. The quiet action of one who endures. She had struggled against a shifting, unpredictable planet once before and endured. She would do so again, or die in the attempt. The fear didn't completely dissipate, but it lost its edge and settled into the background; a thing to be aware of but not to fixate on.

"I think we're going to do fine," Varen said. "This will be fun."

"The thing I'll miss most about Envoy Sardis," Korush said, "is his ability to turn off your voice."

Nyeda chuckled darkly at Korush's words and shook her head.

"I can't believe *this* is the group left behind to deal with this hellscape."

And as she finished her sentence, the sound of *Aterin* and *Vanquin* spinning up their engines washed over them. They all turned to watch as the boarding ramps, now empty, retracted and sealed. Ames was jogging back toward them. And as the two ships roared and lifted off, Elyth had to remind herself that their small team wasn't really stranded. They still had the shuttle. They could escape whenever they needed to.

Even so, she couldn't dispel the foreboding sense that none of them would ever see those ships again.

TWELVE

Once they'd received word that both ships had made it safely off-world, the Arbiter didn't waste any time putting them all back to work. Elyth figured they still had seven hours of good daylight remaining, and Oyuun made it clear he wanted to squeeze the last drop of utility out of every minute they had. None of them wanted to be outside camp after dark.

"Two teams," he said. "I'm open to suggestions as to the arrangement, but don't bother trying to convince me that we should stick together. Sardis showed us that numbers have no correlation to safety."

Elyth felt an unexpected prick in her heart at the mention of the Envoy's name. She hadn't realized the affinity she'd begun to develop for the man, until his absence revealed an emptiness that no one else could fill. Not that she liked him, exactly. But she had come to respect him; his decisive command and willingness to be out front had earned that from her.

And the group was slower to organize without his arrogant certainty. Nyeda was the first to step into the gap.

"Wari Korush, Captain Ames," she said, "you take Varen along with you. The exile and I will travel together."

The suggestion came too quickly to have been well considered, or at least it seemed obviously flawed to Elyth.

"If we're looking for deep analysis of the planet," she countered, "then we should split up, Nyeda and I. We're both trained in the same arts. We'll get more coverage if we're applying them to separate areas."

"You have no authority here," Nyeda snapped.

"And it was a suggestion," Elyth answered, "not a command."

Nyeda scanned the others' faces, and Elyth noticed how her eyes briefly lingered when they met Korush's.

"Yeah, I think that makes sense," Ames said. "Neither of you seem to need much help in the wilderness, so I guess I'm kind of useless on that front. But Korush and I can each run security for one of you. How about I go with Elyth and you go with Nyeda?"

Korush shook his head.

"I will escort the exile," he said.

"Oh, all right, sure," Ames said with a shrug. "Not that you're my second choice, Nyeda. I was just trying to keep things moving. It's an honor either way."

Nyeda dipped her head to acknowledge the courtesy, but was clearly bothered that her recommendation had been so quickly dismissed.

"If that is the group's decision, I'll not challenge it," she said.

"And Varen will come with me as well," Korush added.

"Wari Korush," Varen said, with a half bow. "I'm honored."

The stoic man closed his eyes and exhaled through his wide nostrils.

"Arbiter," Elyth said, "I guess that puts you with Nyeda and Captain Ames?"

"No no," he answered, "I'll stay here to continue working out whatever it is we've already found."

"I'm not sure that's safe, sir," Ames said.

"Of course it isn't," Oyuun said. "None of this is, Captain. But I'll do more good here than I would out there. And it'll be good to have some time to myself for a change, without all these other people buzzing around interrupting my work."

"You gonna grab a nap?" Ames asked, smiling.

"Not my intent . . . but certainly within the realm of possibility. Sometimes I'm better with the math in my dreams."

"What are we looking for, exactly?" Elyth asked.

"The nature of the planet," Oyuun said. "To the best of your unique abilities."

Elyth waited a moment for something more specific, but the Arbiter didn't offer anything.

"That's a broad category, Arbiter," she said. "Do you want to narrow it down for us?"

"Not really, no. I'm likely to tell you the wrong place to look. Better to trust your own judgment, follow where it leads."

"Your findings haven't produced any clues thus far?" Nyeda asked.

Oyuun hesitated, considered his words.

"I will say that the absence of clues is peculiar enough to warrant investigating other avenues."

"Bad data?" Ames asked.

"Excellent data," Oyuun said. "Inadequate analysis, perhaps. A strange world such as this matching so many expected values makes me suspicious. But I haven't had time to focus, and I need that now. I'll leave it to you to figure out how best to proceed from here.

"Captain, perhaps you could take the lead on equipping everyone. Take whatever you need. We should have ample supplies now that we're so few."

"Roger that," Ames said.

Oyuun gave them a curt nod and returned to his research station. When he'd gone, Ames turned to address Elyth and Nyeda.

"Tell me what you need," he said.

"Nothing from you," Nyeda said.

Elyth added, with a smile to soften the words, "Other than your support."

Ames nodded. "You have that for sure. I'm going to gear up heavy, for whatever it's worth. I need about ten minutes. Wari Korush, you good?"

"Yes," he said.

"All right. Let me get my kit. You two figure out where you want to start. We'll take the skimmer out, and I can drop you off. Save a few steps, anyway."

Ames departed, and Elyth and Nyeda curtly discussed their objective and their most effective approach. By the time the captain returned with the utility skimmer, they'd formulated a plan between them that, despite the tension, seemed well-balanced for both efficiency and quality of information. Ames drew up in front of the group, and when Elyth looked in the bed of the craft, she was surprised at how loaded it already was.

"You weren't kidding about running heavy," she said.

"Rather have it and not need it than need it while it's sitting back home," he answered. "But it's not all for me. I know I told you before that I wasn't allowed to arm you, but given our new direction, I figured it'd be best for us all to be shooters, just in case."

He hopped out and produced two rifles from the bed of the skimmer.

"Are you both comfortable with these? If not, I can run you through the basics."

"We're proficient enough," Elyth said. "But we prefer not to use them."

"Preferred or not, I'd feel better if you had them."

"Neither of us are helpless, Captain," Elyth answered. "And our weapons of choice are somewhat greater."

He stood for a moment, rifles still in hand, and Elyth could tell he was trying to decide if he should insist on it, and uncertain whether he could persuade them to do anything no matter how hard he tried. He reached his conclusion to both quickly enough. With a mild shrug, he placed the rifles back in the bed of the skimmer.

"Hey," Varen said, "if they're not going to use them—"

"No," Korush said.

"Believe it or not, Korush, I *am* actually competent with such weapons," Varen said. "And I would *never* shoot you."

"Never on purpose, perhaps," Korush replied. "Subo is sufficient."

"All right, then," Ames said, hopping back in the pilot's seat. "Let's do this."

Nyeda joined him up front, while the others piled in the back. The captain drove them out to the far end of the glade, opposite the cliff face. There, Elyth, Varen, Korush, and Subo dismounted.

"Watch yourselves," Ames said. "Stay on comms. Call if you get in trouble."

"We'll see you back at base," Elyth answered.

Ames looked at her for a span as though he had more to say, but then gave a restrained smile and said, "See you all there."

He pulled away, headed toward the area Nyeda had identified for the two of them to investigate; they would stay closer to base camp, while Elyth led her party deeper into the wild. As the others watched them depart, Elyth activated her local nav tracker and scanned the display, dropping a handful of markers on coordinates where terrain features suggested some promise of useful data. She didn't take long, allowing gut instinct to act before her conscious mind could produce reasons for her choices. Once those were placed, she looked up at her companions and gave them a quick nod.

"It really is a beautiful day," Varen said.

"Keep together," Korush said.

"Follow me," said Elyth.

And with that, she crossed once more from the clearing into the darkened wood. The others followed behind and they moved together quietly, without speaking, for a long while. Elyth was pleasantly surprised at how each seemed to intuit her intent as to when to move, change direction, or pause to evaluate.

It didn't take long for her and Varen to find their shared rhythm; their time together on Qel had demanded close cooperation and forged a deep bond that time apart had been unable to diminish. Korush and Subo, too, might as well have been one, though she noted how carefully they remained on the flanks, bracketing her and Varen. She initially took it as a sign of their diligence in providing security. But she gradually became aware of how intently Korush was watching them, though he tried to conceal it; she realized he was just as ready to respond to *their* actions as he was to any external threat. She'd assumed that the Azirim was focused on keeping Varen contained. She saw now that he was also watchful for any sign of trouble from her. And there was no doubt what his response would be if he thought she posed any threat to the mission.

They traveled for half an hour or so before they reached her first marker, at a small hillock, topped with sparse trees with a large, flat stone in their midst. She signaled for a full halt.

"I need a few minutes here," she said. "Preferably without interruption."

Korush only nodded his assent. Varen looked up into the top of the trees, with a vague smile.

"Fine choice," he said. "You do have a knack for these things."

He smiled at her and then walked to a nearby tree and sat on the ground with his back against it, his legs stretched out in front of him, feet crossed at his ankles.

With a quick scan of the area and her expert eye, Elyth quickly identified several candidates for good samples: a thick, rust-colored moss, a variety of ferns and other such plants, two different kinds of mushroom, and trees with deep root structures. Each would offer her a different perspective on the network of life on the planet surface and beneath it, perspectives she would capture and compare to other such sites when she returned to camp. But before she got to that work, she climbed up to the flat rock to once more attempt her modified technique for touching the essence of the world.

She turned her back to the others, centered herself, and cleared her mind of distraction, and allowed the words of the Deep Language to first imprint themselves on her mind, before she allowed them to take shape in her breath.

"*Dawn chases shadow; blossom greets the day,*" she spoke in a whisper, heavy with the power of the Deep Language.

As before, the unique vitality of Qel's Shadow began slowly to rise to meet her in near-tangible sensations, beyond her physical senses and yet reminiscent enough to trigger close impressions. On this second attempt, however, the escalation came faster, and the substance deeper, as though the planet remembered their first meeting and was eager to pick up where they'd left off. Time expanded, or faded, and soon Elyth found herself attuned only to the voice of the world, and its wordless messages. And now, given the space, Qel's Shadow revealed more of itself to her than it had before.

Deep within its veins, the world had an affinity with Qel, of that there was no doubt. But it was an imperfect reflection of that planet, or an echo of it, as though someone had tried to re-create the same song but couldn't quite recall the precise melody. And underneath, something else that caught her by surprise. A vague but disconcerting hint of deceit, or falsehood; the feeling of beholding a work of art and sensing that it was counterfeit, without consciously being able to pinpoint why. There was life within the planet, but not quite the same life she'd come to know so well through her many years in service to the First House. Though it was too ethereal to grasp, something buried in its core felt artificial. Synthetic.

And as she waited in stillness, searching out the texture and substance of Qel's Shadow, she felt a rising, disquieting sense that it was in return, somehow, growing in its awareness of her. There was a calling hidden within, an invitation to stay, to gaze more deeply into the heart of the world. And that served as warning.

Elyth forced herself to break off the connection. In doing so, she snapped abruptly back into the reality of the wood, became once more aware of the stone beneath her feet, the ring of trees before her, the air around her. But traces of the planet's essence seemed to cling to her for a few seconds more, as though tiny tendrils had begun to wrap around her being and were only now withering away.

She took a moment to gather herself and then turned back to face her companions. Subo stood closer to her than it had been when she began, facing toward the forest; a faithful guardian. But both Korush and Varen had their attention solely on her.

"That's it?" Korush asked.

Elyth nodded. He grunted in response.

"Were you expecting something more?" she asked.

"More than you standing there for ten minutes, yes," Korush said. "But it is not my place to know your ways."

For the first time, Elyth smiled at the Azirim's honesty and humility; both were genuine.

"Perhaps in our time together we can each learn something of the other's ways," she said. She didn't expect any response from him, but to her surprise, Korush tipped his head down in a bare hint of a bow.

"How'd it go?" Varen asked, rising to his feet and dusting off his pants.

Elyth shook her head. "Confirmation that something isn't right about this place. Not much clarity on what."

"Just because it is *different*," he replied, "let's not assume that means it isn't *right*. At least not yet."

"You've been talking to it?" Elyth asked.

"Not exactly, no. I'm just trying to keep an open mind. It might be right for whatever it's meant to do. We just don't know what that is yet."

"Nothing good," Korush said. "Can we continue now?"

"I need to collect a few samples here and then we can move on," Elyth said. "Grief, you want to help?"

"It is my joy to serve," he said, walking over to her. She gave him a tool and handful of collection vials.

"We don't need much," she said. "Just a scraping or cutting will do."

"Of what?"

"Whatever catches your fancy."

"All of it does."

"Then only the things that most greatly capture your grossly indiscriminate heart, I guess," she said.

"Hmm," he said, holding up one of the vials and looking at it intently. "I don't think you'll fit."

Elyth warmed at the unexpected comment, both in embarrassment and rising irritation.

"Don't be useless," she said, and then turned away from him to begin her own work. She could feel his smile behind her but he said nothing else.

While she collected samples from the candidates she'd identified before, Elyth found herself glancing repeatedly at the man. He worked contentedly, focused pleasantly on the environment, seemingly oblivious to her presence now. Occasionally she noticed him pause to gently feel the texture of a leaf between his thumb and fingers, or run his hand over moss or bark. Getting a sense of the world in his own way. Whenever she looked at him, she was torn between wanting to believe his affection for her was genuine and fearing what that might mean. And, as she rolled the thought through her mind, wondering if it might instead be one of his subtle manipulations for some other unforeseen end.

Soon enough, they'd collected all she wanted from the area, and they moved on to her next point. Over the course of a few hours, they repeated the collection process at each location she'd identified. Korush and Ames checked in over comms with each other with each change, keeping each other apprised of their current coordinates and status.

At first, Elyth connected with Nyeda with far less frequency, but as the afternoon progressed, they grew into regular contact, discussing their findings, and adjusting their plans to ensure their joint survey was as thorough and robust as possible. And too, with the distance and cooperation between them, Elyth noticed a gradual change in Nyeda's tone and attitude toward her; where before she'd been closed off and severe at times, the walls that she'd erected seemed to be breaking down. Working alongside each other with common purpose was drawing them back together. Or, perhaps, making it easier for them to ignore the rift that had opened between them.

It wasn't until Korush insisted that they return to base camp that she realized how late it had become. But they still had maybe two hours before sunset, and at least a half hour beyond of workable light, and their camp was no more than an hour of direct travel from their current location. Though she guessed she had enough material to work with, Elyth wasn't quite ready to give up when there was still so much they could gather and discover.

"Let's push on a little farther and see how it goes," she said. "We've got time."

"We have time if there's no trouble," Korush answered. "And it's foolish to expect no trouble."

"Just one more location, then."

"No."

Elyth turned to square off with the Azirim. There was no chain of command between them, and as far as she was concerned, Korush was escorting *her* while she conducted the work Oyuun had directed her to do.

"If you want to head on back, I have no problem with that," she said. "But I'm going to go farther in while I still have light. I don't want to have to come all the way back out here just to collect something I could have picked up on this trip."

The shift in his stance was subtle, but unmistakable to Elyth's keen eye. He wasn't planning to allow any argument, and seemed prepared to use the threat of violence to make his point.

"I have advised our return," he said, the perfect calm in his voice at odds with the coiled energy of his body. "We will do so, whether you are willing or not."

Though there was no obvious command or signal, Subo, too, shifted, turning to face her and seeming to expand to an even more menacing stature.

"Wari Korush," Varen said. "We're all on the same team here."

"I'm not certain of that," Korush responded.

"I am," Elyth said.

The Azirim locked eyes with her; she met his gaze. Long ago, her instructors in the First House had given her a simple heuristic for identifying the greatest potential threat: Whenever a situation grew tense, she always looked first for the calmest person in the room. And in that moment, Korush seemed completely and utterly at ease. Though his hands remained at his side, Elyth wondered just how quickly he could deploy the void-edge. Faster than she could speak?

"Whoa, hey, slow down, guys," Varen said. "You're upsetting Subo."

Neither of them made any acknowledgment of him, nor even took their eyes off the other.

"Subo hates it when Mom and Dad fight."

Still, the standoff continued. Elyth had no intention of backing down, no matter what the Azirim and his machine did to intimidate her.

But Varen stepped between them, facing her, and intercepted her gaze.

"Elyth," he said, with quiet kindness.

"Not now, Grief."

"Elyth," he repeated. "I agree with Wari Korush. We've done enough for today."

The words hit her as half insult and half betrayal. She didn't try to hide the emotion.

"Oh, have we? What exactly would make you think you are the judge of that?" she asked.

He held up a hand, intending to calm her. The gesture didn't have that effect.

"You've done a lot of work today," he said. "I'm sure Nyeda has as well."

"Don't argue this with me, Grief. You're not equipped for it."

He smiled, deflecting the words.

"And," he continued as though she hadn't interrupted, "I may have some additional insight to offer."

Though she'd initially taken his intervention as a mere attempt at peacekeeping, Elyth now saw that he was subtly communicating to her that he had indeed found something. Something he didn't care to discuss in front of others.

"Will you come with us?" he asked, turning his upheld hand over, palm up, and extending it to her. An invitation to join him.

Elyth wrestled with the decision. Korush had turned a simple matter into a war of wills, and that was not an arena in which it was wise to test a daughter of the First House. Returning now would mean submitting to the Azirim, and she didn't like the implications such an action might have in the future. But she knew, too, that selfish pride was rarely a good counselor, and with the addition of Varen's comments, she was no longer certain that raw ego wasn't a factor.

"Come with me," Varen said softly.

Elyth held a moment longer, but finally nodded her assent. She couldn't bring herself to give the Azirim the pleasure of a verbal response. He didn't seem to need it, or to care. Subo resumed its usual size, still hulking but certainly less threatening.

"Captain Ames," Korush said into his comms, as calm as ever. "We're returning to base camp now. We should arrive in about an hour, if we don't run into any trouble."

"Yeah, roger that," Ames replied. "We're wrapping up here too. I'll drop Nyeda off and meet you with the skimmer."

"Thank you," Korush said. And then without waiting for further discussion, he turned and started leading them back to camp.

Subo, however, remained next to Elyth, and didn't move until she and Varen began to follow the Azirim. Once they did, the machine closed in behind them, acting both as rear guard and warden.

They reached the edge of the forest within the hour as Elyth had anticipated, encountering nothing unusual along the way. She felt vindicated to some degree, and mildly frustrated that she hadn't taken the time to investigate one more site as she'd intended. But as they reached the final stretch, she also wondered if Arbiter Oyuun's hypothesis was beginning to prove correct. It was too early to know for sure, but each hour that went by without

EVERY STAR A SONG   187

hearing the strange knocking sound made it seem increasingly likely.

When they emerged from the tree line, Ames was waiting for them in the skimmer, and when they'd loaded up, he took them swiftly to camp. Elyth joined him up front.

"Good day?" he asked, as they crossed the glade.

"We'll see," she answered.

He glanced at her, read her expression, and then said, "Well, looks like we're all going to make it home, so I'm going to count it a good day regardless of whether or not it was productive."

He pulled up in front of Oyuun's station. Nyeda was waiting out front, and Oyuun, presumably, was still inside. The group dismounted from the skimmer, and Ames and Korush started toward the station. But Varen remained next to the skimmer.

"You guys go ahead," he called. "I'd like to talk to the Housemates for a moment."

Ames looked back at him, then waved and said, "Sure, all right."

But Korush stopped and turned around.

"Come on, Korush," Varen said. "I'm not going to cause any trouble. Can't you trust me just a little bit? I did talk Elyth into listening to you, after all."

"You may talk about whatever you wish," Korush answered. "But I will hear it."

"You may hear it, but I don't think you'll understand it," Varen countered.

Korush thought for a moment, then wordlessly turned and walked the rest of the way to the station. He didn't enter, though. He stood watch there, giving them some space, but not so much that he couldn't intervene if he felt it necessary. Subo, of course, remained close by.

"Eh," Varen said, "close enough."

Nyeda walked over to join the two of them.

"You didn't talk me into listening to Korush, by the way," Elyth said. "I just got the sense that you'd found something useful."

"Don't be offended," he said. "I was only trying to make him feel better."

"What did you want to say?" Nyeda asked, with some impatience.

"I know you two have a lot to analyze before you'll make any judgment, but I just wanted to give you my perspective," Varen said. He paused for some response; Elyth just raised her eyebrows, waiting for him to continue. He nodded.

"There's something going on deep in the heart of this planet."

"Wow," Nyeda said. "Great insight. Thanks."

"I don't mean all the weirdness," he said. "I mean, something in its *heart*, in the . . . whatever you want to call it. Essence or spirit of the world. It's struggling."

"Yes," Elyth said. "With us."

"No," Varen replied. "With itself."

Nyeda sighed. "I'm not sure how you would know that, Varen. And I don't think it's going to be relevant to what we need to do here."

"I don't know," he said, shaking his head. "I just can't bring myself to believe this place is entirely evil. It has some purpose. And I think we have a part to play in discovering it . . . or maybe in fulfilling it."

Nyeda scoffed and said, "That's not a surprise. Somehow you always think you're the center of the universe."

"That's because I am," Varen said seriously. "It's infinite in every direction, after all. So wherever I go, I'm the center of it."

He paused a moment, then he smiled and added, "But then, so are you."

"All right, Grief," Elyth said. "Thanks for sharing. Can we get to our work now?"

He looked at her, eyes lingering on hers for a span, searching for something he hoped to find but didn't yet see.

"Sure."

"Thank you," Elyth said, and she moved toward Oyuun's station. The others followed, and when they entered they found Oyuun sitting in front of four active displays, staring intently at them. He made no acknowledgment of them, and Ames, standing off to one side, waved silently at them not to interrupt.

Elyth crossed to him quietly, leaned in close, and whispered, "Can we start setting up our gear, or should we come back later?"

"I think you can go ahead," he said, "as long as you keep it quiet. And *don't* talk to him."

"How long do you think he's been like this?"

"No idea. Maybe since we've been gone."

"Any guess how long he'll continue?"

"Until he's done. Could be hours."

Elyth nodded, returned to Nyeda to explain the situation, and then together they found a quiet corner in the small center to set up their equipment and begin their analysis. They worked in silence for a couple of hours, each analyzing the samples they'd collected and feeding the data into a common pool, where they could begin building a model of the planetary network. But as they added data, Elyth was disappointed to find that the picture didn't seem to be getting any clearer. She knew it would take more time and a wider range of sampling to get a complete and accurate model. But despite having what should have been more than enough data to locate a threadline somewhere in the area, she couldn't find one. In fact, she couldn't identify *any* within the planet.

Every world had its unique pattern of threadlines, fingerprints of its formation, the history of how it came to be and how it continued to exist written within the veins of its internal ecosystem. Understanding those threadlines was the key to Elyth's ability to discern a planet's nature and, more importantly, its vulnerabilities. But no matter how she manipulated the findings she and Nyeda had collected, she couldn't extrapolate even a hint of a single threadline.

Nyeda was seeing the same thing, and after working in silence for so long, Elyth signaled that they should go outside to discuss the matter. Nyeda nodded, and the two of them rose from their workstations to go outside. Oyuun was still at work, apparently oblivious to his surroundings, and Ames had wandered off at some point, likely bored by all the academic work that no one was including him in.

As the two women began to move toward the door, however, Elyth began to feel a strange sensation.

It started beneath her, like a subtle vibration of the ground. She stopped and placed her hand on a nearby table to steady herself, thinking at first that she was feeling light-headed or experiencing some other symptom of fatigue. But when she looked at Nyeda, she seemed to be feeling it too. Oyuun, on the other hand, continued his work uninterrupted.

As the two of them stood there, the sensation grew in intensity, a slowly rising buildup, like static electricity gathering in the air before a storm. It took a moment before Elyth realized that she wasn't feeling physical movement, but rather something deeper within; a familiar resonance folding back upon itself, its amplitude surging in intensity with each cycle of the feedback loop. Familiar, but not the same. The strange qualities of the phenomenon gave it a different energy and texture, but couldn't obscure its foundations. It was the same feeling she had when she uttered the words of the Deep Language. That of cosmic power, flowing through her; or rather, rushing around her from all sides.

When recognition came, Elyth flew to the door, heedless of the noise she created, and burst into the open. Her sudden appearance caused a sharp reaction from Korush and Captain Ames, who were standing together outside.

"What's going on?" Ames said, concerned.

Elyth didn't answer as she jogged to a patch of open ground near the center of the camp. The air vibrated with potential energy. Something was about to happen.

"Elyth? You okay?" Ames called, walking toward her. He was oblivious to the power surge, confirming Elyth's fears. Those who had never experienced the Deep Language had no sensitivity to its impact.

Varen came out of a nearby shelter, alarmed, and looked up first at the night sky above them and then at Elyth. His expression was enough; he felt it too, and it frightened him. He jogged toward her.

"What do you think it is?" he said.

Elyth shook her head as he came up next to her. Nyeda, too, joined them, all three searching the area for any sign of what might be coming.

"Okay, folks," Ames said, "you're kind of starting to freak me out here. What's the deal?"

Before anyone could respond, the stacked wave of energy

vanished in an instant. Not a slow dissipation; rather a sudden release. But to Elyth's surprise, nothing had changed. At least not that she could see.

"What *was* that?" Nyeda asked.

"I don't know," Elyth answered.

"It came from within the planet," Varen said. "Deep, deep within the planet."

Elyth nodded. That was the impression she'd had as well, though she couldn't express why.

"Seriously," Ames said. "What's going on?"

"Some kind of energy pulse," Elyth said.

"I didn't feel anything."

"You wouldn't," she said. "Unless you've been trained like we have."

Oyuun appeared at the front of his station, looking as though he were still struggling to reenter the reality of the physical world after his long stint in an abstract one.

"Is everything okay?" he called to the others.

"As far as we can tell," Ames replied. "But our friends here are spooked."

Korush was the first to notice.

"The sky's different," he said.

"What do you mean?" Ames said, looking at the Azirim and then up at the sky.

Elyth searched the heavens above them, and almost immediately identified what had changed. The realization nearly buckled her knees. She managed to keep her feet, but still she trembled as she told the others what she saw.

"Qel is gone."

THIRTEEN

As impossible as it seemed, the reality of Qel's sudden disappearance was easy enough to confirm. Oyuun contacted *Clariana*, and they verified the planet's startling absence. The research crew aboard the command ship hadn't noted it immediately, since all their attention had been turned to Qel's Shadow, and it took an hour or so to convince them that it wasn't a problem with their sensors. But that was a short time to wait to learn that what Elyth had feared had indeed come to pass.

Qel had vanished without a trace, destroyed by some unimaginable power and design from within the heart of its Shadow.

The team of six had gathered in Oyuun's research station, though none of them really knew what to do other than stand around in shocked silence, half listening to the Arbiter's one-sided communication with *Clariana*.

He sat at his workstation, half a dozen displays open before him and covered with a combination of star charts, orbital imagery, and dense mathematical equations so advanced that it might as well have been some ancient arcane language to Elyth.

"The result of their interaction?" Oyuun asked. "Something like a matter-antimatter reaction?"

Korush was the only one among them who didn't seem dazed by the change in circumstance; he was alert as ever, keeping watch over the group. And, Elyth noticed, paying particular attention to Varen.

"Did you detect any sort of signature at all? . . . Well, that may be something, don't discard it. An event of that magnitude would surely have *some* measurable impact. Perhaps it will make sense later . . . No, we didn't notice anything change here," the Arbiter said, before correcting himself. "I should say that half of us didn't, at least. Varen and our friends from the House seemed to have detected the event as it occurred . . . some sensitivity to the discharge, as I understand it. Not that I understand it. I'll gather more data from them when we have time."

"I need some air," Varen said quietly. "Elyth, care to join me?"

Elyth's initial thought was to say no; there was no telling what she might learn from listening to Oyuun work through the problem in real time. But when she looked over to Varen to decline the invitation, his expression told her he had something he wanted to discuss with her.

"Sure, yeah, okay," she answered. "Might help to clear my head a bit."

He held out a hand, inviting her to lead the way. Nyeda and Ames both glanced at them as they moved toward the door, but neither seemed to have any intent to join them. Korush, on the other hand, silently rose and trailed along behind.

Elyth opened the door and stepped out into the mild night air; Subo was there a few feet from the entrance, facing outward. Their patient and vigilant night watch. Varen paused at the top of the short staircase and turned to address the Azirim.

"Wari Korush," he said, "I don't suppose you would give us the honor of trusting us to be out here together without an escort?"

Korush didn't say anything, but his look was answer enough.

"What harm could we possibly cause that would be worse than what's already happened?"

"I don't care to find out," Korush replied. His eyes flicked to Elyth's and then back to Varen. "But if it's a private conversation, I will allow you some space."

"Thank you, that's very gracious."

Varen trotted down the steps and drew Elyth alongside him, leading her thirty feet or so from the Azirim, well out of the weak pool of illumination cast by the single, sunset-hued light over the entrance of the research station. Korush remained on the top step there, watching them like a hawk eyeing a pair of field mice. Subo hadn't moved, but Elyth knew the machine was also keeping track of them.

For a time, Varen said nothing. They stood there together for a minute, then he sat on the ground and leaned back with his hands behind him, gazing up at the sky, intent, as though counting the stars. Elyth continued to stand a while longer, waiting for him to start whatever conversation he'd been wanting to have. When he didn't, she took the initiative.

"What's on your mind, Grief?"

He glanced at her, his eyes barely visible in the night.

"Many things," he said. "Too many. Will you sit with me?"

Elyth was anxious to return to the station, knowing she was

missing valuable details from Oyuun's work. But Varen's demeanor had shifted, lost its usual lightness, and she sensed how
troubled he was in heart and mind. She glanced over at Korush,
whose eyes were still fixed on them, and then joined Varen on the
ground, cross-legged, hands folded in her lap.

He remained quiet for a span, but just before Elyth prompted
him again, he said, "I can't believe it's gone."

And in those few words, his voice carried a deep, weighty sorrow, a sadness she'd never heard from him before, even in their
darkest time together on Qel. It was a grief too powerful for Elyth
to speak to. She waited in silence, knowing more would come in its
time.

"Such a beautiful world," he continued eventually. "So full of
life. Vibrant. Still so much to give."

"You tended it well," she offered.

He grunted at the comment.

"I appreciate the thought," he said. "But it's not that. I just . . .
Qel had so much potential, and it wasn't realized yet. It was only
just beginning to blossom."

"You saved it once," Elyth said. "Beyond all hope, you stood as
its sole protector and rescued it. You gave it more time than it
would have had otherwise."

"Not *sole* protector."

"I couldn't have done what you did. I never would have even
thought to try."

"And I couldn't have done it without you."

He turned and looked at her in the darkness, his sorrow briefly
tempered by her presence.

"Do you think . . ." he said, then sat forward, shifted his gaze to the ground in front of him, and shook his head. "I've been won-dering."

She waited for him to continue, but probably for the first time in his life, he seemed genuinely not to know what to say.

"Now you're starting to worry me," Elyth said. "Is this the first time you've ever been speechless?"

He chuckled.

"Not the first, no. But perhaps the first to be afraid of what I might say."

"Nothing you can say is going to make me think any less of you, Grief."

"Low bar, huh? Can't go any lower?"

"Just spit it out."

"I don't think it's the kind of thing to spit," he said. "But . . . look, after we made it off Qel, that first little while I spent with the Hezra, was uh . . . notably uncomfortable. I was alone a lot. Almost all the time. And the one bright hope I had, the one that kept me from feeling like I'd failed completely and was at the end of my journey . . . came from knowing that you were out there some-where. And a confidence that I'd see you again, one day."

Elyth felt the warmth of his words, and the discomfort it cre-ated within her. He seemed to be waiting for a response from her, but she had no idea what he was expecting to hear.

"That's . . . very kind of you to say."

"Eh, I don't know that it's *kind*, necessarily," he said, playing off the moment. "I just felt sure we'd run into each other at some point. And I thought maybe when we did, maybe I wouldn't let them separate us again. That maybe I wouldn't let *anything* sepa-rate us again. Unless you had different plans, of course."

This wasn't the direction Elyth had thought the conversation was going to go, and she wasn't prepared for it. They were sitting on a planet that could apparently eat other ones; it didn't seem like the time or place to discuss something as inconsequential as a relationship. And though she wanted to tell herself that it was the inappropriate timing that created her discomfort, she knew there was something else beneath it. Daughters of the First House spent years learning to know themselves, learning how to detect self-deception, and the importance of confronting it.

The underlying truth was that when she had committed her life to the First House of the Ascendance, she had closed off any paths that might otherwise tempt her to consider a life away from it. Especially a life bound to another. But hearing his words, an ember flickered in what she thought was the dead ash of that part of her heart. And that was not something she knew how to cope with.

"Grief, I . . ." she said. "I can't even imagine what will come tomorrow, let alone what a future beyond that might hold."

"Oh, sure, I understand," he replied. "But if you *could* imagine it, do you think you could imagine it with me?"

Elyth had said enough; anything further she might say would only harm more than help. After a few moments of her silence, he nodded, and she saw a deep sorrow wash over him. But he quickly smiled and shook his head, as though he'd harbored no great hope for any particular outcome.

"I'm sorry to put that on you," he said. "I got a little ahead of myself there. Honestly, I just . . . I'm not sure what's going to happen either, and I wanted you to know that. For whatever it's worth. I would hate to get explosively disassembled leaving that unsaid."

She felt him withdrawing, masking the second hurt he'd suffered in such a short time.

"I do hope, at least," he said, leaning back on his hands again and looking up at the sky, "that you and I can stand together on Qel one more time."

Elyth glanced at him, confused.

"Qel was destroyed, Grief," she said. "You just said so yourself."

"No, I said it was *gone*. Not destroyed."

"It vanished in a moment."

"It would certainly appear that way, yes. But I don't think it was destroyed."

"What do you mean?"

"I don't know exactly. I'm not sure I know much of anything, really. But there are certain things to which I am deeply bonded. Certain things, certain *people*, Elyth, who are bound to me . . . or more likely, I to them." He turned to look deeply into her eyes for a moment, ensuring she understood that he wasn't just talking about Qel. But he didn't linger on the point long, and resumed gazing at the stars above. "Whatever it is, somehow that connection gives me a sense of them, no matter how far away they may be. If Qel had truly been destroyed, I would have felt it."

"It isn't there anymore," she said. "We've confirmed every way we know how. What else could have happened to it?"

He shook his head. "Hidden, maybe? Or . . . transformed?"

"Neither of those seems more likely than outright destruction."

"You felt the power this place unleashed. In the face of that, is anything *less* likely than any other thing?"

Elyth drew a breath to argue, but realized it was pointless. Varen was convinced of something that he'd not fully expressed, and there was nothing she could say to move him. And, if she were being honest, his statement had some validity. Anything that *could* be, no matter how minuscule the probability, could be manifested with sufficient knowledge and control over the Deep Language.

"You feel the struggle in it, though, don't you? Whatever this planet is, it's at war with itself." He glanced at her briefly. "I know if I said it to anyone else it would sound crazy, but I think you, of all people, can understand it."

"Even saying it to *me* still sounds crazy."

"Help me understand it, Elyth."

"I *am* trying, Grief," she said. "But I'm not confident we're seeing the same thing."

"I think maybe Qel got into it, somehow. That . . . I don't know, this isn't right but, sort of like Qel was singing into it, the way I sang into Qel. And that whatever just happened wasn't the catastrophe it appears to be."

"There were over a billion people on that planet."

"A billion people the Ascendance was ready to eradicate not so long ago," Varen countered. "And would have, had we not been there to prevent it."

The shift was subtle but uncomfortable. Varen was defending the bizarre world, despite the obvious threat it posed. And Elyth was reminded of her first impression of the man, of his willingness to initiate change recklessly, without regard to its potential consequences, somehow trusting that wherever the new course led would turn out for the better. He hadn't really changed at all.

"What are you talking about? What do you think we're here to do?"

He shook his head.

"I don't know, Elyth. I just have a sense that if we spend

enough time, if I could connect myself to the heart of this planet, we might learn to capture things we currently find inexpressible."

"Truths that can't be spoken?" she asked, recalling his own words from an early conversation on Qel. A reminder of who he'd claimed to be as *eth ammuin*. The Silent One. "I think it's more likely this planet will get into *your* heart. And I shudder to think what change that might bring."

He sat quietly for a span, but then nodded and levered up to standing. He dusted off his pants then offered her his hand.

"You had to dust your pants off *before* you help me up?" she asked, hoping to melt the frost she'd sensed was beginning to form between them.

"These hands haven't been clean in a long, long time," he said, and though the tone was light, there was a darkness lurking beneath that she hadn't seen in some time.

She took his hand, and he helped her to her feet. They stood together, hands joined longer than necessary.

"Grief," Elyth said, "I know how much Qel meant to you. To us. It's okay to grieve its loss. If you aren't sure how, I can teach you." The offer was genuine; in her time in service to the House, she'd taken the lives of a dozen planets, each one a world she'd come to know intimately, and learned to love. Advocates of the Voice carried the heaviest of burdens, and the First House had a long and thorough process to shepherd them through the guilt, grief, and regret that came with every sentence of death carried out.

"Thank you," he said, then released her hand. "But I don't feel the need to grieve a thing only temporarily lost."

He smiled at her sadly, his face shadowed in the night, an expression plain to her only because of how well she knew him. And she felt that somehow she'd caused him greater pain than the loss of his beloved world could have. Varen turned and started toward his quarters, apparently with no intention of joining the others in Oyuun's station.

Watching him go, a thought occurred to Elyth.

"Grief!" she called. "Hold on a second."

She jogged over to her own quarters and pulled out her pack, where she'd stored all her belongings that weren't necessary for her fieldwork. The only belongings she had left now. Deep in an interior pocket was a small, hard-shell case. She removed it, opened it, drew out one of the dozen thumb-size vials within. Once she'd closed and returned the case to its proper place, she rejoined Varen outside. He was still patiently waiting right where she'd left him.

"I've had this a long time," she said. "But maybe now it'll be more use to you."

She handed him the vial, and he left it on his open palm, face close as he studied it.

"Okay," he said. "Thanks. . . . What is it?"

"It's soil," she said. "From Qel."

He looked up at her then.

"A tradition I had," she explained. "Before I . . . put a planet down, I always took some of its earth away, before I spoke its death. So I could remember what it'd been before I'd come to it."

Varen looked down at the small vial with a new appreciation, understanding now what it was that he held. The tiniest sliver of Qel's unique essence. The only sliver remaining, as far as she knew.

"Thank you, Elyth," he said, sincerely now. "Maybe one day we can return it to its home."

He wasn't going to let it go and, in his usual way, he was going to keep subtly hinting and poking either until she came around to his point of view or . . . She didn't know what the other option was. It seemed likely that was the only outcome that would make him stop.

She was about to jab him with a verbal barb, but the words died in her throat. Before she could speak, another surge of power began to rise through the ground beneath her. This one was faster, though, building in intensity at an exponential rate. It was obvious Varen felt it too; he grabbed her upper arm, offering comfort and stability, or maybe seeking them from her.

Common natural instinct would have been to stand in fear and brace herself for the worst, but Elyth's life of demanding study and disciplined training had forged her nature in uncommon fire. Though the fear still rose, this time it triggered a different reaction, calling attention to the opportunity that the dreadful moment presented to her. She pulled away from Varen's grasp and dropped to one knee, placed her hand on the ground, pressed fingertips and palm into the soil underneath.

To kill a planet, she'd been taught the intricate and exacting technique known as Revealing the Silent Gate. And though she lacked the intimate understanding of Qel's Shadow that the technique demanded, in her exile Elyth had carefully extracted a portion of the protocol for different ends.

With the power of the planet growing beneath her, she closed her eyes, inhaled deeply, held the breath, emptied her mind of all but the sealing phrase she herself had created. And in her exhale, she spoke.

"A voice in the void; its song echoes in emptiness."

Her first encounter with the Shadow's power had plunged her into a raging river, throwing and throttling her in its rush along its course. But this time, she voluntarily immersed her hand in that surge and tumble; finely attuned and firmly anchored by the Deep Language, Elyth explored the strength of the flow, its texture and substance. Again, she felt within it the underlying structure of cosmic interaction, but not through any means she could grasp or comprehend. Even so, in the midst of that swirling mystery lay some trace of something familiar, too vague for her conscious mind to identify, too present for her subconscious to ignore, too deeply disrupted by the foreign energy to hold in thought. No, not one, she realized, but two separate traces: a wind and a whisper.

The electric energy stacked upon itself for a full minute, and then, without warning, the surge reversed its course, rapidly depleting at the same rate as it had grown, and Elyth lost contact with its stream. There was no sudden release this time, and the lack of an obvious discharge of power gave her some mild hope that nothing had happened after all. But when she opened her eyes, that hope lasted no more than a second.

Varen stood next to her, staring up. Above them, the sky had changed once more. This time, however, it didn't take a keen eye to notice what was different. The entire expanse of stars had rearranged itself, as though the planet had flipped upside down, or flopped over to some new radical angle. The spread of stars was still separated from a wide swath of emptiness, but the ratio of pinpoint lights to darkness didn't seem quite the same; the band of blank sky was narrower, the stars claimed a greater share of the heavens.

Elyth jogged toward the research center with Varen trailing behind. When Korush saw her coming, he opened the door and stepped aside. Though his face was as stone as ever, his eyes showed that the change in the sky had shaken him in a way Elyth would have thought impossible.

Inside, the others were stirred up as well. Oyuun was fiddling with the gear at his workstation, muttering to himself.

"What's going on?" Elyth asked.

"Dunno," Ames answered. "Lost contact with *Clariana* all of a sudden. Nyeda felt more of . . . whatever that was you guys felt before. Looks like it fried our gear."

"Hmm," Oyuun said. "Something is certainly wrong here."

"What is?" Nyeda asked.

Oyuun looked up from his display, brow creased and eyes narrowed in thought. "Well, my array is attempting to recalculate our location. And it's having . . . a bit of difficulty."

"Like I said," Ames said, looking at Elyth with a half shrug. "Fried all our gear."

"Perhaps . . ." the Arbiter replied, but it was clear his expansive mind was considering other possibilities.

"Well?" Ames asked. "What else could it be besides a busted array?"

"Yes, yes, that would certainly be the most plausible explanation."

"Then why do you make it sound like it's not the *right* one?"

"I suppose I'm not confident we *are* in a known location."

"Look, man," Ames said. "I haven't slept in like sixty hours or something, so maybe I'm even slower on the uptake than usual. But I'm pretty sure I didn't hear you right."

The Arbiter turned away from his workstation and addressed the captain calmly and patiently, like a kind doctor walking a patient through a troubling diagnosis.

"I apologize; I should be clearer," Oyuun said. "The array is re-recalculating our location. It did so once, and I've asked it to do so again. Actually, this is the third time. The array seems to be functioning perfectly well, as is our communications network. So, to use the technical term, our gear is not *fried*."

"Then why'd we lose contact with *Clariana?*" Nyeda asked. "It wasn't destroyed, was it?"

One of the consoles at Oyuun's station chimed, and he looked to it, read the data scrolling by on its display.

"I don't know the vessel's fate. But our communications network has a maximum effective range of about a third of a light-second," the Arbiter answered.

He turned back to face the rest of them before breaking the news.

"And it appears that we are now twenty-four light-years away."

FOURTEEN

The news was so shocking, so bewildering, that even Korush reacted sharply, a level of confusion and dismay on his face that finally revealed the human beneath the iron mask of Aziri discipline.

"Arbiter," he said, and though his voice was even, Elyth could hear the dryness of his mouth in the words, "please explain."

"Oh, I have no way to do that, Wari Korush," Oyuun replied. "Other than to describe what I've already told you. The array contains a full model of our galaxy, and orients based on the bodies around it. Planets, stars, nebulae, those sorts of things. Calculated and confirmed by performing the necessary transforms of course, to match what it sees." He blinked, and seemed to realize that none of the words he was using meant much to his audience. "It's like a fancy star map."

The Arbiter reached over to his workstation and pulled one of the floating displays closer, expanded it so everyone else could see it clearly. It did indeed look like a complex star chart, and as he traced his finger over its surface, labels appeared identifying the celestial body beneath.

"*Tzo ru* oh-one-oh-four," he said, "more familiarly called Avemar. That's the closest planet." He traced farther, to a bright star. "And its gracious host . . . I doubt the technical name means anything to you. . . . Though now that I think about it, I can't recall the colloquial name either."

"You're sure this is accurate, Arbiter?" Elyth said.

"I'm rarely certain of anything, Aspirant," he replied. "But at the moment, this is the only thing I feel strong confidence about."

"You're telling us that this planet just instantaneously jumped twenty-four light-years across the galaxy?" Nyeda said.

"Or was pulled, perhaps. Or the galaxy shifted, and it stayed put. But however we got here, it does appear to be the case that we are some distance removed, yes."

"That makes absolutely no sense."

"I concur with your estimate," Oyuun said. "But to be pedantically mathematical about it, I would say it makes a *non-zero* amount of sense, which, unfortunately, is still the *most* sense, given what we know. Admittedly, what we know is apparently also in the realm of approaching, but not quite, zero."

Everyone seemed too stunned to process anything. But as far as Elyth was concerned, if the impulse from Qel's Shadow had been enough to erase Qel in an instant, then warping across the galaxy, as difficult as it was to accept, was not an unbelievable development. The important question was not whether, but why.

Avemar meant nothing to her. There were so many settled worlds within the Ascendance empire, it was almost impossible to know them all. Judging from the array's display, however, she noted that it was another fringe world, like Qel, far out on the galaxy's edge. Astronomically speaking, it was practically on the border of the Ascendance's governance.

"What's special about Avemar?" she asked.

"Apart from being our only friend out here?" Oyuun said. "Not much. Relatively young in the Ascendance family, I believe, settled perhaps only . . . four, five hundred years ago? I could dig up the details if you like."

Elyth shook her head.

"Grief," she said. "You ever been to Avemar?"

He glanced at her.

"Not that I know of."

"How far?" Ames asked, his voice quiet and heavy.

"I'm sorry?" Oyuun said.

"How far to Avemar?"

Oyuun checked the display and answered, "Eleven point nine four light-seconds, approximately."

Ames had been standing up to that point, but now he lowered himself into a chair, bent forward with his elbows on his knees, and dropped his head in his hands.

"What is it, Captain?" Nyeda asked. He didn't respond at first, just slowly ran the fingertips of both hands across his scalp, front to back, over and over as though trying to soothe a pounding headache.

"Captain Ames?" Elyth said.

He let his hands fall in front of him, clasped them, but didn't raise his head.

"Comm array has a range of a third of a light-second," he said. "Shuttle has a range of about half a light-second. No jump capability."

He took a deep breath, sat up in the chair.

"We're trapped here. With no way to call for help."

Elyth had been so focused on the puzzle of the planet that she hadn't yet thought about the implications for their team.

"*If* we've really moved," Nyeda said, "I'm sure it won't take long for the Ascendance to locate us. It's a whole planet, after all."

She looked to Oyuun, clearly expecting him to agree. Instead, his mouth tightened.

"Arbiter?" she said.

"They will find us, yes," he said. "How long it will take is . . . incalculable at this time."

"I don't understand. You picked it up when it appeared near Qel, didn't you?"

"Yes. But many eyes had already been directed to Qel, for obvious reasons. And, to be transparent, we don't know definitively how long it was there before we noticed it. My associates on *Clariana* did relay to me that the vessel experienced some anomalous feedback before Qel's destruction. It's possible that a similar event might draw their attention, I suppose. But the loss of another Ascendance world seems a high price for the rescue of six, and not one to hope for."

"There has to be an emergency protocol," Nyeda said. "On the shuttle? A beacon, or something?"

"Not one anyone will notice this far out," Ames said. He was keeping his cool, but the effort it took for him to do so was obvious. "It's a ship-to-shore hopper, not an escape pod. It wasn't designed for open space."

"What about our comm array?"

"Linked to *Clariana*. All the long-range gear is on *Clariana*, *Aterin*, and *Vanquin*. . . . I knew we should have kept the gunship."

"You mean we have *no* way of contacting anyone?" Nyeda

said, an accusatory tone creeping into her words. "This whole big Hezra task force had *zero* contingency plan? How can that be?"

"Oh, I'm sorry, Advocate," Ames said, heat rising. "Somehow in all our planning, we made the mistake of expecting a *planet* to stay right where it was!"

"Whoa, let's take it easy here, everybody," Varen said. "There's no need to panic, and we certainly don't want to start eating our own."

Nyeda had more to say, but she wisely chose to leave it unspoken.

"I tried to tell you to keep the gunship, Arbiter," Ames said, quietly, almost to himself, with more regret in his voice than accusation.

"You did, Captain," Oyuun said. "It was my error to disagree. My view of the possibilities was much too narrow, I fear."

The group lapsed into silence, each perhaps sensing how close they were to tipping into a total meltdown.

"On the bright side," Varen eventually said, "Subo is taking this well."

"Grief," Elyth said. "This isn't the time."

"I humbly disagree," he replied. "Optimism is *precisely* for this sort of time. It's not quite as useful when everything is going well, after all. And I would think, at the very least, our circumstances would cheer *you* up in particular, Elyth."

He left the comment dangling there, and she knew it was bait. But she took it anyway.

"Do tell, oh great master of all wisdom and insight, why that would be."

"Well . . . because now we're *all* exiles."

It seemed a particularly flippant remark, ill-advised and maybe ill-purposed. But something about the way he'd set it up triggered a subtle signal in her spirit. On Qel, she'd learned how Varen often buried hints of something deeper in his lightest or most absurd comments. He was making some point, the first brick in a case he was building, though its meaning and significance escaped her for now. There was no doubt, though, that he would circle back to it later. She inhaled, hesitated before making any reply, allowed the words and the tone of his voice to imprint themselves on her mind. And then answered.

"I liked you better as the Silent One," she said. He smiled at the jab but, thankfully, didn't reply.

"Despite our unfortunate lack of an escape plan," Oyuun said, reasserting his authority, "our objective hasn't changed. For the time being, we still have everything we need to continue our assignment here."

"I don't see what good any of that does if the information dies with us," Ames said.

"Yes, true. But best to work one problem at a time, Captain. One problem at a time. And our current priority is to discern what it is we need to know about this planet."

"And once we do," Elyth said, "we might be able to solve the problem of the planet without needing to get off-world anyway."

"How's that?" Ames asked.

"You have an Advocate of the Voice," she said, gesturing to Nyeda. "And a former one. Between the two of us, we'll find a way to kill it."

"Kill it?" Varen said. "Shouldn't we at least figure out what it's doing before we decide what to do about it?"

"Yes, of course, we'll figure out what it's doing," Elyth answered. "And *then* we'll kill it."

Varen's face flickered with a brief expression, displeased or disappointed, but it quickly resolved. He nodded, then withdrew a few paces to a corner and leaned against the wall. Acquiescing. At least for now.

"Okay, then," Ames said, getting back to his feet. "What's our first step?"

He glanced between Oyuun and Elyth; to Elyth's surprise, the Arbiter looked to her.

"We find another place to look," she said. "Nyeda and I pulled together some data, but it's not enough to give us the starting point we need."

"Is that usual?" Oyuun asked.

"Given the amount of ground we covered today, I would have expected to have more to work with. It's not necessarily *un*usual, but I wouldn't say it's common either."

"Could be that its network got disrupted," Nyeda added, "with all the shifting the landscape seems to have done since the first team arrived."

Having some direction and concrete actions to take appeared to be bringing her back to form.

"It'll be helpful to see how varied the flora is across regions, too," she continued. "Better data, clearer picture of what to expect."

"Probably shouldn't have *any* expectations about this place," Ames said. "Seems to get us in trouble every time. And I really don't love the idea of getting too far outside the wire."

"Where do you suggest we start?" Oyuun asked, turning back to his workstation. He dismissed the display with the star chart and brought one of the others around, expanded it for them to see. A detailed terrain map of Qel's Shadow, focused on their immediate surroundings. "Orbital imaging from *Clariana*, overlaid with data from our drones."

The features of the land were sharply defined over the majority of the area, but a few spots were fuzzier than their surroundings. Oyuun anticipated the question before anyone asked it.

"The major discrepancy here is due to the appearance of the cliff. Our local data is good, but *Clariana* hadn't finished reimaging the location before we . . . lost our connection."

Elyth crossed to him, examined the map. The incredible definition of the projection created a powerful sense of physicality, as though if she reached through the display, she'd be able to feel the texture of the terrain beneath her fingertips. Even the planetary intelligence provided by the First House's legendary Order of the Eye had never reached such a level of resolution.

"How much of the area is mapped to this level of detail?" she asked.

With a quick gesture from the Arbiter, the map retreated almost too fast to follow, as though the viewport was being launched into orbit, until the display showed Qel's Shadow in its entirety, floating in space. Oyuun gestured again, and the planet revolved lazily on the screen, completing a full rotation before coming to a stop.

"Pick a spot," he said, nudging the floating display closer to her.

Elyth navigated and manipulated the display using the common gestures of interaction, and was astonished to see that no matter where she looked or how closely she zoomed in, the quality of the image never diminished. Oyuun showed her how to tilt the view as well, to get different perspectives on a location. The near limit appeared to be twenty or so feet above the surface, a range close enough for her to pick out small features that would serve as useful landmarks if she were on foot in the area. She spent a minute or two scrolling around the region, testing out the high-fidelity imaging.

"Are you selecting a location," the Arbiter eventually asked, "or just playing with the map now?"

"Some of each, I think," she said. "Our land-nav instructors at the House never missed a chance to drill into us the difference between map and terrain. I'm not sure they'd be able to argue that quite as convincingly if I showed them this."

"It is indeed a useful tool, generally speaking," Oyuun said. "Though, unfortunately, in our peculiar circumstances, I must admit there's no guarantee that what we see here is what we'll find in person. I wouldn't be quick to discard your training."

Elyth nodded and, now that she was fully comfortable with the map controls, recentered the view over their camp to begin her survey in earnest. She closed her eyes for a moment, cleared her mind.

During her service to the House, Advocates of the Eye had provided her with target packages featuring detailed surface mapping to help her select her points of attack. Had she been on any normal mission, on any other planet, the range of options would have been wide. But here on Qel's Shadow, she knew that every choice they made was critical and any time they lost might lead to another unpredictable catastrophe. She couldn't just find a good location; she had to find the *best* location. And doing so required the perfect balance of conscious analysis and subconscious prompting, gut instinct supported by hard data. In that moment, she felt out of practice.

When she opened her eyes, she pulled the map view out to a distance that looked most familiar, closest to the targeting data her sisters of the Eye used to provide. From there she began a systematic sweep of the surrounding region, a grid-based survey spiraling outward from their base camp. Though she noted several promising areas, the moment the first roots of a mountain range appeared in the view, the image sparked a sharp response in her body. She followed the terrain up to the range and when the display crossed a specific peak, a pair of sensations passed through her like a chill wind.

One was certainty; the other dread.

She spent a long minute staring at the image and its surrounding territory. It was as good a point of analysis as any she'd seen, but nothing about it stood out as an obvious trigger for her reaction. Nevertheless, whenever she returned to that peak, she felt drawn to it, called by it.

Elyth looked over her shoulder at Nyeda and motioned for her to join them at the display. Nyeda came along beside her, and Elyth gave her a few moments to examine the map on her own. Korush stepped closer, watching from the side, unobtrusive but engaged.

"What do you think, Nyeda?" Elyth asked.

Nyeda spent a couple of minutes scrolling around the area, and though she didn't seem to react to the mountain as Elyth had, she continued to return to it as a centering point of reference in her search. The others remained in quiet expectancy while she worked. After a time, she straightened and nodded.

"We have some good options there," she said. "I would agree, I think it's the right place to start."

The range would have been a several-day journey on foot, but it was a short hop for the shuttle. Ames walked over to get a closer look.

"Day trip?" he asked.

"That would be the hope," Elyth said. "But we should pack for longer. Just in case."

"How portable is your gear?" Ames asked Oyuun.

"That depends on how strong we all are," the Arbiter answered with a quick smile. "I can certainly take the essentials. Possibly a few nice-to-haves. The shuttle has *some* storage, of course, but we'll have to weigh trade-offs between equipment and personnel."

"Drones?"

Oyuun shook his head. "Their control base station is too large."

"I've got some dragonflies," Ames said. "Won't be much, but better than nothing."

"Indeed, any data we can collect could be useful. The craft does have a cabin off the main body, and a small emergency medical bay as well. Those could give us a little extra capacity."

"If we're staying atmospheric, we can put some of the gear in a crate, sling it on top," Ames offered. "Might fly a little sluggish, but it shouldn't be heavy enough to cause problems. Could probably toss Varen up there too, if you like."

Elyth glanced over to the corner of the station where Varen had been standing, anticipating his commentary. But Varen was no longer there. She hadn't heard him leave.

"Wait, where did Varen go?" she asked.

Korush went taut, snapped his head around to look at the corner where Varen apparently should have been; a moment later his eyes went unfocused, as if lost in thought. After a few seconds, his shoulders relaxed and his eyes cleared.

"He's outside," Korush said. "Sitting on the ground, near his quarters."

"Subo keeping an eye on him?" Ames asked. Korush gave a

curt nod. And though his face hardened back into its usual expressionless mask, Elyth could tell he was rebuking himself for having failed to notice Varen's quiet departure. And she wondered again about the nature of the connection between the Azirim and his machine, whether Subo had communicated to him in some unheard verbal exchange or if Korush could somehow see what it saw.

"It would be unwise to divide our group," Korush said. "If we're relocating, we do so all together."

"Yeah, I'd agree with that," said Ames. "Safety in numbers, or something."

Oyuun drew the display closer, and bent nearer to examine the area Elyth and Nyeda had selected. After a brief survey, he straightened and nodded.

"Very well," he said. "Everyone return to your quarters, get what rest you can. We'll load at dawn."

The order to rest caught Elyth off guard; everything seemed too urgent, time too short, to allow for any downtime. The Arbiter anticipated her response, his authoritative bearing rematerialized, and he held up his hand to halt her argument before it began.

"That *is* an order," he said. "We've hardly stopped since we arrived, and we're in the range of sleep deprivation where mistakes start slipping into the work of even the most hardened of operators. We cannot afford them."

Oyuun scanned the faces of the others in the room, and then softened slightly, more grandfather than drill sergeant.

"And we've borne a great deal of change today," he continued. "Give yourselves a moment or two at least to attempt to process whatever your minds can handle. We'll all need them as clear as possible to tackle whatever tomorrow has in store."

It took a moment for the full weight of his words to settle on Elyth. Had it only been one day? It could have been a week, and Elyth would have thought that time frame too short. But it had been around the same time the night before that she'd had her first talk with Oyuun, and the cliff had appeared. Since then, they'd found the ship, lost Sardis and Qel, and traveled twenty-four light-years across the galaxy.

Any argument she thought she could make dissipated in the face of that realization.

"You're all dismissed. See you at daybreak."

The others appeared to feel the same as Elyth; hesitant to be the first to leave, reluctant to allow themselves any recuperation with so much work to do, and so many unknowns to contend with. But Ames took the lead, broke the ice.

"Roger that, Arbiter," he said. "I'll bunk with Varen, Korush. Subo can sleep by the door. Get you a moment to yourself."

"That isn't necessary, Captain," Korush said.

"I know it isn't. But it's what we're going to do for tonight. At the very least it'll give you a chance to hose out your armor."

The corner of Korush's mouth curled in an uncharacteristic display of amusement.

"Ooh, that was almost a smile," Ames said. "Now I *know* you're exhausted."

The Azirim bowed his head, touched his heart, and answered, "Thank you, Captain Ames."

"Just here to serve, buddy. Same as the rest of us," Ames replied, then turned toward the exit, speaking over his shoulder as he went. "All right, I'll admit it, I'm the weakest one here, so I'm going to bed. See you all soon enough."

"I'll walk with you, Captain," Nyeda said. He paused by the

door, waited for her to pass through, and then followed her out into the night.

Korush looked to Elyth, offered her half a bow, and then turned and provided the same to the Arbiter.

"Do not hesitate to call upon me," he said.

"Sure," Oyuun said. "Rest well, Lion of the Aziri."

The Arbiter's words stunned Korush, his usually unreadable face momentarily revealing the emotion beneath. But he only bowed once more, and then left without further response. Oyuun's eyes lingered on the door, as though he were still watching the Azirim as he walked away.

"Wari Korush is the highest exemplar of the Way of the Aziri I've ever met," he said, and then turned his attention to Elyth. "He will question himself deeply in the face of what he has suffered today. But he must not be allowed to forget his true standing. No one could do more than he has done. I would appreciate your support in this."

She didn't know exactly what he meant for her to do, but she nodded.

"Of course," she said. "How about yourself, Arbiter? Care for a nap?"

He smiled at her kindly.

"In a bit, dear. In a bit. I have just one more thing I'd like to tie off."

Elyth stood regarding him for a moment, unable to fully reconcile the many dimensions of the man she had discovered. The sting of his confession from the night before remained, but had lost much of its power in light of his actions since then. She knew he was still the man who had recklessly pursued his research and development to near-catastrophic ends. But she also saw the lengths to which he was going to correct his mistakes; and more, the authority he could project when he wished, and the goodness within it.

"Don't ignore your own advice," she said. "You said yourself you'd never ask someone to do something you weren't willing to first do yourself."

"Ah, you are much too sharp for a man of my meager wit," he replied. "Now I suppose I *have* to follow my own command."

She nodded and turned to go.

"Good night, Arbiter."

"Actually," he said, "before you go, could I prevail upon you to answer a question whose resolution has thus far remained beyond my grasp?"

"If there is such a question, I doubt it's within *my* ability to answer," she responded, turning back to face him. "But if I can, yes." And then, after a quick thought, she added, "And if it does not violate any of the tenets to which I still hold."

"Of course. I'd expect neither more nor less of you."

Oyuun paused a moment, formulating the question.

"You, along with Nyeda and Varen, sensed both . . . what shall we call them . . . energy-discharge events, let's say, while the rest of us were oblivious to them. Could you help me understand the mechanism behind that?"

Elyth took a moment to roll the question over, to genuinely consider her response before speaking.

"The simple answer," she said, "is no. But my guess would be that it has something to do with the three of us having been steeped in the power of the Deep Language in a way that few have. There's a quality to it, to the way it folds and shapes the fabric of the universe. I'm afraid it can't be meaningfully described if you haven't experienced it. Though, you might know something like it, if you've ever tried to explain your calculations to someone who lacks the necessary mathematical foundations."

"Ah," he said, and only a few seconds later, the analogy helped him leap to a surprising level of understanding. "Ah, yes, I think I see. There are certain mathematical abstractions—structures, symmetries, that sort of thing—and when one truly grasps the properties of such a structure, one can begin to sense its presence there before the equations ever reveal it. Yet it remains hidden to those who only see the symbols. Something like that?"

"Yes," Elyth said. "That seems like a reasonable parallel."

"Very good, that's helpful. So then would you agree or disagree if I were to suggest that this planet somehow makes use of the Deep Language as you understand it?"

"I would . . ." Elyth began, and then hesitated while she weighed her answer, "disagree, I believe. But only mildly."

He grunted at that.

"Because you say 'as you understand it,' and I can't say that. There is a familiarity there, but also something off about it. Something that . . . *sounds* wrong, I guess."

"Same language, with an accent?"

Elyth shook her head.

"More like different language, same root. Perhaps two branches that share a far-distant but common ancestor. I don't know if that makes any sense. It's difficult to explain."

"Indeed, phenomena outside any previously known experience often are. But the way that those of your House speak the Deep Language . . . I apologize for the crudeness of the analogy, but could it be understood as a manner of precisely describing the reality that you wish to manifest?"

"I suppose something like that. Crudely speaking," she said.

And though she was hesitant to say more about the teaching of the First House, one more detail seemed both important enough to add and innocuous enough to reveal. "Though certain phrases are much more compact, and tied to certain linguistic patterns."

"Hmm," he said. "For ease of use?"

"More for effectiveness."

"Interesting . . . very interesting . . . . so, sorry, last question, I promise. If the general concept is to describe a possible reality precisely, why would metaphor hold such power?"

Elyth had said nothing about metaphor, yet his description as such was shockingly accurate. The insight within the question served as a warning to her; the man's intellect and the quickness with which he could assimilate and integrate information clearly made it dangerous for her to say more. And though he seemed genuinely interested in nothing more than understanding the phenomenon within Qel's Shadow, she suddenly wondered if he had merely camouflaged ill intent beneath his mask of benign curiosity and kindness.

"I fear that is beyond my skill to answer," she said, bowing.

"Ah, I see," Oyuun said, apparently neither disappointed nor interested in pressing the point. "Well, thank you for the lesson. I must admit at the moment my mediocre brain has not yet grasped any of its relevance, but it may prove helpful at some point. One never knows what connections might one day appear between bits of otherwise seemingly useless trivia."

He touched her shoulder lightly in a gentle pat, and added, "Please get some rest, Elyth. You look as though you've been carrying the whole galaxy by yourself. Which would be a silly thing to do, when you have so many others with whom to share the burden."

The Arbiter turned back to his workstation then, and drew up a second display covered with his indecipherable calculations. Elyth left quietly and returned to her living quarters, wondering just how much she had underestimated the man. And what tools she may have given him that might help him discern and deliver forbidden knowledge into the hands of the Hezra. Though the conversation had seemed benign enough, a dark train of thought began tumbling through her mind.

By the time she reached her quarters, Nyeda was already fast asleep, undoubtedly drained by the overwhelming events of the day. Elyth stood at the entrance for a time, watching her former sister and confidante. Nyeda had claimed her continued loyalty to the First House, and the Hezra had treated her as though she were an outsider. But how much had she already revealed to the Arbiter, before Elyth had come along? No one else had confirmed the truth of her claim, and Elyth had no way to verify it on her own.

Nor could she establish for herself that Oyuun's calculation of the planet's new location was accurate, or even that the vanishing of Qel and changing of the sky wasn't part of some vast, simulated projection. The *Clariana* might have such capabilities, regardless of how difficult it was for her to imagine. Clearly the Hezra possessed technology beyond what she had known, and that which she did know was already enough to dwarf any doubt she might have about what was possible for the hierarchy now.

The Ascendance had terraformed countless worlds; given what the Hezra had learned from Qel and potentially Varen during their long separation, it was no longer even a stretch for her to imagine that they themselves might now have the power to *create* one. And how far would the Hezra be willing to go to gain access to, and willing cooperation from, a woman who knew both the secret arts of the First House and the nature of Qel, the only world in history to withstand the full power of the Hezra's dreadful Contingency?

Once she'd opened that door in her mind, the simmering, background disquiet that she'd been carrying erupted into fullblown turmoil, with the thought that nothing was what it seemed, and that she was falling deeper and deeper into the multidimensional intrigues of the Hezra and the House. By the time morning came, she boarded the shuttle with the distinct feeling that she was surrounded not by allies but by enemies of the most cunning kind.

FIFTEEN

They arrived at their designated point of exploration about two hours after sunrise, leaving plenty of time for them to set up the little they needed and get to work. The area they'd selected served as a transition from hill country to a mountain range several miles distant; the air took on a hint of chill that it had lacked before, and though it wasn't uncomfortable, Elyth could easily imagine it becoming so as they gained elevation. The landing zone was a wide natural clearing, elevated above the surrounding terrain, with an ample buffer of open ground between the shuttle and the surrounding trees.

Shortly after landing, the supply crate on top of the shuttle dismounted, autonomously piloting itself to the ground nearby, and unfolded to reveal the neatly organized supply racks within. Ames and Korush had clearly been up early; from the looks of it, Elyth figured they could probably spend a week in the field, or maybe up to ten days if they decided to run lean. In light of her awakening the night before, though, she wasn't sure how many more days she could stand to be in such company. Longer, if she

could find evidence to reassure her; if not, well . . . already a portion of her mind was searching out the possibilities, unlikely as any escape seemed to be.

The group took about an hour to unload and prep for the day ahead, laying out the plan and gearing up to the best of their ability for whatever they might encounter. While they did so, Elyth watched everyone's actions and communications through new eyes, judging intent, searching for signs of deception or conversations staged for her benefit. The team was unusually quiet, though, each member focused on whatever task they had at hand, alert to their surroundings, moving with purpose and efficiency. Varen alone seemed unconcerned with the change of scenery, though he was more distant than usual, more pensive, less engaging.

Elyth was kneeling on the ground, in the middle of packing her gear, when Captain Ames approached her.

"Hey, Elyth," he said. "You doing okay today?"

She nodded without looking up. "Just trying to focus on what needs to be done."

"Yeah, I get that," he replied. He said nothing further, but he continued to stand there, hovering over her. After what should have been plenty of time for him to realize she didn't want to talk, she finally paused and glanced up at him.

"You need something?"

He nodded. "Yeah, I do actually."

"And it is . . . ?"

He dropped into a casual crouch, a few feet away but eye to eye with her.

"I need to know you're on board with this, all the way, one hundred percent."

"Have I given you reason to think I'm not?"

"Not until this morning," he said. "I've been in a few hairy situations before, hairy enough to see some real hard hitters get spooked."

"If you're worried about my courage or resolve—"

"I'm not. I was going to say, I've seen spooked, and that's clearly not what you are."

"Then what do you think I am?"

"I'm not sure. But *I'm* afraid that I might be seeing something like doubt."

"If you're *not* feeling doubt, Captain Ames, then I'm not confident that you've been paying attention to what's happened recently."

"Doubt in us, Elyth. In *me*. And look: I've always figured if I can't be smart, and I can't be good-looking, the least I can do is try to be honest. I'm as straight a shooter as I know how to be, so I can't abide the idea that you might think we're at cross-purposes here."

Elyth held his gaze for a moment, searching for any hidden intent. With every other member of the team, she felt compelled to weigh their words, to search out what meaning might be concealed behind them. But even with her heightened suspicions, Ames seemed nothing but genuine. She shook her head and resumed packing.

"I don't know where you're getting any of that, Captain. We're all on the same team here." The words fell out of her mouth before she realized she was parroting the very thing Varen had said just the day before. She didn't like that.

"Are we?" Ames asked.

"For my part, at least."

"There is no *your* part that isn't also *my* part."

The captain settled back on his heels in a squat that looked awkward to Elyth, but appeared to be perfectly comfortable for him. He held his hands up, palms facing her.

"Just tell me we're good, and I'll take you at your word."

She regarded him once more, and felt some of the tension she'd been holding all morning bleed off. If there was a conspiracy unfolding around her, Ames had clearly been left out of the loop.

"We're good," she said.

He gave her a single, sharp nod, and then stood up, moving from his unusual starting position to upright with surprising fluidity. The man must have had the muscles and joints of a cat. Elyth returned her attention to her gear, mentally rewinding to where she'd been interrupted to ensure nothing was left behind or misplaced in her pack. Once they were out ranging around, she didn't want to lose even a moment to searching for something that should have been at hand.

"I know this is probably weird to say, but I'm kind of looking forward to being out there with you," Ames said. "I really never thought I'd be running around with the Ghost of Qel."

Normally she would have ignored the obvious attempt to pique her curiosity, but given the captain's apparent concerns about her loyalties, she picked up the thread to dispel any misgivings he might have. Even so, she kept her eyes on her pack and continued her work, not wanting to seem overeager.

"Is that supposed to be me?" she asked.

"Yes, ma'am."

"And did you make that up, just now?"

"Nah, I picked it up from a couple buddies of mine. You hadn't heard it before?"

She shook her head. "I guess I shouldn't be surprised that I have a reputation, no matter how ridiculous it may be."

"From what I gather, it was pretty hard-earned," Ames replied, and then by way of explanation, offered, "I was attached to Three Recon for a stint. They had stories."

"Ah, the Fear-eaters," she said, using the storied unit's nickname. One of their teams had been dispatched to track her while on Qel and had nearly caught up with her. Other members had, in fact, subsequently captured her, though she blamed that largely on having had Varen in tow. "If you've been hanging out with them, you must have earned quite a reputation for yourself in the military."

"Oh, I'm not military," he said. "I'm actually on the enforcement side. Conservation officer."

She looked up at him, not sure whether he was kidding or not.

"I figured it was obvious from my lack of discipline," he added.

"Conservation?"

"Wildlife and ecosystems, that sort of thing. You'd be surprised what people will do in protected territory when they think they can get away with it. First gunfight I ever got in was with a couple of big-time poachers. And I'll tell you what, lifelong hunters can *shoot*."

Elyth finished loading her pack, closed it up, and got to her feet.

"Conservation officer," she said, while she pulled her pack on. "How in the world did you end up out here then?"

"Just lucky, I guess," he said. He half turned, making way for her to pass by. She started walking the remaining distance to the designated departure point, and he followed along beside her. The others hadn't yet gathered. "I didn't really know what I was getting into, but when I heard we'd be going out with an Eli, I knew it was going to be a good one. I had no idea it was going to be you, of course."

"An Eli?"

"Oh, ha, sorry, no disrespect intended. That's just what some of us call you guys. Easier than all that Advocate stuff."

"I suppose it's a term of deep affection and honor, then?"

"Something like that. Eli. E-L-I . . . Extinction-Level Individual."

"I see," she said. "Well, I guess that does at least sound nicer than what we call *you*."

"Yeah? What's that?"

Elyth gave him a quick smile but offered nothing further.

"Fair enough."

They reached the gathering point, about twenty feet in front of the shuttle, facing southeast, toward the distant mountain range and the peak she had identified. On the Arbiter's terrain map, the mountains had borne an ancient look, and threadlines often ran along the roots of such megalithic features. But now that she saw them with her own eyes, she felt once more the powerful, uncanny draw toward them. Something more than just instinct and experience telling her the range held within it the connection she was seeking. They *spoke* to her, and the inaudible voice of the planet seemed hidden behind that calling, though she knew in her bones the deceptive nature of the planet. It was a call she would have to resist, for now. Elyth turned her eyes toward the closer surroundings.

The land of the clearing rolled rocky and sparse, ringed by occasional clusters of tall, slender trees like black pines, robed in thin, angular leaves instead of needles, standing watch among other, shorter species with small, unfamiliar characteristics. Beyond that perimeter, the pockets of trees merged with an unbroken wilderness that appeared almost more like a dark sea than land.

The Ascendance's methods of terraforming often resulted in similar plant and animal life, recognizable in form but with sometimes surprising variation. Marks of the family line, revealed in diverse expressions. The same seemed to hold true here on the Shadow, but as she scanned the landscape before her, Elyth was once more struck by an unsettling sense that she was seeing something more like a copy than an original. Her first impression had been one of awe, as though this planet had been the one that all others had been trying to model. Now, it seemed the opposite, that Qel's Shadow was somehow attempting to be so much like all the others, that it had overcompensated and become too vivid, too *real*, for her mind to accept.

"You're sure we're good here?" Ames said, calling her attention back to more immediate matters.

"If you keep asking, Captain," she said, "my answer *will* change."

"There we go," he said, chuckling. "*Now* I feel better. Hang tight while I round up the rest of the troops."

When Ames left her, Elyth returned to her survey, and tried once more to fix her mind on the quality of the world that continued to stick like a burr in her spirit, in her sense of the place. It was there, she *knew* it was, somewhere in the land, not deeply hidden but rather so thoroughly intertwined with its material that she couldn't extract the aberration from its mask of what appeared to be completely natural.

Counterfeit, her inner voice kept whispering, without explanation beyond. It stirred within her the turmoil she'd felt after speaking with the Arbiter, the dread that something sinister swam just beneath the surface, if only she had eyes to see.

Subo slid up next to her, disconcertingly quiet despite its bulk, its method of traversal still not entirely clear. It matched its facing with hers and maintained a stance just off her left shoulder and slightly behind. For the first time, its presence felt more protective than menacing, as though it might be as concerned for her welfare as it had been for Sardis's. Elyth glanced back over her right shoulder to see Korush approaching, and when they made eye contact, he gave her a quick nod. When he arrived, though, he took a place on the opposite side of Subo rather than keeping her in between them. A subtle signal that he no longer felt the need to try to contain her. Elyth wondered if that had been his own idea or had taken prompting from Captain Ames.

Shortly after, the other members of the team joined them and, to Elyth's surprise, Oyuun was there, geared up with light armor, a rifle, and a small pack.

"Question, problem, or concern to voice, Elyth?" he said, when he saw her looking him over. He used what she was beginning to think of as his Arbiter Voice.

"No sir," she said. "I just didn't realize you were planning to go out with us."

"Stick together," he replied. "That was what we agreed. And I didn't spend my entire career in a lab, in case that is the cause of your obvious trepidation."

"I have no concerns about your capabilities, Arbiter."

"Very good. Then lead on. I want to be back at base camp two hours before dark."

The group had gathered behind her, Ames bringing up the rear with Varen just ahead of him. The captain had something in his hand that looked like an oversized egg with a flattened end; he smacked the bottom of it against his thigh, and then threw it to one side, scattering its pieces in a haphazard fan. But instead of falling all the way to the ground, the pieces stuck in midair, as if time had stopped. A few moments later they gently rose, reoriented, and spread out in two identical formations, three in each. One formation held its position off to the right of the group while the other silently glided up and over to the opposite side. Miniature scout drones; Ames's dragonflies.

He gave Elyth a thumbs-up. On his signal, she looked to Nyeda and tilted her head, inviting her to the front. Together, they led the small band down the gentle slope and into the wilderness.

The two women took point, leaving a ten-foot gap between themselves and the others, both as a precaution and to avoid spoiling the ground with too many feet before they had a chance to evaluate it. They had traveled less than half a mile when the first knocking began.

At the first beat, Elyth halted the team; they held position, weapons poised, eyes sharp for whatever the wood might unleash upon them. After a full two minutes without sign of change or danger, she called back to the others.

"Korush," she said. "Subo picking anything up?"

"No," he answered.

"Ames?"

"Not even a fly."

She nodded and resumed their hike, slowly at first, and then eventually back to their normal mode of operation. There was too much work ahead for them to let an uncanny noise hinder them.

Some time later, the knocking was joined by a second and then

third, each at different distances and intensities. The rhythm between the three was mismatched at first, similar in timing, but out
of sync with one another. Gradually, however, once again without
any notable change in their intervals, they merged into a single,
unified pulse, each beat echoing among the hills.

The knocking continued for the next several hours, unbroken
and unabated, but Elyth noticed that, strangely, the sources of the
sounds didn't seem to alter according to their movement. Either
wherever they were coming from was much more distant than it
sounded, or the sources were tracking along with them. Whether
anyone noticed it or not, none said so. Eventually, though they all
stayed alert, the team grew accustomed to the noise, allowing it to
recede into the background as they focused instead on accomplish-
ing what needed to be done.

Elyth and Nyeda continued to guide the group to each point
they'd previously identified. At each location they separated,
working in tandem to gather a handful of samples, and occasionally calling on each other to give a second opinion on unusual or
interesting ecological features. The others followed along, maintaining security while the women worked, except for Varen, who
stayed close but wandered the immediate area, picking grass or
flowers or leaves that caught his interest.

From time to time, Elyth paused her careful work to observe
him, and though he made a good show of studying the environment, it didn't take long for her to see he was doing it solely for
the benefit of the others. Being useful and cooperative. But she
knew him well enough to discern his actual intent, from the way
he moved and the often unfocused, faraway look he took on when
he thought no one was watching.

It would have been concerning if she'd caught him talking to the planet, coaxing it and guiding it the way he had Qel. But he didn't appear to be making any such effort. Instead, it seemed more like he was straining to listen to it. And that was far more worrying.

They'd traveled about seven miles, ranging back and forth across a broad swath of the region when they saw the first sign of wildlife. Ames found a partial print, and afterward they all kept their eyes open for any other hints of the passage of animals. Later, as they came into a small clearing atop a ridge, Elyth was the first to spot the creature that had left the track, grazing along the tree line on a hill some thousand yards distant.

"Hold for a second," she said, and the team stopped at her signal.

"Anything to be worried about?" Ames asked.

Elyth shook her head as she pulled out her monocular.

"Don't think so," she answered.

She locked the monocular's view target on the animal and then activated magnification. The monocular autocorrected for the subtle trembling of her hand that otherwise would have made it impossible to keep the creature meaningfully in sight over that distance. When she saw it, she recognized it immediately. It appeared to be something like an elk, though it was an unusual brindle color, with antlers rounder and flatter. But it wasn't just the species she recognized. Looking at it gave her a sense of déjà vu, a sense that she was looking at not the same *kind* of animal but rather the same animal *itself* that she'd seen once, and only once, before. On Qel.

"Looks like an elk, kind of," she said, but she kept her voice neutral and mentioned nothing else, not wanting to affect the captain's first impression. "What would you say?"

Ames stepped up next to her, borrowed her monocular, and gave a quick assessment of his own.

"Pretty-looking fella," he said. "Maybe not an elk, but definitely kin. I wonder if he's as skittish as the stock breed back home. . . . But yeah, I'd say if he's not the one who left the track, it was one just like him."

One just like him. The words resonated in Elyth's mind, but not for the reason Ames had intended.

He returned the monocular.

"Good eye. Keep moving?"

"In a minute," Elyth answered. "I need a moment to get my bearings."

Ames tapped the local nav tracker clipped to her vest.

"This guy leading us astray?"

"No," she said. "I'm after a different set of bearings."

"Oh," he said, holding up a hand and wiggling his fingers. "Spooky word stuff. Got it."

"It won't be long. But if you want to take a breather, might be a good time for it."

He nodded and returned to the others, spoke to them quietly. None of them looked like they were going to allow themselves even a moment of downtime. Nyeda busied herself scouring the immediate area for useful samples, while the men and Subo spread out to keep watch.

"Grief," she said, "come take a look at this."

He startled at the sound of his name, apparently surprised to be asked to take part in anything. After a moment, he nodded and joined her near the ridgeline. She handed him the monocular, and he gazed through it, following her directions to find the animal.

"Okay," he said, "yeah, I see it. Looks like an elk." He lowered the monocular. "Should it mean something to me?"

"I saw one just like it on Qel," she said. "*Just like it.* And I've never seen another."

"Huh," he said, and he rolled it over in his mind for a moment. "Huh," he repeated. He looked once more through the monocular, before lowering it and handing it back to her.

"I take it you think that's weird," he said.

"You don't?"

"Uh, no . . . I guess not so much. Though I've kind of had my sense of weirdness recalibrated by recent events."

Elyth was surprised at his response; it seemed overly nonchalant, even for him. But he swiveled his head back and forth, taking in a quick scan of the horizon and, apparently, checking on whether or not anyone else was paying attention to them. A moment later, he turned back toward the animal, took her monocular again, and spoke in a lowered voice while he watched it across the hills.

"When you say *just like it*, you mean identical?"

"I do," she said. "Or close enough to count. I still remember the moment vividly, because I'd never seen one before. And because I spooked it from about six hundred yards away. Never figured out how it picked me up."

"Seems like it'd be tough to be sure," he replied. "Been a long time, and if you never really got close to either one . . ."

She thought he was being dismissive, but he brought the monocular down and said, "Climate's different, food sources are different, terrain's different. Same animal, different habitat. I would agree it seems weird, except for one thing."

"What's that?"

"This place is covered in Qel's fingerprints."

He returned the monocular, and she peered at the animal one last time, watched as it wandered up to the top of the hill.

Just before it disappeared down the other side, though, it stopped and snapped its head around, as if it had suddenly detected them. It stared at her for a long moment, its eyes so acutely focused on her that it seemed like it was looking right back at her through the monocular. And then it turned back, and without haste meandered over the ridge. Toward the mountains.

"Something does seem . . . *off* about it, though," Varen continued, still looking in its direction. "I can't quite put my finger on it. Something about the way it's moving, maybe. Or its bearing."

And then, in a louder voice, added, "Sorry, I guess I'm not seeing the same thing you are."

She knew it was no accident that he echoed her own similar statement back to her, his subtle poke and unspoken challenge over their disagreement about the nature of Qel's Shadow. He'd projected his words not for her, though, but apparently for the benefit of the others. No one seemed to be paying much attention to them, except for the ever-watchful Korush.

"What's with the show?" Elyth asked.

He shrugged. "I don't know what anyone wants from me. And no one else seems to know why I'm here either. I figured I should at least *look* busy."

It might have been convincing to anyone else. Elyth waited, giving him a look that demanded the truth. He maintained an innocent look for about five seconds, before a poorly suppressed smile gave him away.

"Still can't get anything past you, huh?"

"Not a thing."

He took a quick inhale, tilted his head from side to side.

"I don't want to give them any more reason to fear this place," he said. "Not until we know for sure that we should. And if I have to argue the point, I won't have much of a leg to stand on if they all think I haven't done anything useful out here."

Elyth watched his face, searched for the deeper intent she knew was there. But she could find no sign of deception in him.

"I have to admit, Grief," she said, "I'm almost starting to hope there really *is* something beyond our comprehension taking place here."

His face subtly lit up at her words, but his voice betrayed no hint of surprise or excitement.

"And why would that be, Elyth?"

She glanced over her shoulder at the others behind them, each still focused on their individual tasks.

"Because the only alternative I can see is too mundane and tedious to contemplate."

When she looked back at him, his eyes were fixed on her, bright and intent. He nodded.

"I think I know what you mean," he said. "To believe we are on the cusp of something extraordinary, only to discover it's an elaborate ruse for a predictable purpose would indeed be a crushing blow." He turned his gaze outward again, taking in the horizon from their elevated vantage. "I do think our friends are here for the wrong reasons. But I have a feeling this is something new, something very real, that we have not yet begun to grasp."

And as if his words had caught the attention of the planet itself, the incessant knocking that had become background noise abruptly ceased. After so long of its steady rhythm, its sudden absence felt both uncanny and ominous.

"Well," Ames said. "I don't like *that*."

The group instinctively tightened up; Ames and Oyuun tucked their rifles to their shoulders, readied themselves. And any doubt that Elyth may have had about the Arbiter's abilities in the field vanished when she witnessed his effortless handling of the weapon. Long-practiced, deeply ingrained.

For two or three minutes, the group held their ground, alert, tense, each scanning for any sign of threat or danger. But nothing appeared, neither shifting terrain nor grotesque creature.

Even so, when Oyuun broke the silence, he didn't sound encouraged.

"It would appear my hypothesis was incorrect," he said.

"Which one was that?" Ames asked.

"The one about the planet's reactions being caused by the presence of so many foreign bodies. It doesn't seem to care much for our little group either."

"Oh, I don't know, Arbiter," Varen said, holding his arms out to either side and twisting slowly back and forth, as if inviting them to behold the beauty around them. "Maybe it's just saying hi. Excited to have such fine company for a change. Nothing horrible's come running at us yet."

"I *really* wish you hadn't said that," Ames said.

They held their position for a minute more, until finally Elyth spoke up.

"We need to push on," she said, "if we want to make it back to base before dark."

"I'm good with that," Ames said. "Especially if you're taking the lead."

He cracked a smile at her, but it was obviously forced.

"I know you'll be right behind me, Captain," she said. "Using me for cover."

"I'm nothing if not tactical."

Elyth stepped forward, resuming their march through the

stretch of woods that stood between them and their next destination. They'd gone about fifty yards when she saw something that paralyzed her and stole her breath.

The silhouette of a woman, standing just beside a tree.

In reaction to Elyth's sudden stop, she heard quick, sharp motion behind her; rifles snapping to shoulders, Subo unfolding its dire weapons.

The woman by the tree didn't respond to their movement; didn't call out, didn't even move.

"She one of yours?" Ames said quietly from behind; he'd closed the gap to her near silently.

Elyth was still too stunned to answer, her mind swirled by possibilities. Could it be one of her lost sisters? Or was this another evil trick of the planet? She took cautious steps forward, hands held out in a nonthreatening manner, looking more closely. Still, the mysterious woman did not move. And with the initial shock wearing off and the change of perspective, Elyth saw that the figure wasn't a human after all, but rather a strange, natural formation. No, not *natural*. Composed of natural materials, but clearly unnatural in design.

"It's okay," she called back to the others. "It's just a bunch of dirt and rocks."

She continued closer to examine it, more quickly but still wary, and stopped an arm's length away from the figure. The silhouette had been so unmistakably human, she'd half expected to discover a statue with finely crafted features. Instead, it looked more like something had scooped a mass of earth into a human-shaped mold and compressed it into form. At first she took it as a haphazard collection of dirt, rocks, roots, and vines. But as she looked more carefully, she found there was more order to it than she'd realized.

There was some attempt at structure there, as if rock had been substituted for bone, roots for muscle, vines for arteries, earth for skin. It was imperfect, patchwork, but disturbing in its incomplete design.

"You think that's what all the knocking was about?" Ames asked, from several yards back. He'd held his position rather than following her over, while his dragonflies performed a silent survey of the area.

"Maybe," she answered.

"It's not the only one," Korush said from farther back. "There, there, and there."

Elyth looked back to him and then scanned the area. There were indeed four of the figures, not quite identical, but of the same uncanny design. Ames moved a few steps closer to one of them, but kept a safe distance, and his rifle firmly planted against his shoulder. His drones shifted focus, pairs of each flitting off to investigate.

When Elyth turned back to the figure in front of her, for a horrible moment she feared that it had indeed once been an Advocate of the House, that somehow the planet had overcome one of her former sisters and this was now all that remained. But as she examined the unnatural statue with a more rational eye, that thought gradually receded, too much the product of awful fantasy for her to accept.

"Like I said," Varen called, "maybe the planet's just trying to say hi. Make us feel welcome."

"Well, it's doing the opposite," Ames answered.

Elyth ignored the commentary, stepped closer to the strange figure, touched the vines, the stone, pressed her fingertips into its soil. The earth was moist and springy, as though it were still part of the forest floor rather than compressed into shape.

It happened too fast for her to react.

A hard impact struck her forearm; crushing pain followed an instant later. Reflexively she tried to cradle her arm, only to find it frozen in place, and to her shock she realized a rootlike hand was clutching it with ancient strength. She cried out, reeling back from the figure, but it held her fast, threatening to powder her bones.

Elyth brought her free arm up, smashed it down on the creature's forearm. The strike did nothing but send shock waves blasting back through her body. She tried to twist, push, kick, anything to gain leverage to break free, but nothing she did had any effect. Still, the figure didn't move, apart from the slow, continually growing pressure of its hand.

Why wasn't anyone trying to help her?

Through her pain, she realized she was hearing gunfire behind her, and had been for some seconds. But it wasn't aimed in her direction. The team was engaging the other figures. Outside the grip of the creature, though, the world seemed distant, fogged. Elyth fought to focus, to reach through the building agony to the place beyond, where clarity of mind and strength of purpose lay. The Deep Language was there, if only she could understand it.

But before the words formed, something shot over her shoulder from behind, narrowly missing her head, and plowed through the abomination, the force of impact disintegrating its head and upper torso and pelting her with a stinging shower of dirt and rock. She stumbled backward, thrown off-balance by the sudden release. Immediately after, the saving blur reversed course, a thick tendril retracting. As it whipped past, she glimpsed the pattern of its metallic surface, and recognition came. Subo.

The remaining portion of the thing staggered away from her and collapsed to the ground, crumbling into a loose pile of stone, earth, and root. Still, the pain remained and to Elyth's horror, she saw that though the creature's arm had been severed just below the elbow, its hand maintained its crushing grip on her forearm. She fought to pry open its rootlike fingers; an instant later, Korush was by her side, lending his strength. Neither of them could relieve even an ounce of pressure, and Elyth felt panic rising, fear that this thing would powder her bones to oblivion and still never let go.

Seconds later, though, it released without warning, dropped to the ground, and, as had its host, deteriorated into its components. Silence followed, heavy and dense. Gradually the world returned, and Elyth became aware of the breathing of her companions, the closeness of Korush, the pressure of his arm around her back, steadying her. She glanced to him, his face inches from hers, his eyes ablaze.

"Are you injured?" he asked.

Elyth looked down at her arm, rotated it gingerly, clenched her hand into a fist, released it, tried to splay her fingers. Movement felt numbed, clumsy. Nothing appeared to be broken, but she found she couldn't fully straighten the two outer fingers of her left hand; while the others straightened fully, her ring and little fingers remained partially curled. When she pressed her thumb against them, it was like touching the flesh of a stranger. Dull pain radiated from the center of her forearm, spreading in both directions, up to her shoulder and down to her knuckles.

"I think I'm okay," she said. "Just need a minute." She looked back at him. "Thank you."

Korush gave a single nod and withdrew his arm just slowly enough for her to test her balance and be confident that she wasn't going to crumple to the ground.

"What . . . in the name . . ." Ames said, breathing heavy, "of Hezra and House . . ."

"I don't know," Oyuun answered. "But we're done here. Back to the shuttle, back to base. We'll formulate a different plan."

"Yeah, roger that," Ames replied.

"Wait," Elyth said.

"No," Oyuun said.

"Arbiter, just a moment," she said. Hands shaking with lingering pain and adrenaline, Elyth pulled out her collection tools and cautiously gathered samples of the earth and root that had moments ago been animated with deadly strength. With that done, she stood and backed off a few steps, but continued to watch, remembering the vile creature that had confronted them before, and its disappearance after its death.

"Can we go now?" Ames asked.

"I want to see what happens to it," she said.

"I don't."

"Two minutes, Elyth," the Arbiter said. "Then we leave, no more questions."

Elyth nodded. Korush remained by her side, and Varen joined them, all three intent on the pile of rubble before them.

"Are you okay?" Varen asked quietly.

"Not happy," she said. "But fine."

He nodded, paused for a span while he wrestled with whatever it was he wanted to say. Elyth tested her arm again. The pain still throbbed; the two fingers hadn't regained sensation. She hoped it wasn't permanent.

Varen still hadn't found his words.

"Spit it out, or don't," she prompted. "Either way, quit chewing your lips."

"I'm sorry," he said. And then again, "I'm sorry . . . I didn't know what to do."

His eyes were still on the remains in front of them, but Elyth saw the shine of tears welled in them; he had feared for her life, and perhaps for the first time, had felt powerless to do anything to save her.

"It's okay, Grief," she said, touching his arm briefly. "I don't think any of us did, really."

"Subo seemed to," he said.

"That is its purpose," Korush commented.

"What happened to the others anyway?" Elyth said. "I was too busy to notice."

"Captain Ames dispatched them," Oyuun said.

"Don't sell yourself short, sir," the captain answered. "You did most of the work, I just finished a couple of them off. Plus, I'm packing heavier rounds, so it's not really fair to compare anyway. . . . Can we please discuss this on the walk back to the base?"

"One minute," the Arbiter said.

Elyth turned her attention back to the pile at her feet. At first she thought nothing was going to happen to it. But her keen eye noticed a few subtle depressions in the earth that hadn't been there before. And as they continued to watch, the remains shifted ever so slightly; a tumble of soil here, a gentle roll of jutting rock or root there.

"Arbiter," Elyth said.

He picked up on her tone and joined them. Together they monitored the micromovements.

"If that thing starts to get up, you better stomp it out quick," Ames said from behind them. "I already dumped a whole mag on them."

They stayed past their deadline, observing whatever it was that was happening before their eyes. Elyth was the first to guess the cause.

"Something's going on with the material at the bottom of the pile," she said. "Sinking into the ground, maybe?"

"Hmm," Oyuun said. "Possible."

"Like the planet's swallowing it back down?" Ames asked. He'd crept closer to the rest of the group and was talking over his shoulder, while keeping his body turned toward the area where the other three figures had been.

With just a few seconds more, the answer revealed itself as the phenomenon reached the stones, roots, and vines on the surface. They began decaying, slowly to the eye, but with time-lapse speed compared to nature, gradually returning to nothing more than dirt and dust.

"I don't much care for that, either," Ames said, still looking over his shoulder.

On a whim, Elyth raised the vial in which she'd stored the sample of soil and root. Though it shouldn't have been a surprise, she was taken aback when she saw that the root remained intact. She shook the vial, heard the clink of the root against the side. It hadn't softened at all.

"I believe I've seen enough," the Arbiter said. "And we're well past time. Captain, if you'd be so kind, I'd prefer you lead us out."

"Sure thing," Ames said. "We all set? Nyeda?"

Elyth didn't hear a response, and for the first time she turned to look for her friend. Nyeda was standing off to one side, a few yards from the group, and a few strides away from one of the disintegrating piles. She had her back to the rest of them, but from her posture, Elyth could tell she had her arms crossed, as if hugging herself against the cold.

"Nyeda?" Elyth called, stepping toward her. "Are you okay?"

Nyeda turned her head as if she'd heard the voice from far away. A few moments later, she looked at the group as if waking from a dream, and then quickly nodded. She dropped her arms to her side and without speaking walked over to Ames.

"Good," he said, "Let's move."

The captain headed off with a confident stride, head up, alert for trouble, flanked on either side by wide formations of his dragonflies. The rest of the team kept pace, silent with focused awareness as they moved. But Elyth's mind kept turning everything over, seeking some foundation for all the phenomena they'd experienced, looking for a common cause or connection. It was all so chaotic, possessing neither pattern nor design. Utterly unpredictable, truly random. An underlying dread bubbled in her heart; anything seemed possible on this planet. And if the world could take any one of them at any time, or all of them at once, she wondered why it had not yet done so.

They safely reached the perimeter of their landing area after the sun had begun its descent, and though they still had hours of daylight left, a wide shadow lay across the ground where none should have been. The Arbiter noted the reason before anyone else spoke.

"Strange," he said. "Another cliff formation. Except this one appears to have been created by rising up rather than sinking down."

Sure enough, off in the direction of the setting sun, a massive cliff wall towered, slate gray, dominating, far higher than the previous one that had formed by their camp. The mountain range had disappeared behind it. Or, perhaps, Elyth thought, the range had broken apart and drawn nearer.

"I guess all that knocking makes sense now," Ames said. "Or at least as much sense as anything here makes."

"Indeed," Oyuun said. "Though such a change should have registered on at least *one* of our instruments."

Elyth scanned the full width of the face; it seemed to stretch across the entire horizon. Here and there across its surface, long silver veins glinted in the sunlight. The shifting light gave the cliff a slow, undulating appearance, almost as if portions of it were still rolling and blooming into formation.

And then it dawned on her.

"Those aren't cliffs," Elyth said. "They're clouds."

An incomprehensibly vast storm wall. And, she saw now, it was racing toward them.

"Everyone get to the shuttle," Ames said. But even he didn't move; they were all mesmerized by the sheer scale of the cloud bank. Moments later he spoke again, commanding, "Get to the shuttle, now!"

The team formation disintegrated haphazardly, some taking a few seconds longer than others to react. Elyth and Korush were the last to move, but soon enough they were all charging across the clearing in a full run, too disciplined to panic, but tested in that discipline. Perpendicular to their course, the storm shadow advanced, as if eating the earth in an attempt to be the first to their ship.

Ames reached the shuttle twenty yards ahead of everyone else, and he shot through its still-opening hatch without breaking stride. By the time Elyth boarded, he was already halfway through the startup sequence, flipping switches and activating drives so fast it almost looked frantic, like he didn't know what he was doing. Elyth pushed through the others to the front, ready to take over, but hesitated when she saw the captain's focused intensity. He most certainly knew exactly what to do. The engines spun up, and the shuttle vibrated as he steadily increased the flow of power to the drives.

"Don't push it too fast," Elyth warned, noting the throughput on the display. "If you burn them out—"

"I know what I'm doing!" he snapped. "Strap in!"

"What about our equipment?" Oyuun called from the rear.

"Already lost!" Ames yelled. "And us along with it if we don't get off the ground!"

The shuttle had no windows; Elyth dropped into the copilot seat and activated the forward array. An exterior view projected up onto the plated face of the cockpit, revealing the fate speeding toward them. Outside, the uncanny darkness of an eclipse consumed the surroundings; the cloud bank had nearly reached the edge of the clearing.

"We're not going to make it," Elyth said.

"We will," Ames answered.

He worked the controls, gaze ping-ponging between the panel in front of him and the display showing the status of the engines. He was pushing power to them just above supposedly max capacity.

"Come on, come on, come on," he urged, one hand poised to launch the craft the instant it was possible. And then louder, "Everyone better be strapped down, this is going to get real rough!"

And without another breath, he punched the engines a few seconds before it was safe, and the shuttle popped off the ground like it had been struck from below. It shuddered with the strain, and hovered a few feet off the ground; Ames rolled it left, trying to bring it around to face directly away from the storm while it continued to struggle to gain altitude. The craft dipped, bumped the ground, and rebounded violently upward again. Elyth swiveled the view to track the storm wall sweeping across their landing zone. The clouds were impenetrable, as though anything beyond had ceased to exist.

Ames fought the controls, racing along the blade's edge between daredevil recklessness and certain suicide. The shuttle quaked with the effort, fighting gravity, rising wind, and the intensity of its own drives. If the storm didn't tear them apart, the captain would. Elyth's instinct told her to seize control, to drop low and turn the craft into the advancing wall; she'd known they couldn't outrun it. The only chance they really had was to land and meet it head on, to let it flow over and past them.

But the second before she acted, she glanced once more at the exterior view and saw now that beyond all hope, Ames had pushed the limit just enough. Even as the churning wall devoured the clearing, the shuttle maintained a bare gap and was starting to stabilize, to gain speed and elevation.

They were going to make it after all.

And then an explosive thunderclap tore through the craft, so loud and sharp that Elyth thought the ship had split in two. The exterior view snapped shut; the interior went pitch black. In the darkness, she could hear Ames grappling with the controls as the shuttle fell into an emergency unpowered glide.

It was impossible to tell whether the next impact came from the storm wall or the ground below.

SIXTEEN

Elyth woke, unable to tell if the impact had struck mere moments before, or if she was just now regaining consciousness after an unknown amount of time; the darkness was so complete, she wasn't even sure her eyes were actually open. Her hearing was muffled, buried beneath a constant rush like heavy, muted static in her ears. It took a few moments before she realized the roar wasn't inside her head, but rather from outside the shuttle, surrounding it, all-consuming. The storm, pouring out its wrath upon them. Its fury shuddered the craft. Gradually, she became aware of the sounds of movement inside the shuttle, and the grunts and groans of suffering stifled.

Something heavy fell on her shoulder, first fumbling, then steady. It took a moment for her to recognize that it was a hand.

"Elyth!" Ames called in the darkness. "Elyth, you with us?"

She couldn't yet find her voice; she nodded uselessly, and then reached up and patted his hand twice, firmly.

"She's all right," he called, words aimed toward the rear. "Or, not dead anyway."

Elyth felt his hands shifting quickly but lightly around her shoulders, her neck, her head; checking for blood, she assumed.

"Can you get unstrapped?" he asked.

She felt around, found the release, and freed herself.

"Got it," she answered. Her voice rasped, as though she'd been struck across the throat with a heavy rod.

"Good," Ames said. "What about your legs? Still got 'em?"

Moving any more of herself seemed like too much to ask, but Elyth tried anyway. First her left leg, then her right. Both felt impossibly heavy, but she managed to lift each foot briefly off the floor.

"Seems like."

A weak light blossomed and glowed from somewhere in the rear of the shuttle; Ames was crouched next to her, half his face hidden in shadow. In the dim light, he gave her a quick smile.

"Good to see you," he said.

"What happened?"

"Total power loss."

"You blow the core?"

"No, came from outside," Ames said. "Something like a lightning strike maybe?"

"Through the shielding? . . . Nothing atmospheric could be that strong."

"Nothing atmospheric *should* be that strong," he said, glancing to the rear. "But here we are."

When he turned his head, the shadow across his face went with him; not a shadow after all. Blood.

"Ames," Elyth said, reaching a hand toward him. He looked back to her, saw her concern, touched the side of his face, then the top of his head.

"Yeah, pretty hard-core, huh?" he said. "Split my scalp or

something. Probably looks worse than it is, but if it makes you think I'm tough, I won't clean it up."

"How's everyone else?"

The captain pushed himself up to standing. "Banged up, but breathing."

Brighter, warmer light rose in the craft, a miniature sunrise in the midnight gloom. Elyth turned to see its source; Subo, in a compact configuration, providing gentle illumination. It sat in the center of the craft, placid. In its light, the other four members of the team appeared.

Korush stood near the rear hatch, gripping a handhold in the bulkhead to keep his balance, but otherwise seemingly as unfazed as his pet machine. Nyeda was kneeling next to Arbiter Oyuun, apparently rendering aid while he remained in his seat. Elyth couldn't tell what had happened to him, but he was breathing through pain, keeping himself calm. Behind him, Varen sat sideways on the edge of his seat, tilting his head slowly back to front and side to side, as if stretching his neck muscles.

"Subo rolled us up," he said, gesturing toward the machine. "Like a crash cage. Probably took the brunt."

He paused and looked back to Korush. "I admit, I may see some evidence to support your perspective, Wari Korush. It was a truly *selfless* act, and saved our lives."

Whatever Varen was talking about, Korush seemed to ignore all but the last four words.

"Storm could still finish us off," he said. As if to emphasize his point, the ship jolted and slid suddenly sideways, like it'd struck a massive pocket of turbulence.

Though she couldn't imagine how it could be, Elyth asked, "Are we airborne?"

"Nope," Ames answered. "We're bellied on the dirt. And the storm's still shoving us around."

At those words, Elyth realized the intensity of the storm had reached an unimaginable magnitude. She didn't know how much the shuttle weighed, but it was wingless and far too heavy for wind alone to move it that way. While she still trying to process the information, a mind-breaking thunderclap ruptured the air inside the craft; it punched through her with such power it nearly stole her breath. The top of the shuttle quavered as though a physical force had hammered them from the heavens. Bright blue sparks spat from the corners of the sealed hatches.

"I think it wants to come in," Varen said, hands over his ears.

The first blast of thunder was followed closely by a second, so intense it could have originated from within the shuttle. Again, the ship quivered and skidded sideways, this time in the opposite direction. Once more, blue-white splinters of shattered lightning burst like shrapnel from the hatches. And though Elyth wouldn't have thought it possible, the roar encasing the shuttle became even more intense, growing to a howl.

"What are we going to do?" Nyeda asked, and then more forcefully, "what are we doing?!"

"What can we do, Advocate?" Oyuun said, his voice thinner than usual. "Other than sit, wait, and hope?"

The shuttle rocked again, this time in a manner different from before. Not like it'd been struck from above; rather as though something had broken in the ground below. Elyth had a vision of the planet opening into an abyssal grave beneath them, swallowing their craft as it had her sisters' ship before.

Nyeda stood, looked intensely at Elyth. Expectantly. There was nothing within First House protocol capable of contending with such raw fury. But Nyeda clearly wanted her to do something, anything, to end the chaos. Elyth stared back at her once-sister, searching her mind for any scrap of teaching or tool that could serve as a foundation for something more.

Another thunder strike detonated, smiting the helpless craft and showering with uncanny fire-rain those sheltered within.

"Anybody got a helmet I could borrow?" Varen asked, projecting above the incessant howl.

Elyth took it as a misguided and flippant attempt at humor; no one else responded.

"Seriously," he said, a few moments later. "Is there any gear I can toss on?"

"For what?" Ames asked.

"I want to try something," Varen answered.

The last time she'd heard him speak those words, he'd invited her to stand together in what she'd thought to be a certain-doomed attempt to turn the annihilating power of the Contingency away from Qel.

"You're not going out there," Elyth said.

"Well, I can't do it from in here," he said, "and I don't really want to just stand around waiting to get exploded."

"Do what from in here?" Ames called.

"Talk to the storm."

"What, like . . . you're just going to go ask it to quit or something?" Ames said, incredulous.

"Something like that," Varen said. "Can't hurt to try."

"It'll *kill* you to try," the captain answered. "And if you open that hatch, it'll probably kill all of us too."

"Subo will help," Korush said.

"What?" Ames said.

"What?" Varen echoed.

"Subo will help," Subo answered politely as it unfolded itself into its usual hulking form. Korush moved away from the hatch and waved Varen over to it.

"Korush," Nyeda said. "Are you sure?"

He gave her a brief, expressionless look before turning his attention back to Varen.

"Stand over there," he said. "And hold still."

Varen did as he was told, taking a position a few feet from the rear hatch.

"You're not going to have Subo shoot me in the back, are you?" he said. "That would be unsporting."

Korush didn't answer; Subo turned and reconfigured itself, enfolding Varen within its structure. Elyth had seen it do something similar when it had encased Sardis during their encounter with the creature in the forest. But instead of creating a protective cage as it had before, this time it formed itself to mimic Varen's shape, enlarged like an imperfect shadow cast on a wall nearby.

"I need to be able to see," Varen said from within his Subo suit. The machine clicked softly, though Elyth couldn't see what had changed. "Neat. Now what?"

"Subo will move as you do," Korush answered. "The rest is up to you."

"Guys, no," Ames said. "This is ridiculous, you're going to get us all killed!"

Elyth touched his arm, spoke as gently as the storm sound would allow.

"He can do it," she said. He looked at her in disbelief; but when he saw her confidence, his demeanor changed. Though he obviously didn't understand how and wasn't happy about the idea, he at least trusted her enough not to argue.

"Well, everyone else better move away from that hatch anyway," he said.

Nyeda helped Arbiter Oyuun up from his seat, and the two of them stood with Elyth and Ames near the front of the shuttle.

"You two get on back there," the captain directed, gesturing to the cockpit. "Might as well put the seats between you and the trouble we're about to eat."

Oyuun made no protest, which told Elyth just how much pain he must've been in. Nyeda assisted him into the pilot's seat, and then stood by his side, facing the hatch. Ames stepped forward and a little sideways, shielding Elyth and the others behind him. Elyth placed a hand on his shoulder and gently drew him back by her side; together they formed a more complete wall to protect Oyuun and Nyeda. For whatever it would be worth.

"All right," Ames said. "I guess do whatever you're going to do."

Korush moved to one side of the rear hatch, by the mechanical emergency release controls.

"Are you set?" he asked Varen.

"Absolutely."

Korush reached up and tapped near the collar of his armor; a section of it around the back of his neck unfurled and re-formed into a faceless, plated helmet, not unlike the one Nyeda had worn when she'd initially fought Elyth. A moment later, he disengaged the hatch, and it unsealed. The sound of the wind surged into the craft, ripping through the cracks around the hatch, singing a banshee's cry.

Varen stepped forward, and it appeared to take all of Subo's strength to force the clamshell hatch open. The instant a gap appeared between its two halves, it was as if an ocean wave had crashed upon the rear; a wall of water slammed the interior, and even encased in the mighty machine, Varen had to lean forward to keep their collective balance against the wind and rain. The storm thrashed its way up the rear third of the craft, soaking the interior, raking Elyth and Ames with arctic chill. And every second the hatch remained open, Elyth felt their danger growing, knowing a lash of lightning would race through the exposed cabin and incinerate them all. But even with Subo's power, Varen couldn't move the doors far enough apart to pass through.

Whether commanded by Korush or deciding on its own, the machine reconfigured its shoulders to form a brace between the doors, and then gradually expanded, forcing the hatch farther open, until finally the space was sufficient. Outside, the storm had blocked all light, and the moment Varen and Subo made it out into that darkness, the hatch slammed violently shut. The shuttle went near-black without Subo's illumination, until their eyes readjusted to the weak light that remained. Elyth realized now that it was coming from a wide-angle flashlight, damaged and dangling from a hook at the back.

In the gloom, Korush resealed the hatch and then stood straighter, deactivated his helmet. It collapsed quietly back into its housing, like ice melting at unnatural speed. Instead of joining the others at the front of the shuttle, he moved two steps back and took a position directly in front of the hatch, facing it, feet apart, arms crossed, as though guarding the entrance. Seeing him that way suddenly made Elyth wonder how much concern he had for his pet machine. From his stance, it appeared that he considered Subo much more than just a tool or weapon.

The group waited together, tense, without speaking, while the storm continued to batter and howl. Elyth could scarcely imagine what was happening to Subo and Varen out there, exposed to its full power. However resilient the machine may have been, it seemed impossible to her that it could withstand so much punishment for long, if at all.

A minute or so after they'd gone out, the air inside the shuttle erupted in a thunder blast so powerful that it jarred Elyth's vision; sparks burst again from around the rear hatch, greater in number and spraying farther into the craft than before. For a strained stretch, no one said anything, until Ames uttered what the others didn't dare.

"Well, we just lost another two," he said grimly. "And I don't see how that was worth it at all."

Indeed, there seemed to be no change in the intensity of the storm outside. Everyone continued to hold their place, though, either hoping for Varen's miracle or paralyzed by the thought that there was nothing more they could do. After two or three more minutes, Ames finally broke away and flopped into a seat in the middle of the cabin, rested his head in his hands. Behind Elyth, Nyeda slid into the copilot's seat. But Elyth and Korush stood together, each intent on the rear hatch. Each believing that salvation was still possible, or, perhaps, each refusing to accept the most likely outcome.

The violence continued around the shuttle long enough, though, that even Elyth's hope began to wane. Her mind couldn't yet absorb the thought that Varen had gone to his doom, but already it was searching again for an alternative, for something she could improvise to get them out of the situation. If Varen had failed, it seemed unlikely she would succeed. But there was nothing else to do, other than try.

Elyth closed her eyes, tilted her head slightly back, strained to reach out beyond herself, beyond the shuttle, and into the storm itself. She had once attuned her senses to the planet; now, she stretched back into that moment, mined the memory of her sensations for any thread she might grasp and weave to her own design. And while she concentrated, she felt a subtle shift in the storm, as though it had become aware of her specifically, and was turning its attention away from the others to take account of her.

Within it, she first felt, and then heard a different tone, edge dulled, anger subsiding; and with it, beneath it, a steady warm drone, gradually growing in volume, not to replace the howl of the wind, but somehow to merge into it. The stability of the droning remained constant as the maelstrom flailed chaotically around it; a hurricane ocean breaking upon an ancient stone seawall. But the fury of the storm threatened to overwhelm and consume it. Elyth bent all her focus to that thrumming, allowed it to form into an image in her mind, and that image to form into something so real to her it became nearly physical. The words of the Deep Language rose to her then, recalling to her the House technique of Observing the Manifold Witness, intended to open the mind to deep insight and revelation during meditation. Though she didn't understand why it had manifested in that moment, Elyth didn't hesitate. Holding on to the droning tone, she spoke the sealing phrase.

"Two mirrors with neither flaw nor shadow between them; light begets light."

The power of the Deep Language flowed through her, and the storm revealed itself to her in new dimensions through new senses beyond the physical. Buried among the fury and chaos, she found a thin, golden thread vibrating harmonically in the raging wind.

The source of the drone. And then instinctively she joined her voice to it, not with the words of the Deep Language, but with a wordless song that felt rooted in it. As she lifted the thread, supported it with voice and will, its resonance grew and expanded, until the wind of the storm began to respond, its glass-edged howl softening and taking on discordant semitones of the droning voice underneath.

At first, she thought the voice was drawing the maelstrom into a matching frequency, but as the metaphysical chorus continued, the dissonance grew louder, more insistent, like a malformed echo gaining strength with each repetition. The storm was indeed reacting, but not in passive response. It was actively resisting.

No, not the storm, Elyth realized. The power of the Deep Language and her technique connected her to the heart of the squall, but such contact with that tempest unveiled something she had not expected to find. Though its rage had a voice of its own, there was something deeper animating it, supplying its breath; the essence of the planet, expressed in the whirlwind, revealed through her cosmic perspective. As before, she experienced it not as a natural, flowing fountain of life but as synthetic, a sensation more mechanical than organic.

And it was winning. The thread trembled, fighting to hold true but nearly overwhelmed. She started to lose her grip, felt the droning slipping away into oblivion.

But in that last battle of tones, Elyth found a third voice emerging, faint and distant, weak, quavering, but striving to match and hold the note. The three voices blended, until she could no longer identify which among them was her own. And gradually, the banshee cry of the storm was bent back on itself, diminishing, until finally it was replaced by the harmonic overtones of the unified voice and all that remained in Elyth's perception was a golden resonance that seemed to vibrate throughout the planet itself.

She had felt something like it before, in the heart of the Qel, when it had turned back her attempt to kill that world.

And then the glorious reverberation vanished in an instant, and she felt a hand on her upper arm, dragging her back to herself. Her mouth was still open, her throat dry and raw, but no sound was coming forth. The world around her remained dark, fuzzy, dream-like. Elyth had no idea how long she had been in that state, and when she followed the hand on her arm up to the face of its owner, she found Nyeda staring at her, eyes wide in shock. Or awe?

"Nyeda," Elyth heard herself say. "What is it?"

"Listen," the woman whispered.

As the trance state faded, Elyth felt herself recentering, her senses returning to their normal state. Her body felt drained, her legs trembled. The familiar aftershock of touching the infinite potential of the cosmos, and of withdrawing from it. Finally, she realized the significance of Nyeda's whisper. She had whispered, and Elyth had heard it. Outside the shuttle, it had fallen silent.

"How long has it been like that?" Elyth asked.

"A minute or two, maybe."

The shuttle interior still had its weak moonlight glow; the hatch was still sealed. Ames and Korush were both looking at her now, the captain in speechless surprise, the Azirim with a mix of newfound respect and heightened suspicion.

"Varen?" she said.

Nyeda shook her head. Despite her deep fatigue, Elyth wasted no time.

"Open the hatch," she commanded, striding toward the rear.

Korush moved to the release, watching her warily, but making no attempt to argue or hinder her. He unsealed the hatch, and Elyth, anticipating the wind, pushed the doors with force. The two halves flew open so easily that they swung the full limit and partially rebounded with a loud clack. Light poured into the shuttle, momentarily dazing everyone inside. The quiet static rush of strong wind through distant trees followed behind, but only a weak, chill breeze entered the craft. There was no rain. Elyth shut her eyes against the brightness, shielded her face with a hand, and stepped out.

Her feet sank immediately up to her ankles in watery mud, as though she were walking along the floor of a shallow, stagnant pond that had been suddenly drained. When she was at last able to open her eyes again, she scanned around her and realized that was almost exactly the case. The clearing lay devastated, pounded into a near-unrecognizable form, churned into a gray-brown sludge with occasional patches of blackened grass laid flat or sprouting at strange angles. And beyond the clearing, two hundred yards into the trees on either side, the granite walls of the storm continued to stream by.

Elyth looked down the center, in the direction of the storm's approach. A channel had been carved through its middle; or rather, it had been parted at a point some two miles distant, like a river branched by a strong and wide delta. The sunlight that had seemed so brilliant before was in fact a late-afternoon hue, half-filtered by the remaining clouds. In its light, about fifty yards from the shuttle, a dark mound lay heavily spattered with mud. It took a moment for Elyth to realize what it was.

Subo.

She rushed to the machine, slipping and fighting against the pull of the muck at her feet. As she ran, she heard the thick splashing of heavy footsteps closing in behind. Elyth reached Subo first, skidding the final few inches and falling to her knees with weariness and fear. Up close, the machine looked like the shell of some enormous sea creature. It had formed itself into a teardrop-shaped bunker with a narrow ridge running from front to back, its point facing precisely in the direction of the split in the storm. She laid a hand on it. It did not respond to her touch.

The approaching footsteps stopped a yard behind her; she didn't need to turn to know who it was.

"Korush," she said. "Is Subo . . . is it damaged?"

Korush didn't answer, but a few seconds later, the machine stirred and re-formed itself into its usual configuration, a little less quickly, a little less fluidly than before.

"Subo is functional," it said, turning to take its place by Korush's side. In the imprint left behind in the mud, Varen lay crumpled on his side, still and corpse-pale.

Elyth remained on her knees, paralyzed at the sight. When she'd realized the storm had subsided, she'd been certain that she would find him standing in its midst, his schoolboy grin greeting her with a mischievous *did I do that?* glint in his eye. Instead, his eyes were closed, and his face slack, with most of the left side sunken in the mire. She could never have imagined that the struggle would cost him his life. A new storm erupted in her heart and mind, battering her with thoughts and emotions too raw and chaotic to process.

"Is he dead?" Korush asked quietly.

Elyth barely heard the words, couldn't have formulated a response even if she'd wanted to. Varen remained utterly still, eyes closed, already half-buried in the mud and pooled water.

"Apparently . . ." Varen said weakly, "not . . . but I think I'd rather be."

His words shocked Elyth with a surging reversal of emotion; hope struggling to replace despair, but failing to find purchase. He didn't move or open his eyes, and went quiet again for so long that she began to think she'd only imagined hearing his voice. She crawled forward, reached out a tentative hand to touch his lower leg.

He didn't stir at the contact.

"I hope . . ." he said, his voice thin and breath strained, "that isn't . . . Korush."

"I am here," Korush said.

Varen rolled his head just enough to be able to open both eyes to look at them; they were glassy and unfocused, but when they fell on Elyth, she saw his gaze sharpen. He might have smiled, if he'd had the strength.

"Please give Subo . . . my deepest thanks," he said, before closing his eyes again.

Elyth squeezed his leg, and turned back to Korush.

"We have to get him back to the ship."

Korush nodded, and Subo immediately stepped forward and crouched next to Varen. Its arms reconfigured, flattening and sinking into the mud. A few moments later, it stood again, lifting Varen with a gentleness and care that seemed full of human compassion. Beneath Varen, Subo's arms continued to re-form into a stretcherlike platform, curved slightly upward to cradle the man.

Varen stirred as he was being lifted, and still without opening his eyes said, "I *really* hope . . . that's not Korush."

Korush extended his hand to Elyth, helped her to her feet in the swampy muck. Subo started back toward the shuttle, its steps even and secure despite the terrain. Elyth nodded her thanks to Korush and began to follow the machine. After a few yards, though, she noticed she hadn't heard the Azirim's slogging footsteps, and she turned back to see what he was doing.

His back was to her, but he appeared to be staring off into the distant cleft in the storm.

"You coming?" she called.

He turned his head just enough for her to see him in profile, but he didn't look at her.

"In a moment," he answered, before returning to his vigil.

Elyth continued to watch him a few moments longer, trying to read his posture. But the man maintained such rigid discipline it was hard even for a master of the art like Elyth to discern much from his body language. Whatever he was pondering, she'd either have to wait to hear it from his mouth or be content with the mystery.

When she resumed her march to the shuttle, she found Subo waiting a few yards ahead. She picked up her pace and as she approached, the machine turned its back to her and reconfigured slightly; two flat protrusions from each lower leg, two rounded arcs higher up near the middle of its back.

"Subo can assist with transportation," it said, and Elyth realized it had created platforms for her to stand on, and handles to hold. She'd grown accustomed to the machine's presence, but the idea of climbing onto it, of being that close to it, struck her initially as distasteful. There was no doubt it would be faster, though, and her weariness clung to her, threatening to drag her down with each step.

"Thank you, Subo," she said, and tentatively clambered aboard. As soon as she had grasped both handles, Subo made its soft-edged clicking sound. Elyth found herself rising quickly but smoothly higher, until her handholds were just behind the machine's massive shoulders, bringing her high enough to see ahead. It began walking immediately, with strides likely twice the length of hers. And though its legs moved with each step it took, the platforms beneath her feet remained stable, or rather continually shifted to compensate for the motion.

They covered the ground back to the shuttle quickly. The other three were all standing outside by the rear hatch, waiting for word. As soon as they were close enough, Elyth called out to them.

"He's alive," she said. "But he needs medical!"

Ames reacted immediately, ducking back into the shuttle. When Subo reached the craft, the captain reemerged with a small, taut pack. Elyth hopped off the machine's back and joined Ames by Varen's side. Subo stood still, continuing to act as stretcher bearer.

"What's wrong with him?" Ames asked, stepping up close.

"I don't know exactly," Elyth said.

"Too many things . . . to count," Varen added.

"Hold this," the captain said, giving her the pack. She held it for him while he unbuckled the straps and started digging through it, and she saw that it was a field trauma kit; lifesaving under the right conditions, possibly useless in Varen's case. Ames pulled out a boxy handheld device Elyth recognized as a flash diagnostic tool. The captain activated it, held it over Varen's chest, and a few seconds later, it popped up a display charting Varen's vitals. Ames let out a concerned whistle as he quickly skimmed it.

"This doesn't look good," he said. "Blood pressure's real low, heart rate's way up. If he'd been shot or something, I'd guess he was bleeding out. But I don't see any signs of internal hemorrhaging."

Varen raised a trembling hand, stretched weakly toward Elyth. When she took it, the coolness of his skin surprised her, as did its ashen color against hers. She squeezed it, uncertain what else to do in that moment.

"Nyeda," Ames said, "see if you can find a couple of blankets somewhere in the shuttle. Med bay if you can get to it, maybe the side cabin. Subo, can you tilt him, feet up, about twelve inches?"

Subo obeyed, carefully lowering Varen's head. Elyth recognized the treatment.

"He's in shock?"

Ames nodded as he fiddled with a setting on the device.

"Yeah," he said a moment later. "Yeah, something's up with his heart."

"I think . . ." Varen said. "She broke it."

"At least his sense of humor's normal," she answered. "Terrible, as usual."

The captain rummaged around in his pack again, and withdrew a flexible black strap.

"Hey buddy," he said to Varen, "I'm going to sit you up in just a second."

"Okay," Varen replied. "Someone be ready . . . to catch my head . . . if it falls off."

Ames slid his arm under Varen's back and cradled him; Subo leveled its arms as the captain lifted Varen into a slumping seated position.

"Hold him," Ames said. Elyth set the pack down and grabbed hold of Varen's shoulders, while the captain wrapped the strap around his chest and clipped it. The moment the ends were attached, the strap cinched itself snugly around Varen. "Okay, easy now, back down."

Together they lowered Varen to lying down again, and Subo

once more tilted its arms. Korush arrived, passing silently by and taking a position next to the hatch.

"Seat belt?" Varen asked.

"Stabilizer. It's going to get your heart straightened out."

"Will . . . it hurt?"

"Might give you a little jolt if it wants to. Shouldn't be any worse than what you just went through."

Nyeda appeared with a pair of rolled-up mats, thin but spongy-looking.

"Best I could find in a hurry," she said, holding them up for the captain to see.

"Close enough," he answered. The two of them each unrolled a mat, and then laid them on top of Varen and tucked the edges under him.

"Nap time?" Varen asked.

"Absolutely not," Ames said. "You're going to stay awake, and you're going to take some nice deep breaths for me."

"Asking a lot."

"There's a reason we didn't bring any lazy people on this trip. Get to work."

Varen let out a gurgling sigh, and then said, "Yes sir . . . roger that."

Ames picked up his pack and headed back into the shuttle, pausing in the entryway. "Elyth, keep him awake. Talking if you can."

"Usually I can't get him to shut up," she said.

"If he's talking, he's breathing."

Elyth nodded, stepped closer to Varen.

"Grief," she said. "I'm cold, muddy, and exhausted, and it's mostly your fault. What do you have to say about that?"

". . . Reminds me . . . of when we first met."

"Nyeda," Ames said. "I need to see what we can do about getting the med bay up and running. Can you help me out?"

"Of course."

"Will he live?" Korush asked.

"Depends on how deep he got," Ames answered. "If we can get him stabilized quick enough, he might. Keep an eye on him?"

"Always."

Elyth heard Nyeda follow Ames into the shuttle behind her. A few moments later, someone came up beside her. Arbiter Oyuun.

"Varen, I'm disappointed," he said. Varen looked up at him with watery eyes. "I had planned to be the focus of sympathy. And you appear to have outdone me."

"I hate," Varen said between breaths, "not to be . . . the center of attention."

"Clearly."

"How hurt are you, Arbiter?" Elyth asked. He shook his head.

"Hardly worth mentioning, dear." But from the controlled way he spoke and how he kept a hand on his ribs, she knew he was in pain. He smiled at her briefly, and then looked back to Varen. "Ah ah, Varen, no closing your eyes. Tell me about your adventure outside."

"It was . . . windy."

"Yes."

"And I . . . got mud . . . everywhere."

Elyth cracked a smile in spite of her worry. Only Varen could sit at the edge of death and dangle his feet over it.

"Mom's going to be upset," she said. "But what did you *do*, Grief?"

"To the mud?"

"To the storm, idiot."

"Same thing you did," he said. ". . . If I had to guess."

"You spoke to it?"

He shook his head slowly, with effort.

"Sang," he answered. "But not to the storm . . ."

She waited for him to continue, but he closed his eyes for a few moments too long. Elyth punched him in the arm, and he jerked at the impact.

"If not to the storm," she prompted, "then to what?"

"The echo of Qel . . . inside it."

Elyth absorbed the words, filtered them through her experience. The golden thread. Qel's fingerprint on the heart of its Shadow.

"Qel was the third voice," she said. But Varen shook his head again.

"The planet?" she asked.

"I only," he said. ". . . I only heard . . . yours."

Though she'd barely understood the event they'd just gone through together, now she felt even more confused. Had she imagined it? Or had she simply heard her own voice reflected back to her? For a span, Elyth disappeared into her own mind, drawing together the fragments of experience she'd had with Qel's Shadow, from her first attempt at reading it, to the data she'd gathered on it; from the strange surges of power that had emanated from within it, to the facet that her contact through the storm had revealed about its essence. She could sense the network there, the interlaced connections that held them all together, but she couldn't see it.

"Your color seems to be improving," Oyuun said to Varen. "I think you're going to be just fine."

"I appreciate the encouragement . . . Arbiter. . . . Though I can't quite . . . believe it."

"I wouldn't have said it if I didn't think it true."

"*Think* is different . . . from *believe*," Varen said. And though he appeared to be responding to the Arbiter, his eyes were on Elyth's. He squeezed her hand as he continued. "Sometimes . . . the voice says one thing . . . while the heart . . . feels something else."

Even now, clinging to fragile life, he continued to call her to himself. But though his words were obviously intended to challenge her previous claims about their potential future together, they had an entirely unintended effect.

His distinction between voice and heart recalled to her the impression she'd felt in the surge of power before they lost contact with *Clariana*. The two traces within the power of the planet, the whisper and the wind. One, a voice speaking; the other, a sensation felt. A lie covering a deception.

"Well," Oyuun replied to Varen, "I *believe* your injuries have made you overly sensitive."

With the lingering effects of Observing the Manifold Witness, Elyth felt the snap of hidden connections revealed, the burst of insight and revelation for which the technique had been crafted. She hadn't been able to see it before, because she'd been trying to force the pieces to fit with what she already believed to be true, to match an assumption she hadn't even realized she'd made. When she let go of that foundational axiom, the most unexpected answer leaped to mind.

The sensation of the planet's release of power wasn't the feeling she had when she spoke the Deep Language herself. She realized now it had been more akin to what she felt during the activation of an aspect drive. Qel's Shadow emanated an energy richer, vastly more complex, orders of magnitude more powerful. But different in degree, not kind. Generated, not spoken.

"Perhaps when you are recovered," the Arbiter continued, "we can have a nice discussion about your experience, and see if we can figure out together why this planet is behaving so strangely."

"I know why," Elyth said.

Oyunn turned to face her with genuine interest and curiosity. "Oh?" he said. "Why is it, then?"

"Because it's not a planet," she said. "It's a ship."

SEVENTEEN

"And I thought this couldn't possibly get any weirder," Ames said, slinging loose cabling out from under the copilot's console. "But sure, yeah, why not."

Oyuun stood just behind him, holding his field workstation, the data modules containing the field analysis of the samples they'd collected, with some other bulky device stacked on top. Elyth, half-dazed and depleted from her encounter with the storm and her use of the Deep Language, sat in a passenger seat in the middle of the craft, watching them work.

"I'm not necessarily agreeing that it's a *ship*, per se," the Arbiter answered. "But the concept that Qel's Shadow may have a *technological* origin is certainly worth exploring."

Ames backed out, sat down heavily in the copilot's seat, and started examining the cables. Nyeda and the captain had managed to get the shuttle's core partially back online, powering the craft enough to run the interior lights and keep the med bay operational. Now, they were trying to patch Oyuun's equipment into the ship's navigational system in order to access its detailed terrain mapping.

Elyth didn't know exactly what they were looking for, or what they would find, but she knew in her heart what the final outcome would be. Qel's Shadow had been constructed, and for a purpose. Whatever else they might discover was secondary to discerning the nature of that purpose.

"I don't understand how any of that could be," Ames said. "But I'm just a grunt, so that's not an indication of anything. Still, though, if it *is* . . . what you said, are you sure it's not one of ours?" he said. "Some extra black-on-black secret program your friends in the skunkworks cooked up?"

"Within the realm of possibility, I suppose," Oyuun replied. "But I have reasonably high confidence that it is not."

"How much juice you think you'll be drawing?" Ames asked, waggling two of the cables in his hand.

"It won't take much," the Arbiter answered. "I just need to be able to see more than what my station can run."

"Well, right now 'not much' is all we can spare anyway. At least until I can get a more thorough look."

In the rear of the craft, Elyth heard Korush and Subo shuttling in and out, moving the few remaining supplies out of the side cabin where they'd been stored. The Azirim continued on as his ever-imperturbable self, focused on doing the next useful thing without concerning himself with debate or conversation. Despite his lingering behind to observe the bifurcated storm front, he'd made no comment about the storm or its division, nor shown any reaction to Elyth's startling declaration as to the planet's true nature.

"I'm not opposed to at least *trying* to recover the base station—" Oyuun said, but Ames waved his hand at him to stop.

"We're not spending hours slogging around out there looking

for something we won't find, and wouldn't be any use anyway if by some miracle we *did* find it. Which we wouldn't. Number one priority is getting this boat running again."

"Our number one priority remains uncovering what we need to know about this . . . place, Captain."

"Tied for first, then. We're not going much of anywhere without the shuttle. Unless you're planning on a few monthlong hikes."

He held up one end of a cable, showed the connector to Oyuun.

"This work?"

"I can make it work, yes," the Arbiter answered.

"Great."

Ames stood and laid a pair of cables over the equipment in Oyuun's arms, and then slipped by him to make room in the cockpit.

"I'm going back out to get a better idea of how bad off we are. Try not to short us out."

"Thank you, Captain," Oyuun said as he sat in the pilot's seat and started looking for a place to distribute his gear. His movements were careful with attempts to manage his pain.

Ames started toward the hatch, but paused by Elyth's side. He looked down at her, started to say something, but then closed his mouth and subtly shook his head. He'd been quick to work with her when she'd brought Varen in, but once they'd gotten him stabilized, the captain had hidden his reluctance to be near her by keeping busy wherever she wasn't. Undoubtedly his view of her had been radically changed when he'd witnessed firsthand the power she could wield.

To ease the awkward moment, Elyth dipped her head in Oyuun's direction.

"Is he going to be all right?" she asked.

Ames glanced back at the Arbiter and nodded.

"Cracked a couple of ribs, but thankfully they're not broken through. Probably hurts like the devil to breathe. The man's tough as an old mountain goat, though."

"And how about you?"

He looked back at her and let out a long breath, like he'd been holding it for an hour.

"A thousand percent out of my depth here," he said. "If I have actual work I can focus on, I guess there's a decent chance I won't go *completely* out of my mind."

She nodded and gave his arm two firm pats with the back of her hand.

"You're doing fine, Captain."

"I must be hiding it well."

"You wouldn't be the only one," she said. "I'm barely holding it together myself."

Ames started to say something, but once more caught the words before they could escape and converted them to a different topic.

"How's the arm?"

Elyth pulled up her sleeve and held up her left hand, opened and closed it for him to see. Six purple-black stripes bruised the middle of her forearm, vicious imprints from her terrible encounter. She still couldn't fully extend two of her fingers.

"Any pain in your hand?" he asked.

She shook her head and said, "Forearm still hurts, but hand seems fine. Fingers are a little tingly."

To her surprise, he reached down and took her hand in his. "Give me a squeeze. Hard as you can."

She did so, feeling the imbalance of strength in her fingers.

"I said squeeze, not crush," Ames said, releasing her hand.

"You said hard as I can."

"Yeah, well . . ." he said. "Seems like I have a habit of underestimating you, huh?"

He gave her a quick, subdued smile, and in it she saw the first signs of a thawing. He'd managed to speak a sliver of what he'd needed to confess but had been unable to admit. He feared her.

"As far as I can tell, your only habit is taking care of everyone around you."

He chuckled, then replied, "Like I said. Keep busy, keep sane. . . . Maybe." He nodded down at her arm, serious again. "But we need to keep an eye on that. If you don't have full use by tomorrow, could mean nerve damage."

"I'm encouraged to hear you thinking about tomorrow," she said.

"Ever the optimist," he answered, and then looked back toward the rear of the craft. "I think Korush and Subo have just about moved everything out of that side cabin. Some spare uniforms in there. You should get cleaned up, get into some dry clothes. Can't have you catching pneumonia."

"Is that an order, Captain?"

"Am I allowed to give those?"

"I'll take it as one. Otherwise I'm likely to fall asleep right here."

"Rest couldn't hurt you either," he said. He gave her a little nod and then left through the rear hatch, calling for Nyeda. Elyth heard the woman respond from outside; it sounded like she was on top of the shuttle.

Like Captain Ames, Nyeda had been avoiding Elyth since her

return, though her response was different from the captain's. Where he had hidden his discomfort in his work, Nyeda just seemed numb and withdrawn. For now, Elyth would keep out of her way, give her space to process whatever it was that she needed to reconcile within her own heart and mind. There was certainly more than enough turmoil to go around and, if she were being honest, Elyth still had plenty to work out for herself.

She pushed herself up out of the seat, stiff, sore, exhausted, and walked to the side cabin. The door was closed but not latched, and she was too much in a fog to think about it. She opened the door and found Korush standing there, armor off, dressed in clean uniform pants, but bare-chested.

"Oh, I'm sorry," Elyth said, startled. "I didn't realize . . ."

She couldn't finish the sentence, and though she'd fully intended to back out and close the door, she found herself paralyzed by the sight of the Azirim.

He stood before her with his arms and torso revealed, and his lean, corded muscles did nothing to dispel the sense that here was a man of living stone. But she saw now that he was indeed flesh and blood; peppered along both arms and in patches across his chest lay a collection of seething welts, angry and raw, looking like a cross between recent burns and early scars.

"Wari Korush," she said, with deep concern. She took an involuntary step toward him, raised her hand in offer of help. "What happened? Why didn't you say anything? We have plenty of medical—"

"These wounds are not new," he answered quietly. He turned his back to her, picked a thin shirt up off the bench next to him, and pulled it on. The same marks scored his back with equal severity.

She couldn't understand; though they weren't bleeding, the livid sheen of the injuries made them seem only minutes old.

"Korush, we have to get you some help—"

The Azirim glanced over his shoulder and shook his head.

"It is not a thing to be fixed, Exile," he said. He stood straight, tucked his shirt in to precise standards, and then donned the jacket to complete the uniform. It wasn't until he finished fully dressing that he turned to face her again.

"My body has its challenges," he said. "But I have borne them long. You need not be concerned with my ability to maintain effectiveness. I will continue to serve, as I have ever served."

At first Elyth thought he was just trying to keep things formal, but after a moment she realized he really did seem to think her only concern was whether or not he was fit for duty.

"Wari Korush," she said, stepping closer, hoping he could sense the sincerity of her compassion. "No one here doubts your abilities, or the strength of your resolve. But no one wants you to suffer needlessly, either."

"It is not needless," he answered. He bent to pick up a thin strap and affixed his sheathed void-edge to it. When it was secured, he put the harness across his chest, keeping the hilt of the weapon grip-down for an undoubtedly quick deployment.

"Does anyone else know?"

"The Arbiter," he said. "And if you have any respect for the Hezra or for its service to the Ascendance, I ask you not to speak of it to anyone else."

She shook her head. "Of course I won't, if that is your desire."

"It is."

"I'm sorry," she said, her heart genuinely moved for the man she'd thought incapable of feeling anything. "I had no idea."

"Then I have honored the Way," he said.

He sat down on the bench and began sorting the components of his armor, placing them in a crate at his feet, in well-practiced order. Unwilling to look her in the eye, perhaps fearing the pity he would find there. Elyth knew he wanted her to leave, that he was chastising himself for allowing her to see him that way. But she knew too what it was to suffer silently, invisibly, and the toll it took to be isolated in one's pain. She closed the door behind her and sat at the end of the bench closest to her, as far from him as the space allowed. For a time, they sat without speaking; Korush tending to his armor, Elyth with her face turned toward the wall in front of her, present but silent.

"I neither wish for your pity nor invite it," he said eventually. "We all bear some cost in our service. Mine is not unique."

"All pain is unique, Wari Korush," she answered quietly. "No one can feel it on your behalf. No one can experience the reality of it as you do. Understanding may be *shared*, but it is never *same*."

He fell silent again, unmoved, she thought, by her words. But after a span his response showed he'd received them and pondered them carefully.

"You know what it is to be set apart," he said.

"Yes."

"You know what it is to serve in a duty that few others have the capacity to fulfill."

"Yes."

"Then perhaps you also know how any physical suffering one might experience is easier to bear than would be the loss of one's ability to continue in that service."

Elyth flashed back to her time as an Advocate of the Voice, how much she had endured in her duty to the First House, and how her identity in the Order had driven her to fight through agony, just to uphold the oaths she'd sworn. And out of fear of losing her place.

"I know it well," she said.

"Ah, yes, of course," he said. He paused his work and turned to look at her. "I suppose you have already suffered the worse fate. And so you quietly bear a pain greater than my own."

She met his gaze and felt a kinship with him she would never have anticipated. He seemed to notice it too, becoming more open to her.

"I'm not so sure of that, Korush," Elyth said. "The pain of exile ebbs and flows, and it has eased over time. Does yours ever subside?"

"When those in my charge face danger," he said, returning to his armor. "Or when meditating on the Way with sufficient focus. . . . Occasionally when I sleep."

"And do you sleep?"

"Occasionally," he said, and though he didn't actually smile, his eyes brightened as if he had. Maybe that was as much of an expression as she was ever likely to see from the man.

"Your wounds . . . they're caused by your armor?"

"A nerve condition, from birth," he answered. "But exacerbated by the mechanisms that enable me to wield Subo, as well as the weapon of the Aziri."

"But there's no treatment?"

"There is, yes. I could have the necessary operations tomorrow, if we were on an Ascendance world. And if I wished to abandon the Aziri. But I cannot have both comfort and the Way. And so I choose the Way."

"You are a true model of the Way of the Aziri, Wari Korush," she said. "Arbiter Oyuun was right to call you a Lion of your people."

He stood and picked up the crate containing the components of his armor and then turned to face her.

"The Aziri are not a people," he said. "And the Way is higher than those who walk it."

Elyth thought he was admonishing her for her attempt at kindness. But then he offered her a bow deeper than mere etiquette required and more sincere than any he'd given her before.

"But thank you," he said, "Daughter of the House."

He exited the cabin without allowing her a chance to respond, closing the door securely behind him.

Elyth remained seated on the bench for a time, considering what had just taken place between them, and what change her knowledge of his secret pain might affect going forward. If any. Though they'd clearly shared a moment, she realized she wouldn't have been at all surprised if he behaved as though it had never happened.

Eventually, she persuaded herself to stand and explore the small cabin. Its decor showed that it was clearly intended for VIPs, but the furniture still bore imprints from the equipment they'd crammed into the space, and several clean uniforms were laid out or draped over various available areas. She found one that fit and carried it with her into the separate lavatory, where she was happy to find that the water was running. It came out almost painfully cold, but it was refreshing to get the mud off her hands and face, and the chill invigorated her. When she had changed out of her mud-stiffened clothes, she felt healthier. Still exhausted, but more like she'd completed a session of hard exercise than the sickening depletion that had clung to her before.

Elyth went then to check on Varen in the med bay and was surprised to find the bed empty. Oyuun was still in the cockpit, deep in thought at his workstation, which he'd managed to get connected to the shuttle's system. Curious as she was, she thought better of interrupting him, and instead stepped out of the shuttle and stood by the hatch.

Outside, the sky had cleared completely, leaving no trace of the storm behind, and the sun was low enough on the horizon that the first stars were just becoming visible. A chill breeze meandered through their crash site, and Elyth noted how much colder it had gotten since earlier in the day. Gone was the springlike mildness, replaced now by a late-autumn edge, herald of a coming winter. The ground had already absorbed most of the standing water, and though she could see patches of thick mud here and there, much of the surrounding area appeared to be merely damp soil rather than the quagmire it'd been only an hour or so before.

And though they'd not intended to make camp, it would have been hard to tell they'd been forced to do so by a hard landing. As hastily as the shuttle had been emptied, she'd expected their supplies to be haphazardly scattered and stacked near the rear of the craft. Instead, she found everything neatly arranged, separated into logical groupings, and organized for easy access. Between that and the work Ames and Nyeda had already done on the shuttle, Elyth felt a vague guilt for not having done more to help. The ship was banged up but intact; whatever damage it had sustained seemed to have been mostly internal, recoverable but tedious to repair.

She could hear Ames and Nyeda working somewhere on top of the shuttle and called to them.

"Can I give you a hand up there?"

"I think we've got it under control, thanks," Ames answered. "Not a lot of room to work. And you ought to be resting anyway."

"I hate to feel useless," she replied.

"Well, you can make yourself useful by rescuing Korush over there. I'm sure he'd appreciate it."

Elyth stepped farther away from the shuttle and found Varen and Korush to one side of it, seated on supply crates about ten yards away, with a portable heating element between them. They'd spread a large ground cloth beneath them, and the Azirim was in the midst of cleaning his armor while Varen appeared to be attempting to engage him in conversation. Beside them, Subo stood watch, silent observer and faithful guardian.

"Grief," she called as she approached. "You sure you should be out here?"

"Fresh air is good for the soul," he answered back, projecting his voice with more strength than she would have expected possible. "Just don't tell Ames."

"I can see you from here," Ames responded from the top of the shuttle. "But if you're dumb enough to die after all the work we did on you, I don't see how that's *my* fault."

"Truly a servant's heart," Varen said, and then to Elyth, "Pull up a crate. It's nice and toasty over here, and full of lively and thrilling debate."

Korush's quick glance told her that the debate was neither lively nor thrilling. Nor, perhaps, even a debate. Elyth dragged a supply crate over and sat down anyway.

"I take it this is more of a sermon than a discussion, huh?" she asked.

"Nonsense," Varen said. "Korush and I were just discussing our differing perspectives on the nature of Subo's interior life."

"I'm already sorry I sat down."

"Well, now that you're here, perhaps you could serve as a neutral party."

"That would only make me even more sorry that I sat down."

"Humor me," he said, inclining his head toward her. "I did just recently almost die, after all . . . not that anyone *owes* me anything."

For a man who had all the look of a corpse not so long ago, Varen seemed astonishingly close to his normal self. His pallid complexion and slumped posture might have been more concerning had they not been counterbalanced by his fullness of voice and lightness of heart.

Elyth let out a dramatic sigh and said, "Fine. But I reserve the right to go lock myself in the shuttle if you get overly pretentious."

"A fair restriction. It's been a long-running disagreement between us, and I would like to finally get it resolved. You know, in case this is the last chance we have."

"That sounds uncharacteristically realistic of you. Are you starting to come around to the idea that this place is trying to kill us all?"

"That's a different conversation," Varen said with a brief smile. "For another time. But my position is that Subo must have some measure of inner life."

"Okay," Elyth said. "May I at least eat something while I listen, so this won't be a complete waste of time?"

"Of course," Korush answered, and he paused his work to point out the correct group of supplies. "Food and water are in that stack. Take whatever you like."

"Can't go wrong," Varen said. "It's all equally terrible."

Elyth opened the top crate and grabbed the first ration she saw without bothering to identify what was in it. As far as she was concerned, food was fuel, and she was too hungry to savor a meal anyway. She returned to the others and, while she opened the container, resumed the conversation.

"All right. And Wari Korush, what is your position on the matter?"

"He's wrong," Korush said flatly, without taking his eyes from his meticulous work.

Elyth chuckled at the response, and Varen replied, "I admit his argument is impressively succinct. But I don't think it's well-supported by the evidence."

"What evidence?" she asked, examining her meal. It appeared to be primarily composed of thin strips of preserved meat in what was probably supposed to be some kind of sauce, but instead had become a beige, gelatinous goo. Underneath, the mushy grain intended to serve as a foundation seemed to be doubling as a sponge to absorb any liquid that hadn't already congealed.

"Ah, the Spiced Slugs over Sludge," Varen said. "A seasonal favorite. The best part is that you hardly have to do any chewing at all."

Elyth picked up a piece of the meat and made a show of dropping it in her mouth to demonstrate how little she cared. And discovered to her displeasure that Varen's description was unfortunately fairly accurate. She tried not to give him any sign that he'd been correct, but his smile suggested he knew.

"Evidence," she said, to get attention off herself.

"Ah yes," Varen replied. "Exhibit one."

He turned toward Subo and said, "Subo, do you have a self?"

"Yes," Subo answered. "Wari Korush is its self."

The statement struck Elyth as a mind-twisting construction; Varen looked back at her with his hands up, as though the response had proven his point.

"I don't . . . see how that helps your case," she said.

"Subo knows it's separate from Korush, but it doesn't consider itself to have *being* apart from him."

"Yes, I picked up on that. It just seems to support the *opposite* of your position."

Korush's face suggested a subdued smile at her response, but he remained focused on his work and offered no further comment.

"I'm just getting started," Varen said.

"I was afraid of that. Wouldn't it be more efficient to just ask Subo directly?"

"Don't try to get philosophical with it," Ames called over from behind her. He was walking away from the ration crate, returning to the shuttle with two meals in hand. "It won't understand, and you'll just break your own brain."

His comment paired with his hasty retreat to the ship suggested that Elyth wasn't the first to be roped into this conversation.

"This is the clever bit," Varen continued, ignoring the captain. "Oh, first, though, should I delve into the dangers that intelligent autonomous weapons platforms like Subo would pose if they were truly self-aware?"

"Please don't," Elyth said, as she worked up the courage to try another bite of her "food."

"Yes, okay, well . . . is it safe to assume that you accept the Hezra assertion that the proper solution to aligning such machines with correct Ascendance values is to assign them a human self?"

"For the sake of ending this as soon as possible? Certainly."

"Good, then we can make sense of Subo's declaration that Korush is 'its self.'"

"Sort of," Elyth said. "Its use of possessive language seems to imply that Subo considers itself a separate enough being to warrant distinguishing ownership of at least *some* things."

"Let's not get bogged down in semantics," Varen said, "lest we lose sight of the higher point."

"You mean so I don't prove you're wrong?"

"You've always had a better grasp of words than I have," he said. "But no . . . Look, if you asked your arm if it had a self, what do you think it would say in response?"

"Hopefully nothing."

"Are you by any chance *deliberately* trying to antagonize me?"

"Me? No, not at all. I just want to sit here and eat my slugs in peace."

"Very well, Elyth, I have noted your objection and will concede the grammatical challenge for the moment, if you'll allow me to finish detailing my line of reasoning."

"How about you just summarize it before Subo gets annoyed and evaporates us both?"

"You're taking all the fun out of this. But *fine*. In *summary*, my theory is that if Subo has no self apart from Korush, then they clearly are a single self. If they are a single self, then if Korush has a soul, Subo must also share it. And thus Subo has a soul. It's much more elegant and compelling in its *detailed* form, I assure you. But Korush disagrees, even though his disagreement is clearly illogical. *Unless* he himself has no soul. Which, now that I say it out loud, I should admit might at least be possible."

"Wari Korush, do you have a counterargument?"

"Yes," the Azirim replied. "He's wrong."

"Sorry, Grief," Elyth said. "Now that I've heard both sides, I'm leaning toward Korush's position."

Varen looked at her with eyes slightly narrowed and waited a beat before asking, "Are you one hundred percent certain that, despite Subo's vast intelligence and obvious capacity for compassion, it has nothing like a soul? Even a tiny fraction of one?"

"To use your analogy, if I lost my arm, I wouldn't think that part of my soul went with it. So I guess I'm pretty certain."

He leaned closer to her, head tipped forward in the manner of a professor challenging a student's too-quick assertion, and said, "Certain enough that you would destroy Subo and feel no more loss or remorse than you do for that shuttle over there?"

For the first time since she'd been taken hostage in the conversation, Elyth felt the gravity of Varen's deeper question. This wasn't a mere thought experiment or debate for distraction to him. And she saw now, too, that the discussion bore all the marks of his circuitous way of talking around a larger concept, leaving it for others to tease out his true message.

"*I* simply think," he continued after she didn't reply, "that we shouldn't be so quick to assume a thing is incapable of possessing an inner quality as unique, precious, and irreplaceable as a soul, whether machine or not."

The look he gave her then confirmed her suspicions, and she understood the real argument he was advancing; even after all they'd been subjected to, he still believed Qel's Shadow shouldn't be destroyed.

"Soul or not," she said, "it is the actions taken that most reveal true intent, and by which all must be judged."

"Oh? You believe our every action is aligned with our every

intention? . . . I wonder, are there any among us who could stand
before such judgment?"

"The Way is higher than those who walk it," Korush inter-
jected, eyes still on his task. "That does not release us from our obligation to strive to uphold it, however faltering our steps may be."

Varen held her gaze for a few moments longer, testing the
depth of disagreement between them. And then, as if it had all
been for fun, he turned back to face the heating element and said,
"Well said, Wari Korush. And it appears you have bested me once
again. In the future, I'll clearly have to select a neutral party in
possession of somewhat less neutrality."

He smiled when he said it, but Elyth knew it was forced by
how quickly it faded. Afterward, the three of them lapsed into
silence for a time, Varen and Elyth each mulling over the implications of their conversation, and Korush just seemingly grateful for
the quiet. But of course Varen couldn't stay silent forever, and
eventually took up a new topic.

"Elyth," he said. "Are you familiar with the honorific that
Wari Korush has earned for himself in his service to the Aziri?"

"Varen," Korush said, with a warning glance. Elyth knew immediately that Varen was up to something; he stared right back
into the Azirim's eyes and ignored the warning.

"Wari Korush," he said. "The Godbreaker."

And then with a sly look at Elyth, he added in a stage whisper,
"I don't think he cares for it very much."

"It is not a name I would choose for myself," Korush said, returning to his work. "And it is more burden than honor. I have
asked you not to speak it."

"Would you like to share the story of how it came to be?"
Varen asked.

Korush stopped his work again and gave him a harder stare than the one before, but whatever point Varen was preparing to make was too important to him to be intimidated into silence.

"An internal matter, if I understand correctly," Varen continued. "Something to do with the Aziri and the previous Hezra-Ka, I believe?"

Elyth glanced at Korush, saw the clenching of his jaw as he struggled to keep his composure in the midst of whatever knife it was that Varen was twisting.

"Grief," Elyth said mildly, trying to relieve some of the tension, "let's not upset the nice man with the void-edge."

"I didn't get many details," Varen continued, his eyes still on Korush while he spoke. "But the ones I did hear gave me an entirely new level of respect for our friend the Azirim. . . . And, if I'm honest, fear. And make no mistake, I was already quite afraid of him. Wari Korush, have you had the chance yet to tell Elyth why you were brought on this expedition?"

"To protect Envoy Sardis," Korush answered, carefully.

"And?"

Korush slammed a piece of his armor into its container, and the intensity of his eyes revealed just how deeply Varen had managed to burrow into a vulnerable part of him.

"And to kill you, Varen Fedic, should the need arise."

At the admission, Elyth's view of the Azirim shifted again. She'd initially thought of him as an overly aggressive guard dog, but recently had gained deeper respect and even some compassion for the man. Now, with the revelation that he was an assassin embedded within the team, all the trust she'd begun to develop in him collapsed, and his actions on-world took on a new light. His constant attentiveness to Varen, his insistence on accompanying him everywhere he went . . . even when he'd allowed Varen out into the storm, it'd been under the supervision of his lethal machine. Korush was no guardian. He was an executioner.

"Indeed," Varen said. "But *only* if necessary. And I do hope so far I've given you no cause."

"There would be none," Korush replied, "if only you talked less." He stared Varen down a moment longer, and then picked up another component of his armor and began cleaning the mud from it to settle himself.

"Believe it or not, my friend, I used to have a *much* worse habit of speaking first," Varen said, and Elyth did not miss his subtle, playful reference to his now-forsaken title of First Speaker. He turned to Elyth and continued, "I have to admit, I actually consider it quite an honor that they would send no less than the Godbreaker himself to contend with me. Not that he'll even need to, of course. Even if it were necessary, though, it's clearly overkill and I'd be no match for a man of his prowess. But it makes me feel special, anyway."

And now Elyth understood Varen's motivation for initiating the strained conversation. The attention that Korush had paid her throughout their time on the planet made sudden sense.

"And, Wari Korush," she said, "I can only assume you have the same directive for me."

He looked up from his work to meet her gaze.

"No," he answered. "That is not my task."

He paused, continuing to lock eyes with her, and then after a long moment, dipped his head toward Nyeda.

"It is hers."

Elyth turned her head slowly to look over at the woman. She was seated on top of the shuttle next to Ames, both eating and dangling their feet over the edge, looking off toward the mountains like they were on a picnic together. And Korush's statement reframed everything in that moment; her concern that she was surrounded by enemies masquerading as allies proved correct, the deal she'd agreed to called into question. Of course they'd never let her go. Despite Sardis's invocation of the word of the Hezra-Ka, she now had to assume they would use her for this task, and then, the moment they were done with her, kill her. By the Voice of her own House. A fitting end.

"Though should she fail," Korush added quietly, "I am sworn to perform the duty in her stead."

He returned to his work dispassionately, as though these were simple logistical matters. Varen looked to Elyth, his eyes communicating everything. He was her only true ally here, and she his.

She was still gazing at him, half-lost in a whirlwind of thought and emotion, when Arbiter Oyuun emerged from the shuttle and called out to them.

"I think I've found something."

EIGHTEEN

The six of them stood in the middle of the shuttle, crowded together as Arbiter Oyuun tried to talk them through his discovery. The ship's main display projected a three-dimensional image of the surrounding area, which Oyuun manipulated with his attached workstation while he spoke.

"These are the areas we examined today," he said. "I pooled the data that you so kindly collected for us there and matched them with some of my own findings from before. But then, Elyth, thanks to your very helpful description of your experience, I filtered all of these using several manipulations and algorithms I developed during my work on . . . on my previous initiative."

"On Deepcutter?" Elyth asked.

"No, I've never heard of that," the Arbiter answered, maintaining the obvious fiction, denying the existence of the Deepcutter Inititative while simultaneously confirming it. "But yes, that one. Taken altogether, I was able to produce this model."

He lightly swept his fingers across the interface of his workstation, and the imagery on the display shifted and rotated to show an isometric view of the land. The detailed terrain features melted away, leaving behind only ghostly outlines in green, something like an X-ray of the region. To the southeast, a small, orange-yellow fireball blossomed underground, with wispy tendrils reaching out in all directions. From beneath the mountains. From within the peak. A shiver spiked its way through her spine.

"What is that?" Ames asked.

"I'm not sure, exactly," Oyuun said. "But I guess I would say it's a rough approximation of what I might call something like a power source."

Elyth flicked a glance at Varen; he was already looking at her, and didn't seem surprised by the finding.

"But this isn't from raw data," Elyth said, returning to the image. "This is from your model?"

"Yes, correct."

"And how confident are you that your model is accurate?"

"Oh, all models are wrong, dear," he said. "But some are useful."

"What do you think it's made of?" Ames asked.

"I'm not even sure it's *made* of anything, Captain," the Arbiter responded. "We could go there and maybe find nothing at all. But then again, we could go there and maybe our gifted friends would be able to sense something the rest of could not."

Elyth stared at the display, filled with dread by what she saw, and knowing she could no longer resist its summons. But she knew, too, that what she would find there would be nothing she'd encountered before.

"It looks like it's underground, though, and pretty deep," Ames said. "Or am I reading it wrong?"

"You are correct, Captain Ames. It does appear to be sub-surface."

"So, we can't *actually* go there, then."

Oyuun focused the map on the mountain range and expanded the image to reveal more detail. The green outlines that had previously been a tangle of confused lines clarified with the closer view.

"Please tell me those aren't tunnels," Ames said.

"I believe they're tunnels," Oyuun replied.

"Noooo thank you," the captain answered, leaning away from the display and stepping back from the group. "The planet's been plenty busy trying to kill us here on the surface. We absolutely should *not* be walking down into its gullet, just so it can swallow us without even chewing. *Especially* if you aren't even sure there's anything there."

"There's something there," Elyth said.

"How do you *know*?"

She held up her hand and waggled her fingers. "Spooky word stuff."

Ames groaned, closed his eyes, and tipped his head back.

"What if those tunnels were made by a billion of those critters like the one that jumped us in the woods? What if it's a *hive*?"

"Then we'll ask Subo to go first," Elyth said. "Captain, if you don't want to go, I understand. But I must."

He looked back at her. "Hey, that's not fair. You *know* if you're going, I'm going. I'm just not going to like it."

"I don't suspect any of us will, Captain Ames," Oyuun said. "But I do believe it's our best chance of finding *some*thing useful."

Ames walked back to the group and leaned closer to the display.

"Going to be a long walk to those mountains," he said. "I don't guess you want to wait until we get the shuttle back up and running?"

"How much longer will that take?" Oyuun asked.

"Couple of days, maybe."

"Then no."

"I figured."

"If we leave at dawn," Nyeda said, "we'll have enough daylight to make it there."

"Yeah," Ames said, "but what about back?"

Nyeda glanced at Elyth, and then back to Ames.

"Yeah," he said. "I figured."

"Very well," the Arbiter said. "We'll leave at dawn."

He shut off the main display and set his workstation aside, then stood to face the group.

"I would be a fool to suggest I had any idea what tomorrow will bring," he said. "But my instincts say that whatever lies ahead, we are at least on the right path. And after all we've been through together, I'm confident we can prevail."

"Glad to hear someone is," Ames said.

"I guess we should set up shelters for the night," Nyeda said. "Are they outside?"

"Yeah, but don't bother," the captain replied. "We've got enough juice now to keep the ship comfortable. Between the main cabin, the side cabin, and the med bay, I think we've got enough space to rack out in here. Save us the time and trouble of breaking camp and loading it up in the morning."

"Sounds like a plan, Captain," Oyuun said. "Thank you."

"Yep," Ames said. He looked around at each member of the group, sighed heavily, and shook his head. "You all look wrecked. If you're going to make me go headfirst into some bug hole tomorrow, the least you could do in return is try to look alert while we're there. I'll get the gear pulled together. Varen, you're sleeping in the med bay, no argument. The rest of you figure out where you're bedding down and then go do it."

"Ames," Elyth said, "we'll all help prep—"

"I got it," the captain said, cutting her off as he started toward the hatch. "You need to recover more than I do."

She followed after him; the man had been working nonstop since their crash, and she knew how hard the next day was going to be.

"We *all* need to recover," she said. "We can work together now, knock it out, and then together we can all rest."

"I said I got it."

"Captain—"

"No!" he barked sharply. He stopped at the hatch, placed his hand on it, and dropped his head forward. After a moment, he half-turned to look at her and then the rest of the team. He took a steadying breath.

"Look," he said, calm and quieter. "I'm in way over my head here. *Way* over. I'm just a guy, I'm not like the rest of you. Come tomorrow, I don't know how much use I'm going to be. Might be none at all. But this is one thing I *can* do, one thing I know I can do that will actually help. So, please, just let me have this."

Elyth stood in the middle of the shuttle, silent. She'd known Ames had been rattled, but now, for the first time, she saw how frayed he had truly become, and got a sense of how long he'd been concealing his fear beneath a mask of good-natured humor and service to everyone else.

"I will assist you, Captain Ames," Korush said. Ames looked like he was about to argue, but he stopped when he realized the Azirim hadn't been making an offer so much as a statement.

"Very well, Wari Korush. We'll see the rest of you at dawn."

Elyth stepped to one side to allow Korush to pass, and the two men exited through the hatch, into the gloaming. When it had sealed behind them, Oyuun took charge.

"Varen, as the captain said, you'll sleep in the med bay. I'd like to keep you monitored throughout the night, so we have a good idea of how recovered you actually are in the morning."

"I feel fine, Arbiter," Varen said. "A little snooze and I'll be right as rain."

Oyuun made a face at the choice of phrase, and Varen flashed a quick smile to let everyone know it hadn't been an accident.

"Nyeda, Elyth," Oyuun continued, "why don't you two take the side cabin. I believe the rest of us can find room here on the deck of the main cabin."

"Neither of us need pampering," Elyth said. "Maybe you and Ames should take the VIP room. Or we can draw names for it if you like."

"Kind of you to say, but it wasn't meant as a chivalrous gesture. I have further work to do with the ship's systems, Korush will insist on sleeping by the hatch for security purposes, and Captain Ames will flatly refuse to take any space in that cabin. If you try to force him, he'll just sit in a seat out here all night in protest. You two *are* our honored guests, after all."

"Well, I guess that's settled," Varen said. "And though I do feel absolutely fine, I think I'm going to go lie down. Doctor's orders and all."

For all his commentary, he was still wan, and Elyth noticed his hands were trembling.

"Good," Nyeda said. "I didn't want to be the first, and I *am* feeling the toll of the past couple of days."

The group disbanded, and the two women retired to the side cabin. And though the quarters were tight enough to require some coordination, they hardly spoke as they prepared for sleep. Nyeda maintained her emotional distance and avoided making eye contact. And Elyth, with her new understanding of Nyeda's true role on the team, knew that any attempt at light conversation would only give her away. Nyeda knew her far too well.

In addition to the cushioned bench, a more proper bed folded out from the bulkhead. Elyth staked her claim on the bench, lying down on it while Nyeda was washing her hands and face in the lavatory. Nyeda paused when she stepped out and saw the bed empty, but made no comment about it. She switched off the light, leaving the cabin in near-total darkness, save for two dim red safety lights over the entryway, like twin stars dying in the void. After Nyeda had climbed into the bed, Elyth lay silently, listening. Ten or so minutes passed, and she could tell from Nyeda's breathing that the woman was also lying awake.

"Nyeda?" she said quietly.

"Yes?"

"I know why you're here."

Nyeda didn't respond for long enough that Elyth assumed her former sister had nothing to say. But eventually, Nyeda answered.

"You should sleep. You'll need to be at your fullest tomorrow."

Elyth woke to the gently rising glow of the interior lights. Nyeda was still asleep, but now that she was awake, Elyth could hear movement beyond the door, in the main cabin. She rose and slipped out, finding Korush, Ames, and Oyuun already suited up and working to make final arrangements. Six large packs rested by the rear hatch, three to each side; none of them were packed quite the same, but the load seemed almost evenly distributed, except for one that was clearly lighter than the others.

"That little one better not be mine," Elyth said.

Ames glanced over at her and smiled.

"Nah," he said. "That one's for Varen. Get any sleep?"

"Plenty. How about you?"

"Enough. Korush kept waking me up with all his snoring."

"That was Subo," Korush answered. And though he said it completely deadpan, it certainly appeared as though he'd just made a joke. Ames and Elyth shared a look of surprised amusement.

"Korush," Ames said, "you are a man of many hidden talents. I had no idea you had a sense of humor."

"My efforts to keep to the Way have sharpened many of my senses, Captain Ames."

Ames laughed and shook his head. "Wari Korush, joking around. I don't know if that's a good sign, or a really, really bad one."

Nyeda came out of the side cabin, and Varen appeared shortly after. When everyone was gathered, Ames pointed toward the forward section of the shuttle.

"I got some goodies over there for each of you. Same things in every pile, and it doesn't matter what size you are. They'll fit."

Elyth, Nyeda, and Varen moved to the front to see what was there. Laid out for them were sets of soft armor, of the same material as Elyth's borrowed vest had been. These sets, however, were complete with an overjacket, pants, boots, and gloves, with the crimson and black markings of the Hezra. All of them felt over-sized when Elyth slipped them on, but just as before, once acti-vated, the material cinched up snugly. She struggled a bit with the glove of her left hand; though she'd regained some movement in her two outer fingers, she still didn't have complete control or sen-sation in them. No one else seemed to notice, though, and she did her best not to draw attention.

A flattened, round-edged capsule rested on the upper back of the suits just below the neckline, about the size of Elyth's hand.

"What are these?" she asked Ames, tapping the one on Varen's back.

"Your hat," the captain answered. He pressed his armor along the collarbone, and in two seconds a helmet had formed, similar to Korush's. The faceplate was smooth with no obvious openings, but when he spoke again, his voice was only mildly changed. "Try it out. Two fingers, anywhere along your collarbone."

Elyth pressed two fingers against her armor as instructed and was quickly enshrouded. The interior of the helmet fit securely along her jaw and the sides of her head near her temples, but oth-erwise left a comfortable air gap around her face. From the inside, however, neither her vision nor hearing seemed affected, and she was able to breathe normally. She turned her head left and right, rolled her neck, testing the mobility. Though she felt some resis-tance, it was light, and certainly less than she'd expected.

"What do you think?" Ames asked, deactivating his helmet.

"Impressive," Elyth said. She tapped her collar again, and the faceplate melted neatly away. "Too bad it comes in the wrong colors."

"Yeah, well, looks good on you anyway."

"How come Korush gets the good stuff?" Varen asked, looking

down at his flexible armor and then over to Korush's sleek powered armor.

"Because he earned it, Varen," the captain said. "If you want to take the oath of the Aziri when we get back, maybe they'll give you your own suit in about twenty years."

"Nah," Varen said. "I'd never be able to stick with it. Too many rules."

"The Way is not a set of rules," Korush commented, as he checked the packs. "It is a direction. It leads us higher, but rarely does it instruct us where our next step should fall."

"Then how do you know where to go?"

"Because it also points away from certain things, and that list is easy to remember."

"Easy enough even for me?" Varen asked, his boyish smile starting to show through; what had started as a gentle jab was turning to genuine interest, taking advantage of Korush's unusual openness.

Korush paused his work and looked directly at Varen as he recited a litany of his Way:

"Eyes that gaze down in arrogance,
A tongue that crafts deceit,
A heart that weaves wickedness,
Hands that shed innocent blood,
Feet that rush to cruelty,
One who sows discord among the people."

Varen stood silent for a moment, absorbing the words, rolling them over in his mind, and, Elyth guessed, memorizing them for later discussion.

Then he blinked and said, "Wait . . . remind me again, that was the list of things to *avoid* or . . . ?"

Korush stared at him a moment and then wordlessly resumed his final check of their gear.

"We really should talk more, Korush."

"I disagree."

"If everyone is sufficiently equipped," Arbiter Oyuun cut in, "we should get moving. We have a long day ahead."

"Breakfast?" Varen asked.

"Eat while you walk," Ames replied. He tossed a small packet over to Varen. From the size and shape, Elyth guessed it was a standard half ration: high-calorie, nutrient-dense, probably chalk flavored.

The team donned their packs and gathered as best they could near the hatch, though given their loads and the size of the craft, they mostly ended up in a crooked line down the center aisle. Oyuun stood at the head of the group, with Korush next to the hatch. The Arbiter turned toward everyone, scanned their faces, undoubtedly preparing to deliver an encouraging speech.

"Let's try not to die before we figure this out," he said.

And then he nodded to Korush, and the Azirim opened the hatch.

The ice-edged air that cut through the ship took them all by surprise; even moreso the thin layer of sparkling white that covered the ground outside. Subo stood watch by the hatch, its head and shoulders frosted with snow.

"Uh," Ames said, "that's quite a change."

The horizon showed the first tinges of color, hinting at a rising sun, and as the team filtered out, the ground crunched beneath each step. As far as they could see, snow hushed the earth and trees.

The group fanned out from the craft, taking in the surroundings, judging the terrain, each attempting to account for the unexpected change in climate. The snowfall was no more than an inch deep, but Elyth knew the cold and the extra care they'd have to take in their footing would sap their energy faster than usual.

"This is lovely," Varen said. "And I suppose we won't have to worry about getting overheated on our journey."

"Well, great," Ames said. "I hope our supplies didn't get all frozen up."

He crunched over to check on the various stacks, and the others maintained their positions while he did so. As Elyth gazed out toward their destination, she couldn't help but feel that this drop in temperature was no natural phenomenon. Some thirty yards away, glinting specks of blue caught her eye, a speckled patch of colored ice fragments atop the surface of the snow. A few moments after she noticed them, they floated up off the ground, scattered and shimmering, and danced gradually toward them.

"Hey," she said, and pointed at the approaching anomaly.

"What do you think that is?" Nyeda asked.

"Fairies," Varen said.

Subo moved forward fifteen feet ahead of the group to intercept the colored lights. After a few moments, though, Elyth recognized what it was.

"Butterflies," she said.

It was a small swarm, comprised of maybe twenty or thirty, and though there wasn't much light yet, the delicate wings of the creatures sparked and flashed a beautiful sapphire blue. The sparkling cloud approached Subo hesitantly, a few bolder butterflies slipping closer before retreating to the graceful dance of their companions.

"What marvelous insects," Oyuun said. "I don't believe I've seen anything of their kind before."

As they watched, the shimmering swarm shifted from a nebulous cloud to take on a more orderly shape; for the briefest moment, they seemed to be mimicking Subo's silhouette. But they quickly returned to their scattered form and flitted away toward one of the supply crates nearby. Captain Ames stood a few yards from the crate, and the butterflies eventually wandered in his direction, pausing a few feet from him. They hovered there for ten or fifteen seconds.

"Yeah, okay, you're very pretty," Ames said, and then he waved his arm vaguely at them. "Now, go away."

The crystal blue of the wings grew vibrant; the captain must have seen something in them, because he turned his head away and started to raise his arm to shield himself just before it happened.

The cloud of butterflies vanished in a lightning flash of white-hot flame so intense that Elyth felt the blast of heat from ten yards away.

Never before had she heard a human make the sound that came from Captain Ames.

Subo was the first to react, covering the ground in what seemed like one step, and an instant later, a thick white cloud billowed from its arm, coating the captain. Nyeda rushed over, and Elyth, stirred from her shock by the motion, followed her to the man's side.

Ames lay on his side, quivering, making a strange half-whistling, half-whimpering noise. He was partially coated with white foam from whatever Subo had sprayed him with, but through the gaps, Elyth could see the damage. The flesh across the entire left portion of his face was flash-burned and blackened; his armor smoked, and appeared to have shriveled and buckled from the heat. The straps from his backpack had disintegrated completely, and the supplies inside popped and sizzled. Around him, the snow had vanished into vapor and the ground steamed with the residual heat.

"Get him out," Nyeda was saying. "Get him out of the armor."

The two women worked quickly to unseal the suit, but as they peeled back the front panel, his scream stopped them cold. Beneath, his uniform appeared to be melted against his skin.

Subo swept in, scooped the captain up, and swiftly moved back to the craft; Korush was already through the hatch. Elyth and Nyeda leaped up to follow as Subo rushed Ames to the med bay, but when they reached it, the Azirim refused to let them in.

"Out!" he shouted. "Stay out!"

The last view they had before he sealed the door was of Subo laying Ames onto the bed and the captain writhing on it.

NINETEEN

"Is he going to make it?" Elyth asked, the instant Korush appeared at the rear hatch. His expression told nothing.

"I don't know," he answered quietly. "He is stabilized. There was sufficient material to dress the worst of his wounds. The next four to six hours are critical, to see if the artificial grafts hold, and if he can withstand the trauma. But if he fights, he could survive."

It had been an hour and a half since the attack, and the horrific injury Ames had suffered seemed to have ripped the heart out of the entire group. They all stood gathered around the rear of the shuttle, waiting for news.

"Subo was quick," Korush added. "And his pack shielded a good portion of him. The two together may have saved him."

Elyth nodded, and the group stood in awkward silence, uncertain what step to take next. The Arbiter didn't let the moment last long.

"We should get underway," he said.

"What?" Nyeda said sharply.

"We've lost time that will be difficult to make up."

"We can't go now!"

"We cannot stay here, Nyeda," he said, kind but firm. "Or there will be no one left to go."

"But what about the captain? We can't just leave him here!"

"No, we cannot," the Arbiter agreed. The remaining team members glanced around at one another, but it didn't take long to draw the obvious conclusion. After a moment, Nyeda nodded her head.

"Is there a way I can track your progress?" she asked.

Oyuun nodded. "Each of our suits has a unique signature, registered to the shuttle. You can follow us on the navigation display."

"And Ames?"

"Monitor him," Korush said. "Encourage him."

Nyeda beheld the faces of the other team members, slowly, each in their turn, and Elyth recognized what she was doing. She and her sisters had often done the same whenever one had been deployed. Weighing the moment, giving it its due, locking in memory the image of each, in case it was the last time she looked upon them. When her eyes at last fell upon Elyth, Nyeda held her gaze for a time, and then gestured to the others.

"May I have a moment with my sister?" she said.

The three men quietly moved off to give them some space, and Nyeda dropped her eyes to the ground and walked closer to Elyth. She stopped about arm's length away, inhaled deeply.

"You said you knew why I was here," Nyeda said. "And when we first arrived, yes. I was prepared to fulfill my duty to the House, and to the Ascendance. To take your life, if necessary, and if I proved capable. But now . . . I don't know what to make of you. They say you have abandoned the First House, but in our time here, I have only seen you uphold the best of it."

Elyth reacted to the statement, and Nyeda looked up at her.

"Not as we were taught, perhaps. But I think, maybe, as we should have been."

It was an astonishing declaration.

"Nyeda," Elyth said. "All this time I thought you despised me."

Nyeda shook her head. "All this time I've been wrestling with who you are, compared to who I thought you'd become. Who they told me you were."

She reached out and took Elyth's hands in hers.

"You can do all that I can and far more. I think maybe you have surpassed even the greatest of our House. My hope now, Elyth-Kyriel, is that you are enough to save it."

It was only the second time since their reunion Nyeda had dared to utter her name, but now she magnified the moment by speaking Elyth's former hidden name, an action tantamount to reinstating her within her Order. Her hidden name was granted by the House and known only to a precious few. And Nyeda *was* precious to her.

"Nyeda-Valanel," Elyth said, embracing the woman. "My strength and my shield."

The phrase was a play on words, capturing the essence of Nyeda's hidden name but with the warmth of a pet name. In their time together in the House, Nyeda had served as her instructor, her training partner, her caretaker, and her guardian during her recoveries. In their shared embrace, all those roles intertwined as though all the sisters of her former House had joined in that one woman, and Elyth felt strengthened, comforted, and charged with a solemn duty.

Nyeda pulled away from her, placed her palm gently and briefly on Elyth's forehead, and then backed away.

"*Sareth hanaan* be your guide," Nyeda said.

"*Sareth hanaan* be our way," Elyth answered.

They shared a final look, and then Nyeda turned and headed back toward the shuttle. Elyth watched her go a few moments longer, strangely warmed by the interaction, but also touched by a vague guilt at having so misread her sister's intentions. She couldn't help but wonder what time she may have lost, if only she had pursued Nyeda's presence, rather than leaving her to her own isolation.

The others had already donned their packs and were clearly anxious for her to join them. Elyth hoisted her gear and buckled the straps around her while she crossed over to them. When she arrived, Korush held something out to her, gunmetal gray and about the size of a large egg.

"What's this?" she said, receiving the device and studying it in her hand. It looked vaguely familiar, but she couldn't place it.

"The captain's dragonflies," Korush said. "He wanted you to take them. For the tunnels."

She looked up to ask when or how Ames had told the Azirim that, but he had already turned away, moving to take the lead headed toward the mountains, with Subo falling into step alongside him. Elyth returned her attention to the device a moment longer. The captain's last effort to be useful, to help guide the way. She clipped the dragonfly pod to her belt, hoping she'd have the chance to thank him. And she moved out, catching up with the others to cross the wide clearing that had been beaten to a marsh just the day before. Now, with the light layer of snow, it felt more like a meadow beneath Elyth's feet.

They kept a good pace, focused now more on covering ground than moving with abundant caution. Though everyone maintained their alertness, Elyth got the sense that they'd all come to accept that Qel's Shadow had too many ways to hurt them to meaningfully predict or adequately protect against. This time, the journey felt less like walking through a minefield and more like crossing open ground in a sniper's known territory. Either they would make it or they wouldn't, and there seemed to be very little they could do about it.

The path they'd followed the day before had been a spline, curving and sweeping through the denser parts of the wilderness, where the range of biodiversity was likely to be highest. Now, they made as straight for the mountains as they could. The forest ebbed and flowed along their way, often opening up into sparse patches that were graciously easy to navigate, and the snow thinned quickly, to the point that it became only an occasional highlight under broad trees or along shaded ridges.

Arbiter Oyuun remained in the rear, and though Varen had started out just behind Korush, he gradually drifted back to walk alongside Elyth. He made it almost a whole hour before he started talking.

"I'm a whole lot sorer today than I expected to be," he said, rolling his shoulders beneath the weight of his pack. "Guess I'm getting old."

"Or," Elyth said, "maybe you were in a shuttle crash yesterday."

"Oh yeah . . . guess that might do it too. I didn't really get hurt that much, so I kind of forgot about it."

"First crash, huh?"

"It wasn't yours?"

Elyth gave him a look, eyebrow raised. He'd been the cause of her first one.

"Oh, right," he said, and grimaced. "Yeah. So how'd this one compare?"

"Other one was worse."

"Glad I wasn't there for that, then . . . and, you know, sorry about that."

He looked up, surveyed the sky above them, then scanned the surroundings, taking it all in as though he were seeing it all for the first time. After a deep breath, he shook his head with a wistful smile.

"It's hard to contemplate that we come from a race that was once planet-bound," he said. "I wonder what it would have been like to stand on a world, believing yours was the only sunrise, the only sunset, the only sea or shore that anyone would ever behold. Can you imagine that?"

"Not really," she said, hoping not to encourage him further.

"Not much of one for imagining, I suppose?"

Elyth shrugged.

"It's our history," he said, peering at her with intention. No matter what she did, he was going to draw her into a discussion, or at least, drag her along with him while he monologued.

"The one we decided to write down, yes," she said.

"You don't believe it?"

"It makes for a nice origin story, if nothing else. Celebrating our great ascension and all that."

"Not that in particular. I mean history."

"I believe its lessons," she said. Varen leaned closer, eyebrows raised, expectant. Elyth sighed and continued, "It has a very long arc, and that's a good teacher. But no one can see history when they're in it. People are blind to the true significance of the events of their day. And later, they tend to imbue past events with what-ever significance they need to fit the story they want to tell. To say nothing of the forgotten stories of those crushed under its weight."

"Huh. True in general, but not in specifics?"

"You know, Grief, the main reason I put up with your lectures before was because I was trying to figure out what you did to Qel, not so much because I actually found you interesting."

"You always were the wiser one," he said, chuckling. "But a rambling fool may prove wise if he rambles long enough." He de-livered that comment as though it were the pronouncement of a philosopher, but then bent closer to her, winked, and added, "That's just statistics."

Mercifully, he fell quiet for a time, as they navigated a denser part of the wood. But when it opened out again, he held out a hand, gesturing at the landscape around them. "Do you think any-one in the future will believe any of this happened?"

"I'm not sure I would believe any of this happened."

"Indeed," he said. He paused to produce something from a pouch on his belt, and added, "That's what makes this such a good idea."

He held the item up between his thumb and forefinger for her to see. It was the vial she'd given him, with the remaining soil from Qel.

"It's good to keep mementos on hand, tangible reminders of what once was," he said. He held it up to let the sun filter through it, gazed at the earth within. Then, as he slipped it back into the pouch, he continued, "Our faith in the past tends to be weaker than our memory of it."

They passed under a large tree with drooping branches, the

lowest of which dangled its long, cedarlike needles an arm's length over their heads. Varen reached up and ran his fingertips along the greenery.

"I've often wondered how long it took our ancestors to first notice the stars," he said.

Elyth shook her head. "We'd be incomprehensible to them now. Except maybe as gods."

"Perhaps," Varen said with a quiet chuckle, "if we were but wiser. As it is, I suspect they would realize very quickly that we are still very much the same."

Elyth let out a single, scoffing laugh.

"Wow, Grief. Even for someone as prone to wild exaggeration as you, that's quite the claim."

He shrugged. "We know how things work to a greater degree of precision, I suppose. We have greater command over our environments. Certainly, we know more of our stars and planets and moons. But just because we can touch them doesn't make us fundamentally superior to our ancestors."

"Oh? Not superior to a planet-bound people, who busied themselves with killing each other over resources they only *thought* were scarce because they didn't know to look at the vast abundance just beyond the borders of their own fragile little atmosphere?"

Varen smiled to himself as she spoke, but, amazingly, didn't say anything.

"What?"

"Oh, nothing. It's just . . . hearing you talk about abundance like that."

"What about it?"

"It reminds me of a conversation we had a while ago."

"I don't know why I bother talking to you," she said. "You

obviously have some point you're enthralled with, why don't you just state it instead of pretending we're having a conversation?"

"Oh, Elyth, come now. I didn't mean to hurt your feelings."

"You're not hurting anything but my ears."

"I'm not enthralled with any point. I would just argue that our ancestors weren't killing each other over bits of dust. After all, these were the same people ingenious enough to create the means to cross every horizon they ever saw. They were constantly seeking out the unknown and confronting it. But it seems to be our nature to seek first to destroy rather than understand. So in that light, I don't think much has changed at all."

Now that she saw where he was really trying to lead her, she cut straight to the heart of it.

"We understand this place just fine, Grief. It *destroyed* Qel. We know all we need to know."

"Hmm. *We know all we need to know*," he said, raising his hand and making a circle with his fingers around a tiny patch of sky. "I wonder if our ancestors ever spoke those very same words." After a moment, he spread his fingers, like a magician making a coin disappear, and added, "Even when we lived on a tiny speck in the middle of nowhere."

Varen went quiet after that, but kept pace with her, not quite lost in thought but not fully present either. Finally, she did some probing of her own.

"I still don't understand what's going on between you and this place, Grief."

"I don't either, exactly," he said. "But then, I tend to be more of a *feel* guy than a *know* guy."

"Tough to tell from the way you act."

"Friendly?"

"Like the rest of us are always behind, trying to catch up to some grand vision of yours."

"Yes, well. If I weren't eccentric, everyone would think I was crazy."

"That's just a nicer way of saying the same thing."

"Indeed," he said. His brow furrowed then, and Elyth recognized the dark edge, reminiscent of the mood that would overtake him on Qel. "It's as it was before, Elyth. There is *purpose* here. I don't know how else to describe it. You must feel it too. Don't you have the sense that all that has happened up to now was leading you here, to this place?"

"All I sense is that I'm here now, and that I need to do the thing that's right, given where I am. That's all I'm trying to do."

"Then we're operating the same way. Maybe I just interpret it differently. But I don't think I could have ended up anywhere else, other than right here, right now. So I feel that my destiny is bound up with this place, Elyth. It's no accident we're here. You and me, together. We have important work to do. And it isn't just breaking this world."

"You're starting to put on your cosmic savior hat again," she said. "That's the part of you I like the least."

"Oh? There are parts you like more?"

"The part where you quietly stare at nature without comment is pretty good."

"Wari Korush," Varen called. "I believe your love of silence is starting to rub off on Elyth here."

"I wish it would rub off on you," Korush replied without turning.

Varen smiled and shook his head, but the look that followed was shadowed once more.

from left to right, but there was nothing that caught her eye as out of place or rose in her conscious mind as an obvious source for the unease. Elyth glanced back at the camp to get her bearings, and looked again at the landscape. It still took her a moment to grasp the fact that she was standing in the same place where she'd performed her meditation the evening before. And recognizing that, she realized that the terrain had completely transformed, as far as she could see.

"Grief," she said. "It's all changed."

He didn't respond to her at all, didn't even stir at the sound of her voice.

"Grief?"

"Elyth," he said, and his voice was burdened with emotion. She stepped up next to him, looked down at him. "Elyth, this is where I was born."

He continued to stare out over the hillsides, eyes shining with a mix of joy, disbelief, and overwhelming memory; the face of a long-exiled man who, beyond all hope, had returned home.

"I mean . . . it's not *really* where I was born, I know that," he added. "But this landscape. This horizon. I spent my childhood staring at this view, dreaming of all that lay beyond it."

He turned to her then, and though his eyes fixed on hers, there was a distance in them that unnerved her.

"I wish you could have seen Markov, Elyth. I wish you could have seen what it had been before I ruined it. And what it could have become if I had not."

"Grief," she said. "What did you do?"

"Nothing," he replied, looking back over the hillscape. "But I think maybe you were right when you said connecting with this world might let it get into my heart. It did. When I stood in that storm . . . I saw it, Elyth. And it saw me. And I think maybe this is its way of telling me I'm in the right place."

Elyth shook her head.

"This world is a lie," she said. "It's not even a *world*, Grief."

"Not as we know them, perhaps. That doesn't make it evil."

"Listen to your own words. Listen carefully to what you're saying. We didn't come here to settle down and make a home for ourselves—"

"And maybe that's why it's reacting the way it is," he said, getting to his feet. He gave her a quick look, folded his hands together behind his back, then began walking slowly along the rim of the hilltop. "I told you before, this planet was struggling with itself. I think maybe we're interfering."

"It's not a *planet*! It's a device!"

He stopped about twenty feet away from her, turned to face her.

"It's not important what it *is*, Elyth," he said sharply. "What's important is what it could *become*. If we just take enough time. Qel is already at work in it, I can feel it. And you and I, the two of us, we can continue that work. We can *shape* this place, Elyth."

There was no madness in his words or his eyes, but she saw that Varen was no longer completely himself.

"Is everything okay out here?" Korush said. She glanced over at him; he was standing off to one side, near the edge of the camp, already in his armor with Subo at his shoulder. And though his voice was calm, his stance emitted a taut, almost tangible energy.

"Just discussing the road ahead," Varen said. "There seems to be a mild disagreement between us."

"There's no disagreement," Korush answered. "There is only what the Arbiter says."

"And what do you say, Arbiter?" Varen asked, his eyes shifting. Oyuun was there now as well, standing by his shelter. With Elyth and Korush, the three of them formed a fan, with Varen the focal point of their attention.

"I say we continue with our plan, Varen," he said carefully. "Just as we discussed."

"You don't believe plans should be adjusted according to new information?" Varen said.

"If new information suggested such adjustment was necessary, yes. I don't believe we've determined that here, though."

Varen looked between the three of them and then gave a casual smile. But Elyth saw the tension in it, how conflicted he actually was.

"Have you told any of them, Arbiter?" he asked. "Or is that another secret you're still keeping?"

"I've shared all the relevant data I know to share, Varen."

Varen chuckled.

"Relevant. I see. Elyth, did the Arbiter happen to mention why it was that he was never successful with Deepcutter?"

"Enough, yes," Elyth said.

"Oh? And what do you consider enough?"

"That the nature of space between galaxies is different from that within one," she said. "And that you were helping them ask the right questions."

"Not between galaxies," Varen corrected. "Only between ours and all others."

He paused, waiting for her to understand, but she couldn't grasp whatever it was he was trying to imply.

"It's a barrier, Elyth. And you know how I feel about barriers."

Her mind couldn't hold the concept. How could a galaxy be

contained? Even so, his face suggested what he said was true; or at least, that he believed it to be true.

"Arbiter," she said, "is this true?"

The Arbiter nodded but didn't take his eyes off Varen.

"Something created a barrier around our entire galaxy?" Elyth asked.

"Or someone," Varen said. "A wall, to keep us in."

"Or to keep other things out," Oyuun answered. "We don't understand what it is, Varen. No one does, not even you. And it's dangerous to pretend otherwise."

"Either way," Varen said, speaking to Elyth, "whatever it was that we did on Qel to deflect the power of the Contingency seems to have poked a hole in it."

"We don't know that either," the Arbiter said. "And Varen, you're starting to give me concerns."

Elyth flicked her eyes to the other two men. Oyuun maintained an easy bearing, not yet ready to exert his full authority. But she was alarmed to see that Korush had subtly moved his hand in front of himself, waist-level, a half instant from the hilt of his dire weapon. She looked back at Varen; surely he was aware of his great danger.

"There's nothing to be concerned about, Arbiter," Varen replied, casually, relaxed. "You know as well as I do that this world came from beyond that barrier. I just wanted to make sure we *all* have the same information. After all, the quality of our information dictates the quality of our decisions."

He looked intently at Elyth as he said the last sentence, testing her once more, attempting to peer into her thoughts. For a span, he just stood on the edge of the hill, facing them, placid. But then he must have seen whatever it was he'd been searching for in Elyth's eyes. He let his gaze drop to the ground in front of him and smiled sadly to himself.

"But this is where I was born," he said. "And I don't think I can let you destroy it."

He inhaled deeply, and Elyth saw his intent.

"Varen, no!"

But it was too late, and many things happened at once.

Varen spoke a single, sharp word, and his voice sounded like a waterfall. A seam raced along the surface of the ground, and Elyth saw Subo wrap itself around Korush an instant before it reached them. The force struck with the sound of thunder, and a dark spray erupted at the point of impact like a wave breaking on rocks, throwing Korush and his machine some thirty feet, dashing them against the tree line. A broad gash in the earth marked where the Azirim had stood moments before. The ejected earth rained back down and in the torrent there were glints of gunmetal gray. Subo's components, shattered.

She looked back at Varen in horror, paralyzed by the shock of the moment. He was staring at the aftermath of the destruction he had unleashed, mouth open, eyes wide. And when he turned to her, she realized tears were streaming down both of his cheeks. He shook his head, though she couldn't tell if he was trying to communicate that he hadn't meant to do it, or if he was just sorry that it had come to this.

And then a rift in the world opened between them, the ground beneath him gave way, and in the cloud of dust that billowed heavenward, he vanished.

TWENTY

Elyth stood stunned, unable to process all that had happened in only a few short seconds. The ground around her looked as though an errant orbital strike had torn a savage bite out the hillside, the rippling wake of its impact scarring the earth with jagged fractures and buckled crests. Motion drew her eye, and she saw Arbiter Oyuun getting to his knees with effort, as though he'd been shot through the gut. He glanced up at her, face distorted with pain, and waved his hand. Signaling he was okay. Or . . . no, calling her attention to the tree line. She followed the gesture, and the trail of debris and damage snapped together into meaning.

Korush.

She sprinted to the woods and found him crumpled on his side at the base of a tree, amid the scattered remains of the machine that had tried to protect him. The moment she crouched beside him, she knew he was gone. The front plate of his armor warped inward just right of his heart, as though it'd been struck by a powerful hammer stroke, and blood trickled in a thin bright line across his lower lip, along his cheek, and dripped rhythmically from his jawline to the ground. Elyth laid a hand on his shoulder, sorrow withheld only by disbelief. To her shock, he stirred at her touch. His eyes fluttered but did not open.

"Take off his armor," Oyuun called from behind her. "The plate is restricting his breathing."

Elyth scrambled, but she couldn't find any latch, seam, or control to open it up.

"I don't know how!" she answered, but the Arbiter was there a moment later, kneeling next to her. He reached down and shifted Korush slightly, and then the upper portion of the armor unsealed and retracted its connectors from its components. Oyuun lifted the damaged plate off and tossed it aside. Korush gasped deeply with the release, but wheezed and gurgled as the air flowed into his lungs. Beneath his armor, he wore a form-fitting layer like a thick shirt, black in color. Through it, Elyth could see that a portion of his rib cage had been crushed inward where his armor had been. The labored breathing and blood in his mouth told her all she needed to know. There was nothing they could do to save him.

"Wari Korush," Oyuun said. "Wari Korush! Wake up!"

Elyth rocked back on her heels, ice-cold, devastated.

"Wari Korush, your commanding officer needs you!"

Elyth laid a hand on the Arbiter's arm. But as she was starting to draw him back, Korush managed to force his eyes open. They were unfocused, wandering, and after a moment of watching him, she realized he couldn't actually see. The Azirim raised a hand, fumbled at his chest, and then reached to touch the Arbiter's knee, and arm, and then the ground nearby. Not checking his wounds, Elyth saw. Searching for his weapon. She reached over and pulled the chest plate closer, and found the mechanism to release the void-edge from its housing on the armor. Then she took

Korush's hand in hers and gently pressed the sheathed weapon into his palm. His fingers wrapped around it, and he drew his arm back to his chest, over his heart. And though his eyes remained open, she knew he saw nothing as the great, final darkness descended upon him.

An overwhelming sense of cruel injustice rent her spirit then, that this man, of all men, a man so devoted to his Way and to a life of service, this Lion of the Aziri, should fall in such a manner. She hadn't recognized it before, but seeing him so broken on the ground before her revealed how much she'd come to rely on his quiet strength as a sign that all would be well. That somehow, as long as he remained, nothing Qel's Shadow had in store would prevent them from completing their task. And now, he lay with the last seconds of his life seeping into that cursed ground, cast there by the planet through the instrument of Varen's hand.

And in that raw emotion, Elyth refused the reality. Not merely refused to accept it, but rather refused its very existence. Long ago the First House had taught her a technique for speeding the healing of her own body. She had never heard of it being used in an attempt to heal another, nor had it been designed to overcome such devastating trauma as Korush had suffered. But she was beyond all that now, beyond being held at the mercy of Qel's Shadow and whatever forces of destiny seemed to be arrayed against her.

"Arbiter," she said. "Move away."

He looked at her, and then rose to his feet and moved back behind her. She laid her hand on Korush's ruined chest. Initially she focused on the image as she'd been taught, that of snow-laden silvergrass, its blades withered by the cold, its fragile life still clinging within them. But now, instead of tightly controlling her focus and filtering out all emotion, she allowed her complete self to pour into the moment, to drench her innermost being in the flood-waters of her unified heart, mind, and body. And from within that torrent, the Deep Language emerged, anchored by her teaching, translated through her inner voice.

"The deep releases its hold; dawn breaks on a world made new."

Elyth felt the release of power flow through her; dust and debris danced playfully away from her in all directions, as though chased by a spring breeze. But there was no other change. Korush didn't stir; his lifeblood continued its slow drip to the spattered ground.

She sank down on both knees, her feet tucked under her, and waited there for a full minute, willing him to move, or blink, or breathe. Waited until she felt the Arbiter's hand on her shoulder. Her head dropped forward, and she closed her eyes.

"Elyth," Oyuun said kindly.

She knew what he was going to tell her. There was not time enough to mourn, not now. And he was right. But the use of the Deep Language was not without cost, and after the shock of Varen's betrayal, she had no strength left to stand.

"I just need a minute, Arbiter," she said. "To recover."

He didn't answer, and he didn't take his hand from her shoulder. He just stood there behind her, present, silent.

Elyth gathered what strength she could, willed it back into her muscles, demanded their submission to her mind. And when Oyuun squeezed her shoulder, she nodded, opened her eyes, and struggled to rise. But as she did, he caught her arm, preventing her from standing, and spoke again.

"Elyth," he said, but this time there was something else in his voice. He'd moved next to her; she looked up at his face, and then followed his eyes back to Korush.

The Azirim was breathing.

She settled back into a crouch, leaned over Korush, and was astonished to find that the collapsed portion of his rib cage appeared to be whole again. His breathing was deep, but not labored, and though there was still blood in his mouth, it had ceased its dripping. Soon after, his eyes opened, fixed first on the ground, and then roving. He rolled away from her slightly, focusing on her face, obviously confused.

"It's okay, Korush," she said. "We're here. You're okay."

He looked at the surroundings, saw Oyuun, touched his chest where his wound had been, and then gingerly patted his torso, undoubtedly searching for the damage. As he did so, he sat up and looked at her again.

"What did you do?" he asked.

"I used my art," she answered, not knowing how else to describe it.

"No, but . . ." he said. "But what did you do?"

She shook her head, not grasping the intent of his question. Korush pushed her gently away from him and carefully got to his feet, keeping his eyes on her. She stood as well, backing up a few steps to give him space. The void-edge was still in his hand when he took hold of the cuff of a sleeve and gently pulled it up, revealing his forearm. He stared at it for a long moment and then looked back at her.

"What did you do?"

It wasn't until he lifted his protective garment up to reveal his torso that she understood his reaction. The lifelong wounds of his flesh were gone; wherever he looked, his skin was healthy, complete, with no sign of scarring. No trace of his long-suffered condition remained.

But when he looked at her again, his eyes were intense, almost wild.

"I can't feel Subo," he said.

"We lost it," she answered.

He ignored the statement, raised his sheathed weapon, and pointed its hilt at her.

"It would have been kinder to let me die," Korush said, restrained anger obvious in his voice and face. But he glanced down at the void-edge, and after a second or two of staring at it, he breathed a sigh of apparent relief and finally relaxed.

"Forgive me," he said, lowering the weapon back to his side. "I'd feared you'd taken this from me."

"We would never take your weapon, Azirim," Oyuun said.

Korush shook his head.

"I meant my capacity to serve," he said. Elyth recalled then his explanation of his condition, and how curing it would have somehow removed his ability to wield his weapons and remain part of the Aziri. From what she could tell, though, his staggering healing had not interfered after all.

"I can't feel Subo," he repeated.

"Subo tried to protect you," Elyth answered. And he nodded. It hadn't been a question, but rather a statement of acknowledgment that his machine companion was gone.

He glanced around at the surroundings, taking it all in for the first time. When he noticed the front plate of his armor on the ground, he nudged it with his foot. Without remark, Korush released the other components of the upper half of his armor. The rear plating connected directly to a portion on his shoulders, and when he lifted it off, he paused to look at it, and then turned it sideways for the others to see. Where the front plate had buckled inward, the rear plate bulged outward in the same location. Elyth could scarcely imagine what must have happened to his internal organs, and the thought made his recovery all the more miraculous.

Korush placed the components in a pile together on top of the damaged plates. Afterward, he reached into the collar of his shirt and removed a triple-looped necklace that she'd never seen before. When he held it up, though, it tumbled into a single large loop, and she realized it was the strap upon which he kept his void-edge whenever he was out of his armor. He placed it over his shoulder, secured it, and attached the weapon in its rightful place. With that done, he detached the rest of his armor and placed it all together on the ground.

"I should have killed him after the storm," he said flatly. He walked a few feet, crouched down, and picked up a handful of Subo's components off the ground.

"You couldn't have known, Wari Korush," Arbiter Oyuun said. "And any blame should rest on me and me alone. I was the one who insisted on bringing him."

"I knew," Korush replied. "He changed after he went out. I could see it. But I hesitated. And now I have failed in both my duties."

He tipped his palm to the side, letting the segmented pieces pour back onto the ground.

"No one could have done more," Elyth said.

"You could have," he answered. The statement wasn't accusatory, nor did he seem to expect a response. But there was a weight to it nonetheless. He stood again, and crossed back over to where she and Oyuun were.

"And you?" he asked her.

"What about me?"

"You've touched this world, as he did," he said. She understood his concern, but she was taken aback by his response to her. Did he not know what she'd just done for him?

"It's not the same," she said. "Varen opened himself up to it in a way I would not invite."

"How can we be certain?"

She held his gaze.

"Was it not enough that I brought you back from the dead?"

His eyes softened at that, his body relaxed. Uncertainty faded.

And so she had no warning when he launched the attack.

Reflex alone saved her from the strike; she twisted her shoulders and tilted her head just enough to take a grazing blow on her ear instead of the stunning impact it'd been meant to have. But at her dodge, his other hand arced and hooked behind her neck, jerked her forward, and a moment later, he had her locked in a clinch, controlling her head. His knee rocketed up toward her solar plexus; she intercepted it with both forearms just before the impact. When he rechambered his leg, she seized the opportunity, wrapped one arm behind his head and locked his opposite elbow against her body with her other hand. She stepped into him, straightened, and the movement broke his grip and threw the man off-balance.

Elyth clasped her hands together and snatched him backward, taking him to the ground. She knew she'd be no match for the Azirim, strength against raw strength, but she'd not met an opponent outside the First House capable of contending with their system of grappling. Even so, it was a mad scramble between them, and though Korush couldn't break totally free, Elyth found herself exhausting every method and technique she knew to maintain control. No matter what lock or hold she put on him, the man seemed to know every counter and escape and could apply them in an instant. She couldn't understand what had set him off, why any of this was happening.

And all Elyth could think was that she had to control his hands, control both hands at all times, because the moment one got free, his weapon would come out and she would die. But they were so fast and he was so technically gifted, it was clear that no matter how hard she worked to trap them, Korush was capable of matching her effort. It would take only one mistake from her to allow him to get them clear. And there was weakness in her left hand; the two damaged fingers threatened to fail without warning.

The two rolled together, weight and gravity constantly shifting; it almost didn't matter whether the man was above, below, or beside her, all Elyth focused on was catching that next shift, that next twist. But for all the speed of the exchange, she was slowly, slowly working her way toward a position that would be her salvation. If she could just reach it in time, she would be able to lock both of his hands away from his deadly blade and choke him into unconsciousness at the same time.

Her body was so empty, though, so depleted, that she could feel her time rapidly running out. Korush seemed tireless, as though whatever healing she had called forth in him had renewed him to the prime of his youth. Elyth's only advantage was that she knew where she was leading the fight, and he remained fixated on trying to reach his weapon.

He managed to create space to get his head away from her body, and an instant later, he slammed it into her jaw. There wasn't enough force behind it to cause any damage, but the impact jolted her, and he was able to get his shoulder into a dangerous position. She could feel his hand twisting and slipping away. Elyth strove to retain control. In a desperate counter, she rolled their tangled knot over; he ended up on top of her, but the movement threw his balance enough for her to snatch his wrist again just as he was about to pull away.

It cost her all the work she'd put in to achieve that final lock. And more. Though she managed to keep his hands captured tight against her body, she lost control of one of his legs. In that one mistake, Korush swiveled his body in a manner she'd never seen. It was enough for him to sling his elbow; the first attempt caught her on the shoulder, but the second landed full against her ear, momentarily blacking her vision. She felt his hand pop free.

And when it went, it took only a half second for him to gain the leverage he needed. Korush ripped his arm fully away from her, straightened it beyond her reach, crushed down on her with all his weight. But he had to angle his body to get the void-edge clear, and that angle gave her an opening. If she could seize it before his hand made contact with the hilt of the weapon, she could trap him in the motion, fold him up, and snap his neck before he could unsheathe it. It would kill him. She would hate herself for it, but it was his life or hers.

But in the instant between thought and action, the image of his opening attack blinked in her mind; an empty-handed strike. If he'd meant to kill her, why not the void-edge? And that thought triggered another . . . he'd made no attempt to attack her ability to speak. Neither could have been an accident.

She shifted her hips, slackened her grip just enough to ensure she could make the move in the right instant, but delayed, giving

Korush a window to test his reaction. The hesitation erased her scant advantage; if he went for the weapon, only the faster of them would survive.

The void-edge was clear; Korush bent his arm. But stopped, hand open.

Elyth didn't perform the killing technique. But she'd already offered him the only chance she'd give.

She rewrapped her legs to gain control of his, launched him sideways, and when she scrambled to take position, he went slack. She didn't dare relax, in case it was a setup for some counter. But after a moment more of locking him up, she realized he was no longer resisting at all.

When she paused her assault, Korush said something she couldn't quite understand; his voice was thin and distorted by the hold she had him in, and muffled by his own arm trapped over his mouth. Elyth eased the hold, just a little.

"Are you surrendering?" she asked.

"You didn't use your Language," he replied, panting. From the rhythm of the words, she knew he was repeating what he'd said the first time.

"You didn't use your weapon," she answered.

He shook his head as much as he could.

"It is forbidden if there is neither cause nor intent to kill."

Elyth kept him controlled, breathing hard, trying to decide whether or not she should go ahead and choke him out anyway.

"Korush," the Arbiter said with obvious irritation. "There are plenty of other, far more sophisticated ways we could have handled that."

"Far slower too."

"You're lucky she didn't break your neck."

Given the conversation, Elyth finally released her grip, and shoved Korush away from her forcefully with both feet. She rolled up to a sitting position, crossed her legs, and waited there with her arms resting on her knees. Her energy was gone, but she didn't want them to know that.

Korush got to his feet and kept his distance. He was winded, certainly, but otherwise stood there as though nothing unusual had happened.

"Am I supposed to believe you weren't just trying to kill me?" she said.

"If I had wanted to kill you," he answered, "I wouldn't have been foolish enough to take off my armor."

"And what if I had wanted to kill *you*?"

"It seems that my armor wouldn't have helped anyway."

"Did *you* put him up to that?" she asked Oyuun.

"Me? Absolutely not. I'm appalled."

Elyth shook her head, incredulous.

"It isn't wise to test an Advocate of the Voice," she said. "Even an exiled one."

"*Especially* an exiled one, I should think," Oyuun replied. He walked closer to her, offered his hand to help her up. Elyth didn't take it. After a moment, he dropped his hand back to his side.

"I overheard your conversation with Varen yesterday," he said. "About the two of you having work to do together. We weren't sure how to interpret it. After his response this morning . . . you understand our concerns."

"Not well enough, apparently," Elyth answered.

"The method may have been crude," Korush said, "but I am satisfied. If you *do* turn against us now, it will be my third failing, and I deserve whatever fate that would bring."

"I hope it was worth it," the Arbiter said, turning to look at the Azirim. "Wasting all that energy when we have a mountain to climb. And what a terrible way to treat the woman who saved your life. *Returned* it to you, by all the look of it."

Korush squared his shoulders and stood rigidly with his eyes locked on Elyth, holding a pose that had become iconic of the Aziri at guard. The sight of such abrupt and powerful formality in the midst of that place stood stark. And then he bowed deeply, bent nearly double; well beyond the range of proper etiquette, and even humble, personal gratitude. It was very nearly the bow of one offering full submission to the authority of a sovereign. Elyth knew there was no mockery in it, but she didn't know what to make of the gesture. The Azirim returned to his upright position, held it for several seconds, and then relaxed and returned to facing Oyuun.

Elyth looked up at the Arbiter, only now picking out the significance of his words. *We have a mountain to climb*.

"You still intend to head to the tunnels, then," she said.

"Unless you see another path," he answered.

"If one existed, I would certainly be on it," Elyth said. "But what are we going to do about Varen?"

It was hard for her to think of him as the same man she had taken to calling Grief.

"What *can* we do, Elyth?" Oyuun said, turning briefly to look at the ruined hillside. "He's buried under half a mountain, and who knows how deeply?"

"I'm not sure he's dead."

"Neither am I. But if he survived, then he is off on his own path once more. If we're fortunate, he may find his way back to us. If not, he'll show up when and where he chooses. Dead, alive, fortunate or not . . . all I know to do is continue."

She remained seated, taking a few moments to breathe and settle her heart rate.

"Is what he said true?" she asked. "About Deepcutter? About the barrier?"

Oyuun weighed the question a moment, but his eyes suggested genuine consideration rather than any sort of intent to deceive.

"Partially, yes," the Arbiter said. "How much of it is true is still yet to be determined. There does seem to be some sort of . . . we're not even sure what to call it, honestly. *Barrier* seems too strong a word for it in my opinion. Neither *matter* nor *energy* seem appropriate. But you could think of it almost like an atmosphere. Except instead of enveloping a single planet, it appears to wrap around our entire galaxy. And every probe we sent to test it, we lost."

"Varen said it was put there. That implies it's artificial."

"Varen is quicker to imply many things than I'm comfortable with. But *artificial* is a funny word. Artificial. Crafted, not natural," he said, and then he stamped his foot three times. "Not so long ago, I would have refused to entertain the idea that what I'm standing on right now could possibly be artificial."

"But now?"

He chuckled. "Now I'm starting to wonder if there's anything that *isn't.*"

Elyth took a moment to breathe. So much had happened, so many extraordinary events had stacked one on top of the other, that she felt she'd finally become numb to them all. Even looking at the scar in the hillside that Varen had left when he disappeared evoked no response from her now. It was just another thing that had happened, and it felt distant, as though it had all happened to someone else.

She clambered to her feet and looked off at the mountain as she walked slowly over to join the two men. This close to that peak, it seemed to exude a dark energy, and Elyth got the sense that she'd been walking in its shadow ever since the moment they touched down.

"Well . . . artificial or not, that mountain's still waiting for us," she said. "I don't think we need to bother with breaking camp. We'll move faster, and if things go well, we'll have plenty of time to get up there and back before we run out of light."

"I don't suspect we should assume things will go well."

"If that's the case," she replied, "then we won't be needing any of this at all."

The three of them returned to their tiny camp, loaded up their essential gear, and secured the rest. As reluctant as they all were for him to do so, Korush was forced to leave his suit of armor behind. The damage to the center piece had disrupted the assisted movement that made the suit fully mobile, and without its support, the suit was simply too heavy for the journey they had ahead. They found Varen's soft armor laid neatly inside his shelter, though, and after some convincing, Korush eventually agreed to wear it.

When they got underway, leaving the clearing behind made Elyth feel unexpected remorse; they'd done nothing to collect any of Subo's scattered wreckage, and it felt too much to her like leaving the unburied body of a companion behind. Korush seemed unfazed by it, though, and she tried not to let it bother her either. Even so, knowing it had only been a machine didn't reduce her sense of loss or guilt. The number of times she'd witnessed it faithfully guarding and protecting them made it seem more akin to a beloved war hound than a piece of equipment.

And Varen. Varen had died there, too. Whether he'd survived the collapse or not, the man she'd known him to be was dead. Korush's words lingered in her mind, that she could have done more to stop him. Could she have? She'd had plenty of warning. But she'd thought, too, she realized, that she would have had more time. That she would see it before the decision point came, and that she would coax him back, or confront him. She'd waited too long, had kept him at a distance while she focused on the planet. Now, it seemed like she should have done the reverse.

After half an hour of walking, her body fell into its normal rhythm, finally beginning to feel stronger. The physical weariness didn't wear off, but it became easier to bear as the aftereffects of her use of the Deep Language dissipated. She glanced over at Korush, recalling the burst of power that had flowed through her and into his broken body. Its toll had been greater than she'd expected. But then, so had its results.

During the hike to the foot of the mountain, her mind leaped from thought to thought in an endless chain, but as they drew near to their destination, the rugged terrain demanded greater attention and she was grateful to have something seize sole possession of her focus.

They reached the point of ascent before the sun had peaked, and after a few minutes of searching, they started up the best route they could find. The path was narrow, steep, and covered with slatelike chips and debris, and all three of them lost their footing at least once in the first fifty feet. They walked single-file, with Elyth in the lead and Korush guarding the rear, leaving enough room between so that if one of them went down, they'd be less likely to take one of their companions with them. She kept her navigation piece readily accessible and checked it frequently. As many times as they were forced to switch tracks, and zigzag up the slope, it would have been easy to end up above their target. And though the amount of elevation they had to gain wasn't extreme, the amount of fight every step required made the journey much tougher than it otherwise would have been. The temperature worked against them as well, especially in the areas shaded from the sun; the chill passed right through Elyth like a wraith.

By the time they were a quarter way up, they were all grateful to have left much of their gear behind. The path was so steep in spots that they often had to brace themselves with their hands on the ground as they made their way up, and even the lightweight packs shifted enough to complicate their already treacherous footing. As they neared their first thousand feet of elevation, Elyth topped a steep incline and nearly let out a little cry of joy. Just ahead of her, the side of the mountain flattened out in a wide, natural shelf, perhaps twenty yards wide.

The area was in full sunlight, and patches of long grass stirred by the ever-flowing air of the mountain rustled and whispered softly. Compared to the worst sections of the climb, the temperature in the sun felt almost balmy. The three companions crossed onto the surface and without even discussing it, dropped their packs for a much-needed break. From the edge of the shelf, Elyth could look back over much of the ground they'd already covered, and seeing their starting point far below reminded her of just how far they'd come. It was easy to lose sight of progress when all she could see was the next step, and it boosted her spirit to see that their efforts had not all been in vain.

After several minutes, Korush joined her at the overlook, and stood silently at her side for a time, straight as a rod, hands clasped behind his back. Eventually, though, he spoke.

"I think perhaps Varen may have been right about one thing after all," he said. "About Subo."

"That it had a self?" she asked quietly.

He shook his head. "That it shared my soul."

There was still no emotion in his voice, no expression on his face to hint at any feeling of loss or grief. But he stared out over the landscape below with the unfocused eyes of a man seeing not that which was in front of him but rather something within.

"Subo was a good protector," she offered.

"I've been its handler for almost sixteen years," he said, and his mouth drew back with a hint of a smile that faded soon after it appeared. "I wonder if this is what it's like to lose a limb."

They stood together in silence again, Elyth knowing well enough how burdensome unnecessary words could be in the midst of pain.

He closed his eyes and lifted his chin slightly; if she hadn't known better, she'd have thought he was mimicking Varen and his habit of pausing every so often to feel the sun on his face or wind on his cheeks. Korush nodded to himself.

"I have no category for you, Elyth," he said, without opening his eyes. "I had forgotten what it was like to feel something other than pain. I can't decide if you've given me a great gift or placed me under a greater curse."

"I'm afraid I considered neither," she said. "My only thought was that a man of your caliber shouldn't suffer such an end. Though I confess, I don't understand how being released from such suffering could be taken as a curse."

"It's only that I see how much of my life I have missed because of it," he continued, serious now. "My life has been small, focused on enduring each day, on doing the task at hand, on my duty. My service has taken me to many worlds . . . . I have no memory of how the wind felt on any of them."

"Your life has not been small, Wari Korush," she said. "Yours has been spent in noble service. And I doubt there is an Azirim more devoted to your Way."

"I think perhaps I am a coward."

The statement struck her as so patently absurd, she made an involuntary sound of disgust.

"You? The man known among his warrior tribe as the God-breaker?"

"It's easier to be a savior than a leader," Korush said. "To rise to one moment, rather than stand unmoving in the tides of many. Even a would-be savior can fail and yet be honored as a martyr. And that is easiest of all. Easiest of all to be a martyr. Easiest of all, to no longer have to live under the burden of your convictions."

"If *you* are a coward, then your Way must be a harsh standard indeed by which to measure yourself."

"The standard of perfection? Yes. Harsh in that the closer you are to it, the more intolerable imperfections become, however slight they may have appeared before. But that is not a fault of the Way. There is no malice in it, it is simply its nature. And beside it, mine stands judged.

"But in this case, I am not speaking of the Way. I'm merely using whatever measure you hold for yourself."

"Korush, either the air is getting thin or you suffered more damage than we realized. I don't think you know what you're saying."

"I do. It makes you uncomfortable to hear it."

"Mostly because a couple of hours ago I thought you were going to kill me."

"I remained because of a duty. I remained here only because my fear of failing the Aziri outweighed my fear of this place. Fear on fear. But you are under no such obligation. You remained solely because of a commitment you made to yourself alone. If I had known such leaders existed in your House, I would have thought more highly of it."

"I'm no longer of the House," she said. "And I've never been a leader."

"You've been our leader since we arrived."

Elyth didn't know how to respond to Korush's sudden torrent of apparent praise and admiration. But she knew the strength of commitment the Aziri made to speaking the truth. He wouldn't have spoken the words if he hadn't meant them. And now that he had, his mood lightened, as if their weight had burdened him for some time. He reached up and grasped the braid of his beard under his chin, ran his hand down it, then nodded to himself once more. Satsified.

"I'm glad that our brief clash wasn't genuine," he said abruptly.

"So am I," she answered. "If it had been, you would have drawn your weapon, and I'd be dead."

"That is far from certain."

She glanced over at him. He was not a man given to flattery; for him, it was a statement of fact. The Azirim caught her look out of the corner of his eye, and though he didn't turn to her, he did respond.

"I have broken one god in my lifetime," he said. "I don't believe I could do it again."

After that, he turned away from her and strode off. Elyth glanced over her shoulder as he walked toward where they'd left their packs and was surprised to find Arbiter Oyuun standing a few feet away with an oddly amused expression on his face.

"Did you catch all of that?" she asked.

"Enough of it."

"Any chance you can explain it?"

"I suspect there are few who can explain their ways," he said, turning his gaze to Korush. "But between that and the bow he gave you earlier, I do believe you've acquired the adamantine loyalty of the Lion of the Aziri."

Elyth looked again at Korush, but his back was to her as he checked their gear.

"Don't abuse it," Oyuun added.

Korush donned his pack; the Arbiter gave her a slight bow and held out his hand, ushering her to do the same. It was time to move again.

Elyth loaded up and took point, crossing the remainder of the shelf to where it once more narrowed and began its climb up the slope. The paths farther up the mountain grew steeper and trickier to navigate, but thankfully the natural terracing proved to be a repeated feature. Their sizes and shapes varied significantly, and it was never clear what had caused their formation. But they provided welcome and much-needed stopping points as the three continued their ascent.

It was early afternoon when they reached their target elevation. All that remained then was to find a way to navigate across the mountainside to the tunnels, and locate the best entry point. Elyth spotted the first craggy mouth within twenty minutes, and though it was much too narrow for them to access, it served as a good landmark by which they could get bearings on the others.

From that first cave, the side of the mountain curved inward before jutting out sharply again some thousand yards distant. The three of them worked together to identify potential access points on their navigation units, and then divided up the visible regions of the slope among themselves to speed their search. On the devices, four of the openings seemed equally viable; now they just needed to identify which of them had the most accessible approach.

They each scanned their designated portions of the mountain with their monoculars for a few minutes, locating two of the four relatively easily. Either seemed promising, but Oyuun wanted to find the other pair before committing, just in case another proved easier to reach. While they continued to search, Korush grunted and lowered his optic. Elyth glanced over at him; he continued to look across the gap to the distant face with his naked eyes.

"Find something, Korush?" she asked.

He raised the monocular again, adjusted it, stared through it for another half minute. Then without taking his eye from the device, he gestured to her.

"Take a look yourself," he answered.

Elyth stepped closer, and he talked her onto the target, until she found the cave entry he'd been staring at.

"That one looks tough to get to," she said.

"About fifteen feet to the right," he said. "There's a white-barked tree with orange leaves."

She followed his directions, found the tree.

"Okay."

"Now look at the face above it."

Elyth followed the tree up, expecting that when she saw the rocky face of the mountain, he would explain what he'd seen. But when her view reached the point, she realized she'd misinterpreted his words. When he'd said *face*, he hadn't been talking about the side of the mountain, exactly. There was a stony outcropping just above the bright orange leaves of the tree, and it was a near-perfect image of a *human* face.

When she saw it, Elyth's legs drained of all their strength, and she felt her knees buckling. Oyuun caught her arm before she sank to the ground.

"Elyth," he said. "What is it?"

"That's Dmini," she said. "That's the face of my sister."

TWENTY-ONE

Once Elyth had seen the face, it didn't matter that the cave entrance below it was the hardest for them to reach, and no one questioned whether or not they should try for it. All that remained was for her to lead them carefully across and up to it. It took constant effort for her to keep her mind focused on the steps ahead instead of on what they might discover at their destination, to control her pace instead of rushing as fast as her heart demanded she move. The likelihood that any of the members from the first landing team had survived this long on the planet was almost assuredly zero, but Elyth couldn't dispel the hope of it anyway. The thought that one of her former sisters might still be clinging to life, enduring even now despite every sign of doom around her, burned away Elyth's fatigue and drove her onward.

It took another hour for them to reach the final climb up to the cave entrance. That last stretch was only fifty yards or so, but the incline was among the steepest they'd encountered and the first seven or ten yards of the path was more like a seam in the mountain than anything anyone but a particularly brave or stupid mountain goat might want to try to walk along. The ledge was about a foot wide and angled the wrong direction, sloping downward, away from the mountainside. It wasn't a sheer face all the way to the bottom from there, but the several-hundred-foot drop was more than enough to send an icy ripple through what seemed like every one of Elyth's nerve endings.

She didn't hesitate when she reached it, knowing that if she did she might not be able to get started again. She sidestepped onto the narrow shelf, pressed as tight as she could against the rock wall to her left, and shuffled up, careful to keep as much of herself in constant contact with the mountain as possible, jamming her fingers into whatever cracks she could find for extra support.

At the far end of the seam, the surface widened rapidly out to six or seven feet across, and when her leading foot finally reached that point, she scrambled to it and dropped onto her hands and knees, grateful for the vastness of solid ground beneath her. She held there for a moment, savoring the feeling of stability, breathing, and wondering briefly if she had taken even a single breath while she'd made the crossing. When she stood and turned back to signal the others to come across, Oyuun was already halfway to her, and she was surprised at how short the traversal seemed to be from her side. It had certainly felt about a mile long while she'd been on it.

The Arbiter made his way to within a few feet of Elyth, and she reached out a hand, expecting only to help him catch his balance when he transitioned to the flat ground. The gesture turned out to be the thing that saved him.

Just before he reached her, a pop sounded behind him and his rear hand snapped off the wall like he'd touched hot steel, bits of rock flying out of his grasp and tumbling the great distance below. The sudden movement spun him away from the mountain face, and both his pack and weapon swung out over the void. Elyth reflexively caught hold of the top of his shoulder strap and just dropped herself backward, dragging the man along with her. His weight didn't land squarely on her, and from the pull she still felt, she could tell he hadn't made it fully onto the landing. She grabbed at his chest, trying to find anything she could grip, and managed to catch the cross-strap of his pack. Oyuun rocked quickly from side to side, feet kicking, scraping, and scuffling to find purchase anywhere they could.

Finally he lurched toward her, rolled off to a side, and went completely still.

A few seconds later he let out a sharp breath.

"Well," he said. "That would have been disappointing."

The words came out so evenly, with such little passion, that he could have just as easily been commenting on having nearly dropped his dessert to the ground. Whether it was from the understatement or just pure relief, a laugh bubbled up from within Elyth, and she made no attempt to stop it. It had all happened too fast for the terror to hit. Oyuun sat up and chuckled as well.

"I hope I didn't damage you, dear."

Elyth scooted up to sitting, still hiccupping short pairs of laughs. The Arbiter got to his feet before she did, and took her hand to help her up. After he'd done so, he turned back and leaned ever so slightly forward to look over the edge that had nearly claimed him.

"I don't believe I'd like to come back this way," he said.

"I don't believe I want to come this way a first time," Korush said from the opposite side.

"Don't dawdle, Azirim," Oyuun answered. "It'll only make it worse."

Korush took a deep breath and stretched out onto the narrow ledge, keeping his eyes firmly locked on the two of them right up until the moment that he'd reached them safely. They all paused there together, glad to have escaped a catastrophe for once. And then Elyth turned and looked up that final stretch, and the weight of what lay ahead fell once more upon her.

"Almost there," she said, though she didn't know who exactly she was talking to, nor if her words had been meant as an encouragement or a warning.

She resumed the climb, scrambling once more on hands and feet up the slope. The last fifteen yards or so mercifully rolled flatter, and Elyth came up over the rounded top to find another wide shelf, carpeted with moss and clumps of the mountain grass they'd seen elsewhere. It was partially roofed by the mountain face arcing out above it, and on the opposite side, where the edge would have normally dropped off, a thick ridge ran along like a boundary fence, ascending to twenty feet at its highest point. Sunlight filtered through the gap between the ridge and the roof, spilling shadows on either side. And through the middle were features that caused her to stop where she stood.

Between her and the far end of the shelf, twenty or so rocky columns rose from the ground at uneven intervals. Each of them were overgrown with thick vines, and had dark patches where moss or soil had gathered between the stones. They were somewhere between seven and eight feet tall, thin for their height. She'd seen something like them once before; the first time, Elyth had mistaken one for the silhouette of a woman.

"We're this close, let's not stop now," the Arbiter said, coming up behind her. But he stopped at her shoulder, seeing now what had caused her reaction.

"Do you think those are the same as what we encountered in the woods?" she whispered. The similarities were undeniable, but they lacked the distinct humanlike form that those of the forest had possessed. The ones here seemed elongated by comparison, long-limbed, erect along the spine, but more hunched at the top where the head and shoulders of a human would have been. In general, they appeared cruder, like a rough approximation or an early prototype, later refined into the horrors that they'd fought before.

"I hope not," Oyuun answered. "But I see no reason to expect otherwise."

Korush drew up on the other side of Elyth.

"The others were smaller," he said. "Just four of them gave us trouble. And there were more of us then."

They all stood watching for a time, looking for any sign that the masses of earth and stone might animate or somehow be aware of their presence. But all was quiet and still.

"You're sure this is the way?" Oyuun asked.

Elyth gave him a sidelong look before returning her attention to the path ahead. The shelf was narrower and far longer than the others they'd encountered, a hundred feet or so. At the far end, the slope resumed its rise, sharper there, with large, towering rocks embedded within it. If there was a path up that didn't demand climbing, it wasn't apparent from where they stood. But at the end of the shelf, twenty feet up, the cave mouth awaited them.

Elyth spotted the orange-leafed tree peeking over the ridge, and she followed it to where she'd seen Dmini's image etched into the mountainside. It took her several seconds to locate the outcropping.

From her vantage point, though, it was difficult to discern any features that stood out as unnatural. Either the mountain had shifted, or the image had been crafted to be viewed specifically from a certain angle. Neither possibility struck her as encouraging.

"I don't suppose there's another way," Korush said.

"Only if we were coming from the other side of the mountain," Elyth answered.

Elyth looked once more across the shelf to the climb leading up to the cave mouth. The only way to reach it was to pass among the columns, and they were hemmed in on either side by walls of stone, forming a gauntlet.

"We didn't hear any of that terrible knocking," the Arbiter said. "Maybe these have been here for a long time."

"Or at least since the first team came through," Elyth said.

The strange structures were mostly on the nearer end of the shelf. If she could make it all the way past them, there would be a fair amount of space separating her from them during the climb. Even if they did wake up or come to life or whatever it was they did, she was confident she could make it up to the cave entrance before they could reach her. She wasn't sure what she would do if they could climb, but she really didn't see any other choice.

"I'll go," she said. "I'm a good climber, I can make it quickly."

"If those things wake up, you won't make it at all," Korush said.

"And if we all go, we'll be trapped," she countered. "At least this way if things go wrong, you can fall back across that narrow ledge."

"We go together or no one does," Korush said. Elyth looked to the Arbiter for support, but she found none there. He already had his rifle unslung.

"Then what's the plan?" Elyth asked. "Fast or slow?"

"Slow," Oyuun said. "In our previous encounter, none of them moved until you made contact with one. With any luck, we'll slip through unnoticed."

"And with no luck?" Korush said.

"I suppose we'll try fast."

Korush grunted.

"I'll still go first," Elyth said. And she took quiet steps forward before either of the others made any reply.

The first column stood ten feet ahead, and as she approached it, she saw that she'd been mistaken to think they lacked the same level of refinement as the others. Just as before, the creations showed uncanny design, reflecting a disturbingly human physiological structure mapped out in earth, plant, and stone. And she realized she'd only considered them crude because she'd assumed they'd been meant to reflect the human form. Now, seeing one from a different angle, she recognized two forms merged into one: the first, Sardis's long features and strict posture; the second, Subo's rounded, humanoid shape. However long these columns had stood, they'd undoubtedly been shaped after her team's arrival.

Elyth kept her eyes focused on the structure as she crept silently by, ready to dodge away at the first sign of motion. Once she made it several feet past it, she paused, waiting, attentive, to see if her proximity had triggered any reaction. But there was nothing. She continued forward, weaving her way among the others, approaching no closer than absolutely required with soft and certain steps.

Though they didn't appear to be arranged in any particular pattern, the columns stood roughly in four rows. As she crossed through the second row, she glanced back to see that Oyuun had begun to follow after her, along the same line that she'd taken. Elyth returned her attention forward, and picked her way across the shelf. The final crooked row of columns had five of the structures, scattered in a loose cluster. She was just passing among the first of them when Korush spoke from behind her.

His voice was calm, even, but clear and direct.

"Run."

Elyth didn't pause or look behind. She just broke into a run, bounding as quickly as the uneven, unyielding terrain allowed, and crossing the last fifty feet in a matter of seconds. When she reached the rock face, it was as she'd anticipated. The only way up to the cave was to climb. She turned back just as Oyuun arrived, and Korush was close on his heels.

"Go," Korush said. "Climb."

"They're coming?" she asked.

He nodded sharply, looking back over his shoulder at the columns. Elyth glanced at them, and though none of them seemed any closer, two had unmistakably changed shape.

She turned back and found two good handholds before starting up the wall. It wasn't the most technical climb she'd ever faced, but her damaged hand and the pressure of pursuit complicated the matter. Even so, she was the first to reach the top; she dragged herself over the lip and into the tunnel opening.

Elyth scrambled up to a crouch, turned back around to lend the Arbiter a hand; he was only a couple of feet from the top, and as soon as he could reach her, they locked hands and she helped pull him up and over the edge. He moved into the mouth of the tunnel, rifle up. She heard him flick a toggle on the weapon, and two thin cylinders ejected from it, one to each side. They hovered two feet from the muzzle, pouring blue-white light down into the darkness ahead.

"Go," she said. "Right behind you."

The Arbiter moved into the tunnel with quick but precise steps, hunched over his weapon. Elyth swiveled back to help Korush clear the last few feet. But he wasn't on the wall.

She looked down to the shelf and found him standing there, twenty yards from the climb, looking up at her. When she made eye contact with him, he gave her a curt nod, acknowledging that she and the Arbiter had made it safely to the top. And then he turned away, to face the waking horrors. Alone.

"Korush!" she called. But he didn't respond. He just held his ground, stance relaxed, hands at his side. The first of the creatures emerged from the group, with long, slow strides, articulated like the many-jointed legs of a spider.

"Wari Korush!" Elyth called again.

He looked back at her then, and smiled, full, genuine.

"Easiest of all."

His gaze lingered for only a moment and then turned to face the stirring constructs.

And in a motion almost too fast to follow, Wari Korush whipped the void-edge from its sheath and held it out horizontally to one side, arm fully extended.

An instant later, the stubby blade unfurled, flowing fluidly into a long, elegant, single-edged sword. The motion of the blade was immediately familiar; it was the same as the reshaping of Subo. When it had fully deployed, Korush brought the blade around and over his head in a slow circle, and then snapped it with precision into its initial position. He repeated the same movement twice more; a ritual, or a salute to his enemies. And then he did the same a final time, but at speed, and the blade flowed with the motion. It sang a clear, thin tone as it stretched, arced around him, trailed through the air like ink from a brush, and then snapped back into its bladed form.

The first construct reached within fifteen feet of him a few seconds later. Korush angled his body, drew the weapon back and in close, blade toward the creature as though he were going to stab it, then dropped his weight backward in a partial crouch, preparing to deliver the strike. Elyth tensed. The construct had greater reach; Korush's timing would have to be perfect.

But before the creature took a second step, the Azirim lunged forward and shot his arm out. The void-edge sang as its blade stretched, streaking toward the construct's torso and passing through it as though it were a mist. With two quick motions, Korush sent a wave flowing along the blade, first vertically, then horizontally. The fluid edge bisected the creature in both directions, before retracting like a lightning strike in reverse. Four large chunks broke away from the top half of the monstrosity, crumbling on impact with the ground. The legs were still connected to a central portion, and took two more steps forward. Korush slashed the air; once more the void-edge lashed out, passing through both stony legs. The remaining structure collapsed ten feet from him.

Elyth had thought the Azirim was making a foolish sacrifice; now, it seemed like he might actually be a stalwart rear guard. She just hoped this wasn't his last stand.

Two more of the constructs were closing in on Korush when Oyuun grabbed her shoulder and pulled her roughly into the tunnel.

"First ten yards or so are clear," he said, half dragging her along beside him until she got fully turned around. His twin lights held steady, showing the way despite the bouncing of his muzzle as he jogged. Elyth kept pace, trying to get her bearings as they moved.

The tunnel surfaces weren't smooth, exactly, but they had a certain regularity of shape instead of the jagged, fractal composition she would have expected. Height and width ebbed and flowed, but those, too, seemed to hold within some invisible metric. After thirty yards of travel or so, Elyth's impression of the tunnel was that they were running down a course left by the root system of some titanic tree.

They reached a branch, and Oyuun stopped and grabbed her arm. At first she thought he was going to say they needed to split up, but what he actually said made her feel even worse.

"You go on from here," he said. He was shoving something into her hands. "Take this. You've got the dragonflies?"

She was still trying to process his first words; the question didn't register.

"What?"

"The dragonflies. Captain Ames's drones. You have them?"

"Yes," she answered. "Yeah, I've got them."

"Sync them with this, they'll get you there and back."

"Where are you going?"

"To help keep the Godbreaker alive, if possible," he said. "And if not . . . to buy you what little more time I can."

"Arbiter—"

"Do what you do, Elyth," he said, already drawing away from her. "And maybe we'll make it yet."

He was backpedaling, keeping his companion lights shining on her while he went, and she realized he was doing it so she could deploy the dragonflies. She reached back and pulled the egg-shaped device off the side of her pack, and held it next to the device Oyuun had so hastily given her; she saw now it was a bulkier navigation unit, running some additional sensor suite she didn't recognize. A single blue light appeared at the top of the dragonfly bundle and then switched green. She'd operated similar drones before; green usually meant good to go, and though she'd never used dragonflies specifically, she remembered how Ames had deployed them. She popped the flat end against her leg, but instead of throwing the bundle aside, she held it up and opened her palm.

The egg fell open like a flower blossoming, six individual pieces separating and tumbling from her hand. They didn't drop far. With a pleasant hum, the dragonflies oriented themselves and moved into formation. Rather than running three on each side of her, though, five moved ahead of her in a fan, each projecting light at slightly different angles to create a wide beam. The sixth floated over her head and stationed itself above and slightly behind her, facing the opposite direction, casting a dim light down on her and sending out a second, more powerful beam to helpfully light the way she'd come.

As soon as that last drone was in place, Oyuun's lights flipped away from her and quickly disappeared. Had it not been for the quiet hum of the dragonflies, the abrupt sense of isolation might have been overwhelming. She'd operated on her own for her entire time in the House, and for security had kept to herself in her exile. It was only now that she realized she hadn't been alone since she stepped foot on Qel's Shadow. The absence of the others felt nearly tangible, and for a moment, she wondered how she'd managed to go so long on her own before.

Elyth turned toward the leading dragonflies and looked at the nav unit the Arbiter had given her. It was locked onto a subsurface location, but the radius of the marked area was larger than she'd expected. He hadn't pinpointed the source. She was going to have to search for it.

With a deep, settling breath, Elyth attached the nav unit to one of the straps on her pack and then looked down the long tunnel that awaited her. Qel's Shadow had thrown so many shocks and horrors at them on the surface, it was hard to imagine anything worse could be under it. But that didn't stop her mind from trying.

But Korush and Oyuun were out there fighting for their lives. Or rather, fighting for hers. Whatever was waiting for her down here, she'd meet it head-on, at full speed. She reached up and pressed two fingers against her collarbone, deploying her armor's helmet, and before it'd even finished unfolding, she began her descent.

The early section of the tunnel system proved easy enough to navigate that Elyth was able to move through it at a quick pace; it took her only about fifteen minutes to reach the perimeter of the Arbiter's search area. He'd already marked up the nav unit's display with grids and an optimized path, so at least she didn't have to concern herself with getting lost or backtracking. The main issue now, though, was simply that she had no idea what she was looking for.

She followed Oyuun's planned route, trailing behind the dragonflies as they faithfully guided her along, and after another ten minutes, she suddenly felt as though she'd crossed a threshold. Nothing obvious had changed; the tunnel continued on just as it had before, the dragonflies hummed gently and flooded the way ahead with light. But Elyth stopped nonetheless, to take stock.

For a full minute, she remained there, searching her senses

and her inner self to identify what exactly it was she felt, and all the while the mysterious reaction crept like dusk's shadows across her heart and mind. When she finally captured the sensation, it seemed to rush upon her then in all its strength, and she could neither deny nor escape it.

It was a presence. The sense that some other being was there with her in the darkness. But not any sort of presence she'd ever encountered before. It had both an unfathomable depth and an overwhelming proximity all at once, as though she were standing at the edge of the highest cliff above the deepest canyon with nothing to cling to. A terrible awe fell over her then, a dangerous, mind-paralyzing awe, without any source or focal point.

And her immediate thought was that the mountain itself had become aware of her.

Elyth felt her training rising to her rescue, could sense it as though the presence had slowed even the speed of her perception. She had been trained to stand before the infinite potential of the cosmos; not just trained, had done so, many times. Whatever it was that she now confronted was less than nothing compared to that all-consuming paradox that contained nothing and everything all at once.

The shift in perspective helped force back the dread that had threatened to overpower her. It was still there, crouching all around her, but she'd gained the strength she needed to move forward.

And twenty feet farther down the tunnel, it was like she'd crossed into an entirely different mountain. Both the size and shape of the tunnel changed abruptly, and appeared as though it'd been twisted at a bizarre angle. She had to clamber through a narrow passage to continue, and from that point on the whole system shared the same properties. It was almost like the interior of the mountain had here been crumpled and compressed. Once Elyth had that thought, she realized it was quite possible that was exactly what had occurred.

She pressed on, and the deeper she went, the greater the weight of the presence became. It was ancient, numinous, and seemed to make the darkness itself dense like heavy smoke or thick incense burning in a sacrificial hall. Though she couldn't see how it would be possible, even the dragonflies seemed affected by it; to her eyes, their beams fell shorter and shorter, until it appeared to her that their light could not even escape its own housing.

Finally, the oppression became so intense she could bear it no longer; it overwhelmed her, and forced her to her knees. Even her will, forged in the refining fire of the First House, was no longer sufficient to raise her back to her feet.

Above her, Korush and Arbiter Oyuun had most likely given their lives just to get her to that point. And the sisters of her House. And her former sovereign. How many of them had attempted to solve the riddle of Qel's Shadow and fallen before it?

She knew she couldn't stand under that terrible presence.

But she had strength enough still to crawl.

She bent forward onto her hands, pulled herself through that crushing, dreadful awe, one hand's breadth at a time. It was all she could manage. But she would give all she had.

And after seemingly interminable effort, she at last broke through. Almost literally. At the sudden release, she pitched forward, through an opening into what felt like the purest, freshest air she'd ever breathed. The dragonflies fanned out again, their light shining forth and illuminating a chamber with a high, rugged, but gently curving ceiling that appeared to have been naturally formed.

Elyth fully expected to find herself too exhausted to stand, but when she tried anyway, she discovered she still had strength in her body. Emotionally and mentally, however, she felt raw and depleted. If there was something important she was meant to find in the chamber, she hoped it would be obvious. She didn't have enough left in her to do much more than wander around.

She walked carefully into the chamber, and gestured to the dragonflies, signaling for them to push outward and automatically perform a survey of what proved to be the first portion of a fairly wide cavern. There was no sign of water nor any life of any kind. She reached up and tapped her collarbone, retracting the helmet so she could get a more complete sense of the environment. With quiet steps, she moved along the edge of the space, scanning the floor and walls, evaluating it. But nothing stood out to her as unusual. The strangeness of the approach to the chamber magnified just how unremarkable the chamber itself appeared to be.

The dragonflies returned and gathered in a circle about eight feet above her, and hovered there, their collective light pooling down around her. She looked up at them, curious. She'd not given them any command to take such a formation.

She turned in a slow circle, looking at the nearest cavern wall, wondering if they'd detected something up there she was supposed to notice. But from what she could see, there was nothing of interest there either.

When she looked back down, however, a paralyzing shock wave ripped through her body; just at the edge of the ring of light, a ghostly, familiar face was peering back at her.

"Elyth," the Paragon said, her voice fragile, cracking. "I knew you'd come."

TWENTY-TWO

Elyth collapsed to her knees, trembling, voiceless, her mind blank and numb, uncomprehending. Surely it was a hallucination, or a vision.

The ancient woman was mostly laying on her side, though she'd pushed herself up with her arms, looking as though she were trying to recover from a fall. Her thin gray hair was stringy, tangled, and matted, and she seemed much smaller than Elyth remembered her.

"Brightest of daughters," the Paragon said. And then she lowered herself back to the floor of the cavern again. "Deepest of regrets."

Elyth opened her mouth, but no words would come forth, and she just shook her head uselessly.

"I'm sorry for the shock," the ancient woman said. "I could think of no way to announce myself that wouldn't have had the same effect."

"Illumined Mother," Elyth heard herself say. She'd not uttered those words since some time before her exile, but they tumbled out almost of their own volition.

"I know you never expected to see me again, child. Though when last we saw each other, if you had known this was the condition in which you would find me, I suspect it might have brought you some measure of joy."

Elyth shook her head again, but this time in actual response.

"No, Paragon," she said, finally in command of her voice again. "No, I never would have wished for this."

She pushed herself up to her feet, still shaken by the encounter, but strong enough to cross over and kneel next to the matriarch of the First House.

"Are you injured?"

The Paragon let out a brittle chuckle. "Not physically. The rest of me . . . is another matter."

Elyth stared at her, at a complete loss of what to do or say. So many questions cascaded through her mind that she couldn't grab hold of even one.

"You made it just in time," she said. "But only *just*, I fear."

How long the woman had been down here, Elyth had no idea; she had no equipment, no supplies, nothing on her other than her blue-gray operations suit, and that was filthy and torn. Elyth unslung her pack, pulled out a canister of water, and bent to help the Paragon drink, but the woman lifted her hand to refuse the aid. There wasn't really anything the ancient woman could do to prevent Elyth from helping her; Elyth slid her arm under the Paragon's shoulders and gently raised her up, cradling her head against her shoulder. Elyth was shocked at how light she was, and how frail.

"Drink something," she said.

The Paragon lay against her, unmoving.

"Paragon, you must drink," Elyth said. "At the very least, so that I may say I did everything I could to save you."

The woman chuckled again.

"Very well," she said. "But you mustn't reveal to any of them that I willingly accepted aid from an exile."

"As an exile, I'm under no obligation to acquiesce to your wishes, Paragon," Elyth said. And she raised the water to the Paragon's lips, holding both the canister and the woman steady while she took two feeble sips.

"No," the Paragon said when Elyth lowered the water. "But you could at least humor an old woman's last wishes."

"What are you doing down here?" Elyth asked.

"The same thing you are, I suspect . . . my best."

"And the team you brought with you?"

The Paragon shook her head weakly.

"I lost them," she said. "All of them. I lost my daughters."

Elyth had known that would be her answer, had thought she'd prepared herself to hear it. Yet once the words were spoken, she felt them as a more substantial reality, as though they alone had transformed the possibility into actuality, and only now had forever closed the door on any other outcome. The loss cut her deeply, despite her expectation. And though she and the Paragon had parted as enemies, in that moment they were united in sorrow; each the only one who could comprehend the depth of the other's pain. Elyth knew nothing else to do, other than to hug the Paragon closer, to draw comfort from and offer it to the matriarch.

"Come now," the Paragon eventually said. "All this will be in vain if we sit here in our grief for much longer. I have discovered many things about this place. Information you will need to carry back with you."

Holding that wight of a woman in her arms and hearing the frailty of her voice rent Elyth's spirit with savage despair. Even at her lowest points, when she'd tried to command herself to accept that the Paragon was gone, she'd pictured the ancient matriarch standing in all her glorious, terrible power, and falling in one broken instant before some incomprehensible force. To find her here, withered, the spirit that once seemed vast and unbreakable reduced to little more than shadow and mist, struck Elyth as a final, intolerable cruelty. The Paragon had stood as the truest example of *sareth hanaan*, the highest ideal of First House doctrine, the living embodiment of wise, quiet action and unyielding endurance. Though Elyth had left that House behind, she realized that she'd never truly left its path; even now, she found herself still in pursuit of *sareth hanaan*.

And the fading of the Paragon seemed to her to be the dissolution of the First House, and all that it exalted, and all that it upheld. The collapse of the First House would be the collapse of the Ascendance itself.

To come so far, to withstand all that Qel's Shadow had thrown at them, only to witness the death of that ancient House was more than Elyth could bear.

No. More than she would allow.

"Listen now," the Paragon said.

"No," Elyth said.

"Elyth . . . you must hear me—"

"No," Elyth repeated. "I didn't allow the Hezra to drag me all this way just to be your messenger girl."

She gently laid the woman down again, and then stood and donned her pack, cinching it up tight. She gestured to the dragonflies, and they resumed their previous formation around her. The Paragon looked up at her, bewildered.

"Elyth, please."

EVERY STAR A SONG 373

"I'm not abandoning you, Paragon," she said. And then she knelt, cradled the woman like a child, and lifted her up off the ground. The Paragon was alarmingly light; in other circumstances she would have been easy to carry. Getting her back through the tunnels, though, after all Elyth had already suffered, was going to be a test of Elyth's true limits.

"Elyth, don't be foolish. My time is done."

"Well, mine is precious, so you'll have to talk on the way."

Elyth carried the Paragon back to the opening where she'd entered and paused there. She'd barely managed to pass through whatever force had bent itself against her the first time. The memory of it, inexplicable as it was, made her reluctant to go back in. And beyond that, what further horrors would she be forced to confront? Even if she managed to make it all the way out of the network of tunnels, all she was likely to find was the ruined bodies of her companions and an insurmountable number of monstrous abominations arrayed against her.

But it was her nature to take the next step, even knowing the one after that might prove impossible. And so she stepped once more into that awful tunnel, embracing the psychic pain she knew would at once envelop her in its oppressive cloud.

Only it didn't.

Whatever threshold she'd crossed over before must have been farther from the chamber entrance than she'd realized. She steeled herself once more and took another step. And once more felt no resistance.

For each foot of distance she gained back up the tunnel, Elyth gained a degree of confidence, until eventually she was able to convince herself that whatever presence had attempted to dominate her before had fled once she reached the chamber. And though part of her mind carried the idea that it might return at any moment, she kept it at bay by focusing herself on navigating the difficult tunnels with the fragile Paragon in her arms.

Despite the matriarch's insistence that she was moments from death and had critical information to reveal before she went, she remained silent through the difficult journey. It turned out to be a good thing; Elyth wouldn't have been able to understand or remember anything she said anyway. Light as she was, she wasn't weightless, and carrying her through the tunnel system took its toll on Elyth's body. Combined with the effects she'd suffered from her encounter with the force beneath the mountain, Elyth started losing faith that she was going to be able to make it. By the time they reached the point of transition from the compressed tunnels into the rounded, easier system, Elyth's legs and back burned white-hot with fatigue. She considered dumping her pack, knowing any weight she could shed would help; but to do so, she'd have to set the Paragon down, and if she did that, she knew she'd never be able to pick the woman up again. So Elyth pushed on, refusing to look at the nav unit clipped to her pack, for fear that seeing how much farther it was to the surface would steal her resolve. She thought of nothing more than just following the dragonflies as they led her onward, and upward, step after step.

When she first saw the light growing ahead of her, hope sprung in her heart. Her first thought was that she must have lost all sense of time and distance; the trip back seemed much shorter than the journey in had been. But when she glanced at the nav unit, her heart fell. She hadn't even made it halfway.

Involuntarily, she stopped. The soft glow ahead was fuzzy, shifting. And Elyth realized she was losing consciousness. As she stood there, swaying but refusing to fall, the strength of the light grew and grew, until finally it became dazzling.

And then a voice called from within it.

"Elyth!"

A man's voice. The Arbiter. Arbiter Oyuun. He was still alive. And he'd come looking for her.

He ran to her and, without question or statement, slung his rifle and took the Paragon in his arms. He stood looking at Elyth for a moment, concern obvious on his face.

"I'll come back for you," he said.

She was too spent to speak, her mind too numbed to find words, but she shook her head. And commanded her body to move.

At her first step, Oyuun turned and headed back up the tunnel, and though he got ahead of her, he glanced back every few seconds to make sure he hadn't lost her. After what seemed like a full hour of trudging along an unchanging corridor in an ethereal fog, Elyth became aware of a change in temperature. A few minutes later, they were coming out of the mouth of the tunnel, onto the small ledge overlooking the shelf.

Down below, the rocky shelf was strewn with shattered stone mixed with earth and vine, the broken remnants of some unknown number of the constructs. There were too many pieces covering too much ground for Elyth to tell for certain how many of the creatures Korush had managed to cut down. He was nowhere to be seen.

She wondered how he had finally died. If the creatures had caught him and crushed him into oblivion, or torn him to pieces, or thrown him from the mountain entirely. Before she could ask the Arbiter, though, a rumble of thunder rolled across the mountain. Another storm coming, she thought, to smash down upon them. At least they could seek shelter in the tunnel this time.

The thunder continued on for too long, though, far too long for a single peal, no matter how severe the storm. And then the sound broke open in the sky just beyond the mountain, and at last Elyth realized it was the sound of a ship's engines. The shuttle. Somehow the shuttle was slowing to a hover, and extending its boarding ramp to the ledge at the tunnel entrance.

The hatch opened, and Korush was there. Bloodied, bruised, left arm wrapped and in a sling. But alive. Oyuun turned and nodded for Elyth to board first, and she staggered up the ramp scarcely able to grasp all that was happening.

Korush caught hold of her upper arm as soon as she was close enough and guided her to a seat in the middle of the shuttle, and then left her to help the Arbiter get the Paragon aboard. Nyeda appeared from the front, a kind smile on her face, tears in her eyes as she looked on Elyth. But when Oyuun came through the hatch and she saw the Paragon in his arms, she let out a cry of indeterminate emotion.

"She's still hanging on," the Arbiter said. "Help me get her to the med bay."

Nyeda didn't react, just stood there staring at the frail woman in his arms.

"Nyeda!" he barked. "Med bay!"

The sharpness of his voice broke through and stirred her to action. She nearly leaped into the medical bay; Oyuun followed close behind her. From her seat, Elyth caught sight of the single med bay bed and saw it empty. Her heart dropped at that, realizing that Captain Ames must not have made it.

She heard the hatch closing behind her; Korush stepped up next to her and touched her shoulder with light fingertips. Elyth looked up at him, saw how drained of color his face was, how flecked it was with small but deep gashes sealed over with medical gel.

"Korush," she said. "After all I did to fix you up, and now look at you."

"Did you find what you were looking for?" he asked.

She shook her head.

"No," she said. "But we might have found what we needed."

His brow furrowed slightly, but he nodded. And then Elyth realized that he was standing in front of her, and Nyeda and Oyuun were in the med bay.

"Korush," she said. "Who's flying the ship?"

"I am," Ames said from the front, his words partially slurred. He leaned around his seat just enough to look back at her with one eye; she could tell from his profile that his face was swollen, and there were bandages running both up under his jaw and over the top of his head. But he did his best to give her a little smile, before he winced in pain.

"Gah, it still kills to turn around," he said, slowly rotating himself back to face forward.

"And if you keep doing it, you'll tear the grafts," Korush admonished, his tone suggesting it wasn't the first time he'd said it.

"What are you doing up there?" Elyth asked.

"Piloting," he said.

"Don't worry," Korush said, in a mock lowered voice, still projected for the captain to hear. "Nyeda's been doing the actual flying. We just let him sit there when it's on auto."

"Keeps me from feeling useless," Ames called back. Despite the difficulty he was having speaking clearly, it was obvious he wasn't letting his injuries dampen his spirits. "And I *do* hate to feel useless. But hey, at least my trigger finger still works."

Korush chuckled at that.

"I thought I had already adequately expressed my gratitude, Captain Ames," he said. "But if not, I remain in your debt."

Ames gave Korush a thumbs-up.

"Truth be told, I was looking for Varen," he said. "Lucky for you, you were wearing his gear."

The shuttle shifted a moment later, accelerated gently, and pulled away from the mountain.

"Don't tell Nyeda," the captain said. "I just want to see if I can keep from crashing this time."

"Where are we going?" Elyth asked.

"Base camp," Korush told her. "Assuming it's still there."

Elyth nodded, and the movement made her head swim.

"Rest," Korush said. "You've done enough today."

She was too exhausted to argue.

Their base camp was still intact and appeared completely untouched since they'd left it. The medical facility there was little more than a field hospital but seemed state-of-the-art compared to the shuttle's tiny med bay. As soon as they touched down, they moved the Paragon into an isolation room in the facility, and got her hooked up to what seemed to Elyth like one of everything. Oyuun took charge of Elyth next, and despite her insistence that she was fine, put her through a battery of diagnostics to ensure her vitals were stable and not at risk of sudden collapse.

In fact, everyone got some sort of treatment, Ames the second-most with Korush close behind. Nyeda was the only exception, who refused to do anything other than attend the Paragon to keep constant watch over her. Once she'd passed her diagnostics,

Elyth, too, tried to stay with Nyeda and the Paragon. But when Arbiter Oyuun discovered her there, he did everything he could to force her out of the facility. Elyth eventually relented and allowed him to order her to sleep and recover from her ordeal, right after she made him promise to come get her the moment the Paragon was stable enough to talk to.

It was ten hours later that Nyeda woke her. The two women walked together to the medical facility, and Elyth was surprised to find Oyunn already in the isolation room. When she and Nyeda entered, it was obvious that he'd been there for a while, and that the Paragon had been talking with him for quite some time. He had a workstation set up, with a number of displays in orbit around it, and was sitting with his face only a few inches from one, engrossed in his work. Korush stood quietly in one corner; he glanced at the women when they came in but said nothing.

"Arbiter," Elyth said, "you promised *the moment* she was stable."

At her words, Oyuun turned his head toward her in what seemed like slow motion, his eyes lingering on the display until the last possible moment, as though bonded to the figures projected there. When his gaze finally fell on her, it was like he'd never seen her before; it took several seconds for him to make the journey from his distant land of pure abstraction back to the physical world. Elyth was sure he hadn't heard anything she'd said, but when his mind at last returned, he smiled and answered her.

"Indeed I did, dear. I *am* sorry," he said, though he clearly wasn't. "Just got wrapped up in my work here. Fortunately, I imagine there was no harm in you getting the extra rest. And you haven't missed anything. The great Paragon of the First House has merely been educating this poor man on the most basic of fundamentals."

The Paragon was propped up in a semi-reclined position and though she looked better than she had when Elyth had found her, she still seemed like she could slip away within the hour. Her hands were clasped in front of her, almost skeletal; her skin was sunken and gray-tinted. But when Elyth locked eyes with the woman, she saw the ancient fire burning there once more, and her initial opinion changed. If death were planning to take the Paragon anytime soon, it would likely need to bring friends.

Even so, that deep well of strength and wisdom was tinged with a foreign quality. Gone was her inscrutable certainty, and the sense that she knew far more than she'd revealed. Instead, her inner being seemed saturated with sorrow; a hopelessness not for herself, but rather for the future.

"Nyeda," the Paragon said, her voice stronger than seemed possible for that frame. She held Elyth's gaze for a moment longer, before turning her attention to Nyeda. "Mighty and faithful Nyeda. I know it hurt you to be denied a place in the first part of our mission. But do you see now the wisdom in it?"

Nyeda bowed her head.

"Yes, Paragon."

"Do not be troubled. Had you been here with me, the outcome would have been the same; only it would have been you that I lost, instead of Umarai. And only *you* could have done what you've done."

"Thank you, Illumined Mother. Your kindness is limitless."

"No one other than you," the Paragon continued, her gaze piercing deeply into Nyeda's. "You have been precisely where you needed to be, doing what you and you alone could do."

Nyeda held the woman's look for as long as she could, but when the tears arose, she closed her eyes and bowed her head. And in that moment, Elyth saw at last the guilt Nyeda had been carrying break off her, and the quiet tears she wept were of relief, and a much-needed release of pain. Elyth turned toward her, laid her hand on her sister's back; Nyeda reached out and took her other hand in her own, held it for a span.

"And you," the Paragon said, returning to Elyth. "The Arbiter here has been speaking quite thoroughly about your actions in support of the mission."

Nyeda squeezed Elyth's hand, released it, and gave her a little nod. Elyth turned and met the Paragon's sharp, unblinking stare.

"Clearly I am fortunate that you chose to accept this operation," the woman added.

"As though you had nothing to do with it," Elyth answered.

"How could I have? I was already here."

She smiled thinly.

"In our last meeting, Paragon," Elyth said, "did I perhaps fail to articulate my feelings about your intrigues? If so, I'd be happy to recount them for you."

"No, no, you made your thoughts on such matters quite plain to me. But mine is a higher duty, and at times the plans of the House must reach out to make use of even the most unwilling of instruments."

"I may have been willing, had I been approached in a more forthright manner."

"*May have been.* But it appears you have nevertheless been useful, and therefore the method by which you were employed is now irrelevant. Arbiter Oyuun tells me you were the one to discern the technological nature of this place."

"I guessed it was a ship, yes."

"Not a ship," the Paragon corrected. "A weapon."

Elyth reacted to the shift in terminology. *Ship* could have meant many uses; *weapon* implied Qel's Shadow had been formed with single intent. Despite her insistence that it needed to be destroyed, the reflexive response revealed how she had yet been clinging to subconscious hope that some other purpose for it might still be discovered. Varen's lingering influence, perhaps, though she'd not noticed it before.

"I know you may find this difficult to believe," the Paragon continued, "but there *are* some things in this universe I take even more seriously than the dance of the Ascendance. Seriously enough, in fact, to set aside past differences, no matter how great. And to form alliances," she said, eyes flicking momentarily to the Arbiter, "no matter how tenuous. After all, there can be no dance if there is no Ascendance."

At the Paragon's last statement, Nyeda looked up. "Is that truly what we're facing, Illumined Mother?"

"It is the role of the First House to consider all possibilities, child. It is what brought me here, to study this place for myself."

"And having studied it," Elyth said, "you believe it remains a possibility."

The Paragon shook her head. "A certainty."

"Then we've been right all along. We have no choice but to destroy it."

"We have no choice at all," the Paragon said. And then she added a statement that Elyth never imagined she would hear uttered by that great woman.

"It is beyond us."

The Paragon's quiet declaration thundered as a sentence of

death, issued by the last and greatest judge. There was no sorrow in her voice, no sense of despair. She was merely stating a fact, confirming a truth none of them wanted to accept. And with her words, a heaviness settled in the room, a finality that robbed all hope of victory over Qel's Shadow. The ancient matriarch of the First House was not one to readily allow defeat nor to relent, no matter how long or how much she needed to endure in order to prevail in the end. To hear her speak with such finality, such grave resignation, filled Elyth with cold dread; this, then, was the source of the Paragon's great sorrow. Perhaps the First House had indeed died down in that cave. And with it, the Ascendance.

Korush glanced toward the door as though he'd heard something outside, looked back to Elyth for a moment, and then wordlessly left the room. Overcome by the heavy proclamation, maybe, and unwilling to allow the others to see his genuine reaction. It wasn't until after the door had closed behind him that anyone else responded.

"So, then . . . what?" Nyeda asked. "What do we do?"

"Endure," the Paragon said. "Endure, until the very end."

She paused and looked around at each of them gathered there.

"Whatever its origin or its nature, unless this . . . adversary . . . turns aside of its own volition, then it is likely the end of our race. But it is *our* nature to endure much, even in the face of final defeat. We will not allow it to rob us of that as well."

The matriarch spoke with stern assurance, as though exhorting a unit of troopers before they made their last stand. Commanding them all, hers the final word.

For a time it seemed to be the end of all discussion. Until the Arbiter spoke up.

"Forgive me, Paragon," he said. "I know it is the ultimate

foolishness to contradict the Seat of Wisdom, but I am nothing if not the greatest of fools in the history of our people. There may yet be a way."

"You've found something?" Elyth asked.

"No," Oyuun admitted, turning back to his displays. "But there *is* structure in it . . . I can sense it there, somewhere. And so I feel that I *should* find something, given enough time."

The Paragon lowered her eyes to her clasped hands in front of her. Whatever she had revealed to the Arbiter, she'd done in an attempt to convince him of the futility of their efforts. And Elyth realized that for all the physical deterioration the Paragon had suffered under the mountain, it was her loss of hope that most made her body seem so small and fragile.

"Whatever solution you believe you might find, Arbiter, you must be certain of its success before you attempt it," the Paragon said. "There is no room for error against this foe."

He glanced back over to her.

"I'm afraid I'm not wired for certainty, Paragon. But I take it your caution has something to do with the Shadow's inner workings?"

She nodded.

"It is a mimic," she said. "How it learns, I could not discern. But the longer I engaged with it, the more apparent it became. There are elements of Qel within it, yes, drawn from its long study of that world. And elements of each of us who have interacted with it deeply, I fear. I did what I could to restrain it. Each touch only expanded its capabilities."

"Varen must have sensed your influence," Elyth said. "He told me more than once that the planet was at war with itself."

The Arbiter winced at her words.

"Varen is alive?" the Paragon asked, her voice even, despite her obvious displeasure.

Oyuun held Elyth's gaze for a moment before answering, like one sibling caught in a lie because of the other.

"He was," he said, "the last time we saw him."

"I see," said the Paragon. "Of all those lost, I suppose I should not be surprised that he alone would find a way to survive. But if he is loose on this planet, then our danger is even greater than I feared."

She lifted a hand and with one finger traced a line across her forehead.

"I strove with this world, searched for a weakness, or way to turn its power against itself," she said. "Some of its capabilities can be temporarily overridden or diverted, but neither for long nor with great control. And every attempt to disrupt it only seems to make it stronger."

"Diverted in what way?" Elyth asked.

"You found our ship, I presume?"

"Parts of it, yes. But not when we landed. It had been buried, and only uncovered when the surface shifted." A moment later Elyth made the connection. "*You* formed the cliff."

The Paragon nodded. "My intent was to reveal the vessel to you. The method was . . . imprecise."

She reached over to take a canister of water from her bedside table, sipped from it, cleared her throat. And continued.

"I sensed your arrival, through the planet. And with what little energy I could spare, I did what I could to assist you. To lead you to me."

With that revelation, Elyth's mind sorted through the anomalies they'd encountered, extracted the few that had been useful, or at least had caused no harm. The bird singing Umarai's song; the elk from Qel, leading them toward the mountain; Dmini's monument in the cliff face. And another.

"It was your voice," Elyth said. "Your voice I heard in the storm."

"I followed what I heard," the Paragon said, with a careful nod. "Though I did not understand. I am not convinced it was of any use."

Korush returned, slipping quietly once more into the room and remaining by the door, present but removed from the conversation. He caught Elyth's eye and tipped his head back in a subtle signal; he had something to tell her, when the time was right.

"As I believe you have experienced for yourselves," the Paragon added, "the mechanisms of this . . . this place, this device, *can* be resisted, for a time. But not finally overcome."

"What if we brought more—" Nyeda started.

"Not if all the skill and craft of the House were to combine with all the might of the Hezra," the Paragon answered before she could finish. "I thought perhaps with . . . her," she said, dipping her head toward Elyth, "we might find a way. But in the time since, I have learned that *if* there is a vulnerability, the means to exploit it remains well beyond our grasp."

She returned her full attention to Elyth.

"It seems that our understanding is not as complete as we once thought."

"Paragon," Elyth said, "I find it difficult to believe you brought us here, through all of this, merely to tell us our race is doomed."

"I don't need you to believe it for it to be true."

Elyth looked around at the others in the room. Nyeda was

withdrawn, her gaze cast down to the floor in front of her, having heard and, it seemed, accepted the final word of her sovereign. Arbiter Oyuun sat with his head turned halfway between the Paragon and his workstation, staring at nothing in particular, his brow furrowed as his expansive mind searched for some solution out there in his most abstract of realms, to no avail. And Korush stood at silent attention, stoic in service as guardian.

Seeing him there, Elyth was struck by his commitment to the moment, his willingness to withhold any thought, advice, or opinion, and to remain content in his duty no matter what fate might have in store for him. But there was more, too. He wasn't looking to the Arbiter or the Paragon. His eyes were on her. Waiting for *her* to lead, she realized. The Azirim's words came back to her then, when he had described his Way not as a set of rules to follow but rather as a direction to face.

And while Elyth couldn't be sure where exactly her next step should fall, she knew for certain which way she should go.

"Well," she said, looking back at the Paragon. "I'm sorry to reject your judgment a second time, Illumined Mother. But if we are unable to *find* a way, before we declare defeat perhaps we should try to *make* one."

She held the matriarch's gaze, the two women locked once more in a contest of wills over nothing more than who would be the first to look away. And in that contest, Elyth caught the spark of the ancient woman's once-indomitable spirit. The heavy despair still clung to her, but something else seemed to be taking the most fragile root, so vulnerable and delicate that a harsh breath might yet wither it. It was not true hope in Elyth or even in a future, but a hope that such hope might exist. Or, perhaps, that it might be called forth into existence, if only the right voice cried out.

In other circumstances Elyth would have refused to concede to the Paragon, but for now she bowed her head in a show of respect to the Paragon's office within the First House, if not to the woman herself. Afterward, she nodded in turn to the Arbiter and to Nyeda.

"Where are you going?" Nyeda asked.

Elyth moved toward the door, answering over her shoulder.

"To find Varen."

But as she reached the exit, Korush held up a hand.

"If that's your intention," he said, "you may not need to go far."

"You think he's close by?" she asked.

Korush nodded.

"He's standing at the edge of the clearing."

TWENTY-THREE

Korush stood with Elyth near the edge of the base camp, both of them looking out across the wide clearing to the figure standing just outside the distant tree line. Without optics, he was little more than a dark shape standing out in the glade, but Elyth had no doubt it was Varen. The air itself seemed bound in ice; motionless, heat-sapping.

"How long do you think he's been there?" she asked.

"I have no idea," Korush answered. "But I think he tripped the perimeter warning a few minutes ago. That's what I left the Paragon's room to check on. He hasn't moved since I first saw him."

"Well," Elyth said. "I suppose I should go see what he wants."

"I'll bring the skimmer around," Korush said. "We'll go together."

But Elyth shook her head.

"It's okay. I'll walk."

"Elyth."

She turned and looked at the Azirim.

"You've done your part, Korush. Time for me to do mine."

He regarded her for a long moment, but apparently recognized she wasn't going to let him come with her no matter what.

"Be safe," he said.

She turned to face Varen, some five hundred yards away.

"I don't think there's any way to do this safely," she said. "But none of us came here expecting safe, and I think we've done all right so far. See you in a bit, Wari Korush."

Elyth strode off then, eyes fixed on the distant figure, mind fixed on her purpose. It'd been a long time since she'd first clashed with Varen, when he had ceased resisting her attempts to delve into his being and had nearly overwhelmed her with the force of the chaotic power within him. But she had studied the source of that power since that meeting, tested it systematically, found its deeper presence hidden in the folds of her First House training. Whatever Qel's Shadow had done to him, she knew he had not lost himself entirely to it. And as long as some of him remained, there was something within him she knew she could contend with.

For most of her journey across the clearing, he kept his place, as still as if he were feeling the sun on his face with eyes closed. Despite his stillness, as she crossed the halfway point, she felt an unease that grew as she continued her approach, as though some sort of pressure were emanating from him. Within the first few moments, she recognized the sensation. It was the same as the heavy presence she'd felt beneath the mountain, though here beneath the open sky it had lost its overtly oppressive nature.

As she reached a distance where she could just begin to make out some of his features, Varen stepped forward, walking slowly to meet her. He had his hands behind his back, the way he often did whenever he adopted his philosopher-teacher persona. But as he approached, the invisible, alien cloud advanced with him; it filled

Elyth with an inexplicable, sharp-edged energy, awe blended with a heightened sense of danger, as though she'd been sent out alone to meet the first native emissary of Qel's Shadow.

They stopped with about twenty feet between them; she unwilling to enter farther into whatever presence clung to him, and he seemingly wary of approaching within her range of physical attack. Though he didn't smile at her, she saw a lightness in his eyes that suggested he was still more himself than whatever the planet had enticed him to become. At least for now.

"Was that Korush I saw?" he asked, his voice quiet and concerned.

"It was."

He nodded, and his shoulders relaxed with some small measure of relief.

"I was afraid I had killed him."

"You did," she answered.

Varen looked at her for a long moment, reading her face.

"You . . . restored him?"

"Not me," Elyth said. "I may have spoken the words, but it was the Deep Language that did the work."

He smiled at her then, subdued but pleased.

"You've come so far in such a short time, Elyth. Yours is truly a gift."

"And you seem to have to returned to the worst version of yourself, Varen."

At the mention of his name, all light left his eyes and he seemed to look right through her. Not as though he were mesmerized but rather as though her physical form had lost its substance, and he was seeing something more fundamental. His face changed so dramatically to an expression so unnatural for him that it struck her like looking at his corpse, as if embalmed and prepared by those who had never known him.

"That name no longer has meaning," he said.

"You got tired of that one again?" she replied. "Then which one should I use? Grief? *Eth ammuin*? The First Speaker? You've had so many, it's hard to keep up."

"I'm afraid there is no name by which you may know me now."

"Ah. Because you've transcended such trivialities, I suppose."

"No," he said. "Because mine is beyond your comprehension."

"As is the extent of your arrogance, apparently. I'd guess even the Arbiter couldn't calculate enough dimensions to measure it now."

Varen smiled at the barb, but the distance remained, as though he were humoring a child.

"You must recognize," she said, "that you aren't yourself."

"Myself?" he said. "No. I'm much more than that now. Something closer to what I'm meant to be."

"Then what are you doing here?"

"I told you before," he answered. "I cannot let you destroy this place. And since I was unable to prevent you from reaching the Paragon, I knew I would need to join you here, in hope of persuading you to choose a different course."

"That was you, under the mountain?"

"In a manner of speaking."

"Then you should have known you'd have to try harder than that if you wanted to kill me."

"Kill you?" he said, apparently genuinely alarmed by the sentiment. For a moment, he was fully himself. "I was *protecting* you, Elyth."

"Strange method."

"Did it not occur to you that it would have been nothing for this creation to crush you beneath the weight of that mountain? And it would have done so, had I not prevented it."

He took a step toward her, but stopped at her reaction; the psychic distance between them opened again, the man receding under whatever influence the planet maintained over him, or within him.

"Elyth . . . Elyth, do you still not see that I don't want this world to destroy *you* any more than I would have you destroy *it*?"

"You'll have to pick one," she said, "because you can't have both."

"If it must come to that . . ." Varen answered, and it sounded like he was about to say that he'd already made his choice. But instead he stopped himself and said, "I don't want it to come to that, Elyth. It doesn't need to come to that."

And in that moment, she saw what she'd been looking for, hoping for. Conflict within him. The shifts in his demeanor and responses to her had signaled that some measure of his true self remained intact, but now she heard genuine struggle in his words.

"You're right," she said. "It doesn't need to come to that."

And Elyth reached back into the training of her House, to the technique called Unwalling the Garden; she had used it on him once before and had nearly broken under the strain. But she was stronger now, and she knew him better. Knew him well enough to plunge into his psyche and find him among whatever alien thoughts held sway over him.

She spoke the words in the Deep Language.

"A once-hidden garden, sunlight permeates."

Varen smiled, recognizing her intent, welcoming the connection she was creating between them; he didn't resist, but in fact embraced the communion. As before, the intensity of the effect was vastly beyond that of any she'd experienced with any normal human being; she felt as though she were falling from a great height as the physical reality disintegrated into a psychic one, an internal space shared by the two selves enmeshed by the technique. Through the connection, she immersed her being fully in his and entered into a constructed reality, a projection of his mind and his heart.

The last time she had engaged him this way, she'd found herself on her back, surrounded by a vast, sun-blasted plain under a depthless void.

But this time she landed on her feet. And all around her, lush, emerald hillsides stretched as far as her eye could see, beneath a sky laden with a seamless, unending gray-green cover of clouds that hinted of a gentle rain soon to fall.

And before her stood Varen.

"I'm glad you're here," he said.

In their last such meeting, chaos had raged around her, and threatened to overwhelm her. Now, there was only peace. Or rather, a display of peace. Elyth could sense a tautness in the idyllic scene, as though it were straining to hold together against an unseen power.

"Where's your friend?" she asked. He looked at her, puzzled. "You know, whatever it is that you invited in, that drove you to betray us."

"It's unfair to characterize my decision as a betrayal. From the beginning, I was honest about my intentions. But I *am* sorry, Elyth. I'm sorry to have left you in that manner. If I'd had any other choice, I would have made it. But Korush would have killed me if I had stayed."

"Can you blame him?"

Varen chuckled. "No, I suppose not. At least, I hope no more than you blame me."

"You can't compare yourself to him. You're nothing alike."

"I disagree. He and I are both just pursuing our purpose, Elyth. Of the three of us, *you're* the only one out here running *from* something."

Varen had never hesitated to challenge her before, but his manner was typically gentle, playful. Now his words had taken on an unusual acidic edge, meant to bite deeply, intended to wound. And despite his efforts to keep the mask of control on, she saw through it to the force animating him, exploiting him. Even here in his own mind, he seemed oblivious to how his interaction with Qel's Shadow had subverted his will. Or, perhaps, he still believed himself capable of overcoming it, and turning it to some good he alone could see.

Elyth ignored his cutting remark and looked out over the projected landscape. The same sickly energy that permeated the physical realm of the planet saturated his psychic space; she felt the same intangible quality of the counterfeit.

In that thought, Elyth realized the Paragon had captured the truer essence of Qel's Shadow. Not a counterfeit. A *mimic*. The Shadow's dark imitation of what it had studied, an imperfect echo. In evaluating that ethereal space, Elyth recalled the last conversation she'd had with Varen before his disappearance, and she recognized elements of what she saw.

"This isn't Markov, Varen."

The comment caught him off guard as though it'd been a non sequitur; after a moment, he glanced out over the hillsides, considered her words.

"No," he finally admitted, looking back to her. "No, it isn't. But it *could* be. It could be whatever we want it to be."

"Okay," she said. "I want it to be vapor."

"Oh, Elyth," he said, smiling again. "Always so quick. And still too quick to grasp for simple solutions where there are none. I thought Qel had taught you a valuable lesson about being open, about listening. But I suppose you haven't learned very much at all."

"And you seem to have unlearned everything that made you redeemable."

His eyes narrowed while he absorbed the punch.

"Then why are *you* here?"

"For you, and you alone. There's still time for us to stand together, you know. Still time for you to find your way back."

"You speak as though I had a choice."

"And you hide behind empty concepts of fate to escape accountability."

For a moment he seemed to hear her, to actually be considering her words. But then he shook his head.

"It reached out to me, Elyth. Before we ever touched its atmosphere, this world sought me out and spoke to me."

"Or maybe you wanted so badly to return to Qel's work, you imagined a voice speaking what you wanted to hear."

"No. While I was in stasis, I dreamed of it."

The claim struck her with force; it should have been impossible. Stasis suspended all but the most critical, automatic functions of the brain. But given all she'd experienced on the Shadow, *impossible* no longer had meaning.

"Tell me," he said. "Is there a particular reason we couldn't have had this conversation in the real world?"

"Yes," she answered. He waited for her to continue, but when she didn't, he prompted her.

"Care to share it?"

"I needed to see for myself how deeply entwined you are with Qel's Shadow."

"Oh," he said. "Why didn't you just say so?"

With that, the veil of green hills and gray clouds tore apart, and all around her the cosmos swirled, wild, limitless, mind-breaking. But it was not the pool of infinite potential as she had come to know it through the Deep Language; it was nearly unrecognizable, alien, as though she were viewing infinity transformed through too many dimensions, as thought-crippling as the first time she'd uttered the fundamental language of the universe and felt its energy move through her. And within it something writhed snakelike, somehow the size of the cosmos itself and yet contained by it, unleashing upon her an ancient, instinctual fear.

"Varen," she said, horrifyingly entranced. "What . . . what is this?"

"I told you," he said. "Much more than just myself."

He remained unmoved as he spoke.

"But not yet what I can become."

The distorted cosmos churned in every direction, but rather than reject the sensory overload as incomprehensible, her mind twisted as it fought to decipher what it beheld. There was structure within it, patterns within patterns, a complexity that bordered on madness. And now she understood what the Paragon had tried to tell her; whatever *this* was, it was beyond them. Elyth tore her eyes away from the tormenting vision, forced herself to focus on Varen's face and his face alone.

"It sears the mind," he said. "You feel as though your thoughts might wrench from their moorings."

She couldn't respond; the effort to filter out all else was too great, too consuming. Varen nodded anyway. He could see her struggle; she could see he had once felt it himself.

"It pains you," he said, "only because you still think that concepts like *distance* have meaning."

And just as suddenly as it had all appeared, the warped universe vanished, replaced not by the idyllic hills of a false Markov, but by a flat, featureless plain, under a sky radiant with galaxies.

"Still clinging to old ways," Varen continued. "But if you would just listen, truly listen, to what this place can teach us . . . oh Elyth, the future it would open to us is . . . indescribable."

"Varen," she said. He closed his eyes at the use of the name, but didn't correct her. "The Paragon has delved far deeper than you have, and she understands. Whatever Qel's Shadow is, we cannot shape it to our own ends. We cannot turn it from its purpose."

"Perhaps she was too intent on resisting it to consider learning from it."

"It's a weapon, Varen. A *weapon*. There is no option *but* to resist it."

He shook his head, agitated.

"What you call a weapon, I call an instrument. A tool, whose *purpose* depends on its wielder. It transcended the barrier between our galaxy and what lies beyond. Imagine what we could do, you and I, with such an instrument."

"Call it whatever you want. It destroyed Qel. It's going to destroy Avemar. And every other world it chooses."

"No, Elyth," he said sharply, "I tried to explain before, it isn't a world-killer. It's not like *you*."

His stinging comment targeted a place in her heart where he knew she was vulnerable; a cruel twist of a knife she herself had first buried there. In it, the Shadow's influence was laid bare in him.

"*You* might think of it more like a world-*stealer*," he continued, "though that, too, is a small-minded perspective. After all, we didn't make these worlds. We found them. We may have cultivated them, but they existed long before we did. It's only taking things that were never truly ours to begin with."

"Taking them where?"

"It doesn't matter!" Varen shouted, and the violence of the statement seemed to surprise even him. He took a moment, recovered. "Here, there . . . the distance between any two points is much smaller than you realize."

"This Shadow," Elyth said carefully, "is a fundamentally destructive force. It will dismantle the entire Ascendance. And no amount of your semantic gymnastics can change the fact that *you* are siding with my *adversary*."

"Would you not have said the same about me once, that *I* was a fundamentally destructive force? And yet *I* learned what it was to be generative. You helped in that work. And you can continue that work. If only you would let go of what came before.

"Elyth, I told you some time ago that the foundation of the Ascendance was going to be shaken. I didn't know how, I didn't know when. But I knew it couldn't stand forever. This is that moment, Elyth. This is the shaking, and the time for old things to pass away, in the light of something new. *We* can shepherd this future into existence. The two of us, together."

"And if I refuse, Varen? What then?"

He sighed, genuine sadness in his eyes; and they were *his* eyes for a moment, truly Varen's eyes. And in them was the same sorrow she'd seen pass over him when he'd sought some promise of a shared future, and she'd answered with silence.

"I extended my hand to you once, on Qel," he said. "I'm doing so once more, here on its Shadow. . . . I won't do so again."

Elyth felt a surge in her heart then, an unexpected swell of emotion. She'd come looking for him in order to accomplish her purpose; to bring him back, and to use him to prevail against a foe that even the Paragon thought invincible. She'd let herself believe that had been the only reason. Seeing him here, now, ensnared, she could no longer deceive herself, could no longer deny how deeply she cared for him, how she too had wondered what future might have unfolded for them, if she had chosen a different path on Qel. And Elyth realized, too, just how savagely wounded it would leave her to stand against him, to be the one to overcome him.

"Do you remember the story you told me on Qel," she said, "about the spear that couldn't be stopped, and the shield that couldn't be broken? How both could hold true, as long as they never clashed?"

"I do."

Elyth nodded.

"I don't want to lose you to this place, Grief."

The nickname resonated with him, called him back to the man he'd been when they'd parted on Qel; to the man he'd been before the Hezra forced him to become Varen once more, before he'd stepped foot on this cursed world.

"I'm not lost, Elyth," he said. "I'm right where my destiny has been leading me all along."

Elyth gave him one last moment, held his gaze, willed him to throw off the deception and stand once more with her. But she saw his true self receding, saw him *allow* himself to recede, to merge again with whatever force lay behind him, and his eyes became shadowed.

"Then," she said, "this is where our paths diverge."

She closed herself off from him immediately, dispelling the psychic connection, snapping them both back into the physical reality. All that they'd experienced together in that space had taken a single instant.

In the next, she launched herself at him.

But just before he was in arm's reach, she was repelled, thrown back by the dense presence around him as forcefully as if the air itself had flashed solid and punched outward. The impulse knocked her to the ground; she rolled backward up to her feet, hands up to defend herself. Varen hadn't moved to close the distance.

His mistake.

Elyth made the hand sign of her own design, spoke words she had carefully crafted, and called the Deep Language to her aid.

"Lightning seeks its course."

The technique sped through her, unifying her senses, quickening her perception. Varen's face showed his momentary confusion as he tried to interpret her intent; his was readily apparent.

Anticipating another direct attack, Varen clapped his hands together and then raised them skyward. In the motion, Elyth saw the effect it would produce; she danced sideways as the ground beneath her began to surge upward. He had intended to throw her. Instead, she used the cresting earth's momentum to spring forward at an angle, taking his flank. The movement surprised him; he swept his hand around, dragging a wave of land to intercept her. But he was too slow. She crossed the gap, snatched his wrist, continued the motion around behind him, yanking and twisting his arm to off-balance and trap him.

Varen had never been a fighter. His instinctual reaction was the same as any untrained human, and Elyth easily followed his attempt to turn and pull away. Before she could exploit the opening, though, he spoke.

"Elyth-Anuiel!"

His voice was many voices, and the echo of her true name resonated through the planet and back again, with a power amplified by the essence of Qel's Shadow.

And now it knew her name.

The full weight of the planet bore down on her in its oppressive power, seething with terror and unearthly malevolence. As if the dread birthed from an abyssal deep had become a tangible force, driving down upon her from above. Beneath it, no human strength could stand.

Elyth felt the effect of the Deep Language drain from her, replaced by or transformed within the terrible presence; where she had processed Varen's small motions with enhanced speed, now instead her mind was forced open as witness to a celestial power before which all worlds stood still. She had perceived the raw substance of the universe, had stood in the midst of infinite possibility unmoved, had wielded its energy to weave subtle designs within its fabric. Never before had she encountered it so acutely focused in such vast scale.

Varen turned easily, tore his wrist from her grasp, seized her upper arm, and with otherworldly strength ripped her from the ground, wrenching the bone from its socket. Elyth cried out in pain as he threw her ten feet from him. Too disoriented to break her fall, she impacted violently, head dashing against the earth, face clawed by its frozen surface. Immediately the awful hand of Qel's Shadow fell upon her, crushing her into itself, commanding her submission to its might, dominating her once more with a collective will. With Varen's will, multiplied, amplified beyond measure.

There were no techniques, no tactics, no skills by which such empyreal force could be overcome, or even resisted. But in raw fury, Elyth denied its dominion.

She cried out again, not in pain but in a pure, unconstrained expression of her full being, driving herself up first to a knee, then to her feet, bent double beneath the weight of oppression. But she had held that position thousands of times; the stance of her meditation, Titan Bears the World. And though now it seemed she bore the cosmos itself upon her back, Elyth straightened and threw off its burden.

Her right arm hung immobile, dislocated, bone grinding against bone. Her left hand still had only half its strength and motion. And Elyth found her spirit strained beyond its limits by a righteous fury of inexpressible magnitude. The labyrinthine deception of Qel's Shadow entangled Varen's mind inextricably, and even in the Deep Language she could find no words capable of unleashing the full measure of her wrath.

So instead she sang out, releasing every ounce of herself into calling on a fullness of the Deep Language unrestrained by a sealing phrase or even any clear direction or focus. On Qel, she had improvised to hold a world together. Now, she did so to obliterate the pure essence of one.

"Elyth-Anuiel!" Varen called again, and even her deepest cry caught in the gale force of his magnified power. He made subtle signs with both hands, held his arms up in gentle motion. Despite the chaotic vortex of cosmic energy clashing between them, he stood calm, untouched and untested. And she saw then the full, terrible expanse of potential within him, and for the first time glimpsed the man he had once been, as Varen Fedic, First Speaker, Desolater of Worlds. This was his method, amplified by dire means into something wholly insurmountable. Her shield could not hold.

"Elyth-Anuiel," he said again, quietly. The frozen earth crackled beneath her feet, spiderwebbing throughout the clearing; the surge passed so powerfully that Elyth felt her very spirit might be torn from its roots, and she was once more cast down in its wake.

Varen walked toward her then, stood a few feet away, looking down on her, projecting hideous power upon her.

"Elyth," he said, voice his own.

Her strength was gone, her being depleted by her attempt to wield the power of the Deep Language with desperate, reckless abandon. And in that moment, she knew she had truly given all she had. The Paragon had been right after all. This foe was beyond them. If there was any solace to be found, it was only that she would not live to witness its victory.

Qel's Shadow would use Varen to deliver her death stroke, and she was helpless before its wrath.

But she would allow neither that Shadow nor whatever it had forced Varen to become to dictate the manner in which she received it.

Elyth forced herself up from the ground for the last time. But instead of standing, she remained on her knees, back straight, hands in her lap, in the calm, relaxed posture of an Advocate of the Voice at formal rest. No sign of fear, resignation, or submission. Simply one demonstrating full confidence in her place and standing within the universe. The quiet action of one who had endured.

She looked up at him, held his gaze, and neither fear nor awe could touch her now. If Varen wanted to kill her, he would have to do so facing no resistance, no threat, with neither reason nor excuse but only because he himself chose that path. And though she was at his mercy, the peace within her emanated outward, radiated against whatever awful presence clung to him.

Like a single dying star holding back all the weight of darkness in the cosmos, she waited.

For a moment of pure clarity, Varen emerged once more, wholly himself, forcing his way out from under the Shadow's influence to look upon her one last time. To plead with her from the deepest recesses of his heart. She could see that he knew in destroying her, he would destroy himself. And she could see the genuine struggle within him, as he fought to choose between sacrifices. But what end could be worth such a sacrifice?

"Elyth," he said again, tears in his eyes. "I've already destroyed the first jewel of my heart. Please don't make me destroy the last."

In his words, she perceived the two realities branching before him. Varen had hoped to unify them rather than choose only one; now, he would be forced to destroy his last jewel, if there was to be any hope of recovering the first.

His mind unfolded before her then, why he had dared to open himself to Qel's Shadow, why even now he *chose* to believe its deception . . . all in an effort to repair the great ruin he had brought upon his home world, and six others beside. And she saw for all his great love for her, how profound was his longing for home. Indeed, her own life would seem a small cost if such an atrocity could truly be unmade. But there was no such power in the universe, no matter how greatly one might distort its fabric. Yet still Varen clung to the false hope that maybe here, within Qel's Shadow, some means of reparation could be found.

He had already made his decision. He just hadn't yet brought himself to pay the price.

In him, Elyth beheld her end. But in that final moment, she recognized a chance to plant a seed in his mind that might one day grow into redemption. Not in time to save her, but, with time, to deliver the Ascendance. And perhaps even Varen himself.

Her last, quiet action that would endure into eternity.

Varen's wild power, made godlike by the incomprehensible mechanisms of Qel's Shadow, could in some distant future be undone by the simplest technique of her House. A basic training tool called Mirroring Sun and Moon, the very first she'd been taught upon her induction into the Order of the Voice.

She raised her left hand, made the simple hand sign, spoke the sealing phrase that she had recited times beyond counting.

"A quiet pool reflects the heavens; within, the deep revealed."

It was a barely perceptible draw upon the Deep Language, its effect was straightforward, its intent pragmatic. Simply, it aligned a student with her instructor, to establish a shared connection: the student in stillness, mirroring the essence of the instructor, to gain insight beyond mere teaching; the instructor, witnessing that reflection, to judge the clarity and purity of her own purpose.

But here, before her coming doom manifested, she took on the image of her destroyer's inner being, and in turn revealed the immortal, immutable truth of himself back to him. It would take time to grow beneath that Shadow, but even its great deception could not prevail forever.

Varen's face twisted as his raw pain intensified to fathomless anguish; he saw that she knew his mind. Worse, perhaps, that she understood.

Elyth smiled to herself. Content.

Now she had given all that she had.

She closed her eyes. And in stillness, heard him draw in the breath to speak her ruin.

TWENTY-FOUR

The planet itself could not withstand the cataclysmic energy unleashed in Varen's inhuman cry; Elyth felt herself lifted as the ground beneath her ripped from its moorings, assaulting her with a jagged spray of rock and ice that tore her face and hands. Her eyes flew open as the earth broke and tumbled away; the sky swirled above a shattered horizon. Gravity fought centrifugal force over her body and limbs, each striving to rip away the greatest share. She was airborne, riding a wave of invisible power; she realized it an instant before she impacted.

And the cosmic veil tore before her eyes. Gone was Qel's Shadow, replaced by an infinite expanse laid open. It beckoned her to the place she had visited through the Deep Language, the place she had fought to resist each time it had called her to release herself to its depthless pool. Elyth had no strength to resist now. Nor any need.

Her work was done.

Her final thought was of the Paragon, her once Illumined Mother, and whether the ancient matriarch of the First House would feel sorrow over Elyth's sacrifice, or only relief. Regret, perhaps, once Elyth's final act manifested, and she at last understood how Elyth had once again made a way where no other could.

At that, Elyth released herself, felt the cool embrace of death close around her. She found it had an unexpected sweet aroma, like fresh earth after a spring rain, and within it lay the settled peace of a quiet stream beneath a star-kissed sky.

The weighted darkness pressed upon her, so tangible she could nearly feel it in the palm of her hand. She grasped it, felt its texture, damp and sponged.

And realized that somehow her breath persisted.

Though she knew it would be impossible, she tried to raise her head, only to discover it was not impossible after all. Darkness receded, her vision returned clouded. She was lying amid a deep pile of loose, soft earth. And she became aware of her tightly clenched left hand. When she relaxed her grip she discovered there a small mound of the soil, marked by the strength of her touch.

She turned her hand, let the earth rain from her palm. If only she'd had one of her vials to store it in.

In the distance, she heard the howl of a wild animal, melancholy, lonely. It wasn't until a gentle wave of power washed over her that she realized it was no animal she heard. Varen still raged.

Elyth struggled to sit up, feeling every muscle and bone in her body as they strove to remember their roles and how to work together. She went to raise her right hand to wipe the dirt from her face, and cried out at the lightning pain that struck her. The dislocated shoulder became a focal point of her body's diffused hurts. Its sharpness made the rest dull, and thus manageable. And she found strength enough to clamber her way up to her feet.

With her left hand, she gently cleared the dirt and dust-infused tears from her eyes. Once she'd restored her vision, she still wasn't sure she was seeing clearly.

Varen stood some forty yards away in the middle of a shallow crater, his back to her and looking out over a landscape transformed. At first, she thought he must have wandered away after striking her down, and was now wrecking the land in violent lament. But then she realized that he was still in the same place, and that she was the one who had moved. His intended killing blow had thrown her an incredible distance; how she'd survived it was beyond her.

On the opposite side of him, the land had changed so much that it was difficult to tell he was standing right where she'd knelt in front of him, awaiting death. A savage rift had opened almost at his feet, narrow at its origin but widening as it stretched away from him, and continuing to do so all the way it seemed to the horizon. Elyth couldn't judge its depth; from where she stood, it appeared that it could have been down to the very core of Qel's Shadow. She recalled the hole he'd opened in Qel to swallow a unit of troopers sent to capture them, and, too, the channel he'd cleaved in the titanic storm here on its Shadow. The canyon he'd carved seemed a combination of the two, and dwarfed both.

He continued to howl, wordless, mindless rage and grief pouring out from him, rippling energy across the surface of the planet and causing the unstable edges of the chasm to shudder and crumble. Elyth stood stunned for a time, witnessing the overwhelming ferocity of a soul gone supernova.

But when he finally fell to his knees and quieted, she felt stirred to action. She crossed the distance to him, uncertain of what that action would be.

Varen's head was tipped forward, a man filled with despair and too spent to release any more. He seemed so crushed beneath the weight of sorrow that even knowing he'd just tried to annihilate her, Elyth couldn't help but feel pity prick her heart. She crept forward, careful in her trembling steps to avoid revealing that she'd survived.

At the lip of the shallow crater, she stopped and stood watching him, wondering what she should do. Call his name? Invoke the Deep Language upon him? Sprint forward and smash in his skull with a rock? There were plenty of good ones at her feet, churned up by his devastation.

"Elyth," he said, sending a cold shock through her. He'd given no sign that he'd heard her approach; his voice betrayed no surprise at her presence. "I can't."

She didn't know what he meant or how to respond. She glanced down at a rock, bent, and quietly picked it up. Just in case.

Varen raised his head, gazed out over the rift he'd torn in the planet's surface, or perhaps gazed into it. After a few moments, he picked up a rock the size of a small apple and slung it into the chasm. All the energy had left him; the awful presence had lifted. And he seemed so small and broken, it was difficult to believe he'd ever presented any sort of threat.

"I can't," he repeated.

"Sure looks like you did," she answered.

He let out a punctuated breath, the ghost of a sad chuckle, and then turned his head; not far enough to look at her, but enough to speak over his shoulder.

"I'm glad you're okay," he said.

Elyth imagined the rock sailing from her hand and dashing his skull in.

"I needed to move you," he said. "I just . . . pushed a little harder than I meant to."

"When you killed me?"

"I wasn't trying to kill you, Elyth. That might be hard to believe, I guess."

"Good guess. Especially since you actually *told* me that's what you were going to do, right before you did it."

"I know . . . but . . . I mean, you were sitting right there," he said, and then flicked a hand at the ruin in front of him. "If I'd meant to kill you, do you think I would have missed this badly?"

"You want the honest answer?"

"Not really. Are you going to put the rock down?"

"Not yet."

He nodded and returned to looking over his handiwork.

"I didn't know I was going to do . . . all this . . ." he said. "I wonder if you'd be able to see it from space."

"Varen?"

"Yes?"

"*Are* you Varen?"

"Him and him alone. Or you can call me Grief if you like. Before you smash my head in, I mean. Or while doing it, if that's your preference."

She stepped down into the crater, crossed its soft surface; a cold unease rose in her, as though she were walking on an immense, recently filled grave. He didn't turn at her approach, and she stopped a few feet behind him and off to his left.

"Where's your friend?" she asked.

He raised his hand, waggled it at the chasm.

"Gone for good?"

Varen shrugged.

"That's not encouraging."

"Neither is sitting here, having to live with myself."

"Might not have to for much longer."

"It would be justice served," he said. "But far too small a sliver. And I fear I don't have a sufficient number of lives to pay the full debt."

"All this time, you've been working to let Qel's Shadow in," Elyth said, wary, "and then you turn around and throw it off that quick? That easy?"

"Time doesn't mean what you think it does, Elyth," Varen answered, then pointed at the new canyon. "And you think that was easy?"

"No, I think *that* was an accident."

"Yeah, well . . . still took a lot out of me. . . . And, you know what you did. What you did to . . . force me back."

"I didn't force anything," Elyth said. "And I didn't expect it to have an effect that soon."

"Quick learner," he said. "I guess it's possible I had a choice. Maybe I could have done it, could have . . . you know, followed through, taken that path. But if I did, it didn't seem like it in the moment."

"You love to talk about destiny. And never about your responsibility to it."

Varen closed his eyes for a moment, then ran a hand over his face before he responded.

"Do you know what the odds are that when I first started this journey, I should happen to uncover the bits of the Deep Language that I did, in the order that I did, at the time that I did?"

"I'd guess slim."

"The Arbiter calculated it for me once. Instead of an answer, he just told me there aren't enough zeroes in the universe to account for it. Change any one of those by even the slightest amount, and I would have destroyed only myself instead of seven worlds."

"And yet your words were under your power to control at every point along the way."

"So it would seem."

He went quiet for a span, but when he spoke again, he raised his hands above his shoulders, just high enough for her to see. Elyth saw he was trembling.

"These hands wrought something . . . horrific. Something so hideously abhorrent that I think there is not a word even in our great Language that can fully capture its scale. And it is a thorn in my heart, Elyth. Buried deep, deep within it. I have spent . . . lifetimes trying to remove it."

Varen dropped his hands into his lap again, shook his head.

"I tried with Qel," he said. "I wanted to try again with its Shadow. Desperately, *fiercely* wanted to try again. I still want to."

He sank into himself at those words, eyes focused on the ground ahead of him but seeing only something within himself.

"Then what did you see in yourself that made you stop?" Elyth asked.

At the sound of her voice, he blinked a few times and then answered.

"It wasn't in *me*, Elyth . . . it was in you. I saw the same thorn in *your* heart. . . . But I saw, too, what you have learned that I have not."

Elyth couldn't follow what he was saying, what he thought he'd seen in her that could have had such a profound effect upon him.

"And what was that?"

"Simply that it cannot be removed," he responded. For the first time since she'd walked up behind him, he turned to look at her fully. "You carry the same burden. For different reasons, I know, and for reasons that may even be just. But it's the same."

There was no doubt as to which burden he meant; even at the mention of it, she felt the familiar wave begin to rise within her. It recalled to her the many worlds that had died by her hand.

But now it recalled to her, too, what Varen had said when the Shadow had destroyed Qel, how he wouldn't grieve a thing only temporarily lost. And she realized how that statement had merely been a shadow and an echo of the one he'd crafted and clung to in his search for his way back home.

"Seeing it in you made it somehow more real in me," he continued, turning his face once more toward the chasm. "And I was wrong to believe only I carried it."

Elyth watched him, evaluated him. He did seem like himself again, but the change had been so sudden it was difficult to trust.

"I'd like to believe you. But I'm still not sure whether you were using Qel's Shadow, or it was using you."

"I'm not sure it matters. We were after the same goal, in a way. Trying to preserve it."

"I don't know why it needed *you* for that."

"*You're* still standing, aren't you?" he said. "And I don't think it was quite prepared for things like us to be walking around on it. Things so small, but so resilient."

"And what about you? I need to be sure you don't need *it* anymore."

"Can any of us be sure of anything, Elyth?"

She threw the rock; it smacked the ground right next to him, so close it made him jump.

"Nice throw," he said, looking down at it.

"I meant to hit you," she replied. "Do I need to pick up another one?"

He shook his head.

"I won't deny the temptation, Elyth. Even now. There is power there, *such* power, that could be harnessed. Mysteries that call to be unraveled. And I had hoped that by unraveling them, I might find a different answer there. But I know I won't. I think maybe I've known it for a long time.

"There is no . . . ." he started, but the words caught in his throat. Even now he could barely bring himself to speak them. "There is no reality in which I will be able to correct what I've done. . . . I *know* that. I'm just afraid of what it might mean if I allow myself to believe it."

In his confession, Elyth heard both the fullness of his pain and his reluctance to approach it. And she got the sense that he was still teetering, dangerously close to tipping into some other place. She didn't know what that place might be, but glancing at the rift he'd torn in the world, she didn't want to find out.

"You're right, Grief. It *is* the same burden I carry, and will always carry," Elyth said. "But it is not one I have ever had to carry alone."

Varen took a deep breath and exhaled, and then did so again several times in a row. And she realized how close to the edge he was, how fragile the moment.

She reached up and touched her collar, switching on her comms to call back to base camp.

"Korush," she said. "Korush, I need you to bring Nyeda and the Paragon out here. Right now."

The three women knelt in a circle around Varen, each with a hand on his shoulder. Korush had reset Elyth's arm in its socket, and she hoped the lingering pain wouldn't distract her from the task at hand. She still wasn't confident that the attempt was truly wise; normally the technique required six Advocates of the Voice, and as far as she knew, it had never been performed on anyone outside the House. But then, wise or not, the Paragon had agreed to it, and they really didn't seem to have any other options.

After a successful operation to put a corrupted planet down, the Advocate who had carried out the sentence underwent an extensive recovery protocol. Dividing the River was used during the period of healing and through it, the small cadre entered into the returning Advocate's experience, each taking on a share of the negative impacts of so intense and consequential an event. Though the fragments of experience were imperfect, they made known the inexpressible, and bound the group together to ease the terrible sense of isolation that inevitably accompanied the aftermath of the Advocate's grave duty.

The Paragon looked to Nyeda, then to Elyth, and with a nod signaled the beginning. Together, the three women spoke in the Deep Language.

"A torrent cascades; through many streams it quiets."

The response was immediate and excruciating, as though liquid fire had coursed through Elyth's hand into the veins of her arm and throughout her body. But even before she could react, the physical pain vanished, replaced by a whirlwind blast of image and emotion as the technique took hold and drew out fractured memories too often relived. The visions came too fast to retain and Elyth had only impressions and sensations: the nameless panic of a small child lost in a crowd; the paralyzing shock of a sudden betrayal; the helpless longing unleashed by the image of a loved one taken too soon. None of the feelings came attached to specific events. Or rather were all part of the same event, rehearsed countless times. And the weight of Varen's great burden made itself fully known, pressing down upon her, threatening to crush the breath from her lungs.

Never before had Elyth experienced so vast a range of such acute sensations; the flood overwhelmed her, overran her ability to process, rendered her incapable of doing anything more than squeezing her eyes so tightly shut that she thought they would burst. The darkest aspects of Varen's life poured into her with immolating intensity, and within them she felt the lingering influence of Qel's Shadow. Indeed, it was part of him now, its tendrils intertwined with vivid experience.

Beyond the violent surge of memory and emotion, Elyth heard a voice speak, sharp, commanding. And a moment later, the searing stream dissipated like mist under a swift sunrise.

Once more, they were just three women in an open, devastated glade; the Paragon was standing now, her hand atop Varen's head. The old matriarch was dressed in a plain service uniform, brown, unremarkable. Even so, she radiated authority and splendor of a measure that would shame all but perhaps the Hezra-Ka. And Elyth understood then that whatever she herself had suffered under Varen's pain, the Paragon had borne the greatest share, and had commanded it.

"I believe that's enough for now," the Paragon said. She lifted her hand from his head and motioned for Nyeda and Elyth to rise. As they did, the two women exchanged a look; Elyth saw that Nyeda had endured the same trial.

"For now?" Varen asked.

"It will be a good long while yet before you notice any change," the Paragon answered. "Wounds that deep take a great deal of time to heal. Even after you stop reopening them."

Outwardly, nothing about him had changed that Elyth could see. But she could sense the shift in his energy; though the power remained in him, it had lost some of its wild edge. Not that he was at peace, exactly. It just seemed far less likely now that his potential would manifest in its most destructive forms. And Elyth felt that perhaps for the first time, she was finally getting a glimpse of who Varen was as his truest self.

"I see," Varen said. "And um . . . forgive me, this is embarrassing to ask, but . . . was I supposed to feel anything?"

"Grateful, at least," the Paragon replied.

"To have been honored to partake in so sacred and secret a ritual?"

"To be alive. Were I in Elyth's place, I would have smashed your head in with the rock."

Varen got up from the ground and looked at Elyth.

"I see where you get your quick tongue from."

Elyth glanced at the Paragon.

"I didn't smash his head because I thought he might be useful," she said. And then she looked back at Varen. "Now I'm not so sure."

"We have time and plenty of rocks," he offered. "But if you're going to do it, you should probably do it soon."

"Yeah, why's that?"

"Because Qel's Shadow still has many ways to hurt us," he answered. "And I was the only thing holding it back."

———————

The seven of them stood gathered in Oyuun's research station, six of them watching as the Arbiter flipped through a dozen or more displays, looking for the relevant ones. Apparently he'd been struck by a notion while Elyth had been away, and had relocated to his main work area in hope of working it out. On their return, it had taken a great deal of convincing by Elyth before Korush or Ames had agreed to let Varen anywhere near the camp. When the knocking sounds started up again, though, the conversation had ended quickly.

Now, Varen wisely kept himself small, seated on a stool in the corner farthest from the door. Elyth stood near Oyuun hoping to catch a glimpse of whatever he'd found or at least hurry him along in his search, while trying to ignore the throbbing in her shoulder.

Outside the knocking continued, and it seemed new sources sprung up every minute or two. However many were out there, they hadn't yet fallen into sync; together they produced a short, strange pattern like the random scatter of raindrops on a hard surface, recorded and played back in an endless loop. Over time, it did seem to Elyth to have shifted, with one single stroke falling more strongly than all the others. The convergence point, she assumed, emerging gradually from the chaos. She didn't want to think what else might emerge from the planet, once the sounds had aligned and then stopped.

After what seemed like an eternity, Oyuun finally stopped cycling through displays and closed most of them, leaving only four open, which he'd arranged in a square in front of him. He stared at them, eyes rapidly shifting back and forth as he tried to retrieve from his mind whatever it was he was looking for.

"Someone," he said abruptly, without looking away from the displays, "at some point said something about . . . what was it . . . the systems, or . . . or . . . capabilities! Yes, capabilities, I think it was . . ."

He trailed off, apparently oblivious to anyone else in the room. About fifteen seconds later, it was clear he was not.

"Well?" he barked, firing a glare off at the middle of the room but hitting no one in particular before he turned back. "What was it? What about the capabilities?"

The group stood in startled silence for a moment, trying to figure out what exactly he was asking.

"That they can be disrupted?" Nyeda offered.

Oyuun waved his hand and shook his head, his brow furrowed.

Elyth saw the intensity on his face, the frustration that something useful was just beyond his grasp. And though she didn't know what he was reaching for, she replayed as much of the conversation from the Paragon's isolation room in her head as she could recall, parsing the words that might have caught in his subconscious. Moments later, one leaped forward.

"Overridden?" she said.

Oyuun's head snapped around, his eyes finding hers immediately.

"Overridden," he repeated. And then he plunged back into his collection of displays, quickly rearranging them, which made no difference that Elyth could see. "Overridden made me think of 'hijacked,' and hijacked made me think . . ."

He swiveled around to face them all, but he focused on the three women.

"You were all here when we jumped across the galaxy. You, great Paragon, you must have experienced its mechanism at work."

"Yes," she answered.

"Did you ever try to move it yourself?"

The Paragon's eyes narrowed as she shook her head.

"Good," Oyuun replied. "You recall the work we did that allowed us to pinpoint the location of the Paragon?"

"The work *you* did, yes," Elyth answered.

"Obviously I was incorrect about it being a power source," he said, and then winked at Elyth. "As I said, wrong, but useful. I built it on a foundation of computations from the Deepcu—er, rather, from my previous research. What made it useful, though, was its combination with the analysis that our two Advocates provided. My hope is that between the Paragon's familiarity with Qel's Shadow and my work on certain projects, we can override its method of transport to send it away."

"Away where?" Nyeda asked.

"Somewhere beyond the barrier, of course."

"Of course," Nyeda parroted. The tone should have made it clear to the Arbiter that no one else knew what he was thinking, but he didn't notice.

"Look," Captain Ames said, "I know I'm the dumb one and all, but I can't possibly be the only person here who doesn't understand what the Arbiter's talking about. Can I?"

He glanced around the room for some support.

"What is it you don't understand?" Oyuun asked.

"I mean, pretty much everything that's happened since I got hooked up with you. But what I've put together so far . . ." Ames said, and he held up his fingers as he counted. "One, something or some*body* put up a fence around our galaxy. Two, this rock we're on isn't a planet. Three, whatever Varen and Elyth did on Qel punched a hole in the fence. That part right?"

"Roughly speaking, yes," the Arbiter said.

"And now you're going to use fancy math and spooky word stuff to hijack a world and pop it back out of our galaxy?"

"See, you understand just fine."

"I don't even understand what I just said, Arbiter. But when you say *send* it away, you do mean we're not going with it, right?"

"That would be the intention, yes, Captain," Oyuun answered, swiveling back around to face his workstation again. "Or at least, not all of us. But let's focus on solving one problem at a time. The trouble is we'll need strong anchors to serve as both an origin and a destination. I could perhaps rig up something to give us what we would need to use Avemar as an origin. It's gathering sufficient data to formulate a destination that I haven't cracked yet."

"What do you mean not all of us?" Ames asked.

"You need a destination?" Varen asked from his corner. The Arbiter glanced over at him.

"Yes," Oyuun said.

Varen smiled.

"I can take care of that."

"Arbiter," Ames said, louder, "what do you mean, 'not all of us'?"

Oyuun ignored Ames, too intent on Varen's words.

"By what means?"

"Qel's out there. I can feel it. I can still feel it just as strongly as when I was walking in its mountains and sitting in the warmth of its sun. It's a long, *long* way from us . . ." Varen answered, pausing just long enough to catch Elyth's eye. "But that's only a problem if you still think concepts like *distance* have meaning."

He looked back to Oyuun, and added, "There is one problem, though."

"Only one?"

Varen nodded. "I don't think I can do it alone."

He was careful to keep his eyes on the Arbiter, but there was no doubt to anyone in the room what he was saying.

Since she'd arrived on Qel's Shadow, Elyth had imagined many different outcomes at many different times. But through all they'd experienced, never once had it entered her mind that she would remain on the false planet's surface while it sped away to some distant galaxy. Nor, for that matter, that she would play any role in piloting it there. There may technically have been a choice for her to make, but like Varen before her, in that moment it didn't seem like she had one.

"That's all right," she said. "I didn't have anywhere else to be anyway."

"Whoa, hold up now," Ames said. "Oyuun, you said *send*, not *pilot*."

"I brought it here," Varen said. "It's right that I should return it to its proper place."

"*We* brought it here," Elyth said. "When we resisted the Contingency."

"We're not leaving you two here," Ames said. "Arbiter. We're not just leaving them, right?"

"If there were any other way we most certainly wouldn't, Captain," Oyuun replied. "If there were any other way."

"Well, there's got to be *some* other way—"

"It's okay, Captain Ames," Elyth said. "Varen and I have done this sort of thing before."

"Listen," Korush said, interrupting. Everyone turned to look at him, expecting to hear what he had to say. But he only held up a finger, pointing toward the door.

Outside, the dreadful rattle of knocks had unified into a single rhythmic pulse.

Ames was the first to move to the door, but once he opened it, the others followed after. None of them went very far.

What appeared to be a single, nearly black cloud the size of the sky itself spiraled above them with terrifying speed. But despite its movement, the air at ground level stood still as a grave. And as though it had been waiting for them to step outside, the thrumming of the planet ceased.

"I'm too late," Oyuun said. "I won't have time to run the calculations for Avemar . . ."

"Oh, don't worry, Arbiter," Varen replied. "I can still do it."

The others all looked to him.

"Least I can do after all the trouble I've been," he said. "Still going to need some help, though."

Elyth nodded.

"The rest of you better get to the shuttle," she said. As she spoke, the wind began to stir. "And if you want to have any hope of getting off this planet, you've got to go right now. None of you want to get stuck here while we do this."

Varen looked to her and smiled.

"Not we," he said. "Or, at least, not you."

She glanced at him, certain she'd misheard him. "I'm sorry, what?"

He didn't repeat himself, just tipped his head at the Paragon, who stood a few feet away talking quietly with Nyeda; she walked over and joined him. They had clearly discussed some matter beforehand.

"Paragon?" Elyth said.

"You were never as deep into the Shadow as either of us," the Paragon answered.

"And as the Arbiter said," Varen added, "we need a destination *and* an origin."

"What are you talking about?"

"I'm going to need you to give us a little push."

"What? No," Elyth said, shaking her head as it finally dawned on her what they were saying. "Paragon, you're barely standing as it is. I'm more than capable of taking this on."

"You are more than capable of many things," the Paragon said. "Which is why you must remain within reach of the Ascendance."

"But what about the House? You can't just abandon it—"

"My time there is done, and it will continue on quite well without me. It will find its new Paragon, just as it always has when the seasons change."

The wind continued to gather strength at an alarming pace; the already low temperature seemed to drop another ten degrees in an instant.

"This won't work," Elyth said. "It is utter foolishness for you to stay—"

"You *are* aware, I hope," the Paragon said, and her voice rang with power and authority, "that outside the First House I am known as the Seat of Wisdom." She paused just a moment before adding, "And Wisdom is proved right by her actions."

A sharp-edged growl sounded from behind Elyth; the shuttle engines spinning up.

"Illumined Mother."

"Come now. A day ago I was as good as dead. You should celebrate the fact that this old body has strength enough yet to be of such use."

Without any explanation, the Paragon removed her brown uniform jacket, under which she wore only a short-sleeved shirt, exposing her frail arms to the vicious cold. She stepped close to Elyth, and uttered a phrase in the Deep Language that Elyth had never heard before.

"Void without limit, voice without sound, strength within stillness, heavens unbound."

As the final syllable left the Paragon's lips, silver fire streaked bright in intricate designs from the backs of her hands, up her arms, across her shoulders, along her neck, and framed her face with lines too fine and delicate to have been etched by any craft other than the calligraphic imprinting of the First House. The brightness of them shone through her thin shirt, and even Varen was taken aback by their sudden appearance, though he had once witnessed Elyth perform the same unveiling. Within those markings were written her history and standing within the House; why she had chosen to reveal them here and now escaped Elyth's understanding. The Paragon's purpose became clear a moment later, when she grasped Elyth by the shoulders firmly and fixed her with a piercing gaze.

"I am Shali-Orinel," she said, speaking her own hidden name. "Watcher over Hand, Eye, Voice, and Mind, Seat of Wisdom, Eighty-eighth Paragon of the First House of the Ascendance. By my hand and will, you stand anointed."

The Paragon leaned forward and breathed on Elyth, and in so doing completed a ritual that Elyth had only read about in the great Library of the First House. It did not reinstate Elyth's former position as an Advocate of the Voice, but it did mark her as a trusted ally of the House, as one who could call upon it in time of need. Elyth trembled at the magnitude and shock of the moment. The Paragon released Elyth's shoulders and donned her jacket; as she did so, the designs faded until no trace remained.

"Elyth-Kyri—" the Paragon said, beginning to address Elyth by her former hidden name, before catching herself. And though she was under no obligation to do so, she instead spoke Elyth's chosen name. "Elyth-Anuiel."

"Yes, Illumined Mother."

"Do be a dear and see that someone with a keen eye and a quick hand looks after my garden."

With that, she moved some distance away, leaving Elyth alone with Varen.

"I'm not sure what to make of that," he said.

Elyth shook her head, too dazed by the convergence of events to explain. She could never have anticipated any of this, and it was all happening too fast.

"I should go," Varen said. "And so should you."

She blinked at him, trying to regain her footing in the moment.

"Don't worry, it'll be okay. I'm kind of excited to be one of the first humans outside our galaxy," he said. "I feel good about it. I think it's going to be fun."

"This isn't the time—"

"Probably not. Still, isn't it funny that a thing meant to be an attack against us should turn out to be the very thing we needed to move forward?" he said, and he mimicked a pose from Elyth's moving meditation routine. One he had demonstrated before.

Watcher Greets the Storm. "One never knows what our abundant universe might provide, if only we're willing to receive it."

"Grief, I can't . . . . I told you I didn't want to lose you to this place. And you said yourself, if we ever found our way back together, you wouldn't let anything separate us again. Not after last time."

"Well, yes, but last time there was a choice," he said. "This time there isn't."

He took her hand between both of his, clasped it tightly.

"Come find me."

"I don't know the way."

"That's all right," he said, flashing his grin. "Just make your own."

He looked into her eyes for a moment longer, then pulled away from her, turned his back, and began walking swiftly toward the Paragon awaiting him some yards distant. Elyth watched him go, watched him while her mind raced to find the words that would call him back, that would be enough to convince him to find another way. That would finally break open the wall she'd built and let free the heart she had for him. But language failed her there, the words all escaped her, all betrayed and fled from her, and as the wind built into a rage around her, she realized it was already too late. Varen and the Paragon were walking together now. Walking into the coming storm, and she would not see them again.

"Elyth!" Korush called over the sound of the engines and the rising wind. She heard his call and knew what it meant, but could not find it in herself to move. Would not allow it, until she had firmly secured in her mind every detail of that final vision of the woman who had most shaped her, and the man whom she most loved.

"Elyth," Korush repeated, closer now and gentle, and she felt his hand on her arm. And though she was still reluctant to turn, she allowed the Azirim to lead her back to the shuttle and to her seat. It wasn't until the hatch had closed and the ship had begun its climb that Elyth realized she was clutching something in her hand. In the hand that Varen had held. She opened it, and when she saw what he had placed there, tears stung her eyes.

It was a small vial, filled with the last of Qel's soil that remained in the galaxy.

But, she felt for the first time, perhaps not in the universe.

Elyth had no memory of the flight from Qel's Shadow, of passing through its bleak and blackened sky and into the open space beyond. How long she sat lost in her thoughts, she didn't know; after she'd found the vial, her next moment of awareness came when Nyeda knelt beside her and touched her arm. Elyth looked at her, and it took a few seconds for recognition to come.

"Nyeda," she said.

"We've passed the gravitational threshold," Nyeda said. "We're clear."

Elyth nodded, though she didn't immediately understand. It wasn't until she looked up at the forward compartment where Ames had the exterior view projected and saw Qel's Shadow hanging there that she absorbed the significance of Nyeda's words.

They'd made it off the planet. They'd escaped that terrible Shadow.

But not all of them.

"Any idea what we should expect now, Arbiter?" Captain Ames asked.

"None," Oyuun said.

It was less than a minute later that Elyth felt a subtle pulse move through her, as though someone had whispered the Deep Language in her ear. In the same instant, Ames let out a startled cry that sounded like a group of meaningless syllables jammed into the broken shells of two or three different, partially uttered profanities.

Qel's Shadow had vanished from the screen. Blinked out of existence. Or, rather, most likely blinked *into* another galaxy, across some unfathomable distance, taking with it Varen and the Paragon of the First House. And though at the time she hadn't fully grasped what Varen had meant when he'd said they needed a destination *and* an origin, it was now painfully clear to her.

He had once told her that he could sense those things to which he was deeply bonded no matter how great the distance between them. Qel had served as the anchor point for his destination.

She, of course, had been his origin.

After a brief conversation between Nyeda and Oyuun following Ames's outburst, no one spoke for a time. It was perhaps due to the fact that the dire nature of their situation was only now truly setting in for each of them. They had escaped Qel's Shadow and all its terrors, and had together discovered a way to banish it from within the borders of the Ascendance empire. But having done so, they now found themselves floating in deep space, aboard a tiny vessel with barely a week's worth of support.

Captain Ames was the first to break the silence.

"So, uh . . . I don't suppose you guys have any spooky word stuff for this sort of thing?"

"No," Nyeda answered.

"Yeah, I figured you would have said something by now if you did. Sounds like we're going to have to go with plan B then."

"Do you have a plan B?"

"Sure. We aim at Avemar, get the Arbiter to do some fancy math for a trajectory, do a full burn for a day or so, and then coast our way there."

"That's a long way to coast, Captain," Nyeda said. "You think we can stretch supplies out until we make it?"

"Oh no, we'll be long dead by then. But after everything we saw on that planet, a slow, quiet death sounds pretty good to me. And hey, at least this way maybe we'll end up getting a proper burial."

"I don't understand how you can make jokes right now," Nyeda said.

"Has a lot to do with me being an idiot, I'd guess," he answered. "What about you, Arbiter? Any ideas left in that big old brain of yours?"

"Nothing useful, I'm afraid."

"Korush?"

"One," the Azirim replied.

"Let's hear it."

"We could preserve air by taping your mouth shut."

"There it is," Ames said. "Glad at least one of us remains consistent."

For the next two hours or so, the group alternated between brief bursts of conversation followed by long stretches of silence. It was during one of the silent bouts that Elyth caught a glimpse of something on the viewscreen.

"What was that?" she asked.

"What was what?" Ames said.

"I thought I saw a flash. Real small, upper left corner of the display."

"Don't mess with me, Elyth. I can't handle it right now."

"Wait," Oyuun said. "I believe there *is* something there."

Ames sat up straighter, attentive but not yet ready to hope for anything. Elyth expected Oyuun to target the exterior array on whatever had caused the flash, to try to get a sensor reading or something that could confirm whether or not they'd imagined it. Instead, though, he just started keying codes into the communications network.

"I don't suspect that's going to do us much good, Arbiter," Ames said. "At least, not unless by some—"

"Arbiter Oyuun?" a woman's voice said, coming across the open channel, trembling with an obvious mix of shock, hope, and disbelief. "Arbiter, is that you?"

EPILOGUE

Two weeks after their rescue, Elyth found herself dressed in formal attire, standing outside the command chamber of the Hezra-Ka himself. Arbiter Oyuun, Captain Ames, and Nyeda had all preceded her, and now she and Wari Korush awaited their turns to enter the chamber to face the sovereign of the Hezra in person. Their three companions had gone in one at a time, each about half an hour apart. None of them had yet come back out.

Elyth glanced over at Korush for the hundredth time since they'd been escorted into the antechamber and left alone; seeing him in the High Guard dress of the Aziri made her painfully self-conscious, but she couldn't help checking again to see if his uniform was really as perfect as she kept thinking it was. And every time she checked, she realized it was indeed just as perfect as she'd thought.

Being neither of the Hezra nor the First House, Elyth had been unable to rely on the traditional regalia reserved for such a rare and elevated audience. Arbiter Oyuun had graciously called in a few favors to secure her clothing that friends and family of

particularly high-ranking Hezra officials were allowed to wear; it
was all black, sharply cut, but most important, not likely to draw
any undue attention. Even so, the understated splendor of the
High Guard dress was hard to stand next to. She smoothed her
outfit, tugged at its sleeves, and reminded herself no one on the
other side of those doors was going to care about what she was
wearing.

"No one will care about your attire," Korush said quietly.

"That's easy for you to say," she answered. "You look like the
iron discipline of the Hezra incarnate."

"It is about as comfortable as that as well."

He maintained his stance at attention, eyes forward. But the
corner of his mouth that Elyth could see curled up slightly, and it
made her relax. She'd only seen him one other time since their return, and it was good to be with him again, even in such a
high-pressure setting.

Their recovery by the *Clariana* had turned out to be less im-
probable than she'd first believed. After Qel's Shadow had seemed
to destroy Qel, the crew of the research vessel had detected anomalies; and once it vanished, the crew had begun monitoring widely
in hopes of locating it. Oyuun had thought it might take the destruction of another Ascendance world to attract their notice, but
as it turned out, the discharge of power that had returned the
Shadow to its distant origin had proved enough to alert them.

Now, after having been through a short quarantine and an
excruciatingly thorough debriefing, she had been summoned to
appear before the Hezra-Ka for reasons unknown. Elyth desperately hoped he wasn't going to ask her for another account of
their trials.

When the doors to the chamber finally opened, the speed with which everything unfolded seemed shocking. Two Envoys stepped out, and though Elyth had expected that Korush would be admitted first, they were swiftly ushered in together. The command chamber was neither large nor grand, but its simple aesthetic had a rounded precision that struck Elyth with as much gravity as any throne room.

An elevated station dominated the rear section of the chamber, ringed by a halo of wide floating displays. And at the station sat the Hezra-Ka. His back was to Elyth and Korush, his attention fixed on one of the displays. They were directed by the Envoys to stand in specific spots; Korush seemed to know exactly what was expected of him before anyone guided him, but he patiently followed their instructions nonetheless. Nyeda, Ames, and Oyuun were nowhere to be seen, and Elyth scanned the chamber for another door, but couldn't identify one.

Once Elyth and Korush were in place, the two Envoys moved quickly off to join four others to one side of the room, where they all stood at attention. Despite all the haste, the Hezra-Ka took no notice of any of them for several minutes. Based on the reactions of everyone else in the chamber, Elyth guessed this was how things usually went. And though she maintained her focus and discipline, she found herself growing less impressed and intimidated by the circumstances.

But when the Hezra-Ka stood, any intimidation that had waned came rushing back. He had to have been over seven feet tall, though he was built so proportionally that it was difficult for Elyth to wrap her mind around just how massive he was. He had an athletic look, well-muscled in a military, functional way, and though the lines in his creased face hinted at his age, both his light movement and sharp eyes gave him a youthful energy that made it impossible to judge exactly what that age might be. To Elyth's eyes, he seemed nearly the complete opposite of the Paragon, and that made him, perhaps, the perfect complement.

As he stepped around from behind his station, one of the Envoys spoke loudly.

"Wari Korush, of the Aziri."

"Yes, thank you, I recognize my own bodyguard," the Hezra-Ka said, his voice a booming baritone. "Wari Korush. Good to see you."

Korush bowed, but said nothing in response.

"Still a man of few words, I see," the Hezra-Ka continued. "My apologies to you both; I know it is extremely rude to keep one's guests waiting, and now I've been forced to see you together rather than take time to address you individually as is warranted. Unfortunately, a great many matters demand my attention of late, as you might imagine. This shouldn't take but a moment."

He turned to the Azirim and said, "I've been reviewing all the details of the *ru het* eleven-seventeen operation, Wari Korush, particularly your two personal assignments during it. On that pair of tasks, it doesn't appear that you had very great success. I've suffered the loss of my trusted Envoy Sardis. The criminal Varen Fedic has apparently been released to the wild. Given those facts, tell me, Azirim, do you believe it's right that you should continue to bear the title Wari?"

The great man's eyes narrowed as he evaluated Korush, and Elyth had to fight to keep herself from glancing at the Azirim to see how he'd taken that unexpected onslaught. She felt the urge to speak up, to explain and to defend Korush, but she knew anything she said would only make matters worse.

"I believe it is right that you should judge, Hezra-Ka," Korush said, his voice as calm and even as she'd ever heard.

"Then I judge that you shall bear it no longer."

The Hezra-Ka stood silent once more, a severe look on his face. And then after several seconds, he broke into a smile, obviously amused with himself.

"You truly are a man of the Way, Korush," he said. "I thought for certain I could get some reaction from you with that. Inappropriate, I'm aware, but I couldn't miss the opportunity. I am serious, however, that I cannot allow you to carry the name Wari with you anymore. You now stand peerless among your storied tribe, and to allow others to bear *your* name strikes me as unfair."

The Hezra-Ka glanced toward his line of Envoys.

"Envoy Ridla, we'll need to find a new title to bestow upon the Azirim, if we can find one above *Wari*."

"Yes, Hezra-Ka," the Envoy replied with a quick bow.

"Until then," the Hezra-Ka said, returning his attention to Korush, "I don't believe we can go around calling you Korush Korush or some such thing. For the time being, Godbreaker, I think I'll decree that you be known as Korush, Hand of the Hezra-Ka. How does that strike you?"

"As an honor, Hezra-Ka," Korush answered, and Elyth detected the sound of raw emotion in his voice.

"Fine. So it shall be."

The Hezra-Ka turned then to look at Elyth, and the good humor left his face as he waited expectantly. Elyth, too, waited for one of the Envoys to announce her, until it became clear that none of them had any intention of doing so. She didn't know what the protocol was for such a situation, but given the look on the man's face, she felt she had to say something.

"Hezra-Ka," she said, bowing as etiquette dictated. "I am Elyth, exile of the First House of—"

"I know who you are," he interrupted sternly. "And I am offended that you would refuse to introduce yourself appropriately."

His comment threw her off; Elyth glanced quickly at Korush to see if he could offer any clue or support, but he maintained his rigid stance.

"My apologies, Hezra-Ka," she said, and then tried again. "I am Elyth, former Advocate of the Voice—"

"*Exile, former*, such titles," the Hezra-ka said, stepping toward her. He covered the distance in three long strides, and stopped six feet in front of her. "If the First House refuses to recognize the value of someone such as yourself, perhaps there should be a *next* House."

Elyth looked up at the man towering over her, uncertain how to read his words, and of his true intent.

"Yes, I know who you are," he repeated, smiling now. "Young Paragon."

ACKNOWLEDGMENTS

If I tried to thank everyone who deserves to be thanked in a manner suitable for their contributions, this bit would be longer than the book, and I'd still probably miss a few.

So, here's the very short list, with apologies to all the people I've left out. All the most highest and greatest of thank-yous to:

Jesus, first and best Word.

My superhero wife and our amazing children, who continually shower me with gracious love, affection, patience, and understanding. And sometimes delicious baked goods.

Both sets of my parents, for your never-failing support and many kindnesses.

Sam Morgan, trusted ally, for your support and encouragement and for taking care of so many important things that would never get done if they were left to me.

Mike Braff and Vicky Leech, for being such skillful and kind champions and advocates.

All the many other folks whose work went into taking this file off my computer and turning it into a real book that's so much more enjoyable to hold and look at.